Gone Without a Trace

Gone Without a Trace

Maddie Baker Mystery
Book Two

Denise
Grover Swank

Other Books By
Denise Grover Swank

Rose Gardner Mystery

Rose Gardner Investigations and Neely Kate Mystery

Carly Moore Mystery

Maddie Baker Mystery

Magnolia Steele Mystery

Darling Investigations

Harper Adams Mystery
Probable Cause (short story)
Little Girl Vanished
Long Gone

Chapter One

Maddie

When are we gonna learn how to kick some *real* ass?"

I took in the blond woman with flushed cheeks and eyes bright with excitement. *Oh crap.*

"Yeah," a small chorus of other women sang out.

"We want to kick some ass!" another woman shouted.

We were standing in the dining room of Deja Brew, the coffee shop where I worked most weekdays. It was early December, and in a nod to the season, Christmas lights and tinsel garland were strung around the windows. Eight stockings were taped to the counter, each bearing the name of an employee. I, my boss Petra, and co-worker Chrissy had transformed the dining room into a dojo of sorts so we could offer our first-ever women's self-defense class. The coffee shop was still open, but the customers only had two-top tables to sit at in front of the windows overlooking Main Street. Tony, the high school junior who worked weeknights and weekends, was gaping at us like we were an invading army of Huns. As aggressive as this group of twelve women was, I wondered if he wasn't half right.

"Well," I said hesitantly.

"I want to break some boards," another woman said. "When do we start that?"

I waved off her question. "This isn't a martial arts class. It's a self-defense class. If you want to learn martial arts, you should go to Ken's Tae Kwon Do down the street. In fact, I plan to join myself."

There was some grumbling from the crowd.

I *did* plan to join, but not in the foreseeable future. My salary at the coffee shop was barely above minimum wage, so I had no budget for incidentals. This class wasn't helping my financial situation since Petra had convinced me to offer it for free as a community service. Chrissy, who wasn't required to be here, had grumbled over the fact that *she* wasn't getting paid. In fact, she'd told me to stand up to Petra and insist that I needed the money, which wasn't a lie. Beyond my thirty or so hours a week at the coffee shop, my only source of income came from occasionally driving for Uber. I wasn't exactly raking in money, particularly since so few people in Cockamamie, Tennessee's population of twenty thousand used rideshare apps. While I never would have gotten rich off my salary as a middle-school librarian in Nashville, it had definitely paid better than this.

Still, I'd gone along with Petra's plan willingly enough. My life had been shaped by my mother's murder, and I knew better than anyone that learning self-defense was a necessary life skill for women. Hell, it had saved my life—twice—just a month ago. Besides, most residents of Cockamamie weren't flush with cash, which meant half the women in this room might not have come had we charged. If I could keep one woman safe, then it was worth it, and Petra had put up with a lot from me over the past three months that I'd worked here. I owed her.

Now I needed to convince these women to take this class seriously. "If an attacker is swinging a board at you, your first thought shouldn't be how to break it. It should be how to dodge it. What we *are* going to teach you is how to protect yourself by getting away. But sometimes you have to inflict some pain to do that, which means you *will* learn how to flip people over your head."

Most of the dozen women in the group let out a cheer, while a few looked more reserved. One, a young woman with black hair who appeared to be in her mid-twenties, stood at the outer edge of the group, looking downright scared.

"But you won't be flipping anyone tonight," I added. Which seemed self-explanatory since there weren't any mats on the wooden floor.

A few women booed, but they'd signed up for a three-night course, and this was the first night. Honestly, I was surprised so many women had signed up—even if it was free—particularly since we were starting the first week of December. Of course, the news reports of how I'd fought off my attackers last month —not to mention the videos showing me and a Cockamamie police detective demonstrating self-defense moves at a women's club meeting—were still fresh in their minds. Especially since I'd pretty much kicked Detective Noah Langley's ass.

They might not be taking this seriously, but I definitely was, and the responsibility was starting to make me nervous.

Petra stood behind me. She had a habit of reading people's emotions, so it didn't surprise me when she said, just loudly enough for me and Chrissy to hear, "You're doing great, Maddie."

I swung my head to get Chrissy's reaction, and she stared at me for a moment before turning to face the women. "Look, y'all. Do you think Maddie learned how to kick Detective Langley's ass in one session? I mean, *really?*"

A grumbling acquiescence rippled through the crowd.

"This is my first class, so y'all are my guinea pigs," I said with a warm smile. "You're helping me figure out how to teach the basics."

"Plus, you're getting it for free," Chrissy stated firmly behind me. "Don't forget that."

"And a five-dollar Deja Brew gift card," Petra quickly added.

"Yeah," Chrissy said with a sneer. "You're basically getting *paid* to learn how to kick someone's ass."

A few heads bobbed, and almost everyone's faces brightened. The dark-haired woman in the back still looked scared.

"Okay!" I said brightly. "So tonight, we're going to practice fending off someone who tries to grab you from the front. Tomorrow, we'll work on attacks from behind—which *will* involve flipping people over your back—"

Cheers broke out. These women were vicious.

"—and Wednesday, we'll practice what we've learned before trying something new."

I demonstrated how to break the grip of someone who grabs your arm, then had everyone pair off and practice on each other. There were a lot of giggles and halfhearted attempts while I walked around and gave tips and suggested adjustments to their stances. They all seemed to pick up on it fairly quickly. I instructed the mock attacker to reach across the attackee's body, then taught them how to get out of that as well. Once they had that move down, I had them switch it up, so the attackee didn't know how the mock attacker would reach for them and needed to figure out how to break free on the fly.

"You want this to be instinct, y'all," I said. "And remember, once you get free—"

"You run like hell," Chrissy said, her eyes dark and menacing. "You can get even later."

I stared at her for one long second, then said, "After you get free, you call the police."

Chrissy shrugged. "Or you can do that." But the way she said it suggested it was the chicken shit way out.

At the end of the hour, I thanked everyone for coming and reminded them we'd be meeting tomorrow night at the same time.

As they grabbed their coats and purses to leave, the dark-haired nervous woman hung back, wringing her hands in front of her. "Excuse me," she said in barely a whisper. "Miss Maddie?"

Something about her made me want to wrap her up in a hug. The other women were here for entertainment. I sensed she was here for very real reasons.

"It's just Maddie," I said. "No miss. What's your name?" Petra had planned to get nametags, but we'd run out of time, and I'd forgotten to ask everyone to introduce themselves.

"Amy," she said.

"How can I help you, Amy?"

Her gaze shifted to the women who were leaving, then Petra and Chrissy, who were starting to move the tables and chairs back to their usual places. "Are you going to teach us how to get out of a chokehold? You know...like you did with that police officer in the video? The one where you were on your back?"

Noah and I had demonstrated how to break free if an attacker had gotten you onto your back and was strangling you. Amy's turtleneck sweater made me wonder if she was asking for a reason other than curiosity.

"I hadn't planned on it," I said. "There's not enough time in this class, and that maneuver's a little advanced, I think." I held her gaze, worried that I'd scare her off, but I needed to ask anyway. "Are you okay?"

Her eyes flew wide, but I could see fear in their depths. "Of course. Sorry I asked." She turned to snatch up her heavy sweater and purse.

"Amy," I said, following her but keeping my voice low. "I can teach you privately."

She turned back at that, and the hopefulness in her gaze formed a thick lump in my throat. This woman was in danger, and she was desperate for help. Maybe I *could* do some real good here.

"I wouldn't want to be any trouble," she said, but eagerly enough that I knew she'd do it if I agreed.

"It's no trouble at all," I said. "What's your schedule like? When are you free?"

"Tomorrow morning? I don't have to be at work until three." She looked worried. "But if that's too soon..."

I shook my head. "Nope. Not too soon at all. I just so happen to be off tomorrow." Technically true, but I'd hoped to get in a few Uber rides. Dropping a passenger off to his murder a month ago had made me less eager to give rides, but when a girl was in need of money and had limited sources of income, she did what she had to do. Well, everything short of moonlighting at Glitter Palace, a new strip club outside of town. Besides, the can of pepper spray I kept next to me in the car made me feel a *little* safer.

"Are you sure?" she asked.

"Positively sure," I said. "But I'm not sure where we can practice, so let's meet here at, say, nine or ten? I should have a place figured out by then, and we can head there."

"Ten would be best. Thank you, Maddie. *Thank you.*" The relief in her voice made me want to whisk her off and call the police because it was obvious she didn't feel safe.

"You don't have to go home tonight," I said, lowering my voice. "If you're in danger—"

Her eyes shuttered. "I never said I was in danger," she stated, sounding slightly panicked.

"No, of course not," I soothed. "I'm just saying if you ever feel like you *are* in danger and you don't feel comfortable calling the police, you can always call me. Do you want to program my name and number into your phone? In fact, I can just text you where to meet tomorrow once I get it figured out. Then we can skip meeting here and get straight to work."

Her gaze dropped to her feet. "I didn't bring my phone. I don't always have it with me."

That was weird. Was she purposely avoiding giving me her number? But I recognized that she needed to be in control of this situation and getting my number but not giving out hers was her way of maintaining it. "That's okay," I said. "Why don't I give you one of my Uber business cards? It has my cell phone number on it, and you'll have it in case something comes up. Just give me a second."

I hurried to the breakroom in the back to grab the card from my bag. I was scared to death Amy would run off while I was gone. Frankly, I was surprised she was still in the seating area when I came back, albeit closer to the exit and wearing her winter jacket with her purse strap slung over her shoulder. The Christmas lights in the window glowed behind her, making her appear even paler. She looked like she was about to bolt at any second.

"Here you go," I said cheerfully, handing her the card. "You can call me if you need to change the time, or if you need anything at all, okay?"

Taking the card, she looked it over, then stuffed it into the pocket of her coat, keeping her gaze down. "Thank you, Maddie."

"Of course. I'll see you tomorrow," I said, trying to sound breezy even though I wanted to snatch her up and make her tell me what was going on.

She bolted out the doors into the cold night, and I watched her through the windows. Should I follow her and make sure she was okay? Should I call Noah and tell him about my concerns?

No, you are not calling Noah Langley.

You'd think a month would be long enough for my heart to accept that Noah Langley wanted nothing to do with me. He'd made that perfectly clear after I'd been kidnapped and shot at for the second time in a matter of days. Sure, he'd seemed concerned about my welfare, but he'd turned right around and ghosted me. We'd shared some intimate moments, even sleeping in the same bed, when he'd stayed overnight to protect me, so his behavior had hurt. A lot. And no, we hadn't *slept* together. We hadn't even kissed, but we'd shared a deep connection that was both chemistry and something else, like two lost souls who understood each other. But he'd run scared as soon as he knew I was safe.

It was for the best. I wanted a family someday, and he'd told me that he'd broken up with his last girlfriend because she wanted marriage, and he didn't. In my thirty-four years, I'd learned that if a guy tells you something, you believe it. You don't fool yourself into thinking you can change them. I'd learned that lesson the hard way with my last boyfriend, Steve.

So why did my heart ache for Noah?

Didn't matter. I would *not* be calling Noah Langley. Besides, what would I tell him anyway? That a woman showed up at my class wearing a turtleneck and asked if I was going to teach her how to get out of a chokehold? I didn't know anything about her other than that her name was Amy.

Then a thought hit me. I could find out her full name, email address, and phone number from the sign-up form Petra had posted.

"Petra," I said, whipping around to face her. "Can I look through the roster for tonight's class?"

Confusion crossed her face. "Sure. Why?"

"I want to find out more about the woman who stayed after class was over."

She walked over to the counter and pulled out a folded piece of paper from underneath the register. "Here you go," she said as she handed it to me.

Opening the paper as I took it, I quickly scanned the list. The first thing I noticed was that fifteen people had signed up for class, but only twelve had shown, which was actually a decent turnout, considering they hadn't been required to pay anything to reserve a spot. But the second thing I noticed was that there was no one named Amy on the list.

"Petra, Chrissy," I said. "Did either of you recognize that woman who stayed after to talk to me?"

They both shook their heads. "Never seen her before," Chrissy said.

I stared at the door, my stomach flip-flopping. I was going to have to wait until tomorrow morning to find out more about her, but that didn't mean I wouldn't be worrying.

Turned out, I had good reason to be concerned.

Chapter Two

Maddie

When I got home, my Aunt Deidre was working on a jigsaw puzzle with our next-door neighbor, Margarete.

Back in early September, I'd come home for Uncle Albert's funeral and had quickly discovered Aunt Deidre was incapable of taking care of herself. While I'd known she had dementia, I hadn't realized how far it had progressed. Uncle Albert had done a good job of keeping it from me. It would have been too hard on her to move to Nashville with me, so I gave up my job and moved into Cabbage Rose House. Aunt Deidre and Uncle Albert had raised me like the daughter they'd never had after my mother was murdered, so it was the least I could do. Now I worked two jobs to live in Cockamamie and took care of her.

I was surprised to see her up at this hour. Now that it was getting darker earlier, she tended to go to bed even earlier, but she was probably excited to have someone other than me hanging out with her after dinner.

"How did it go?" Margarete asked, looking over her shoulder as I walked in, slipping off my coat and hanging it on the coat rack.

"Pretty well," I said, heading over to check on their progress. They'd finished the border and were working on something pink. "The women seemed excited to learn things, but they were disappointed I didn't teach them how to flip an attacker over their heads. I told them we'd get to that tomorrow."

Aunt Deidre chuckled. "Maybe we can go watch your class. I saw Andrea flip some guy over her head. He didn't look like he was expecting it."

She was referring to a demonstration I'd held with Detective Langley—not something my mother had done—but I decided not to correct her. "Well, we might not be flipping anyone unless I can get someone to loan me some mats."

"I thought you were going to ask that karate place," Margarete said.

Tae kwon do, but I didn't correct her. "I did, and Ken was really nice about the whole thing, but he said he couldn't spare any on weeknights. He needs them for his own classes."

"Well, where did Noah get them for his demonstration at the Women's Club meeting?" Margarete asked. "Why don't you ask him?"

The mention of Noah tweaked something in my chest. "I don't know where he got them. He made it perfectly clear he's not interested in seeing me again, though, so I won't be asking him."

"I'm sure he'd want to help the women in the community," Margarete insisted. She'd met Noah the night three men had broken into our house to try to kidnap me, and now she thought she was an expert on Noah Langley. "He's a nice man, Maddie."

That was part of the problem. He *was* a nice man, and I suspected he didn't come back to see me because he thought he was sparing me. Or maybe he was sparing himself. All I knew was I didn't want to see him again—not because I hated him, but because I'd only *just* stopped hoping to see him walk up to the counter at Deja Brew to order an Americano instead of drinking the gas station coffee he claimed to like. There hadn't been enough distance for me to see him again and be okay.

My phone rang in my pocket, and I pulled it out, smiling to myself when I saw my friend Mallory's name on the screen. She hadn't been so generous in her interpretation of the way things had ended between Noah and me. She had a lengthy list of names she liked to call him, most of which she couldn't say in front of Aunt Deidre and Margarete. Then again, she was fiercely protective of me and threatened anyone she saw as a danger to me.

"Who's calling you so late?" Aunt Deidre asked.

"Mallory."

She squinted at me. "Who?"

Margarete shot me a sympathetic look.

"Just a friend," I said, my heart hurting.

Aunt Deidre had known Mallory since she and Uncle Albert visited me for parents' weekend during my freshman year at the University of Tennessee. Mallory had been my roommate, and we'd been best friends ever since. Mallory had been here countless times, yet Aunt Deidre had forgotten her. But then again, she'd forgotten who I was two days ago and nearly called the police because she thought I was an intruder.

She was losing more of herself every day.

I gestured to the kitchen. "I'm going to answer this and make myself a cup of tea. Would either of you like one?"

"No, thank you, dear," Aunt Deidre said, waving her hand.

Margarete shook her head. "No, thank you, Maddie. I'll only be staying a few more minutes."

I accepted the call as I walked into the kitchen. "Funny, Mal, I was just thinking about you."

"Then maybe you were channeling me because I've been

dying to call you for the past two hours, but I knew you had your fighting thing."

"Self-defense class."

"Same difference."

"Not really, but tell me why you were dying to call me."

"Steve sold that monstrosity of a house."

I stopped next to the sink as my mouth dropped open. "His flip house?" Steve was the ex-boyfriend I'd left in Nashville, and the house had been his brilliant investment idea. He'd been working on it for nearly two years and had convinced me to drain my savings account to help him.

"Yep. And my friend Genie, who's a real estate agent, said he got five-fifty for it."

"Five hundred and fifty thousand *dollars?*"

"No, gumballs. Of course dollars. He paid three hundred for it, right?"

I sank back into the edge of the counter, rubbing my forehead to focus. "Uh...yeah."

"How much did he put into it?"

"Including my fifteen thousand? About one hundred. And maybe another twenty to finish after I left."

"Has he contacted you?"

I barked a short laugh.

"So that's a no," she said, her voice vibrating with anger.

"You know I'd tell you if he had. I haven't heard from him since I moved out and put all my furniture into storage—which I need to sell soon, by the way. I can't afford to keep paying those storage fees."

"You can afford it after you make Steve pay you back with interest."

I laughed again. "I'd have to hire an attorney, and those cost money. Since there was no contract and we were in a relationship, it's murky territory."

She sighed. "You've already contacted a lawyer."

"Two. And both said I'd spend at least half of what he owes me in legal fees."

"Half is better than none," Mallory protested.

"If I even *get* half. Then there's the emotional cost of a lawsuit dragging on and on. It could take years." I drew in a deep breath. "We'll call the whole thing a very valuable—and expensive—lesson and move on."

"Maddie..."

Picking up my electric kettle, I said, "I'd rather talk about my class tonight. We had a pretty good turnout." While I set about preparing the tea, I told her how everything had gone, then about the woman who'd stopped me afterward.

"Do you think her husband or boyfriend is abusing her?" Mallory asked, alarmed.

"Maybe worse. She was wearing that turtleneck and wouldn't give me her phone number. I think whoever she's scared of tried to strangle her. I'm really worried."

"Well, you're supposed to see her in the morning, right? Maybe she'll share more then."

"Yeah," I said, but I doubted it. I knew most women in abusive relationships were secretive about it. "I still need to find somewhere to take her to practice."

"What about that Ken guy? The one with the dojo?"

Pressing my lips together, I considered it. "I can at least ask him if he'll let me rent the space for an hour or two, although I hope he doesn't charge much."

"Don't worry about that. I'll send you the money. And don't consider it me giving you money. Consider it a charitable contribution to saving someone's life."

I sagged against the kitchen counter. "Thanks, Mal. You're the best."

"I've been telling you that for years. It's about time you finally got it."

"I already knew. I tell you all the time." I laughed. "But thanks for everything. I'm not sure I would have gotten through any of this without you."

"Obviously, you're doing just fine. But you know I'm here for moral support. Now go get Aunt Deidre off to bed."

We hung up, and I carried my tea out to the dining room. Margarete looked up from the puzzle, put both hands on the table, then started to rise. "Well, I'm off. You two ladies have a good night."

"Thanks, Margarete," I said, grateful she was so willing to help when I needed it. As Margarete saw herself out, I turned to Aunt Deidre. "What do you say we get ready for bed?"

She gave me a defiant look, and I was sure she was going to protest, but then she said, "I want to take a bath."

"Oh," I said in surprise. "Okay." She hadn't taken a bath since I'd moved back, but I knew she used to love them.

We headed upstairs, and I started to fill her clawfoot tub, scooping some lavender bath salts into the water. She stood in the doorway, watching.

"I need help," she said, sounding embarrassed. When I gave her a blank look, she said, "Getting in and out. Albert used to help me. But..."

"Oh." Aunt Deidre had always been a modest woman, and I knew she'd be embarrassed for me to see her naked. No wonder she hadn't taken a bath. "Of course I can help. How about you put on your robe, and I'll help you in and turn my back. Then you can hand it to me, and I'll leave the room? I can wait in your room for you to finish."

Tears filled her eyes. "I don't want to be a bother."

"You're not a bother, Aunt Deidre. I would love to do this for you. In fact, we should put it on our schedule."

"More about the schedule," she groused.

I bit back the urge to tell her that a schedule had helped with her confusion. She already knew that, but just because you know something doesn't mean you like it. Just like I knew Steve had made a tidy profit on his house and had no intention of paying me back.

I stayed in the bathroom and lit a few candles while Aunt Deidre changed. When she walked in, she smiled in delight. I helped her step into the high-sided tub, then turned my back and took her robe when she handed it to me.

"I still need help," Aunt Deidre said, sounding small. "Sitting down."

"Oh." Then I forced brightness into my voice to keep her from feeling uncomfortable. "How about I close my eyes and give you my hand, and you can use it to help yourself down?"

"Okay."

Pinching my eyes closed, I turned sideways and held out my hand. She took it and lowered herself into the tub.

"Thank you, Maddie. This is so..." Her voice broke. "Nice."

"Of course, Aunt Deidre. You let me know when you're ready to get out."

I left the bathroom, leaving the door open a crack behind me. I was about to sit in the wingback chair by the window when something on the dresser caught my eye. I moved closer and realized it was a neatly folded, deep forest-green woolen scarf. It tugged at a memory that refused to surface. I fingered the wool fibers, trying to remember why the scarf seemed significant, but nothing came to mind.

Sometimes this house had too many memories, both good and bad. I wasn't sure what to make of this one.

Pulling out my phone, I sat in the chair, then sent an email to Ken from the taekwondo dojo about possibly renting his space for an hour or so in the morning. I included my phone number and suggested that we could text if it was more convenient.

I was surprised to get his text a few minutes later.

> This is Ken. It might be better to discuss this over the phone. Are you free to talk?

I called his number. "Hey, Ken. Thanks for answering so promptly."

"Of course," he said. "I heard your class went well tonight."

"You heard about it already?" I asked with a laugh.

"Small-town gossip is not to be underestimated. I wanted to apologize again for not being able to loan you some mats. It's just that—"

"Ken, it's okay. You don't owe me anything."

"I know," he said, his voice warm. "But what you're doing is important. That's part of the reason I wanted to talk and not do this over text." He paused. "You can use my space tomorrow, free of charge—to make up for me not being more supportive."

"Oh, Ken. I wasn't asking for that, and besides, I understand why you can't spare the mats."

"I know that wasn't why you were asking," he said. "And that's part of the reason I wanted to make the offer. After your session tomorrow morning, I'd like to talk about your defense classes. I have an idea that might benefit us both."

I frowned in confusion. "Uh...yeah...sure."

"Great!" he burst out enthusiastically. "I planned to go in at nine tomorrow to catch up on some paperwork. I'll leave the door open so you and your client can just walk in and get straight to work."

"Thank you, Ken," I gushed. "You have no idea how much I appreciate this."

"Not a problem. I'll see you tomorrow."

Chapter Three

Maddie

I spent the next ten minutes looking up Steve's flip house. Sure enough, my real estate app showed that the house had been sold nearly a month ago. It had been listed at five-sixty, so I suspected he actually got five-fifty for it.

Asshole.

I considered writing him an email to ask when he planned to reimburse me, but I didn't feel up to dealing with it now. Maybe tomorrow.

After I got my aunt out of her bath and into bed, I activated the alarm system I'd had installed a few weeks ago. Back in early November, she'd gotten out of the house without her home health worker noticing. It had scared the daylights out of me. The alarm was set to go off if the outer doors were opened, but it also sent an alert to my phone if Aunt Deidre opened her bedroom door in the middle of the night. I hated monitoring her like she was a prisoner, but it was better than letting something disastrous happen.

I read in bed for a while before falling asleep. But around two in the morning, I was woken up from a deep sleep by my phone ringing with a number I didn't recognize.

"Hello?" My heart raced as I answered, terrified. Middle-of-the-night phone calls never brought good news.

There was only silence on the other end.

"Hello?" I repeated several times. All I heard was someone breathing.

"Is someone there?" I asked, but the line went dead.

I was about to write it off as a prank when a terrifying thought hit me. What if Aunt Deidre had gotten out somehow and found a phone to call me? Panicking, I jumped out of bed and ran to her room, nearly falling over with relief when I opened the door and saw she was still in bed. A ding went off on my phone after I opened the door, so I quickly quieted it, hoping I hadn't disturbed her, and went back to bed.

Who had called me?

The thought kept me awake for about ten minutes before I fell back into restless sleep. It wasn't until I woke the next morning that I thought about Amy. What if she'd called me but hadn't been able to talk?

What if she really was in trouble?

After I got ready for the day the next morning, I went downstairs to grab a cup of coffee and found Aunt Deidre sitting at the kitchen table, writing on a small notepad. She was humming a happy tune under her breath. The scarf I'd seen the night before sat on the table beside her.

She glanced up with a bright smile as I reached for a cup in the cabinet. "Oh, good. You're up. I'm working on my Christmas list. We need to figure out which day to go Christmas shopping. We also need to figure out when to have the Christmas tree delivered."

I stared at her like she'd asked me to grab her breakfast from the moon. "Christmas tree delivered?"

Her brow furrowed. "We order a Christmas tree from Mr. Henderson's tree farm every year." Her eyes flew wide. "Tell me you ordered the tree, Maddie." Her disapproving tone cut me to the quick.

"Uh..." I hadn't ordered a Christmas tree. I hadn't even known I needed to. "It's taken care of." Or it would be as soon as I made that call.

"Thank goodness," she said with an exhale of relief. "We don't want to ruin Christmas."

Great. No pressure, Aunt Deidre.

"What's that?" I asked, pointing at the scarf. "I saw it on your dresser last night."

"Oh." She frowned at it for several seconds. "It's yours, I believe."

"Mine?" I shook my head. "No, it's not mine."

"But it is," she said, suddenly insistent as she pushed it toward me. "You have to wear it. It's cold today."

I picked it up, a vague memory rippling through my mind again, but it was still too faint to grasp. I knew this scarf had meaning of some kind. It was important, although I didn't know how.

"Thanks, Aunt Deidre," I said, picking it up and looping it around my neck. "I can't find my scarf, so this will come in handy today."

As soon as Linda, my aunt's home health aide, showed up, I planned to run over to Margarete's and ask her about the Christmas tree situation.

Twenty minutes later, I was on Margarete's doorstep, ringing the doorbell.

She answered the door, and before she could even say hello,

I blurted out, "Please tell me it's not too late to order a Christmas tree from Mr. Henderson's tree farm."

Sympathy filled her eyes. "Oh dear. Mr. Henderson's farm has been closed for five years."

My eyes sank closed, and I felt a lump in my throat.

"She's getting worse, Maddie."

"No," I insisted as my eyes flew open. "She's just confused because it's her first Christmas without Uncle Albert."

The look on her face suggested she wasn't buying it.

"They've always had a real tree," I said. "I've been back the last three Christmases, but is there somewhere special Uncle Albert got them after Henderson's closed down?"

"Albert, the stubborn old goat, insisted on chopping their trees down himself. Mr. Henderson sold his land, and the new owners let people come out and chop down trees."

"But they don't deliver?"

"Nope."

I cast a look at my small Ford Focus. There was no way I could get a Christmas tree to the house with that.

"Okay," I said, forcing a smile. "I'll figure it out."

"Don't be a slave to her whims," Margarete said. "I love that woman to death, but you're runnin' yourself ragged trying to take care of her and everything else. Do yourself a favor and order an artificial tree from the internet. Have it delivered to your front door. That's what I did last year, and I have no regrets."

"Thanks, Margarete. I'll consider it."

She nodded toward the scarf that was still looped around my neck. "I see she gave it to you."

I reached for it, stroking the waffle pattern. "She said it was mine, but I don't remember having a scarf like this."

Sympathy filled her eyes. "That's because it was Deidre's."

"Oh." For some reason, that disappointed me, although I had no idea why.

"Andrea made it right before she died."

My heart stuttered. "Oh."

It was stupid to be overwhelmed with emotion. My mother had been dead nearly half my life, yet the reminder that she was dead—and of how she'd died—still hit me like a bolt of lightning sometimes.

"Deidre found it yesterday and wanted to give it to you. I suppose she wasn't lucid enough to tell you the rest."

I swallowed the lump in my throat. "No. She gave it to me this morning and just insisted it was mine. No explanation."

Margarete put her hand over mine. "She found it in a box in the attic, and it brought her to tears."

"She was in the attic?" I asked in alarm.

"Don't worry. Linda was with her. She was looking for some of Albert's old clothes to send to the clothing drive. In any case, she remembered that Andrea had knitted it for you, but you hadn't wanted it, so she'd given it to Deidre instead."

My blood ran cold. "What?"

Concern washed over her face. "Oh dear. Maddie, you were sixteen, and your mother had just learned to knit. *Of course* you wouldn't want to wear it."

My eyes burned as the memory came back, still vague but now more fully formed. I wasn't ugly to my mother when she offered it to me, at least. Yet, there was no denying I'd been ugly to her the night she was murdered. My last words to her had been full of anger and resentment. I'd always resented that my mother devoted so much time and attention to her students at the high school where she taught, more so than she did me, and I'd let my feelings spew out before she left that night.

She'd gone off anyway, saying her errand was important, and we'd talk when she came back.

Only she never came back.

I'd give *anything* to take back the ugly things I'd said.

My fingers sank between the strands of yarn. *Oh, Mom. I'm so sorry.*

Margarete pulled me into a hug. "There, there, Maddie. You loved your mother, and she knew it."

I buried my face in her shoulder. "I was so mean to her before she died."

"She knew you loved her, Maddie. I promise. Mothers always know."

I pulled away and wiped my face, grateful I hadn't put on makeup, or it would likely be smeared everywhere. "Thank you, Margarete."

She stared up into my eyes. "You carry a heavy burden, Maddie. You always have. I worry about you."

I gave her a weak smile. "I'm fine."

She looked dubious but didn't say anything. Still, she stayed in the doorway, watching as I got into my car and shut the door.

I sat in the driveway, trying to gain control of my emotions. I didn't need this today, not on top of my worries about Amy and my aunt, who might need to go into residential care sooner than I'd hoped. I owed it to her to keep her home as long as possible, but how long would that be?

Long enough. Suck it up, and get on with your day.

Taking a deep breath, I shoved all my feelings down deep and turned on my Uber app. I still had nearly two hours until I met Amy, so I was hoping to get a few rides in. I never got a lot of requests, but mornings often yielded the most rides, and they usually came from the downtown area, so I drove to the library and parked. While I waited, I looked up Christmas tree farms and artificial trees online to fill the time. After almost an hour, a request finally showed up—a short ride from a house to the library. It took all of ten minutes and earned me nearly four dollars. That was barely going to pay for the latte I planned on getting at Deja Brew before my lesson with Amy.

I really needed to consider looking for another part-time job. Or two. Christmas *was* only three weeks away, and I could use some spare cash.

A little before ten, I walked into the coffee shop. The morning crowd had thinned to its usual midmorning size. Cynthia, the other part-time employee who worked on my off days, seemed excited to see me when I stopped in front of the register.

"Maddie! Welcome to Deja Brew..." She frowned. "...where everyone's always chatty."

Cynthia loved to welcome customers with original greetings.

Chrissy, who was making a drink, shot her a dark look. "That has to be your worst one yet. Give it up, Cyn."

Chrissy was right. It *had* been terrible.

She looked dejected. "I'm having an off day."

"*Day?*" Chrissy challenged, her brows halfway up her forehead.

"You do you, Cynthia," I said encouragingly. "I'm sure even Shakespeare had his off days. Can I get a latte?"

"You want a chocolate croissant today?"

"Nah, I had breakfast at home."

"I like your scarf," Cynthia said, gazing from my neck to my face. "It really brings out the green in your eyes."

I self-consciously reached for the scarf. "Thanks." For some reason, I added, "It was my mother's."

Chrissy's gaze jerked up and met mine. I understood why. I rarely mentioned my mother.

Feeling uncomfortable, I grabbed a five-dollar bill from my wallet and handed it over.

Chrissy took it from Cynthia and shoved it back at me with

a fierce expression. "Girl, you taught a self-defense class outside of work hours for free. You're not paying for this coffee."

I made a face. "That doesn't seem right."

She looked over her shoulder at the window to the kitchen in the back, where Petra made breakfast sandwiches, but our boss wasn't in view. Chrissy turned to me, lowering her voice. "What doesn't seem right is you teaching that class for nothing. You could have easily charged those women twenty dollars each —bare minimum—and made eighty dollars last night." She gave the money a hard shove. "Take it, or I'm not making this drink."

Sighing, I tucked the money into my wallet.

After Chrissy finished my latte, I carried it over to a table and sat down, waiting for Amy to arrive. When she didn't show by five after, I figured she was running late, but by ten-fifteen, I was starting to grow concerned. I wasn't sure how long to wait, and I had no way of getting ahold of her. By ten-thirty, I was very worried but unsure what to do about it. She could have forgotten or blown me off, thinking she'd over reacted, but I couldn't stop thinking about how scared she'd looked and that phone call I'd received in the middle of the night.

My gut told me that Amy was in trouble, and I had to help her.

After an internal battle, I pulled up Lance Forrester's name on my phone and placed the call. He was Noah's partner, and I'd gotten to know him during the murder investigation of the guy I'd dropped off to his murder. Lance and I had gone to school together, but he was a couple years younger than I was. In fact, he'd told me that my mother's murder had affected him so much it had inspired him to become a police officer. I knew he'd be receptive to my call.

"Maddie, is everything okay?" he asked as soon as he answered.

It was a fair question. I hadn't spoken to him since he'd

taken my statement about a month ago. "Actually, I'm concerned about someone, and I'm not sure what to do about it."

"I just sat down for a late breakfast at Benton's Diner. Are you on a break? Do you want to come over and tell me more about it while I eat?" Then he added with a laugh, "Of course you can eat too. You don't have to watch me."

"It's my day off, so that's not a problem, but I'd hate to interrupt."

"You're not. It's my day off too, and I'd love to have some company. This way, I don't have to eat alone."

"Well, if you're sure, but my concern would be work-related for you."

"That sounds troubling. Come over, and we'll talk. I was just about to order, but I'll hold off until you join me."

"I'm at Deja Brew. I can be there in a few minutes."

"See you then."

Benton's Diner was a two-block walk. It was a cool morning, but I walked quickly enough that my cheeks were flushed by the time I walked into the restaurant. Lance was sitting in a booth, holding a coffee cup. He smiled and lifted his free hand in greeting.

I unbuttoned my coat as I headed over, shrugging it off before I slipped into the seat opposite him. I left my scarf around my neck, not ready to lose contact with it yet.

"Thanks for meeting me," I said, folding my hands on the table.

"Hey, you're doing me a favor. I hate eating alone," he said as he set his cup on the table. "But let's order before we get to the reason you're here." He motioned the waitress over, and Lance ordered a sampler breakfast. I ordered an omelet and a carafe of coffee.

After she walked away, Lance gave me a warm smile. "How are you doing, Maddie?"

"Good."

He gave me a scrutinizing look. "Are you sure? You had two kidnapping attempts. Any lingering anxiety?"

I stared at him in surprise. "A little, I guess."

He lifted the cup to his lips. "You seeing anyone?"

I froze.

Was this about Noah? Oh, God. Was *Noah* seeing someone, and this was Lance's subtle way of breaking the news to me? But the concern in his eyes registered, and I felt like an idiot. "Oh. You mean a therapist?"

A huge grin lit up his face. "Yep. What else would I mean?"

My cheeks heated up.

His eyes danced. "You thought I was asking you out."

I shook my head vigorously. "No. I swear. That's not what I thought."

Still looking amused, he said, "You're a very attractive woman, Maddie Baker, and if a certain someone doesn't get his shit together, I might want to revisit this topic again in the future, but for now, yes, I was talking about a therapist."

The waitress showed up with the carafe of coffee, and I set to work on pouring a cup and doctoring it, thankful to have bought myself a few seconds.

"No, I haven't," I finally said. "But I'm fine. And I'm not here about me."

"Maybe not, but we've got plenty of time, and I wanted to ask. How'd your self-defense class go last night?"

"You knew about that?" I wasn't sure why I was surprised. It was a small town.

He studied me as he said, "Noah told me."

My heart skipped a beat. "Oh." A million questions raced through my head. How had he known? Why had he told Lance? How was he? Did he regret walking away?

But of course, I couldn't ask any of them.

"It was good," I said. "Great. Actually, that's kind of why I wanted to talk to you."

He laughed, shaking his head. An infectious smile lit up his face. "I'll preempt the question by saying I'm not letting you flip me. I've seen those videos of you flipping Noah over your head onto his ass more times than I can count. In fact, when I need a pick-me-up, I whip out my phone and watch. I have it bookmarked."

"You do not," I said with a scowl.

He picked his phone up off the table, and with a few swipes, pulled up one of the many videos of the training. Only instead of the video itself, it was a Boomerang of me flipping Noah over my back, then him going in reverse, back and forth, multiple times.

"He hates it," Lance said with a chuckle as he set his phone down. "Which is why I show it to him every few days."

My cheeks flushed again, this time not from physical exertion or cold air. It was the idea of Lance shoving me into Noah's face. He said Noah hated it. Was it because he didn't want to be reminded of me?

"That's not what I wanted to talk about, although if I can't get someone to lend me some mats, there might not be any flipping at all."

His face perked up. "You need mats?"

"I asked Ken from Ken's Taekwondo if he could loan me some, but he needs them for his night classes." Which reminded me: I needed to let him know I wouldn't be using his space this morning after all.

"I've got you covered," he said. "Noah borrowed some from the station for his demonstration at the Women's Club. I can bring them over for your demonstration and pick them up after."

I breathed a sigh of relief. "Are you sure it won't be any trouble?"

"None at all. Now we can eat without that hanging over your head."

"That wasn't all I needed to talk to you about, Lance. It really is something sort of official."

He leaned his arms on the table, turning serious. "I'm listening."

"There was a woman in my class last night...I think she's in an abusive relationship."

"Go on." I was about to, but his gaze lifted, and his smile fell slightly as he said to someone behind me, "I thought you weren't coming."

I froze, because without turning around, I knew who Lance had to be talking to.

"I got done with my report faster than I thought," said a deep male voice from behind me. "If I'd known you were replacing me, I wouldn't have come."

It *was* Noah.

My heart started to race. I wasn't sure I was up to facing him, but that was too damn bad because there was no getting out of this, and I wasn't backing down. I hadn't done anything wrong. He was the one who'd ghosted me.

"Don't be stupid," Lance told him, forcing a smile. "This was an impromptu thing, and you should probably hear this too."

Noah moved next to the table, with his face locked in an expressionless stare. "I don't want to interrupt."

"I'm not staying long," I said. "I just need to get Lance's advice, and then I'll be gone. Please. Have a seat." I started to slide out of the booth, but Noah lowered himself onto Lance's bench, shoving him over none too gently.

I tried to hide my reaction to seeing him—not an easy task. Absence must have made my appreciation for his appearance even stronger, because I could have sworn he looked even better than he had a month ago. His thick, brown hair was longer than the last time I'd seen him, and he still had the same sun-kissed blond streaks. His dress shirt stretched across his broad chest and shoulders, and his open collar gave a peek at his chest underneath. I could see a hint of stubble on his previously clean-shaven face.

But it was his eyes that held my gaze. They were a deep blue today that had an icy edge, which might have been because they were missing the warmth I'd grown accustomed to.

Noah wasn't pleased to see me, even if every part of me was drawn to him.

"Maddie was just telling me about her self-defense class," Lance said in a breezy tone, as though the tension between me and Noah wasn't sucking all the air out of the room.

"More like telling him about one of the attendees," I said, forcing myself to hold Noah's gaze. It was cold and distant, making something inside me break a little. "She's young, probably in her mid-twenties, and she looked anxious the whole time. Some women were understandably nervous about trying the moves, but it was more than that with Amy. Now that I think about it, she looked like she was scared to be there." Crap. That made sense. She hadn't signed up for the class and was there hoping to learn how to defend herself. If the person abusing her found out she was learning self-defense, they'd probably be pissed.

"Maddie?" Lance asked gently, and I realized I'd fallen silent for a few seconds.

"Sorry." I shook my head to focus. "After class, she asked me when I'd be teaching them how to get out of a chokehold. It really worried me because she was wearing a turtleneck sweater." I took a deep breath. "I told her I wasn't sure if we'd have time to get to that in a three-night, one-hour class, but when I saw how disappointed she was, I told her that I could teach her privately. She looked so relieved. She said she didn't have to be at work until three today, and since it was *my* day off, we agreed to meet at Deja Brew at ten. I said I'd take her somewhere for our private lesson. Only she never showed up. I gave her my business card with my phone number, but she didn't call to cancel."

"You think something happened to her?" Noah asked, his voice neutral.

"Maybe. I also got a phone call in the middle of the night. Around two. When I answered, no one responded. Even after I said hello a few more times. The call cut off after a few seconds, but afterward, I wondered if it had been Amy."

Noah pulled out his phone, opened an app, and started to type. "Her name's Amy?"

I nearly cried with relief that he was taking this seriously. "Yeah, but I don't have a last name. She only told me Amy. When I looked at the sign-up list, she wasn't there at all. She'd just dropped in for the class. Not that we minded," I added. "We only had the sign-up list to make sure we had enough room. I asked Petra and Chrissy if they'd recognized her, and neither of them had seen her before. I sure hadn't. She wouldn't give me her phone number, and I don't have a last name. I don't know anything about her. I only know she's in trouble."

Noah glanced over at Lance, and they exchanged a look.

"I know it's not much to go on," I said, "but my gut says she's in trouble."

"We believe you, Maddie," Lance said, "but you're right. It's not much to go on. Do you have a photo of her? Are there CCTV cameras in the coffee shop that we can grab some images from?"

"No," I said. "Petra doesn't have anything like that."

"Did you happen to see what car she drove?" Noah asked.

I shook my head, glancing down at the coffee cup in front of me. "I should have followed her."

"No," Lance said insistently. "Why would you follow her? She didn't do anything wrong."

I looked up at him, my eyes burning. "But I suspected she was in trouble. I flat-out asked her, which, in hindsight, was a stupid thing to do. It put her on the defensive. But I got her to agree to meet me today. I was going to try to find out if she really was in trouble, then convince her to talk to you, Lance. But it wasn't enough."

"Maddie," Lance said, giving me a soft smile. "This isn't your fault."

"Like you would tell me if it was," I said, reaching for a paper napkin from the dispenser at the end of the table and dabbing at my eyes.

He didn't respond, and neither did Noah.

I took a deep breath, trying to control myself. "Maybe Petra took some photos for her website. I admit that I was concentrating on the class and not what she and Chrissy were doing. I can ask her."

"That's a good idea," Lance said. "If we have a photo, we can show it around."

Noah shifted in his seat, looking uncomfortable. "In the meantime, why don't you give us a description of her?"

"Yeah. Okay. She was about my height—five-six. She was really thin, so maybe one-twenty? One twenty-five? She had black hair. It was thick and a little wavy, but it was hard to tell how long because she had it up in a messy bun during the lesson. She's white, pretty pale, and she had gray eyes. Her eyebrows were pretty thick, and she didn't have much makeup on, but she had long, dark eyelashes."

"What was the shape of her face?" Noah asked.

I pictured her in my mind. "Heart-shaped? Her chin is narrower than her forehead, and her lips are full." I gave him a wan smile. "She's pretty."

"What was she wearing?" Noah asked.

"A black turtleneck, like I said, and jeans. She was wearing a pair of really worn white athletic shoes."

He nodded as he continued tapping. "You said she mentioned that she had to be at work at three. She didn't say anything else about her job?"

"No, nothing."

"Anything else you can think of that would be helpful?" he asked, keeping his gaze on his phone.

"No."

His gaze lifted to mine, apologetic. "I'll ask around, but there's not much to go on here. If you come up with a photo, let us know, and we can show it around."

"Thanks," I said, my thoughts in turmoil. Why hadn't I asked her to stick around the shop and have a cup of coffee with me? What if Amy was in trouble? Or dead?

Our food hadn't come out yet, but I'd lost my appetite, and I couldn't handle sitting with Noah now that there was nothing else to tell him...which wasn't entirely true. There *was* something I'd been wanting to tell him and Lance for a month, but I'd sat on the information, unsure of whether I was ready to open Pandora's box again. But now I wanted them to know the whole truth. It was up to them to decide what to do with it.

"There's one more thing. Unrelated to Amy." I kept my eyes on Noah's face.

"Go on," Noah said, unblinking.

"Lance said you were both certain that Martin Schroeder killed my mother. That you thought she went to the school to confront him about his pedophilia, and he killed her for it." Martin Schroeder was the man I'd driven to his murder. I hadn't recognized him at the time, but he'd been a teacher at the high school where my mother had taught and I'd attended. While investigating his murder, Noah and Lance had discovered that he'd molested several female students. Unbeknownst to me, my mother had worried he was molesting *me*. She'd planned to confront him the night of her murder, so I understood why they'd come to that conclusion.

There was only one problem.

I drew in a breath and said, "He didn't kill her."

Lance's eyes flew wide, and he shot a look at Noah, who was staring at me, still expressionless.

"Why do you believe that?" Noah asked, his tone steady.

"Because Martin Schroeder has an alibi for that night."

"We never heard of an alibi," Noah said.

"It's legit. Trust me. After everything came out, one of Schroeder's victims came to see me. She told me he had taken her to a motel the night my mother was murdered. There was no way he could have killed her."

"The vic could have gotten the night wrong."

"No," Lance said with a grim look. "Trust me. No matter who it was, they would have remembered. Everyone knew what they were doing the night of Andrea Baker's murder."

"Before you ask," I quickly added, "no, I won't tell you who she is. I'm protecting her privacy, but I'm telling you she's trustworthy. He didn't do it."

My high school best friend had shared her secret in confidence after the investigation of Martin Schroeder's murder. She was ashamed she'd been caught up in his manipulations and worried it would destroy her marriage and her relationship with her kids. I wasn't sure I agreed, but then, I didn't know them. It was her call to make, and I'd keep her secret. Even if it hurt to do so.

I grabbed my coat and purse and started to slide out of my seat.

"Maddie," Lance protested. "You can't drop a bomb like that and just leave."

"I'm not hungry," I said. "Besides, there's someone else I need to meet." Then, without another word, I got up and walked out the door.

Chapter Four

Noah

"Why didn't you tell me she was coming?" I demanded through gritted teeth.

"I didn't *know* she was coming until about fifteen minutes ago," Lance snapped. "I'd been here at least ten minutes by then, so I presumed you were a no-show. When she called and told me she needed to talk to me, I invited her to meet me here. So cool it."

"She wanted to tell you about that woman?" I asked, unable to stop myself from watching her from the window as she crossed the street.

"No wonder you made detective," he teased. "You're so perceptive."

"Fuck you," I grunted.

He laughed. "No thanks. Now go sit on the other side. You're crowding me." His eyes danced. "Although, I admit it *will* be harder for you to watch her from over there."

Shit. He was right. I was watching her as closely as if I were an undercover cop, except anyone this obvious would never last long undercover.

I got up and nearly walked out the door, partially because I didn't feel like having this conversation with Lance but also because I wanted Maddie to explain the bombshell she'd just dropped about her mother. Okay, the main reason was because I'd thought of her every day since I'd seen her a month ago. Having her so close had been painful. Watching her walk away had been excruciating.

"What do you make of her saying that Schroeder didn't kill Andrea Baker?" Lance asked, pretending to be oblivious to my struggle. He was no slouch in the observation department. He knew full well what I was going through.

I settled in the seat opposite him, resisting the urge to glance over my shoulder out the window. "That someone approached her and gave her an alibi? I'd like to speak to the alibi myself, but I'd be the first to admit we had no hard proof that Schroeder killed Andrea Baker. Everything was circumstantial."

"Which means we need to find her case file," Lance said with a grim expression.

Easier said than done. We'd tried to get our hands on that case file when we'd started to see connections between Maddie, her murdered mother, and Martin Schroeder. Andrea Baker's murder case had been run by a crooked cop in the department who'd made more than a dozen cases—that we knew of—disappear. Several of them had been related to Schroeder, a retired high school chemistry teacher who had been protected by the detective. After we'd wrapped up Schroeder's murder, we'd helped the Feds deal with his murderers. They were involved in a plot to steal and sell pharmaceutical information and were thus above our paygrade. Part of our clean-up work had involved paying a visit to retired detective Howard Bergan's home. He was currently residing in St. Vincent's Village, a residential care center that had a wing devoted to patients with dementia, but his wife hadn't touched his home office. We'd gone through everything in the room—a tedious endeavor, considering the mess that had been left. Although we'd turned up information on a few cases, there'd been nothing on Andrea Baker.

"I think he might have shredded it," I said sullenly. "Which is further reason to believe it was tied to Schroeder." I leaned back in my seat, furious with myself. I knew I had blinders on when it came to Maddie Baker. I hadn't realized they were so big they'd hide the facts of her mother's unsolved murder.

Lance studied me for several seconds. "It was a logical conclusion—even the chief agreed—but the logical conclusion isn't always the right one."

"Despite what you think, Maddie's secret witness alibi might not remember correctly," I protested. "It was over a decade ago, and she must have been a teen."

Lance just gave me a dead stare.

I drew in a deep breath. "Okay. The alibi is reliable. Maddie, of all people, had reason to believe Schroeder was her mother's killer. She wouldn't accept someone else's word for it unless she trusts them or they have proof."

The back of my neck strained as I fought the urge to turn around and see her one last time.

Lance picked up his coffee cup. "She went inside the dojo."

I blinked. "What?"

"Maddie walked into Ken's Taekwondo." A grin spread across his face. "I know you were dying to know where she went."

"I don't give a shit what Madelyn Baker does." Which was a flat-out lie. I'd kept tabs on her—discreetly, of course. I'd needed to make sure she was okay after everything she'd gone through, and to all appearances, she was fine. She hadn't even taken any time off from the coffee shop, not that she could afford to.

During the investigation into Schroeder's murder, she'd confessed she was cash-strapped. I'd actually dropped by Deja Brew a few times, but only when I knew she was off. The teens who worked the late afternoon/evening shift had no idea about my connection to Maddie, and on the few occasions I'd run into Petra, she'd agreed not to tell Maddie I'd been in. Or that I'd asked about her.

Petra didn't tell me much. Only that Maddie seemed to be handling everything okay and had recovered from her injuries. She didn't know how Maddie's aunt was doing because Maddie rarely talked about her, and when Petra asked, Maddie always demurred that her aunt was fine. I'd been tempted to call Margarete, Maddie's next-door neighbor, but had decided that would border on stalking. At least I got an Americano every time I talked to Petra, so I could justify it as a customer making casual conversation with the owner.

Why was Maddie going to the dojo? Was she taking classes? It was none of my fucking business.

"So?' I said, glancing around for the waitress. "What does it take to get a cup of coffee here?"

"You should ask Maddie out for coffee," Lance said.

I scowled. "She works at a coffee shop. I'm not going to ask her to sit at the place where she works."

His face lit up as he pointed a finger at me. "Ah-ha! So you *do* want to ask her out!"

I narrowed my gaze, giving him my best glare, but he seemed totally unfazed. "It's not a question of me wanting to ask her out, it's that I can't."

"Why not? It's as obvious as shit that she likes you and you like her. She's not a person of interest in any of the cases we're working, unless she's involved with those break-ins."

"We're work partners. My love life is none of your concern."

"Wrong," Lance said, stretching his arm casually across the back of his seat. "We're not just partners. We're friends. Hell, you're practically my adopted brother, given the way my mom has taken to you. She claims she sees more of you than me. Way to make me look bad, by the way."

It was true that I saw a lot of his mother. After we'd tied up the Schroeder case, Lance had taken me to his mother's tavern for dinner and a few beers. It had taken all of five minutes for Matilda Forrester to proclaim herself my second mother. I went there at least a few nights a week, even if Lance didn't.

"Still..."

"Nope, I'm not agreeing to this *none of my business* bull-shit." He dropped his arm from the seat back and leaned forward. "Why won't you ask her out?"

I'd answered the question before, not that he'd accepted my answer. I was messed up—from trust issues to paranoia—after being shot seven months ago in my previous life as a detective in Memphis. Maddie didn't need to deal with my emotional issues. She deserved someone who could give her what she needed and wanted—like a family. I never wanted to get married, and I was *never* having kids. I didn't need to ask Maddie to know she wanted both. I'd heard it in her voice when she'd told me how alone she felt in the world.

Bottom line—I couldn't be the man Maddie Baker needed, and she deserved nothing less.

I rubbed my eyes, a headache beginning to form. "I don't want to talk about Maddie."

"Okay," Lance said. "But that Ken is a pretty good-looking guy who happens to be single. And I know for a fact he doesn't have morning lessons."

I hated the stir of jealousy in my chest. "Maybe she's talking to him about her class."

"She's not getting mats from him. She asked, and he can't

loan her any. She was worried she wouldn't be able to teach her students how to flip an attacker who comes at them from behind."

I scowled. "Why won't he loan them to her? It's not like she's made of money and can just go buy some."

"If only she could get them some other way," Lance said with a frown.

"We've got them at the department," I said, getting pissed that she was having to search all over town for materials for a class she was offering as a community service. God knew she needed the money and should be charging for her expertise. "Why didn't she ask us to loan her some?"

Lance shrugged. "Her next class is tonight. I told her we could get some to her, but I can't take them. I have a date."

My brow lifted. "*You* have a *date?*" I asked skeptically.

"Hey," he protested. "Don't look so surprised. Women find me relatively attractive."

I snorted, mostly because they found him *more* than relatively attractive, but he was currently single. "Why haven't you mentioned this date before now?"

"Maybe I have a few secrets of my own," he said with a laugh. "But if we're going to get those mats to Maddie, you'll have to be the one to take them."

I started to protest, but then stopped. I could send a uniformed officer to do it, but if they got sent out on a call, they might be late. I could run the mats over early, but Petra didn't have room to store them. It would have to be right before class. "Fine," I grunted. "I'll do it."

"If it makes things easier, I'll text her and let her know she doesn't have to worry about it anymore."

"Fine."

"So what do you want to do about the woman in her class?"

I pushed out a breath. "We don't have much to go on. No

one's filed a missing person's report since Maddie's aunt took off a month ago. I guess we'll sit on the information and ask around when we have the opportunity."

"Maybe Maddie's overreacting," Lance said.

"No," I said with a frown. "That's the last thing I'd accuse her of." All the more reason to deliver the mats myself.

Chapter Five

Maddie

I arrived at Deja Brew at seven so I could help move the tables and chairs to make room for our class. When Lance hadn't shown up by seven-fifteen, I started getting nervous.

After leaving Noah and Lance at the diner, I'd stopped by Ken's Taekwondo to tell him I wouldn't need to use his space. He'd apologized again for not being able to spare his mats, but he'd offered to let me use his mats *and* his space if I offered my classes on Sunday nights. *And* charged for them. He thought there was a real interest in the community, and such an arrangement would help us both. We'd talked about the possibility for a little while, shooting ideas back and forth, but I'd gotten the vibe that he was about to ask me out, so I'd beaten it out of there.

Stupid me was still hung up on Noah.

But Ken's offer about Sunday classes wasn't going to help me find mats for my class tonight. I grabbed my phone to text Lance, but before I could type a single SOS, I caught the door opening out of the corner of my eye. I shifted my gaze to see Noah walking in, carrying a mat.

My stomach did a few cartwheels across the now empty

floor. He looked good. *Really* good. Of course, he'd looked good this morning in his dress pants and shirt, but now he was wearing jeans that hung on his hips, and a black Henley that clung to every muscle of his arms and chest, which made my heart join in the anatomical gymnastics my stomach was still performing.

Noah Langley was an exceptionally fine-looking man. It was impossible not to notice.

He gave me a hesitant look as he stopped at the edge of the empty dining space. "Lance couldn't bring the mats, so he asked me to do it."

"Oh," I said with a frown. "Did something come up?"

"He claimed to have a date, but I'm highly suspicious that he was lying."

I didn't ask why he thought Lance was lying. I suspected we were both thinking the same thing.

"Thank you," I said. "I'm sure you had better things to do."

"Not really," he said quietly. "I think what you're doing is a good thing, Maddie. Plus, I figured I'd see if your mystery woman shows. If not, I can ask some of the women whether they know anything about her."

I stared at him in surprise. I knew he'd taken me seriously at the diner, but I hadn't expected him or Lance to do much, since they were hamstrung by the lack of information.

"You're really going to make sure she's okay." It was a state-ment, not a question, and it meant more to me than it probably should. I still remembered the way I'd been ignored and side-lined by the investigators who'd tried to solve my mother's murder. It was gratifying that someone on the force took me seriously. Then again, it was Noah, and he'd never failed to take me seriously. That wasn't our problem.

"I'm going to try," he said. "We'll see if I can get more information tonight." He walked over to the open space, spread out the mat, then headed back out to his car.

Chrissy walked out of the back and sidled up next to me, watching Noah go out the door. "Detective Americano brought you some mats?"

"Yeah," I said with a frown, watching his backside as he walked out the door. His butt really filled out his jeans nicely. "He said he's going to stick around for the class."

Her face lit up, and a maniacal look filled her eyes. "Does that mean we get to watch you flip him over your shoulder in person?"

"No," I scoffed. "I'm not flipping him over my shoulder. If anything, he'll probably want to flip *me*."

"I'll bet he does," she said with plenty of innuendo before she headed to the back, fanning her face.

Great. Was it wrong that part of me didn't hate the idea?

Two women walked in together, their eyes bright with excitement. "Oh! A mat!" one of them, Roxie, if I remembered correctly, said. "Does that mean I get to flip Marissa tonight?"

I couldn't help laughing. "Everyone'll get the chance to flip someone."

They turned to each other and started to argue about who got to do the flipping first, then stopped short when Noah walked through the door, carrying a second mat. He moved past them, giving a nod as he said, "Ladies," and continued to the open space.

"Oh my God," Roxie whispered. "Is that *Detective Langley?*"

Her friend Marissa stared at him, her mouth hanging open. "Can we pick our partners?"

I could see why she was asking. Noah was laying the second mat out next to the first one, the fabric of his Henley stretching across his biceps and back. It was hard to look away.

He stood upright and turned to face me.

I pulled myself together, but the two women didn't bother to hide their interest. Despite the wedding rings on their fingers.

Marissa's arm shot into the air. "Can I be your partner, Detective Langley?"

Noah gave me a helpless expression, and since he *was* here to help me, I decided it was my duty to save him. "Detective Langley is helping *me* tonight."

They grumbled, murmuring about it not being fair, as more women entered the coffee shop. They were all just as excited to see my partner.

Noah pulled me aside. "How do they know who I am?"

"Are you kidding? They've all seen the footage of us demonstrating these moves. Those videos are probably the whole reason they're here."

His lips pressed into a scowl. "Maybe knowing who I am will make them more willing to talk to me about Amy." Several more women walked in, and Noah went back to arranging the mats.

Petra walked out of the back, and her face brightened when she saw Noah. "Detective Langley's helping tonight?" she asked.

"He brought the mats," I said, gesturing to the floor. I glanced up at the clock. Somehow, it was already seven-thirty. I searched the group to see if Amy had shown up, not surprised to see she hadn't. My stomach dropped nonetheless. I had a feeling something terrible had happened to her, but there was nothing I could do about it now. I had a class to run.

"Okay, ladies," I called out. "Let's get started."

Noah moved to the front of the store, leaning his shoulder against the edge of the window in the corner. The Christmas lights strung around the frame cast a glow around him. Our eyes met for several long seconds before I forced myself to turn away and focus on the group.

The women gathered in a semicircle, and a quick count told me that we were missing one other person besides Amy.

"Welcome back," I said, forcing a smile. "Tonight, we're going to learn how to get away from someone who attacks you from behind." My smile brightened. "And yes, you *will* be learning how to flip someone over your back."

A few women released excited squeals, but a couple of them looked nervous.

"Everyone pair off, and then I'll show you how to get away from someone who grabs you from behind." Then I added, "In case you haven't noticed, Detective Langley is in the back, observing. He'll be my partner when I need one, which means he's not up for grabs."

A collective groan rippled through the room.

"I don't have a partner," one of the women said. "My friend had to stay home with her sick baby."

I darted a glance to Chrissy, who nearly turned me to stone with her glare. She was out, and I couldn't imagine Petra volunteering.

"I'll be your partner," Noah said, taking a step forward and standing next to the woman. "I can help Maddie demonstrate the maneuvers, and then I'll be—?" he glanced down at her, lifting his brow in question.

"Diane," she said, her eyelashes fluttering.

Noah's mouth tipped up into a smile. "Diane's partner."

Several women shot Diane jealous looks.

Roxie shoved Marissa's arm. "Don't you need to head home and put your kids to bed?"

"I think you need to go home and make sure that husband of yours hasn't plowed through his nightly six-pack yet," Marissa retorted, shoving her back.

My eyes flew wide because I wasn't sure they were joking. "*Okay.* Now that *Detective* Langley has agreed to work with Diane, let's get started."

"Be right back," Noah said, flashing Diane a smile while striding over to me. Diane looked like she was about to faint, but Noah didn't seem to notice as he stopped next to me and turned to face the women.

I was nervous. I hadn't touched Noah since he'd tackled me a month ago to protect me in a crossfire of bullets. The last time we'd demonstrated self-defense moves, some major chemistry had sparked between us. Nothing had changed on my end. In fact, I was pretty sure it had intensified, and although I might be stupid with men, I'd bet money that Noah was still attracted to me too.

I wasn't sure I was up to this.

I drew a deep breath, and then an idea hit me. "*Actually...*I just remembered that Chrissy said she was going to help me, and she'll be really disappointed if Noah takes her place." I spun around to give her a beseeching look. "Isn't that right, Chrissy?"

She couldn't have looked more unhappy if a clown had invited her to join him in a balloon-tying act.

"Please," I mouthed.

Forcing a smile, she walked over to Noah and elbowed him in the side. "You're standing in my spot, loser."

Noah's eyes widened slightly, but then a blank expression settled back over his face. He headed back over to Diane.

She looped her arm around his, gazing up at him with a dreamy look. "Back where you belong."

A few women grumbled about the unfairness of life.

Noah's bland façade broke, panic peering through, but I ignored him, thankful I'd dodged a lust bullet. I'd spent too many nights thinking of him while using my vibrator. I was pretty sure that if he pulled me close to his body, it would make me do things I'd regret. With witnesses.

"Now that *that's* settled," I said, "Let's start our first demonstration. I'm going to show you how to get away if someone wraps an arm around your stomach from behind. Chrissy, you get behind me and grab me."

She pinned me with another dark stare before putting an arm around my waist and hauling me to her. "I swear to God," she hissed in my ear. "If you flip me, I will *end* you."

I was fairly certain she was kidding but decided not to take any chances. I showed them how to immobilize an attacker by twisting a leg around theirs and then dropping down quickly enough to throw off their center of gravity. I stopped short of flipping her and then took my turn as the attacker, talking Chrissy through what to do. She flipped me over her back like I weighed nothing, then stood.

A huge smile lit up her face as she brushed her hands together. "And that, ladies and gent, is how it's done."

I had the others practice and walked around to give them suggestions and corrections. Several of the women kept suggesting Diane share Noah with them, but she kept grabbing his arm in a death grip. I showed them two more moves and wrapped up the session.

"Great work, ladies!" I said enthusiastically. "We'll finish our lessons tomorrow night."

"And we'll give you graduation certificates!" Petra called out. "And your Deja Brew gift cards."

"Will Detective Langley be here again?" Roxie asked hopefully.

"Will he hand out our certificates?" another woman asked.

"Forget the certificates," Marissa grumbled. "You better bring your partner tomorrow, Diane. The rest of us want a turn with the hot detective."

Noah shifted on his feet, his trademark blank expression on his face.

I brought the students' attention back to me. "Detective Langley is here because he brought us the mats that cushioned our falls tonight, so let's give him a round of thanks." I started to clap, and the women enthusiastically joined in.

Noah grinned, then lifted his hands in surrender before lowering them. "It was no big deal. Maddie's the true hero for offering you this class. I'm just happy to help."

"But are you coming back tomorrow?" Roxie pressed.

"No," I interjected. "Noah was doing us a favor tonight. We couldn't possibly ask him to give up another free night."

Several women gasped in disappointment.

"Noah?" Marissa asked, glancing between Noah and me.

Noah took a few steps toward me, then turned to face the woman. "I'll be here tomorrow night to help out again. Maddie mentioned that a couple of women were missing tonight. Diane's friend has a sick kid, so hopefully she'll be back, but it sounds like another woman is missing. Amy? Do any of you know if she'll be here tomorrow?"

I had to admit that he'd slipped that in expertly. Maybe he *did* know what he was doing.

The group looked stumped as they glanced around at one another.

"Does anyone know her?" Noah asked.

"She was the woman in the back," I added. "Last night, her black hair was up in a messy bun, and she wore a turtleneck. She's young, and she was pretty quiet."

They were silent again until another woman said, "I don't know her, but I saw her at Bob's Market last week."

"Grocery shopping?" Noah asked.

"No," she said. "She was stocking shelves."

Hope sprung to life in my chest.

"Does anyone else know anything about Amy?" he asked.

"You must really want her to come tomorrow night if you're going to this much effort," Marissa said.

"I firmly believe that the citizens of Cockamamie should do everything they can to learn how to protect themselves," Noah said.

"You're really dedicated," Diane said, in a wistful tone.

"You're married, Diane," Roxie quipped.

"A girl can dream," Diane said, staring up at Noah. She looked like she was close to suggesting they run off to a Caribbean island together.

Noah shot me a glance, then turned back to the women. "Okay. Thank you for your help, ladies. I'll turn it back over to Maddie."

"That's it, ladies," I said. "See you tomorrow."

They started to grab their purses and coats, stopping by Noah as they headed for the door. Every last one thanked him for his help before they left.

Chrissy grumbled behind me as the last woman walked out the door. "You're the one teaching them how to save their lives. Detective Americano is just eye candy."

"She's right," Noah said with a frown.

Chrissy cocked her head. "So you *admit* that you're eye candy?"

His face went blank. "What? Not that part."

"Whatever," Chrissy said, flicking her hand in the air as she spun on her feet and headed to the back room. "See you tomorrow, Badass woman."

Noah watched her walk away for a few seconds. Grimacing, he asked, "Why do I always feel like I've been beat up every time I talk to her?"

"Chrissy's harmless...mostly. She's just protective of the people she cares about."

One of the women, Amber, came back inside the coffee shop. "Detective Langley, I had a question about that last maneuver."

He gave me an apologetic look and said, "Maddie's the one you need to talk to. I'm just a helper." To prove his point, he turned his back to her and started to fold up a mat.

Amber's face flooded with disappointment as she studied his backside.

"What can I help you with, Amber?" I asked politely even though I knew she hadn't come back in to ask about the move. Her left ring finger was bare, so unlike the other women, she actually had a shot with Noah.

It was hard to ignore the jealousy burning in my gut.

"I...uh..." she stammered.

I decided to cut her some slack. "You mean the move where you twist the attacker's arm?"

She dragged her gaze from Noah's butt as he stood with the mat and headed for the door. "Yeah. But I think I just figured it out. Thanks, Maddie." Then she bolted out the door after Noah.

Pushing out a sigh, I folded the remaining three mats and stood them on end against the wall. I'd begun moving the tables and chairs back in place by the time Noah came back five minutes later. He'd been gone longer than it should have taken to carry his mat out to the car and come back, which meant he'd probably talked to Amber.

Without a word, he started moving a table back in place.

"You don't have to do that, Noah."

He didn't respond and continued helping me move everything back to where it belonged.

When he finished, he grabbed two of the mats, leaving one against the wall.

"Thanks for helping with the tables," I said.

"Yeah," he said, keeping his gaze on me. "No problem."

"Let me carry that last mat out for you."

He glanced over at it, then back at me. "Okay."

I picked it up and headed to the door. He set one of his mats down and held the door open for me to go out. Then he followed, easily carrying his two mats while I struggled with my one.

His car was a half-block down the street, and I dropped the end of the mat on the sidewalk when we finally reached it.

"I would have carried that out, Maddie," he said softly as he set his mats next to mine.

"It was the least I could do after you brought them."

He opened the trunk and tucked one of the mats in before rising up and holding my gaze. "Does Chrissy really see me as a threat to you?"

I made a face. "She's upset about a lot of things about this class, and the women giving you credit was the icing on the cake."

"I didn't mean to take credit," he said with a stricken expression. "That wasn't my intention."

"I know," I assured him. "But Chrissy...she's kind of sensitive about the whole topic of the class." I shrugged. "Don't worry about it. Seriously. I'm just grateful you brought the mats."

"You should have asked me, Maddie," he said, sounding frustrated. "You have to know I'd support you on this."

I stared at him in disbelief. "Why in the hell would I call you? You totally ghosted me. I got your message loud and clear."

He inhaled sharply, then his face turned expressionless. "You should have asked Lance. You two seem to have hit it off."

Leaning my head back, I released a groan, then leveled my gaze with his. "Noah, I'm too tired to do whatever this—" I gestured between us "—is."

He started to say something but stopped.

I needed to change the topic and focus on what was important. "So we got a lead on Amy," I said. "That's great."

"Yeah," he said. "I'll check on it first thing tomorrow."

"Tomorrow?" I asked in dismay. "Why not tonight?"

"Maddie, this isn't even an official investigation."

"You weren't the one who had a phone call in the middle of the night." I drew in a breath and pulled my shoulders back. "But you're right. This isn't an official investigation, which means I won't be out of line when I stop by Bob's Market on the way home to ask about her."

His jaw dropped. "Have you lost your mind?"

"That was the whole point, right? To follow up on her whereabouts? If I'd found out on my own, I wouldn't have thought twice about going in and asking about her."

"But you *did* involve me, so let me do my job."

"Unofficially," I said with more bitterness than I'd intended.

"You know that you don't know her well enough to file a missing person's report," he said with a sigh. "It *has* to be unofficial."

"Sure. Which means there's no reason I can't go ask about her."

"You could get yourself into trouble, Maddie."

I lifted my chin. "I'm capable of taking care of myself. I think I've proven that."

He turned to face the street. "Maybe so, but it's still foolish to purposely put yourself in danger."

"By going to the grocery store?" I asked incredulously.

He turned back to face me. "You *know* that's not all this is." His jaw set. "I'll go with you."

"I don't need you to *go with me*," I spat in frustration. "I'm going to a grocery store for heaven's sake, not Cock on the

Walk." A rough biker bar on the edge of town I never hoped to set foot in.

A frustrated look filled his eyes. "That's not it, Maddie."

"News flash. I don't know what *it* even is. You don't have to help me, Noah. You don't have to do *anything* for me, including bringing me those mats." To my irritation, I was close to tears. I wasn't doing this. I wasn't going to let him see how much he'd hurt me. So I spun on my heels and left him there on the sidewalk.

I'd do this on my own. Just like I did everything else.

Chapter Six

Noah

I felt like shit, which was exactly what I deserved. She was right. I'd ghosted her and obviously hurt her, but better to be hurt a little now than heartbroken down the road. I couldn't be the man she wanted. The man she deserved. Yet, I couldn't keep myself from helping her. Or wanting her.

She may have thought she'd ditched me, but I wasn't shaken off so easily. After she was safely back inside the coffee shop, I headed to Bob's Market, parked in the back of the lot, and waited.

To be honest, I was frustrated. I should have just told Maddie I'd stop by the store on my way home, but I had a shit-ton of paperwork to get through, and I hadn't planned on spending an hour and a half at the coffee shop. I'd planned to drop off the mats, leave, then show up again at the end to collect my mats and ask some questions. But I couldn't summon the will to leave her.

I'd missed her more than I had any right to, and while I couldn't act on my feelings, I had rationalized that it would be good community outreach for me to stay and help. Even if it meant I'd be up until midnight or later, going through the paperwork. We'd had multiple residential break-ins over the past two weeks, and I was trying to stay on top of it.

Being around her was torture. She was wearing yoga pants that hugged her ass, and watching her bend over multiple times had brought a few X-rated thoughts to mind. I couldn't help wondering what she'd discussed with Ken Park this morning. He was single, and I knew women found him attractive. Did Maddie? I couldn't imagine why he *wouldn't* ask her out.

How would I handle it if I saw them together in town?

Releasing a sigh, I considered going into the store and making inquiries about Amy before Maddie got there, but I didn't see any reason to piss her off more. So I waited for another ten minutes before her Ford Focus pulled into the lot. I was out of my car and walking toward her vehicle before she'd parked it near the entrance.

"Detective Langley," she said dryly as she got out and clicked her key fob, making the car chirp. "I thought you were too busy to stop by the store tonight." She lifted her chin in defiance.

"I just remembered I needed more coffee to stay up and finish all that paperwork," I said, holding her gaze as we stood in the middle of the parking lot.

During the class, she'd pulled her long, dark hair into a ponytail, but it was loose now, hanging past her shoulders. The parking lot was poorly lit, but I could still see her eyes were bright, and her cheeks were flushed. A long, deep green scarf hung around her neck and over her short, light-gray dress coat. She wasn't just beautiful; she was stunning, and my heart ached with the knowledge that I couldn't have her.

After I helped her with this, I'd have to go back to avoiding her at all costs out of self-preservation, but for now, I'd see this through.

She lifted her shoulder in a half-shrug as though saying *do whatever you want*, then turned and walked toward the entrance. I easily fell in step beside her.

"How's your aunt?" I asked.

She didn't spare me a glance. "Fine."

"No more episodes of running off?"

She pulled to a halt in front of the automatic doors, spinning on her feet to face me. The doors opened for us, but neither of us moved forward. "Stop it," she said, her eyes glittering with anger.

"Maddie..."

She crossed her arms as her brow lifted, waiting for me to continue.

"It's not personal," I said, knowing it was the lamest thing I could have said, even as the words fell out of my mouth.

Her brow shot even higher. "Which part? Ghosting me for a month? Or having the audacity to ask me about my aunt? Which one of those isn't personal?"

She was right, and I felt like a first-class asshole.

The automatic doors closed.

"You took the chicken shit way out, Noah Langley. I thought you were a braver man than that."

I gave her a sheepish look, because she was right, but an apology would have felt pretty damn empty.

Shaking her head, she turned to walk inside, growling when she realized the doors had closed.

I took a step back and then forward to activate the motion sensor. The doors opened, and she shot me a dark glare before going inside.

I decided to let her take the lead, but I kept in step beside her as she marched up to the service counter. No one was behind the counter, and the two cashiers on duty were too busy checking out customers to spare us a glance.

She speared me with another dirty look before pushing

away from the counter and starting down an aisle, presumably looking for an employee to speak to.

It's not how I would have handled it, but it didn't seem like a good idea to tell her so.

She wandered two aisles before we came across a teenage boy placing cans of soup on a shelf.

"Excuse me," she said as she approached him. "I was wondering if you could help me."

When he glanced up, an appreciative smile spread across his face. "Sure." His smile faded a bit when he saw me standing off to the side, but he ignored me and gave Maddie his full attention. "What can I do for you?"

"I'd like to talk to one of the other employees. Amy."

The eagerness in his eyes faded a bit, and he darted a glance at me before turning his attention back to Maddie. "I ain't seen her for a couple of days, and that's the truth."

His reply seemed suspicious as hell.

"So she *does* work here?" Maddie asked.

"Well, yeah," he responded in confusion. "You're asking about her, ain't ya?"

"Has anyone else been in looking for her?" I asked.

His eyes shuttered. "Um...no."

He was lying or hiding something. "Does Amy have a husband or boyfriend?"

"I'm not interested in her like that," he said in a rush, holding up his hand.

"I never suggested you were," I said. "But I'm guessing there's a jealous husband in the picture."

"I *think* he's her boyfriend. I don't think they're married. She doesn't have a ring or nothing. But he doesn't like it when other guys look at her. Or talk to her. Or even talk *about* her."

I nodded. "Did he come in and threaten anyone for looking at her?"

"Once. He's a scary dude."

"Do you know his name?"

He shook his head. "Amy's never told me. She doesn't talk much when she works. Just does her job, then leaves."

"What does her boyfriend look like?" I asked.

His brow furrowed. "He's about as tall as you and nearly the same size." He motioned to me. "He has thick arms, though. Bigger than yours."

I worked out regularly, so my arms were hardly sticks. That suggested her boyfriend worked out a lot, or took steroids. "What color was his hair? Did he have any facial hair?"

"Dark brown, and he had a short beard and mustache."

"How old did he look?"

He shrugged. "Dunno. Maybe in his late thirties or forties."

"What was he wearing?" I asked, wishing I'd brought in my notebook.

"Greasy jeans and work boots. One of those brown work jackets."

"Was there a logo on it? A business name?" I asked.

The kid pondered the question for a moment. "No. Not that I remember anyways."

Maddie had been standing to the side, listening, but she shifted her weight as she asked, "Did Amy show up for work today? I know she was supposed to come in at three."

He shrugged. "I don't know. She wasn't here when I got in at five." Worry filled his eyes. "You know, I don't think I should be talking to you guys about her."

I reached into my back pocket and pulled out my wallet, flipping it open to show the kid my badge.

"Eddie," I said, reading his nametag. "I'm Detective Noah Langley with the Cockamamie Police Department." I gestured to Maddie. "And this is Maddie Baker. She teaches a self-defense class your coworker's been taking, but Amy didn't show tonight. Maddie's worried, so I'm helping her follow up to make sure Amy's okay."

A bewildered look flitted across his face. "Shoot, when I skip my English class at the end of the day, the school doesn't send the truant officer looking for me. Does Amy owe you money or something?"

"No," Maddie said. "Nothing like that."

His face softened, and his appreciative look was back, probably because he'd realized we weren't together. His gaze dropped to her chest.

I stifled the urge to throttle him, deciding to remind him that Maddie was too old for him. "*Ms. Baker* has a gift card to give Amy for her attendance, but it expires soon. She'd like to drop it off at Amy's house. Is your manager around to get that information for us?"

"What kind of gift certificate?" he asked. "Because if you're handing out gift cards to Walmart, I might want to sign up for your class." He cocked his head toward Maddie. "I wouldn't mind so much if *you* flipped me to the ground and straddled me."

"It's for women," I growled as Maddie said the same thing.

"That's like reverse discrimination," he sulked. "My daddy says feminazis have ruined America."

"Tell you what, Eddie," Maddie snapped before I could respond. "The next time you're scared to walk to your car in the back parking lot because you're worried about being attacked, then you track me down at Deja Brew, and we'll talk about self-defense classes, okay?"

He looked like he was about to make a smart-ass comment before I interrupted. "Dude, if you're smart, you'll let it go. Now where's your manager?"

"Gene's in the back doing paperwork."

"Thanks for your help, Eddie," I said cheerfully, then

turned my gaze to Maddie and motioned to the back. "Let's go talk to the manager."

She looked surprised, likely because I was including her, but this wasn't official, and she was the one who'd gotten this ball rolling. Besides, if I insisted on handling it myself, I'd just have to fill her in later.

She headed toward the end of the aisle, and we walked side by side until we reached a short hall that led to a swinging door marked *Staff only.*

I pushed open one of the double doors and walked through, holding it for Maddie to follow. I planned to take the lead on this, since I was the one carrying the badge.

We walked into a large storage area with shelves and pallets of grocery items. A light shone from an open door to our left. I headed in that direction, letting Maddie follow, and stopped in the doorway.

An older man wearing a white short-sleeve dress shirt and jeans sat at a worn metal desk, punching keys on an adding machine. He glanced up with a stern look.

I reached for my wallet again and showed him my badge. "I'm Detective Noah Langley from the Cockamamie Police Department. Are you the manager?"

"Yeah," he said warily. "Gene Hamilton."

"How long you worked here, Gene?" I asked, shoving my wallet back into my pocket.

"Going on thirty years, seen a thing or two, but I'm guessing that's not why you're here. Is this about the shoplifting case?"

I lifted a brow. "Shoplifting case?"

Gene let out a frustrated groan. "Someone stole a hundred dollars' worth of steak a few weeks back. I talked to your other detective. Showed him the video feed, but I ain't heard from him yet."

"Sorry," I said, making a mental note to check in with

Detective Cuso, the other detective in the department. "I'm here to ask about one of your employees—Amy."

Releasing a weary sigh, he pushed his chair away from his desk. "Amy Davis. She in trouble?"

"We're not sure," I said. "Did Amy show up for work today?"

He shook his head. "Nope. Didn't call in either."

"Does she do that often?" I asked.

"Not show up or not come in?"

"Either."

He turned his chair to face me. "She's only worked here a few months, and she's had the flu more often than one person has a right to, if you know what I mean."

"Yeah," I said, not liking the implications.

"But she's a good worker when she's here, and those are hard to come by, so I've let it slide. She always lets me know so I can get someone to cover for her, but not today. We tried her number, and it went straight to voicemail."

"Do you think you could give me her number and her contact information?"

"Yeah," he said, turning to his computer. "You planning to check up on her?"

"We'd like to make sure she's okay," I said as he started typing. "Has she ever shown up to work with bruises?"

"On her face? Once, but she said she'd gotten hit by a flyball in a softball game, which seemed strange since she's never talked about playing softball."

"I suspect the other employees talked about her showing up like that," I said. "Must have been big gossip."

"Not in the way you might think," he said with a hint of defensiveness. "The girls were genuinely concerned about her. Her boyfriend isn't the most loving guy, if you know what I mean."

"How so?"

"He's been in a time or two. He threatened Bill behind the butcher's counter. Claimed he'd caught him staring at Amy's ass. I had to talk to Amy about it and tell her I couldn't have her boyfriend threatening the other employees."

"*Was* he staring at her ass?" Maddie said from beside me.

He glanced at her in surprise, as though just noticing her. "Probably." He shrugged. "There's no crime in looking."

I could feel Maddie's body stiffen next to me, but thankfully, she didn't respond. We couldn't afford to alienate a potential source of information, especially since he'd agreed to give me Amy's contact information. This wasn't official, so he wasn't required to cooperate.

"Do you happen to know her boyfriend's name?" I asked, hoping to get the questioning back on track.

Gene shook his head. "You know, I never heard her say his name—she always just referred to him as her boyfriend—but one of the girls might know. She's closer to Gloria and Amber, although I'm not sure how much she shares with them."

"Are either of them working tonight?" I asked.

"Gloria's working one of the registers up front. Mindy's working the other. She was supposed to go home at five, but she's covering for Amy."

I nodded, making a sympathetic face. "You mentioned that Amy showed up one time with a bruise on her face, but did you ever notice bruises elsewhere? Say on her arms or legs?"

"Or her neck?" Maddie added.

"It's hard to say," Gene said, pausing to consider. "She always wears long-sleeved shirts under her work shirt. Lately, she's been wearing a lot of high-neck stuff, so I guess it's possible she had bruises on her neck, but we didn't see them."

"I'd sure like to see what paperwork you have on her," I said.

"Specifically if you have anything with her address and perhaps a photo?"

He frowned. "Now you're worrying me."

"We're just trying to cover all the bases," I said. "Is there anything else you can think of that sticks out about Amy?"

He shook his head. "Nothing comes to mind. She's usually a quiet thing, but everyone likes her."

I pulled out my wallet again, removed a business card, and handed it to him. "If you think of anything, don't hesitate to give me a call."

He took it and looked it over. "Sure thing, detective."

"Now about that contact information for Amy..." I said, hoping he still planned to give it to me.

His brow lifted. "Oh, sorry." He pulled up a form on his computer, then pressed a button on his keyboard. A printer whirred to life, spitting out a piece of paper. Gene grabbed it and handed it over. "This is a copy of her application, which has a photo. I hope Amy's okay. If you see her, tell her that even though she didn't call today, we're still hoping to see her on Thursday."

"Sure thing. Thank you for your time," I said, shifting my gaze to Maddie before I turned and guided her toward the exit.

Chapter Seven

Maddie

I had to admit that Noah had gotten a lot more information than I likely would have on my own. Once we'd left the back room, I tugged him to a halt. Grabbing my phone out of my coat pocket, I pulled up the call I'd received in the middle of the night.

Noah must have realized what I was doing because he held the paper toward me. "Is it the same number?"

A quick glance confirmed that it was. Nodding, I looked up at him with dread.

"She might still be okay," he said, his voice soft.

My voice shook. "The manager said her phone is going to voicemail."

"Hey," he said with a tender smile. "Maybe she sent it to voicemail because he's her boss, and she doesn't want to deal with him. Why don't you try calling her?"

"Yeah. Okay." I pressed the call button on her number, putting it on speaker. When it went to an automated voicemail, panic shot through me.

"Leave a message," Noah said. "Ask her to call you back."

I nodded. After the beep, I said, "Hey Amy, this is Maddie. I missed you this morning and tonight in class. Give me a call back so I know you're okay." I rattled off my number even though it was on her caller ID because my measly message didn't feel like enough. I had a feeling something very bad had happened to Amy, and I had no idea how to help her.

I hung up and drew in a shaky breath.

"Don't freak out," he said. "For all we know, she might have gone camping and is out of cell reach, or maybe her phone died."

"Do you really think she's gone camping?" I asked in a flat tone.

He paused, then said, "No."

I grabbed the edge of the paper and skimmed it. Amy Davis lived at 14560 Harrington Road. The official address was in Cockamamie, but I was fairly certain Harrington Road was outside city limits. After some simple math, I figured out that she was twenty-three, about to turn twenty-four in February.

"I'm going to talk to Gloria and Mindy up front," Noah said. "They might know something their boss doesn't."

"I want to be with you when you talk to them."

Indecision filled his eyes before he reluctantly said, "All right, but only because I'm still not ready to declare this an official investigation. Not until I get more information. Let me do the talking."

"Okay," I said, anxious to find out anything that could be helpful. At least he was letting me participate. I'd feel so damn helpless if I couldn't even do that.

We walked up to the front of the store, and I was grateful to see that one of the cashiers was free. Noah approached her, flashing the badge in his wallet.

"I'm Detective Noah Langley with the Cockamamie Police Department."

The middle-aged woman looked nervous.

"Are you Gloria?"

Her name tag read "Gloria," but I supposed Noah needed official confirmation.

Her gaze shifted to the vacant customer service desk, then back to Noah. "Yeah."

"Gloria," Noah said, "I'd like to ask you a few questions about Amy Davis."

She visibly relaxed when he mentioned Amy's name, making me wonder what had made her so anxious. Did she have something to hide?

"She didn't show up today," she said, "but that doesn't seem like grounds to call the police."

"I'm just asking questions," Noah assured her in a friendly tone. "How well do you know Amy?"

"Better than most here, but not all that well. She keeps to herself."

"How long has she worked here?"

She shrugged. "A few months. She started after Labor Day, if I remember right."

"Do you know anything about her home life? Who she lives with? Whether she has a boyfriend?"

Her lips pinched. "She's not one to volunteer much information, if you know what I mean. But I'm 99% sure she lives with her boyfriend."

"Do you happen to know his name?"

She shook her head. "She only ever called him her boyfriend, which I thought was strange, but I never called her on it."

"I heard her call him B once," the other cashier said. She was at the register behind us and didn't have any customers waiting in line. She was leaning an arm on a low partition separating her space from our lane. This woman was younger than

Gloria, maybe in her late twenties or early thirties, closer to Amy's age. Her nametag read Mindy.

"B?" Noah asked, turning to face her. "Is that his name or an initial?"

She shrugged. "Dunno, but she looked like she wanted to swallow her tongue after she said it."

"When she mentioned him, what did she say?" Noah asked.

"In that particular instance, we were talking about what we were having for dinner, and Amy said she was making a marshmallow salad. When I said something about that being an odd choice for dinner, she said she was making it because *B* liked it."

"Any idea why she doesn't talk about her personal life?" Noah asked.

Mindy shook her head. "Like Gloria said, she keeps to herself, but if I had to guess, I'd say she's scared."

Noah shifted to face her more fully. "What do you think she's scared of?"

Mindy's mouth twisted to the side. "Her boyfriend, if I had to guess. I saw him once. He came in to talk to her, and he thought Bill, back at the butcher's counter, was looking at her the wrong way."

"What does *the wrong way* mean?" Noah asked.

"You know," she said with a slight shrug. "Like he wanted to screw her. Anyway, her boyfriend told Bill that if he looked at her like that again, he'd gouge his eyes out."

"We were sure Amy would quit," Gloria said. "She didn't come in for a few days after that. When she did come back, she was different."

"How so?"

Both women were quiet for a moment before Mindy said, "It's hard to describe, but it's like a piece of her was gone. Like part of her had died inside."

Gloria nodded in agreement.

My chest tightened, and air stuck in my lungs. Amy had started working here around the same time I'd moved back to Cockamamie. It sounded like she lived with an abusive asshole who retaliated against her whenever she showed any signs of independence. Had he found out she'd come to my class? Had he hurt her over it?

Or worse?

Feeling lightheaded, I rested my hand on the edge of the conveyor belt to hold myself upright.

"Has Amy ever come to work with bruises?" Noah asked.

"Once she had a black eye," Mindy said. "About a month after she started working here." She repeated the softball story the manager had told us.

"Did you believe her?"

"Not really," Mindy said, "but I didn't know enough about her home life to know for sure. Now, I don't believe it for a minute."

"I *never* believed it," Gloria said. "Someone hit her. Probably her boyfriend."

"Did she ever have bruises after that?" Noah asked.

"It's hard to say," Gloria said. "She started wearing long sleeves after her face bruise, but if I had to guess, yeah."

"I saw a bruise on her side once," Mindy said quietly. "She bent down to grab a few boxes of mac and cheese that had fallen off a shelf, and her shirt hiked up. I could see the purple splotches on her skin. Right here." She turned to her side and pointed to the side of her waist.

"Did you say anything to her about it?" Noah asked.

Mindy looked sheepish. "No, it seemed like an awkward conversation. She was really defensive about the bruise on her face."

"Weren't you worried about her?" I blurted out before I could stop myself.

Mindy turned a cold stare on me. "*Of course* I was worried about her, but I've been around enough women who've been beaten by their husbands and boyfriends and daddies, and God knows who else, to know there wasn't a doggone thing I could do to help her. The only thing I can do is be her friend, and she makes that task hard enough."

I felt properly and justifiably chastised. "Sorry," I said, swiping a hand over my forehead. "That was my own guilt talking. I have no right to judge you."

Mindy's eyes widened. "Guilt?"

"She showed up for my self-defense class at Deja Brew last night," I said. "I knew she was in trouble when she asked me—"

Noah's face darkened. "Thank you for your help, ladies." He pulled out his wallet and handed each of them a card. "If you think of anything else about Amy, please don't hesitate to call." Then he placed a hand on my lower back and ushered me to the door.

"What are you doing?" I whisper-sneered under my breath.

He kept his mouth pinched tight until we were through the automatic doors and in the parking lot, standing next to my car.

"Maddie, you can't volunteer information like that," he said in exasperation.

"Why not? They were volunteering information to us."

"Look," he said, holding my gaze. "You let the witness tell you everything they know without sharing what *you* know. Otherwise, you might bias their statement or unintentionally give them information they don't have, which would be detrimental to the case if they happen to be the guilty party."

"You honestly think either of those women had something to do with Amy not meeting me this morning or showing up tonight?"

"No, but it's bad form."

Nodding, I turned to the side and ran my hand over my head as my brain went into panic mode.

"Talk to me, Maddie," he said insistently. "What are you thinking?"

"I'm sorry," I said. "You're right. I should have kept my mouth shut."

He paused, then his voice softened. "Amy's disappearance isn't your fault, you know."

I didn't say anything, but I couldn't bring myself to look at him.

"I want you to say it," he said.

I snapped my gaze to his. "Say what?"

"That this isn't your fault."

"Of course it's not my fault. I didn't stop her from coming into work."

He continued to stare at me with a patient look.

"Don't patronize me, Noah."

"I'm not. But you told those women you felt guilty." He placed his hands on my shoulders. "What is it you feel guilty about?"

His hands felt too good there, as if they belonged on me. Which was such a stupid thought that I immediately shook him off and reached for the car door. I wasn't making myself vulnerable again. I wasn't setting myself up to be hurt by him again.

I started to open the door, but he held it shut. "Maddie."

Pushing out a sigh, I said, "I'm tired. I just want to go home."

He hesitated a moment before removing his hand. "Tomorrow morning, I'm going to drop by the address listed on Amy's application to see if she's there. I'll let you know what I find, okay?"

I nodded but refused to look at him. "Yeah, okay."

"Her boyfriend sounds like a first-class asshole who doesn't have any qualms about hurting women. You need to stay away from him and let me take over."

I nodded, still looking away.

"She could be all right, Maddie. Don't give up hope."

But it was hard to find hope when it all seemed so hopeless.

Chapter Eight

Noah

I woke up early the next morning despite having slept poorly. What little sleep I'd gotten was filled with dreams of Maddie—until they shifted to the night last spring, when my entire world had come crashing down.

I left my house by seven-thirty. Amy's address was just outside town, so it wasn't in my jurisdiction, but it wouldn't be out of bounds to stop by and ask about her.

Harrington was a country road, and the houses were somewhat sparse. Most of the terrain was empty fields interspersed with wooded sections. The day was overcast, giving the landscape a depressing, abandoned feel.

I didn't have to drive long before I pulled into the empty gravel driveway of 14560. The first thing I noticed was the overgrown bushes in front of the one-story house, which looked like it needed a coat of fresh paint and a new roof. There were houses on either side. The one on the right was about thirty feet away, with a yard linking the properties. The one on the left was about a hundred feet away, with a line of trees standing between them. Amy's address had an outbuilding with double doors that sat about twenty feet behind the house, which could have been used for either a garage or a workshop. A similar structure stood behind the house to the right, although it looked like it had been built for a tractor or motor home. It was also in better shape.

I got out of the car and walked up to the front porch. An elderly woman holding a watering can emerged from the house to the right. She started to water the dead plants in pots on her porch, but her gaze was firmly on me.

So the neighbor was a busybody. That could work in my favor.

I knocked on the front door and waited for half a minute before knocking again with no answer. When I knocked a third time, the woman next door called out, "They're not home."

I stepped down from the porch and started walking across the yard toward her. "I'm looking for Amy Davis. Have you seen her recently?"

The woman lifted her hand to shade her eyes even though the sun wasn't out. "Whatcha want with Amy?"

I pulled out my wallet and showed her my badge, holding it up as I continued to move closer. "I'm Detective Langley with the Cockamamie Police. Amy didn't show up to work yesterday, so I'm doing a welfare check."

"You're out of your jurisdiction, ain't ya?" she asked. "We live out of city limits. The sheriff's department handles cases out here."

"True, but like I said, this is just a welfare check. Have you seen Amy recently?"

She leveled the can while eyeing me suspiciously. "Maybe."

"Do you know if she's lived here long?"

"I saw them move her in right after Labor Day. I was kind of surprised because those two boys lived there a couple of years, and I hadn't seen a woman living there since the last one moved out a year ago."

"Two guys, you say? Do you happen to know their names?"

She pursed her lips. "One of them is Jake. The other is Boomer. I'm guessing it's a nickname."

Boomer. According to Mindy, Amy had called her boyfriend B. "You happen to know their last names?"

"Nope. I didn't even know Amy's last name until you said it."

On the off chance we were talking about another woman named Amy, I pulled out my phone and showed her the image I'd taken of Amy's application photo. "Is this the Amy you know?"

She took my phone and brought it closer to her face, then moved it half an arm's length out. "Yep. That's her."

"Do you know anything about her?" I asked as she handed the phone back to me.

"I met her soon after she moved in. She was outside planting some chrysanthemums in the flower bed out front, and I wandered over to introduce myself. She said she'd just moved here from Georgia to live with Boomer. She was kind of shy but sweet. Then one of the guys came home and got pissed at her for wasting money on flowers."

"Did they get into an argument?"

"No, she just looked upset, like she was about to start crying. He asked if his dinner was ready, and she scampered inside. Kind of like a little kid who got in trouble with her parents."

"Do you think it was Boomer?"

"Yeah, she called him by name."

The example she'd given—a kid with her parents—struck me as strange. "Is he older than her?"

"Yeah. I'd say he's in his late thirties. Same as the other guy, Jake."

"Do you know if the two guys are friends or related?"

"Don't know," she said. "They were never too friendly

before Amy moved in, and I took it they didn't want Amy to be friendly with me either."

"What makes you say that?"

"A few weeks later, Amy was outside raking leaves, and both guys came out with some fishing poles and loaded them in their pickup truck. The other guy, Jake, looked at me, then hollered at Amy, telling her she had some housework to do inside. She said she needed to rake the leaves so they didn't blow into my yard, and they told her it wasn't her concern. Then they watched to make sure she went inside before they left."

These guys sounded like a couple of sweethearts. "Did you talk to her any other time?"

"Yeah, I was making some bread the day of the leaf incident, so I took it over to her a couple hours later—after making sure those guys weren't back. She met me at the front door but wouldn't let me in. I could see past her though, and the house was neat as a pin. The furniture was old and worn, but it smelled nice, and it was clean. She loved the bread and thanked me up and down. I took her more baked goods after that, maybe a couple times a week—always making sure the guys weren't home—and it was always the same way. Clean and fresh smelling."

"When was the last time you saw Amy?"

"I saw her a few days ago. I could hear shouting outside and poked my head out the front door. Amy had just gotten home from work—she was still wearing her apron—and Boomer came outside, shouting at her, asking where she'd been. I could still hear shouting for a while, but then it went quiet."

"What day was that?"

She tapped her chin with her finger. "Last Sunday. I was getting ready to head out for evening church services, so about five-thirty."

"Do you know of any instances of domestic violence?"

She frowned. "Are you asking if they beat her? I can't say for sure. I've seen bruises on her arms and face, but she never called the police. Wait a minute. I know I said Sunday was the last time I saw her, but come to think of it, I saw her Tuesday morning—yesterday. She was putting a bag and a suitcase in her car."

My brow shot up. "You think she was moving out?"

"She didn't have much when she showed up, so maybe so. She waited until Boomer and Jake had left to bring her things out. They'd been gone about a half hour."

"Did the two guys leave together or separately?"

"Together. In a blue pickup truck."

"Do they have another car?"

"Yeah, a red car, but it's pretty old, and I ain't seen it for a few weeks."

"Do you know what time Amy left yesterday morning?"

Her lips pressed tight as she frowned. "Around nine-thirty or so. Definitely before ten. My talk show comes on at ten, and it happened before then."

Which meant Amy either left to go meet Maddie and never made it for some reason or decided she was done with Boomer and Jake and headed out of town. "What kind of car does Amy drive?"

"I'm not good with makes and models," she said dismissively. "They all look the same to me."

"Can you tell me what color it is? How big? Two doors or four?"

"It's a little silver car. But it does have four doors."

"Does it look older or newer?"

"Definitely older. It has some rust spots by the back wheels."

That narrowed it down to about a million cars, but it was

better than nothing. "Do you know anything about Boomer or Jake? Where they work? What they do?"

"I've seen Jake drive a work truck home a few times. Emerson Auto Parts."

"When was the last time you saw it?"

"Maybe a week ago?"

"Is there anything else you can remember that might help me find Amy?" I asked.

Worry filled her eyes. "Why?"

"I just want to make sure she's okay."

"Those two men are bad news, if you ask me. Amy's a sweet girl. She deserves better than that lot. She left those boys, so she's safe now."

I pulled a card from my jacket pocket and handed it to her. "Maybe so, but if you think of anything else you might find helpful, please don't hesitate to call me. My name's Detective Langley, and my number's on the card."

She took it and looked it over, then tucked it into her pocket. "Barbara Johnson. And I don't think anything else will come to me, but if it does, I'll let you know."

"Thanks for your help." I headed back to Jake and Boomer's property and looked around the front yard. Dead flower plants were in the bed lining the front walk. I climbed the front porch again and peered in through the front window. A small Christmas tree sat on an end table that had been pushed to the corner. It was decorated with sparse, cheap-looking ornaments, and there weren't any wrapped gifts. Fast food wrappers and glass cups were strewn across the coffee table. The place looked like a mess.

I headed back to my car and pulled out the copy of Amy's application to Bob's Market. She'd listed a woman named Shelly Tillman—her cousin—as her emergency contact. I tried the number, but a recording said it wasn't a working number.

Had Shelly Tillman lost her phone contract, or had Amy made her up?

Even though Mrs. Johnson had seen Amy leave, I wanted to make sure she'd arrived at her destination. I called Lance next. When he answered, I asked, "Are you at the station?"

"Yeah, why?"

"I need you to find out who owns the house at 14560 Harrington Road."

He paused. "Isn't Harrington Road outside of Cockamamie city limits?"

"Yeah, but it's the last known address for Amy Davis."

"You got a last name and an address?"

"I found out she works at Bob's Market, and the night manager gave me her employment information. I just talked to a neighbor." I filled him in on what she'd told me, then said, "I'm on my way to Emerson Auto Parts to see if I can talk to Jake."

"Need backup?"

I considered it. "No. It's just a friendly visit. No need to stir up trouble. Yet."

"You think she left town or moved in with someone else? Or are you thinking this is something worse?"

"I don't know. The neighbor thinks she's safe now, but I'm not ready to let it go yet."

"I'm sure Maddie will appreciate it."

I scowled. "How'd your *date* go?"

"She was a no-show."

"I'll bet, since I suspect she doesn't exist. Where would you have met a woman?"

He chuckled. "There's this new-fangled thing called internet dating, gramps."

"I'm only a few years older than you."

"Which makes it that much more amazing that you act like a seventy-year-old man instead of a thirty-seven-year-old."

I absently reached up to rub the scar on my chest from the bullet wound I'd received last spring. Getting shot by a kid you'd mentored for over five years and then being forced to kill him would do that to a man. "I'm not interested in dating, and now's not the time to bring it up. I'm headed to the auto parts store. Let me know when you find out who owns the property."

He chuckled. "Will do."

Lance could handle my grumpiness like a champ.

I headed toward the auto parts store and pulled into the parking lot. The store was also outside the city limits, and the building looked like it had been there for a few decades. I was new enough to the area that I didn't know the history of a lot of places like a local would, which was both a blessing and a curse. A couple of cars and a pickup truck were parked in the lot. A truck with the company's logo was parked in a space apart from all the other cars to the left of the building. I wasn't sure if that meant Jake was here, but I took it as a good sign.

When I went in, an older man was finishing up a transaction with a guy who looked to be in his early twenties. I waited until the customer took his receipt and bag and headed for the door.

As soon as the door started closing behind the customer, I held up my badge to the cashier and introduced myself. "I'm looking for Jake."

The guy leaned closer to study my badge, then lifted his gaze to mine with a panicked look. "Jake?"

"I was told you have an employee named Jake who works here."

"We ain't in Cockamamie," he said defiantly. "You're a Cockamamie cop."

"That might be true, but I still have some questions. Is Jake here?"

A smirk spread across his face. "Nope. He's out."

"Do you know when he'll be back to work?"

"Hard to say. Heard he might have the flu. It might be a few days."

I shifted my weight, not amused that he was lying. "That's too bad. You got a home address on him so I can drop by and make sure he's okay? Or maybe a phone number so I can call him and not catch whatever he's got?"

He lifted his chin. "Nope. The manager has that stuff, and he's not here right now."

"And when will your manager be back?"

"Dunno."

I leveled a stern gaze at him. "What's your manager's name and number?"

"Danny, but I'm not allowed to give out his number."

I gave him a withering glare, and he shrank back a little but kept his mouth shut. Frustrated, I pulled out a business card and put it on the counter. "When he comes back, please have him give me a call."

"Yeah," he said with a smug look. "Sure thing."

He wouldn't tell him, which meant I'd need to follow up later.

I was outside, about to open my car door, when Lance called. I answered as I got in. "What have you got for me?"

"The owner of Amy's residence is Peter Castillo. Not Boomer or Jake. He's owned it for ten years."

"Boomer's gotta be a nickname, and his real name could be Peter. See if you can get more information on him."

"What's your gut saying on this?" Lance asked in a subdued tone.

"I'm not sure. It worries me that Amy's emergency contact listed on her employment application is a non-working number, and Amy's not answering her phone. But she might have ditched hers to keep her boyfriend from finding her. He might have some kind of tracking app installed."

"Who's her emergency contact?"

"A cousin in Georgia. Or at least the number has an Atlanta area code."

"Huh." He was quiet for a moment. "You think her boyfriend might have found her *and* her cousin?"

I frowned, tapping the steering wheel. "I don't know. It's too early to say."

"If she's dead, that'll be Cockamamie's second homicide in a month. Before Martin Schroeder's death, we hadn't had a murder in years. You must be some kind of bad luck charm."

"Very funny," I said dryly. "Or maybe I'm just that good at picking up on cases. No one else would be chasing this down. And I'm not even doing it officially. If she disappeared after she left home, that would make it a case for the sheriff's department."

"You gonna call and see if someone'll take it?"

I frowned. "Not yet. I doubt there's enough to convince them, but if I can get a little more...I'm heading back to the grocery store now to see if anyone else knows something."

"I'll help by looking into Peter Castillo."

"Thanks, Lance."

"Yeah, no problem."

I hung up and was pulling into the grocery store parking lot when I got a call from my sergeant.

"Noah, we just got another residential B&E call."

I groaned inwardly. My investigation into Amy would have to wait. "Shit. Same as the others?"

"This one's a bit more...weird."

That didn't sound good. "I'm on my way."

Chapter Nine

Noah

Weird didn't even begin to describe the scene. The four previous break-ins had all been your garden variety B&Es—houses hit during the day while the homeowners were at work. The perp entered through the back door, grabbed their loot, then left. You wouldn't have even known the houses had been invaded, other than a busted back door and the missing electronics and jewelry. One couple's Christmas gifts had been taken from under the tree as if the Grinch had struck. Another homeowner had only been gone for half an hour before returning to a house stripped of valuables.

It wasn't uncommon for the thieves to strike during the day, and we believed they'd taken to pulling their vehicles into the garages to hide their activities from their neighbors. This led us to believe there were at least two perpetrators—one to break in the back and open the garage door, and the driver who pulled into the garage. In fact, one of the homeowners had found his garage door open when he came home from work. None of the homes had security cameras, alarms, or even dogs. That, along with the short window of the one robbery, led me to believe the homes had been specifically targeted. The frustrating part was that we had absolutely no leads. No fingerprints had been left behind, and up until this point, there hadn't been any witnesses. There weren't security cameras on any nearby houses either that could have picked up unfamiliar vehicles.

Two patrol officers were at the house when I arrived. One of them was talking to a distraught woman in yoga pants and a long, thick cardigan sweater next to the street. The other officer approached as I got out of my car. "What have we got?" I asked, grateful it was Neil Erickson. He'd only been an officer for six months, but he was thorough. Much more so than some of the tenured guys.

"Mrs. Gibbs arrived home at approximately nine-o-five a.m. after taking her kids to school. She said she had only been gone twenty minutes. When she came home, she saw a white van pulling out of her driveway headfirst. She thought that was odd, of course, but then she went inside and freaked out."

"The sarge said it was weird. What makes it weird? Was the home vandalized?"

He took a breath, then said, "Maybe you should see for yourself."

Now my curiosity was really piqued.

Lance pulled to the curb behind my car, so I walked over to him and filled him in on what little information I had.

"Both the sarge and Neil said it was weird?" Lance asked, then made a face. "That doesn't sound good."

"Tell me about it. Let's go check it out."

We headed toward the house, and Neil joined us, saying, "Mrs. Gibbs entered and exited through the garage door, but the entry for the suspects is the same MO as the others—through the back door."

An older green minivan was parked in the open bay, so we

walked around it to the door leading into the house. It had been left open, so we climbed the two steps and walked straight into the kitchen. Lance and I stood close to the door and looked around.

"What's weird?" Lance asked.

"Check out the counter," Officer Erickson said, pointing to something next to the sink.

As we got closer, I caught a look at a polaroid photo of a hand holding a pair of black lacy underwear...in front of a jeans-covered crotch.

"What the hell?" Lance muttered under his breath.

"Mrs. Gibbs saw it, freaked out, then ran outside and called police. She said she thinks it was a pair she wore yesterday and left in her laundry hamper. When Officer Martinez and I got here, we cleared the house and found another photo. The one in the bedroom is even worse."

Lance shot me a worried look.

"Where's the bedroom?" I asked.

Officer Erickson grimaced. "This way."

We followed him through a living room that had a big gaping hole in the entertainment center where a TV would go, but we ignored it and headed down the hall to an open door at the end that led to what I presumed was the master bedroom. The dresser drawers were open, with clothing scattered all over the floor, but several pairs of women's underwear had been arranged under a polaroid photo in the middle of the bed.

We leaned over the bed and got a good look at a man's very erect penis under his tighty-whities with a strip of the black panties sticking out of the top of his elastic band. A male-looking hand gripped the base of the penis through the underwear.

"Jesus," Lance muttered under his breath.

"Shit," I growled. We weren't just dealing with burglary. This was a sexual predator.

"This isn't the only thing different from the other cases," I said. "In the previous four, the houses were left undisturbed, other than the missing items. It was as though they'd tried to be as neat as possible. This room is a mess."

"So's the bathroom," Officer Erickson said, pointing to a partially closed door.

Lance and I walked inside and stopped as soon as we entered the room. The perps had vandalized this room, dumping out drawers onto the floor, along with the contents of the cabinet below the sink. A red heart had been drawn on the mirror with what looked like lipstick.

"We think some drugs are missing," Officer Erickson said. "We couldn't find any pill bottles, and Mrs. Gibbs said her husband had knee surgery a few weeks ago. He definitely had some of his pain medicine left over, as well as a muscle relaxer he'd gotten around the same time for his back."

"They haven't taken drugs before either," I said.

"It's not the same team," Lance said.

"Agreed," I said. "This is way too different."

And a whole lot more fucked up. This guy—or guys—was potentially dangerous.

What would have happened if he'd still been inside when the homeowner had gotten home?

"You said she took her kids to school," I said over my shoulder to Officer Erickson. "Have you checked their rooms?"

"They're missing electronics, and the rooms are a mess, but there's no photos or anything disgusting. At least not that we've seen."

I gave him a sharp nod. "I take it the crime scene unit has been notified?"

"Yeah, but they're tied up with a murder case over on the other side of the county."

My mind instantly jumped to Amy. "A murder? Know anything about the victim?"

"White guy in his twenties or thirties. They found him on a walking trail over by Maguire Lake. They think it's a drug deal gone wrong."

At least it wasn't Amy.

"They said the unit has been out there a while, so they should be here soon."

"Has Mrs. Gibbs's husband been called?"

"She called him before we got here. She said he had a meeting to wrap up, but then he was heading home."

"Do we know what time he left for work?"

"About seven."

"Let's follow up with his employer to make sure he's been there all morning," I said, heading out of the bathroom and back into the master bedroom.

"You think her husband did this?" Neil asked in surprise.

"I have no idea who could have done this, but until everyone has been cleared, everyone is under suspicion."

"Even Mrs. Gibbs?" Neil protested.

"She could have set it up," Lance said. "She likely didn't, but we can't overlook the possibility."

"Still," I added, "we won't be treating her like a suspect, particularly when we tell her what we found. I doubt she had anything to do with it, but we still need to rule out her involvement."

Neil nodded.

"Let's go check out the other rooms."

The three of us went through the rest of the house together. Thankfully, there was nothing perverted in the two children's rooms, but their drawers had been dumped, and there weren't any electronics.

When we finished our walkthrough and went outside, I saw a man sitting on the street curb with Mrs. Gibbs. Officer Lou Martinez walked over and told us the man was the woman's husband, Andrew Gibbs, so I sent Neil to take his statement while Lance and I talked to his wife.

I knew Jennifer Gibbs was either innocent or a skilled actress within a few minutes of talking to her. She was pissed that someone had violated her home and just wanted to go inside to inventory what had been stolen. Lance told her that we needed to get a statement from her before we moved into a discussion of what was missing. I was grateful he didn't allude to something bigger going on.

She said her son had dragged his feet getting ready for school that morning, so they'd been late getting out the front door. She hadn't hit any traffic or made any other stops, but she got home about five minutes later than was typical.

"Did you notice anything unusual when you got home?" I asked.

"Just like I told that nice young officer over there"—she pointed to Neil—"a white van was in the driveway, pulling out headfirst, and the garage door was open. I know for a fact I closed it, because I nearly forgot, and Hunter—that's my son—reminded me. I saw it closing as I drove away, and when I stopped at the stop sign, I checked in my rearview mirror to make sure it was shut."

"Did you get a look at the driver or a passenger in the van?" I asked.

Her eyes filled with tears. "There was a guy in the driver's seat. He had a bushy red beard. I think he was wearing a black T-shirt."

"You only saw the one guy?" I asked.

She nodded.

"And how long were you gone?"

"It takes me about six or seven minutes to get to school, then about the same coming back. I only spent a couple minutes in the drop-off line, so about fifteen to twenty minutes."

I looked at Lance. Was fifteen minutes long enough for one guy to go in and steal everything and take those photos? I was leaning toward him needing help. It would be extremely difficult for someone to break in the back and then have to pull the van into the garage.

"Have you noticed any unfamiliar cars in the neighborhood lately?" Lance asked.

It was a great question. The perpetrators had to be doing surveillance to know that the targets and the homes nearby didn't have exterior video cameras.

"Are you asking if I've seen any white vans lurking around? No, but I haven't been looking either. My kids keep me busy. Can I go back into my house now? It's cold out here."

She was shivering in her light sweater.

"It's probably going to be a while," I said. "Perhaps sit in your car or get a neighbor to bring you a jacket or blanket."

She made a face, then let out a sigh. "The only one who'd be home is Mrs. Buttrum across the street. The woman who's spying on us through her front door. She's not exactly friendly, if you know what I mean. I'll just call my friend Val."

"I'll check on Mr. Gibbs," Lance said. "Then we'll start knocking on some doors while we wait for the crime scene team to get here."

"CSI?" Mrs. Gibbs said in shock. "Like those people on TV? My friend Penny's house was broken into last week, and she said they barely looked for fingerprints."

I paused in my tracks, and Lance gave her his full attention.

"Penelope Waterson?" I asked.

She nodded. "Yeah, that's her."

Penelope Waterson's house had been the second one hit in this string of burglaries.

"How do you know her?" I asked.

"We go to church together. Same as Valerie Dillingham. Cockamamie First Baptist Church."

I shot a pointed look at Lance, then turned back to Mrs. Gibbs. "Do you know Mike and Martha Middleton?"

Her nose wrinkled for a moment. "No. Doesn't sound familiar."

"Excuse me for a moment," I said before turning to Lance. We moved several feet away and turned to each other.

"I'll call the church," Lance said under his breath, "but it's pretty big. I'd guess a good portion of the town attends church there, so it might be purely coincidental."

"The burglaries have taken place in four different neighborhoods," I said. "We thought the vics were chosen at random, but what if that's not true? What if they were targeted not only based on their homes' locations and the lack of exterior cameras but also because of something else?" I glanced to the other side of the street, and an older woman glared at me from the window. Was this the Mrs. Buttrum Mrs. Gibbs had mentioned? "I'm going to head across the street and see if the neighbor saw anything. You call the church and see how many of the previous homeowners were members."

"On it."

When I stepped onto Mrs. Buttrum's front porch a few moments later, the door opened before I even had a chance to knock. The woman who answered was medium height and overweight, with graying hair and a red, pudgy face. I guessed her to be in her fifties.

"I didn't have nothin' to do with nothin'," she grunted in disgust.

This interview was going to be as pleasant as trudging through mud uphill, but I gave her a warm smile and introduced myself.

Mrs. Buttrum started to shut the door, but I held up a hand. "Mrs. Buttrum, I need to ask you a few questions."

"I told you I didn't do nothin'."

"You're not a suspect," I said. "I just want to know if you saw anything over at the Gibbs's house."

"I can see all kinds of things goin' on at the Gibbs's house right now." She gestured toward their front yard.

I restrained a sigh. For some bizarre reason, I'd thought people in this town would be more receptive to questioning than the citizens of Memphis. While some were, I'd found that many were just as suspicious of law enforcement.

"Did you see Mrs. Gibbs leave her house this morning?"

Her brow lifted. "You think I spy on my neighbors?"

The binoculars on the entry table behind her suggested she did, but I kept that to myself. "Of course not. But you might have seen something as you walked past the window." My conversation with Amy's neighbor this morning came to mind. "Or maybe while you were out watering your flowers."

Her chin lifted in defiance. "In December? You see any flowers out there? I didn't see that woman leave her house."

"Did you see *anyone* there this morning?"

She hesitated. "I saw a white van pull into the driveaway right after she left."

She'd just contradicted herself, but I didn't want to call her on it in case she clammed up. She must have realized her mistake because she added, "I didn't see her leave the house, but I saw her green minivan turn the corner, and the white van pulled into the open garage less than a couple minutes later."

"Did you say the van pulled into the driveway and pulled straight into the garage? It didn't pause for the door to open?"

"I don't think I stuttered," she grumped. "The garage was closed, then it opened, and the van backed inside. Then the door closed behind it."

So they'd been waiting for her to leave. As I suspected, a second person had likely gone around the back and broken in, then opened the garage door for the van. Pretty slick, and likely why no one had seen anything going on at the other houses. That was if this break-in was connected to the others. I was still struggling to understand the change in MO.

"Have you noticed a white van hanging around the neighborhood this week?"

"No."

"What about other vehicles that don't seem like they belong?"

"Nope."

"Did you see anything else unusual at the Gibbses's house?"

She crossed her arms over her chest. "Nope."

"Mrs. Gibbs saw the van pull out of her driveway when she got home. Did you see the white van leave?"

"I saw the door open and the van pull out."

"Did you happen to see the people who arrived with the van? The driver? Any passengers?"

"I saw a ginger driving—had a big beard in need of trimming —and that was it."

"Anything else you can think of that might help?" I asked.

"Nope. I told you my side of the story. Now it's time for you to tell me what's going on. Did the Gibbs family get robbed? I'm the former president of the neighborhood watch, you know. I need to be informed of these things."

I stared at her, incredulous. "You're the former president of the neighborhood watch, and you didn't think to call the police when you saw a suspicious white van pull into your neighbor's garage?"

She lifted her shoulders into a defiant shrug. "I warned those fools they'd regret voting me out of the presidency, and lookie here. I stopped watching over the neighborhood."

Or more like she was still watching, but she was using her information for her own purposes. "What I hear you saying is that you failed to notify the police because you were voted out," I said dryly.

"Heard Jennifer voted for Miriam too. Maybe you should be talking to Miriam since she's the new president. Miriam Brewster. Lives five houses down." A smug look crossed her face. "Oh, wait. She's at work, so she didn't see nothin'." She shook her head in irritation. "I warned those fools they'd regret voting me out. Told them I'm home and can watch over everything better than anyone else could, and it looks like I was right."

"You mean to say that you watched your neighbor's house get broken into and did nothing *on purpose*," I said, trying to rein in my disgust. "Do you know if Mr. or Mrs. Gibbs has any enemies? Have they pissed off anyone in the neighborhood?"

Other than you.

She gave me a haughty look. "I know that the Harmons, their neighbors to the right, don't like when that Gibbs boy goes outside to play basketball in his driveway. Henry doesn't like the sound of the bouncing ball. Complained to Andy about it a time or two. The last time—a few weeks ago—Henry shouted at Andy to be more considerate of his elderly neighbors."

"So Henry Harmon is elderly?" I asked.

"He's seventy-nine."

It seemed unlikely that Henry Harmon was the culprit—the hand in the photo looked like it belonged to a younger man—but I wasn't ready to rule anyone out yet. "Anyone else?"

"Nope."

I pulled a business card from my pocket and handed it to her. "If you think of anything else, don't hesitate to call."

She took the card and looked it over. I suspected she might be calling in the future about things unrelated to the Gibbs situation. I had no doubt I'd be on her speed dial if she was voted in as president again.

I headed back to Lance, who was lowering his phone from his ear.

He gave me a grim look. "I talked to the church secretary. She seems to know something about everyone in the church. She said four of the five families with burglaries attend First Baptist, all with varying levels of participation in the congregation. Fred Myers is a deacon, and his wife is a Sunday school teacher, but the Gibbs family barely attends. The other two families are somewhere in the middle with attendance."

I took in the information before I said, "So like you suggested, it's probably just a coincidence, but we'll keep it in mind anyway." I cast a glance at the Gibbses's house. "Did Mr. Gibbs have anything helpful to add?"

"Nope. He hadn't heard or seen anything unusual around the neighborhood for the past few days, and he doesn't know of anyone who has a grudge against either him or his wife."

"He could be lying," I said.

"Or she could. It was definitely a dick pic, even if it was covered. Maybe she was having an affair and broke it off."

"Maybe..." It warranted some investigation, but the idea didn't seem to fit. My instincts were usually right, or at least they had been until the incident in Memphis last spring. That night, my instincts had gotten my dog killed, along with the kid who'd shot him.

"Any word on the crime scene team?"

"Sarge said they're about fifteen minutes out." He paused. "When do you want to tell the Gibbses about the other photo?"

"After the crime scene team is finished, we'll take the couple on a walkthrough to get an inventory of what's missing. Then we'll tell them about the second one. And we'll ask again if they know of anyone who could have done this."

A couple of hours later, we'd sat the Gibbses down and told them about the second, more vulgar photo. They'd been horrified, and both had insisted they couldn't think of anyone who would've done such a thing. They came up with a list of missing items—including the black pair of underwear—and I told them we wanted to keep possession of the house a little longer so we could do a few more walkthroughs of our own. Mrs. Gibbs readily agreed, saying she refused to stay there and would be at her parents' house for the foreseeable future.

I had Officer Erickson monitor their actions while they packed a few bags, and Lance and I waited outside to discuss theories.

"Any new thoughts?" he asked as we stared at the house.

"I sure as hell hope we get some prints from this one. The guy obviously wasn't wearing gloves when he took the photo we found on the bed." Sometimes cocky assholes were careless in their arrogance.

"I'll start calling pawn shops to see if any of the stolen items have been brought in. I know we haven't recovered anything from the previous burglaries, but since this case is different, we might get something."

"Let's hope."

The Gibbses walked out of the house, looking like they'd just stepped out of a war zone. Mrs. Gibbs appeared on the verge of falling apart, but her husband had an arm wrapped around her shoulders as they headed down the porch steps. Officer Erickson had two duffel bags slung over his shoulders.

I walked over to them as they approached their minivan.

"I want to burn the place down," Mrs. Gibbs told me, with a haunted look in her eyes.

"We're going to do everything within our power to catch the perpetrators," I told her, looking her square in the eye. "I'll do everything I can to make you feel safe in your home again."

She gave me a tearful thanks before her husband helped her into the passenger side of the minivan.

He pinned me with a menacing glare. "You find the bastard."

Chapter Ten

Maddie

On Wednesday, everyone and their brother wanted coffee. I was tired after working, hosting self-defense lessons, and dealing with both the strain of Aunt Deidre's fluid memory and my worry about Amy. Oh, and the resurfacing emotions regarding my mother. I was pretty sure I had dark circles under my eyes because Petra made me down two double-shot espressos during my shift while working on the line.

It was two o'clock before I could take a break and check my phone, eager to see if Noah had called with an update after checking at Amy's address. I was ticked to see I hadn't missed any calls or texts from him. Had he not gone after all, or had he just not bothered to call me? While I knew that wasn't fair—he'd taken the case seriously at the grocery store—I realized I was still irritated with him over everything that had gone down a month ago. It was just bleeding into this situation. Still, knowing something and dealing with it are two different things.

I didn't waste any time calling him.

He answered, sounding distracted. "Hey, Maddie. I

planned to call and let you know what I found, but I got called in on a case, and it's kept me busy for the last few hours."

Guilt washed through me, but it was quickly followed by fear. "There hasn't been another murder, has there?" Even though Noah and I had met because of a homicide investigation, murder was extremely rare in Cockamamie. "Oh, my God. Was it *Amy*?"

"No. No. Just a home burglary, although the homeowners feel violated, of course."

"Of course." While I'd had a security system put in after our break-in and my near kidnapping, I still struggled to sleep some nights. "Did you find out anything about Amy?"

"I did, but not much. What time do you get off?"

"Three."

He hesitated, then said, "Do you want to meet somewhere after you get off so I can fill you in?"

It was my turn to hesitate. Couldn't he just tell me whatever he'd discovered over the phone? Then I realized the police liked to deliver bad news in person. "You found out something bad," I said, my voice quieter than intended.

"What? No. I promise, Maddie. I *did* discover a few things, but let me tell you in person, okay? How about we meet at Lucky's Tavern?"

"A bar? Won't you still be on the clock?"

"I'm starving, and they have a great lunch menu. The food's good if you're hungry. Plus, it'll be quiet. It's usually pretty dead in the middle of the afternoon."

He was obviously speaking from personal experience. Despite everything, I wanted to see him. Which was why I needed to stay away. "I don't know. Why can't you just tell me?"

"Meet with me, Maddie. I'll be waiting to see you when you get off work."

Against my better judgment, I agreed.

The next hour seemed to crawl, leaving my overactive imagination plenty of time to go over all the possible horrible things Noah could have found out about Amy.

At three, I didn't waste any time leaving the coffee shop and sent a text to Aunt Deidre's home health aide letting her know that I was taking care of a few errands before going home.

I'd never been to Lucky's Tavern before, but I knew where to go. When I got there, Noah's car was in the parking lot, along with two other cars. I was walking toward the front door when my phone rang. I took it out and glanced at the screen, stopping dead in my tracks and staring at it in disbelief.

Steve.

Why the hell was he calling me? I hadn't talked to him since I'd left Nashville in September. Was it about the house? Did he actually intend to pay me back the money I'd given him?

I stopped in my tracks and answered. "Why can't you just text like a normal person?"

"Well, hello to you too, Maddie," Steve said in his infuriatingly condescending tone. "Nice to know you missed me."

Hearing his voice and tone reminded me of how embarrassed I was that I'd put up with his crap for so long. What an idiot. "I missed you like a toenail fungus. Are you calling to tell me when I can expect to see my fifteen thousand dollars plus interest?"

"So you heard I sold the flip house."

"I heard you sold it a month ago. Why am I just now hearing from you?" I ran a hand over my head. "You know what? Who cares? I'll text you my aunt's address so you can mail the money to me."

I didn't feel like dealing with his asshattery right then, so I hung up, rapid-fire texted my new address to him, then stuffed the phone in my purse.

After taking a deep breath to center myself, I walked into

the tavern, letting my eyes adjust to the light as I slipped off my coat and scarf. The place was cozy, with high-backed stools at the bar to the right and a row of booths with high wooden backs along the left wall. A couple of rows of tables and chairs filled in the middle.

Noah was sitting at a booth, deep in concentration, with an open laptop in front of him. He was wearing a brown sports coat and a light blue dress shirt, but today he was minus a tie.

No one else was in the place—not even a bartender—and it felt eerily intimate.

He didn't notice me until I was halfway across the room. He glanced up and slid out of his seat to greet me. "Thanks for meeting me here, Maddie. I haven't eaten since this morning, and I like how quiet it is here in the middle of the day."

"Looks pretty private," I said, glancing around the space.

"Are you hungry? Matilda should be out any minute with my burger and fries."

I lifted a brow, irritated by the zing of jealousy shooting through me. "Matilda?"

He grinned. "Lance's mom. She owns the place." He motioned to the seat opposite where he was sitting. "Have a seat."

Lance's mom owned the tavern? I slid into the booth and put my coat and purse on the seat next to me as Noah sat across from me. He closed the laptop, pushed it to the side, then took me in for a long second.

A rush of heat swept through me. I'd been right. Meeting Noah like this was a bad idea. It was too intimate, too much like a date. "You said you had information about Amy," I prodded.

His gaze dropped to the table before he lifted it, looking more guarded. "Not much, but I wanted to fill you in. Amy wasn't home when I showed up at her address this morning. In fact, no one answered, but I talked to a neighbor who said Amy had moved into the house in early September. The neighbor said she came from Georgia. Amy lives with two men—Boomer and Jake—and she said Boomer is her boyfriend."

"Mindy said Amy called her boyfriend B, so that fits."

"Agreed. The two men aren't friendly with the neighbor, and she doesn't think much of them. They're short with Amy, she said, and they don't like it when she talks to anyone other than them. She's seen Amy with bruises from time to time. She also said that last Sunday, Boomer got mad when Amy came home from work. He met her outside and was shouting, asking where she'd been. The neighbor said there was also a lot of shouting when they went inside, and then it was suddenly quiet."

My stomach dropped. "Did he hit her to get her to shut up?" I asked. "Or maybe he choked her?"

He gave me a sympathetic look. "It's all speculation. There's no point in going there."

"She wore a turtleneck and asked me to teach her how to get out of a chokehold, Noah. What else am I supposed to think?"

He started to answer, but a woman emerged from the back, carrying two plates with burgers and fries. She set them on the table in front of each of us and said, "Noah told me he was expecting someone to join him, so I brought out another plate of food." She stepped back and looked me up and down with a delighted smile. "And who might you be?"

"Matilda," Noah said, "this is Maddie Baker."

Her eyes widened slightly. "You're the woman who drove that guy to his murder."

"That's me," I said in a glib tone even though I hated it when anyone brought it up. It made me feel like the Uber of death.

"Sorry," she said, looking apologetic. "It's just that Lance worked your case with Noah, and that's how he started working investigations instead of being out on patrol."

"Oh," I said in surprise. I hadn't known any of that. "He was very kind to me through everything."

"I'm sorry about your mother's death, too," she said hurriedly, reminding me of my other nickname around town: Andrea Baker's orphaned daughter. "It really bothered Lance that they never found her killer. Of course, it bothered all of us, but it really affected my boy. It's a big part of why he went into law enforcement." She cringed. "Oh, dear. I'm sure you don't want to be talking about your mother."

"That's okay," I said. "I'm used to it."

She shook her head. "You shouldn't be. Can I get you something to drink?"

"Some iced tea would be great."

Her head bobbed with a crisp nod. "Coming right up." Then she hurried behind the counter.

Noah picked up a ketchup bottle and handed it to me. "She means well."

"I'm sure," I said, opening the top of the bottle. "It's just strange when everyone knows such a big thing about your life. It's part of the reason I moved away after high school." I squirted ketchup onto my plate and handed the bottle to Noah. "Did Amy's neighbor say anything else?"

"She said she saw Amy yesterday morning."

My back stiffened. "She did? When? Where? What was she doing?"

He poured ketchup on his open bun, then on his plate. "She saw Amy leaving the house around nine-thirty. She was carrying a suitcase and a bag out to her car."

"She was moving out?"

"Either that or going on a trip," he said. "The question is, where did she go? Did she head back to Georgia? Move in with friends?"

"Maybe she was going to ask me to help her."

"Maybe, but it could also mean that attending your class and asking you to meet her gave her the courage to leave."

"What about the middle of the night call?" I asked.

He grimaced. "Maybe it was an accidental call. You said no one said anything. Or maybe she called you intending to ask for advice and realized how late it was and then hung up."

"You really believe that?" I asked sarcastically. "You think she accidentally called me at two in the morning?"

He drew in a breath, then let it out. "No."

"What do you think happened?"

"I think she was in trouble when she called you, but the neighbor saw her leave, so we know she was..." He grimaced.

"Alive," I filled in. "We know she was alive on Tuesday morning at nine-thirty."

"She probably left town, Maddie. She probably went back to her family in Georgia."

While I hoped so, we didn't know for certain, and I couldn't let it rest until we did.

Noah dipped a fry into the ketchup on his plate. "I called the emergency contact on her employment application. She listed Shelly Tillman as her cousin, and the phone number had an Atlanta area code, but the number was out of service."

I narrowed my eyes. "Why would it be out of service? She just listed that number a few months ago."

"That's a good question," he said. "She could have made it up. Or it could have been a working number at the time, and Shelly either changed numbers or stopped paying her phone bill. Another possibility is that it was a pay-as-you-go phone, and she ran out of minutes."

"But Shelly Tillman would likely be the person who'd know

if she's okay," I said. "Can't you just call to find out what happened to her phone?"

"Not without a warrant. And this isn't an official case. Even if it were, it would be out of my jurisdiction."

Which meant his hands were tied.

Matilda came out from the back, carrying a glass of iced tea. Noah and I remained silent as she set it on the table in front of me.

"Something wrong with your food?" she asked as she took in my untouched plate.

"No," I said, offering a smile. "I was just busy talking to Noah."

She frowned. "Would you rather have something else? We added a crispy chicken sandwich to the menu about a month back."

I shook my head. "No. This is great. Thank you, Mrs. Forrester."

With a stern look, she pointed her finger at me. "That's Matilda. And if you want something else, don't be shy about asking."

I picked up my burger and took a bite. "Mmm," I said through a mouthful of food.

Grinning, she turned and headed into the back.

"Matilda's got a thing about feeding people," Noah said, his affection for her obvious.

"I'm glad you let *someone* look out for you," I said after I swallowed.

His face clouded over. "What's that mean?"

Were we going to have this conversation? Now seemed as good a time as any. I set the burger on my plate and wiped my fingers on my napkin. "I know why you ghosted me, Noah."

"I didn't—" He stopped and drew in a breath, keeping his

gaze on the table. "I thought it would be easier to make a clean break."

"Easier for *you*." I shook my head. I changed my mind. This was a terrible idea. "Nope. Not doing this." I looked him dead in the eyes. "I'm only here because I want to know what you found out about Amy. This isn't personal. Now, did you find anything else?"

He looked like he wanted to say something, then thought better of it. "There's not much else I can do. I found out where the roommate works and went to talk to him, but he wasn't there."

"Where does he work?"

He gave me a look of warning.

"I'm just asking," I said defensively.

"He works at Emerson Auto Parts."

"Okay," I said. "That's an easy place to go back to when he *is* working. Or you can go back to his house and talk to him and Boomer tonight."

He gave me a troubled look. "There's another reason I asked you to meet me. I wanted to tell you this in person." He paused. "The case I've been working on all day is pretty big. It has to take priority right now."

"You're saying you don't have time to look for Amy." I couldn't say I wasn't disappointed, but I wasn't upset with him either. "I understand. I knew you were looking into it unofficially."

"Since she lives outside the city limits, and the last place she was seen was pulling away from her house, I called a sheriff's deputy I've gotten to know since I started on the Cockamamie force."

"Is he taking the case?"

He shook his head. "No. There's no reason to suspect foul

play, and no one close to her has reported her missing. But if something comes up, he'll be aware of our concerns."

"So that's it?" I asked, feeling defeated.

He leaned closer. "I know you're still worried, but I suspect Amy's back in Georgia with her family, safe from those assholes she was living with."

That painted a pretty picture, but I knew that life usually wasn't that generous.

"That's about all I know," he said, sounding apologetic.

It wasn't much, but it was something. I had her address. I knew her boyfriend's first name and also that the neighbor had talked to Amy on multiple occasions.

People were often more willing to talk to friends of the victim than the police. The neighbor was a good place to start.

I reached into my purse, pulled out some cash, and put it on the table.

"You're leaving?" Noah asked in dismay. "You've barely touched your food."

"I'm not very hungry, and I have a lot to do before my last class tonight."

He grimaced. "There's one more thing. I know I told you I'd bring you mats again, but I might be tied up with this case. But I *promise* you'll have mats. Even if I have to ask one of the patrol officers to bring them over."

I gave him a sincere smile. My feelings for him were complicated, but he was helping me, despite the fact he didn't have to. I couldn't ignore that. "Thanks. I really appreciate you looking out for me."

Grabbing my things, I slid out of the seat and headed to the door, but I could have sworn I heard him say, "I'll always look out for you, Maddie."

Chapter Eleven

Maddie

I knew Noah would likely be pissed that I headed straight over to Amy's house, but, like he'd said, there wasn't an official investigation underway, and I wasn't willing to blindly accept that she'd left town. I couldn't see the harm in talking to her neighbor.

Amy's house was set off the road by about thirty or forty feet, and the closest neighbor was to the right. I suspected they were the neighbor Noah had spoken to since the house to the left looked rundown and abandoned.

I parked my car on the side of the road in front of Amy's house—not an easy task since there wasn't much of a shoulder. There weren't any cars in Amy's driveway, and Noah had said no one was home when he came by in the morning. I hadn't intended to approach Amy's house, but now that I was here, I was strongly considering it. What if she'd been inside earlier but had been hesitant to open the door to a man? She didn't know Noah, but she *did* know me.

I walked to her driveway and headed toward the house, trying to figure out a cover story in case Boomer or Jake answered. By the time I reached the porch, I had a vague excuse about the grocery store. I knocked on the door multiple times, though, and no one answered.

Still, I couldn't shake the fear that Amy was inside and injured. If Boomer really did choke her, who knew what else he was capable of?

I knocked again, then called out, "Amy? It's Maddie from the self-defense class. Are you home?" I waited several long seconds before banging the door again. "Amy?"

There was still no response. Either she really wasn't home, or she couldn't answer. The latter thought made me shudder. I tried the front doorknob, not surprised it was locked.

Time to try Amy's neighbor. The house to the right was painted a pale yellow with white trim and had a cheerful air despite the two pots of dead plants on the front porch.

I walked across the yard and up to the front door.

An elderly woman opened it before I could lift my hand to knock. "Are you having car trouble, dear?" she asked with a worried look.

"No. Actually, I'm here to talk to *you*."

Irritation pinched her mouth into a firm line. "I don't need any siding, new windows, yard service, or pest control, so you can head right back out to your car."

"I'm not selling anything," I said in a rush, holding up my hands in surrender. "I wanted to ask you about Amy."

She turned wary. "Amy's a popular girl today."

"I'm a friend of hers," I said. "She didn't show up to work yesterday, and I'm worried about her."

She pushed out a heavy sigh. "It's cold out here, and I've been standing on my feet a lot today. Why don't you come inside?"

"Thanks," I said before walking into the dated living room. The only thing that didn't look two decades old was a large-screen TV sitting on an old cabinet. I took a seat on a sofa with upholstery covered in pink and blue roses, and the woman sat in a worn blue recliner, tittering as she lowered herself to the seat. She turned down the sound on a game show she was watching. "I love me my talk shows and game shows. Have you seen this one?"

I glanced at the screen for a couple of seconds. "I think my aunt watches it." I gave her a warm smile. "I'm Maddie, by the way. I realize I didn't introduce myself."

"I'm Barbara. And I talked to a detective this morning. He told me all y'all at the grocery store are worried that Amy has missed some work."

Barbara thought I worked with Amy. I knew I should be truthful, but I didn't think it would hurt to let her continue believing that. It seemed better than saying I'd met her in my self-defense class and had known her for less than two hours. "The thing is, the detective said he can't do much. No one close enough to her has reported her missing, but we're still worried. Amy's taken off work before, but she's always called in. She didn't show up yesterday, and she didn't call. She's not answering her phone, and she doesn't seem to be home."

"Oh, honey. You don't need to worry. She left town," Barbara said with a sympathetic sigh. "I saw her leave the house yesterday morning with a suitcase and several bags. She waited until after those two lowlifes left the house." She wrinkled her nose in disgust. "I'd say that's probably the smartest thing she's done in her life."

"I know that Boomer was abusive," I said, hoping to prod her into volunteering more.

Shaking her head, she clucked her tongue. "That man has a temper. Amy isn't the first girl to move into their house. There was another about two years ago. I didn't see her nearly as much as Amy, but one time, *that* girl ran out of the house, and Boomer ran after her and dragged her back in by her hair."

I gasped. "Oh, my gosh! Did you call the sheriff?"

"Oh no," she said with a frown. "I'd tried calling them before when I heard her screaming bloody murder. Two sheriff's deputies showed up but didn't stick around long. They came over and told me that she didn't want to file a complaint. Plus, Boomer knew I was the one who called, and the next morning, the tires on my car were slashed. I called the sheriff about *that*, but they said there was no proof, so they couldn't do anything to him." She frowned. "But I sure learned my lesson. I'm a sickly old woman living alone. Those boys could hurt me, and it could be days or weeks before anyone found me."

"You could move."

Anger filled her eyes. "I was here first. I raised my kids in this house. I buried my husband, may he rest in peace, in this house. It's bad enough my social security is barely enough to make ends meet, let alone pay the taxes on this place. Those lowlifes have only been there just over two years. I'll be damned if I let *them* run me off."

She had a point. "You're right. You shouldn't have to move because you have bad neighbors. I'm sorry."

She waved her hand. "It ain't your fault. I told that detective this morning all about what they did to Amy, including their big fight on Sunday night, and he didn't do diddly. The police and the sheriff never do shit."

I understood why Noah hadn't done anything—his hands really were tied—but that was poor consolation to Barbara. "What big fight on Sunday? Amy never mentioned it at work, not that she told anyone much about Boomer." Noah had told me they'd fought, but I was hoping Barbara would be willing to share more details.

Barbara pushed out a sigh. "Like I said, I told that detective all about it, but he didn't seem too concerned." She drew in a breath and leaned closer. "Amy came home right before I was leaving for Sunday night services. Boomer came running out of the house, angrier than a fire ant. He was shouting at the top of his lungs that she'd gotten off work over an hour ago, demanding to know where she'd been. Well, that poor girl tried to answer, but he never really gave her a chance. He hit her across the face, then grabbed her by the throat and dragged her into the house. There was a lot of screaming and shouting before it all abruptly stopped." She paused, looking devastated. "I nearly went over to check on her, but I was scared." Her hand began to shake. "And I was scared to call the sheriff. You know, after last time I called."

I nodded, telling myself I didn't know what I would have done if I'd been in her shoes, but that was a lie. I would have done *something*. Still, I reminded myself that this was an old woman living alone, and it sounded like Boomer was terrifying.

Tears filled her eyes. "I was so grateful to see her yesterday morning when she was cartin' her stuff out of the house." She bit her lower lip as she wrung her hands in her lap. "I lied to that police officer, and I'm feeling mighty guilty about it."

My eyes flew wide. "Lied? What about?"

She shook her head and drew in a deep breath. "I actually talked to her as she was loading her car, but I didn't tell him because I didn't want to get into the middle of it. I'm worried that maniac Boomer will come after me if he thinks I know something."

"What did she say?" I prodded.

"She told me she wished she'd never moved to Cockamamie, and she was leaving Boomer. I got the impression she was headed back to Georgia. She said something about her cousin."

"Do you happen to know her cousin's name? I'd really like to talk to Amy myself and make sure she's okay."

Frowning, she said, "Seems like you and your friends at the

grocery store would know better than me. She only mentioned her cousin in passing—no name or nothing."

I didn't try to hide my disappointment. "She never talked about her life before Cockamamie, and she barely shared anything about her life here." At least, that was what her coworkers had said. I was somewhat relieved to hear that Amy had probably gone back to Georgia, but I was still concerned. "Do you know how Boomer reacted to Amy coming home on Monday night?"

"Are you asking if he lost his temper and started yelling? No, I didn't hear a peep out of them, which seemed weird. He liked her being home. He'd usually yell at her for not having his dinner on the table when he got home. I could often hear him all the way over here."

"Can you think of anything else that might help me find her? I'm *really* worried about her."

"I can see that you are," she said, reaching over to pat my hand. "But you don't need to be. She's just fine. You should thank the stars she got away. That's a rare thing, you know, for a woman to get away from an angry and controlling man. At least she was one of the lucky ones."

Maybe so, but I couldn't leave it like this. I needed to be sure. "Do you happen to know much about Boomer and Jake? Like where they work or where they're from?"

Her brow furrowed. "I don't know anything about those two boys, and I've tried to keep it that way."

"But surely you've noticed a pattern for when they come home." She sure seemed to notice a lot about Amy.

She made a face and tilted her head as she considered it. "Now that you mention it, I have. They usually leave around seven-thirty or eight in the morning and get home around six."

"What about company? Do they have friends over very often? Do their parents or family ever come around?"

She released a nervous laugh and patted her hair. "You make it sound like I'm a snoop. I'd have to be to know all those kinds of things."

"Oh no," I assured her. "Just a conscientious neighbor looking after the neighborhood." I leaned in closer. "I mean, knowing when something is out of place means knowing the routine of things."

She pursed her lips in disapproval, most likely because I'd insinuated she was a snoop, even if I'd dressed it up in pretty words. Her gaze drifted to the muted TV. A woman on the screen was jumping up and down in excitement.

"Well, crap," Barbara groaned. "I missed the winning question."

"I bet you can rewind it," I said.

Her eyes narrowed. "Hmm." It was obvious she didn't seem to believe that was possible.

I considered offering to show her, but I suspected I wouldn't get much else out of her, so I stood up. "Thank you so much for talking to me, Miss Barbara. You've helped ease my fears. If you hear from Amy, would you give me a call? I can write my number down, if you like."

"Or I could just give you a call at Bob's Market," she said. "I can look up the number."

I needed to shut that idea down quickly. "I'd rather you just call me directly, if you're okay with that. Our boss doesn't like us getting personal calls at work." Then I added, "Even if it's about Amy. He's a little sore that she hasn't been covering her shifts."

"Yeah," she said with a frown. "I can see how he might be. Let me get a paper and pen." She struggled to get out of her seat, then hobbled into the kitchen and came back with a used envelope and a pen. "Just jot your information down there."

I wrote my first name and my phone number, then handed

the envelope and pen back to her. "Thank you, Miss Barbara. I really appreciate your help."

"Of course," she said with a wave of dismissal, "but like I said, don't worry so much. Your friend got herself out of a bad situation. You should be happy for her."

And I was, sort of. Except, for some reason, I still couldn't let this go. The fact she had called me in the middle of the night and never said a word haunted me. I wasn't stupid. I knew it was also tied to complicated feelings about my mother's unsolved murder. I always felt like they had never tried very hard to find her killer, so this was probably me overcompensating.

I walked out of Barbara's house, intending to head back over to Amy's place, but now there was a blue pickup truck in the driveway.

"Oh dear," Barbara said, in a worried tone. "It looks like Boomer's home. I wouldn't go over there if I were you. He's liable to be angrier than a bear in heat."

"Thanks for the warning," I said as I walked down her porch steps, but what could he do to me in broad daylight? I could tell him I was a coworker checking on Amy. Surely he didn't know everyone she worked with.

Drawing every bit of courage I had, I marched back over to Amy's house and up to the front porch. After I knocked on the front door, I moved to the bottom step. I figured it would be good to have some distance, even if I had to look up at him. Just to be safe, I grabbed the can of pepper spray out of my purse and gripped it inside my coat pocket. The temperature was dropping, so it wouldn't look suspicious to keep my hands tucked away, out of the cold.

The door opened, and a clean-shaven man opened the door. He looked to be in his thirties and was wearing dirty jeans and a dirty white button-down shirt with the name *Boomer* embroidered over the left side of his chest. He had a tight hold on a can of Budweiser, and his eyes were narrowed in fury. He had an overall rough look that scared me, and I wondered what had drawn Amy to him. Had he been different with her in the beginning?

"Whatdaya want?" he grunted.

"Hi," I said, forcing a smile. "I'm Maddie. I'm looking for Amy. She hasn't shown up to work, and she's not answering her calls. We're worried about her."

He released a growl, then spat into a bush next to the porch. "Well, you're asking the wrong person. She ain't here."

"Do you happen to know where she might be?"

"How the fuck would I know? She took off for work on Monday and never came home."

His statement caught me off guard. "You're sure she never came home on Monday night?"

"Did I fucking stutter?" he shouted. "I said she *never. Came. Home.*"

He was lying, but *why* was he lying? "Was her stuff missing when you came home?" Maybe Barbara had gotten the day wrong. It made much more sense for Amy to have left on Monday morning if he'd attacked her on Sunday...except she'd shown up at my self-defense class on Monday night. Maybe she *had* left Monday, and she'd come to my class to learn self-defense in case Boomer came looking for her.

His eyes turned murderous, and he looked pissed enough to hit me, but instead of coming down the stairs, he turned around and went back inside, slamming the door behind him.

I drew a deep breath. Why was he lying? Was he trying to cover up hurting her?

My gaze darted toward Barbara's house. She was standing on the front porch, gripping tightly to the railing. I headed back over to her yard, and she limped down her steps toward me. We met a few feet from her steps.

"You shouldn't have talked to him," she said, casting a worried look at his house. "As I'm sure you figured out, he's not a nice man. He could have hurt you."

"He said Amy didn't come home on Monday night."

Her brow lifted, and she eyed me with a smirk. "And you're surprised he lied?"

"But why would he? Could you have gotten the day wrong? Is it possible she left on Monday morning? The day after their big fight?"

She shot me a look of disgust. "I may be old, but I ain't senile. It was just yesterday morning, and if you don't believe me, you can verify it with my friend Connie. We always meet for coffee at my house on Tuesday mornings."

"Connie saw her?"

"Sure did. She saw Amy pulling out of the driveway when she was in front of Amy's house. Amy nearly hit her in her haste to get away."

None of this made sense. I ran a hand over my head. "But why would Boomer lie about Amy not coming home on Monday night?"

Barbara made a face as she grabbed my coat sleeve and tugged me closer. "There's something else I didn't tell you or that detective."

"Oh?"

"I know I should have told him, but like I said, I don't want to get in the middle of this. It never went well before, and... well..." She drew in a breath. "Amy's face was looking pretty rough when I talked to her on Tuesday morning." She gave me a sympathetic look. "These things escalate, you know, which is probably why she left."

That asshole had beaten her and then tried to cover his tracks by saying she hadn't come home that night.

"I gave her all the money I had for gas, although it wasn't much with my fixed income. She thanked me, then took off. Like I said, she pulled out of the driveway so fast, she nearly T-boned Connie."

"Has Amy called to check in with you? To let you know she made it okay?" I asked, glancing over at Boomer's house.

"I don't think she has my number. We talked when she was outside, and I dropped off cookies and such for her, but we didn't have each other's numbers." She gave me a warm smile. "Amy's lucky to have a friend like you. I don't think she had many of those here. But I'm sure she's safe." Her face hardened as she glanced at the house next door. "At least much safer than she was living here."

Maybe so, but I still wasn't satisfied.

Chapter Twelve

Maddie

I wasn't sure what else to do, but I figured it wouldn't hurt anything to drop by Emerson Auto Parts and get a look at Jake. Noah had said he was off today, but he hadn't been home. Besides, it was only about four-thirty, and if Barbara had been right about his schedule, the store probably didn't close until at least six.

I figured I had the perfect cover—the weather forecast was calling for snow later tonight, and I needed new windshield wipers. No harm in dropping by to pick up a pair.

But as I pulled away from the shoulder, I drove slowly past Boomer's driveway and snapped a photo of the license plate on his truck.

Several cars were parked in Emerson's lot when I arrived, and I parked to the side of the lot, out of sight of the front door. No need to flaunt my presence.

When I went inside, several men were milling about the place, checking out car batteries and car parts, or whatever they were looking for. I headed for the windshield wipers. It felt like a normal, run-of-the-mill car parts store. Nothing suspicious. But then again, it wasn't the business that had drawn me here.

There were multiple kinds of wipers to choose from, and I had no idea which kind fit my car, so I stood there for a good half a minute before a guy walked up next to me and said, "You look a little lost, sweet thing. Can I help?"

I turned to him, and my stomach somersaulted when I saw his nametag read *Jake*. That was way too easy.

I gave him a bright smile and infused my voice with a strong Southern accent. "Goodness me. I hope so. My windshield wipers are a mess, leaving big streaks across my windshield. The last time it rained I could hardly see out the window. But I can't figure out what kind I need."

"Well, let me help you with that," he said in a smooth tone that made my skin crawl. He was a little under six feet, but he was stocky, the muscle kind, not fat. He was wearing a T-shirt with short sleeves, and his arms were decorated with tattoos. His brown hair was shaggy and covered his ears and the top of his collar, just enough to give him an *I don't give a shit* attitude, but not so out of control he looked disheveled. He sported a trimmed beard that proved he actually *did* give a shit. He was good looking, and his arrogance suggested he knew it. "A pretty thing like yourself should have a man to help you with things like that. Where's your man?"

I fought to hide my disgust. "He's too busy to help, so I said I was just gonna do it myself."

"You need to find you a man who will take care of you, baby," he said, leaning in close. "What kind of car do you drive?"

"A Ford Focus."

"We have just what you need right here." He reached around me, his arm wrapping around my back in a possessive manner as he grabbed a package of wipers. He held them, his arm still around my back. "This pair should do the trick. Do you need anything else?"

I was trapped. With the display in front of me and him caging me in, I couldn't step away unless I was willing to create a scene. "Nope," I said cheerfully, hoping it didn't sound forced. "That's it."

"We have a sale on air fresheners over here." He gestured down toward the end of the aisle. "How about we go take a look?"

I considered my options for a moment. Finding him had been ridiculously easy, but now I wasn't sure what to do next. I couldn't ask him about Amy, and he wasn't her boyfriend anyway. Coming here had probably been a stupid idea, and Noah would likely crap his pants if he ever found out, but I decided to let this play out. "A girl can always use a new air freshener."

"They can be priceless when the rug rats drop french fries and crap in the backseat," he said, ushering me down the aisle, his arm now around my lower back.

"Oh, no kids for me," I said glibly.

"Your man firing blanks?" he asked with a laugh as he stopped in front of the air fresheners. "You really should dump that guy."

I laughed and turned to face him, daring to look him in the eyes because a plan was starting to hatch. "Maybe I'm waiting to find a man who can take care of me before I start popping out babies."

His eyes widened, and a lazy grin spread across his face. "Sweet thing, you've found the pot at the end of the rainbow."

"Oh yeah?" I asked coyly.

"Yep. What are you doin' Friday night?"

I gave him a flirtatious look. "My momma told me not to trust silver-tongued devils like yourself."

He spread his hands out at his sides. "You can trust me, baby. I swear."

I snatched an air freshener from the display. "That's what all you playboys say." Then I walked past him and headed to the register to stand behind a man holding a car battery.

Jake followed and walked behind the counter, still holding my wipers. He moved to an available register and motioned me over.

"But there's a line," I said, going over to him anyway.

"Baby, I'll take care of *all* your needs." The innuendo was so strong I was sure the stench of it reached the sidewalk outside.

"You really think you can handle me?" I asked with a laugh as I set the air freshener on the counter.

"I'm willing to put my money where my mouth is. And plenty of other places."

Gag. Did he realize he'd just told me that he'd put his money in plenty of other places, not his mouth? I looked up at him through my eyelashes. "Friday night, huh?"

I needed to be nominated for some kind of acting award for this.

"Yep. I can pick you up at eight. All you have to do is tell me where you live."

There was no freaking way I was giving this guy my address.

I made a face. "I don't know. My cousin's comin' to town, and I can't just ditch her."

"Is your cousin as hot as you?"

Did he seriously just ask me that? "Hotter," I said. "And single. But now I'm worried you'll like her better than me."

He leaned a forearm on the counter and stared deep into my eyes. "No way that could happen, baby. You have me mesmerized."

I let him continue staring for a few seconds. "Well, I can't leave her at home. You got someone who could come with us?

I'm not into three-ways." Then I grinned mischievously. "At least not on the first date."

He was practically drooling.

"Are you gonna just eye fuck 'er, or are you gonna ring her up?" the other employee asked as customers lined up behind me.

Jake glared so hard the other employee took a step back, but then he rang up my items and told me the amount.

Crap. I couldn't use my credit card, or he'd find out my name. I dug my wallet out of my purse, relieved that I had enough cash to cover it, even if it meant I'd be strapped until I got paid next week.

I handed over the money, and when he gave me the change, he let his index finger stroke a line from my wrist to my palm. He placed the money inside and then curled my fingers around it.

"Your skin is silky smooth," he cooed. "Is it smooth like that everywhere?"

I winked. "If you're lucky, maybe you'll find out on Friday. But you never told me if you have a friend for my cousin."

The corner of his mouth ticked up. "Lucky for your cousin, *my* cousin just became single."

"Is he as hot as you?" I asked with a grin as I picked up the wipers off the counter.

"Nah, but you deserve Grade-A Prime Beef. What's your name, sweet thing?"

Shit. Nothing came to mind, so I gave him a sexy smile. "Maybe I'll tell you on Friday night. If my cousin and I decide to meet you and *your* cousin, that is. Where exactly are you planning to go?"

"Cock on the Walk. Nine o'clock."

First, there was no way I was going to Cock on the Walk. It was a notoriously rough biker bar. And nine o'clock? I'd rather be in bed binge-watching something on Netflix, but I beamed at him because I wanted to keep my options open. If I still felt uneasy about Amy by Friday night, I could meet with him and see if I could find out more. Or the smarter thing would be to send Noah or Lance, not that Jake or Boomer would be inclined to talk. "It's a date, Jake."

His brow lifted, and a hard look filled his eyes. "How'd you know my name is Jake?"

"It's on your nametag, you idiot," his coworker said in disgust. "And unlike you, I suspect she passed reading in the first grade." Jake shot him a glare, but the other guy ignored it. "I thought you were gonna stop wearing that after that cop showed up this morning."

Noah.

"You in trouble with the law?" I asked breathlessly.

Jake's eyes glittered with mischief. "Always, baby."

I turned and glanced over my shoulder. "Good. I like my men to be *bad*." Then I headed out the door, praying he didn't follow me.

He didn't.

I got in my car, tossed my purchases onto my seat, then pulled out of the parking lot, using the side entrance so he hopefully wouldn't see what I drove.

You already told him what you drive, you fool. When you were looking for the windshield wipers.

Okay, but I hoped he didn't see the color of my car or, more importantly, the license plate.

I wasn't sure where that performance had come from, but one thing was for sure—I wasn't the same woman who'd moved back to Cockamamie in September. Facing those kidnappers last month had changed me.

Only I was starting to wonder if it was for the better.

Chapter Thirteen

Maddie

A few hours later, I backed into a parking space behind Deja Brew with about twenty minutes to spare before my self-defense class. After leaving the auto parts store, I'd barely had time to go home, make dinner for Aunt Deidre, and change while I waited for Margarete to come over. Aunt Deidre hadn't been happy to see me go. She was used to me being home just about every night—a sad testament to my lack of a social life—and she'd thrown a small fit. Which meant I hadn't had time to change my wiper blades, and even though I should have gone inside the coffee shop to see if a patrol officer had dropped off the mats like Noah had promised. With the looming snow forecast, I decided to tackle changing the wipers first.

With my car still running, I pulled up an instructional video on YouTube, then turned off the engine and hopped out to get started. I'd just begun struggling with the first one when Noah pulled into a parking space on the passenger side of my car.

I lifted my gaze as he got out.

"I thought you weren't coming," I said in a snotty tone. "I thought you were sending a patrol officer." I wasn't sure why I was pissed at him. Because I'd found out more about Amy than he had? Because I was still hurt that he'd blown me off last month? Did it matter? After tonight, I wouldn't have to see him again.

"I decided to take a break and come help you."

I shrugged, then turned my concentration to the wiper blades.

"What are you doing?" he asked, his voice dripping with suspicion.

I snorted. "And here I thought you were a better detective than that."

"I'll admit the question wasn't phrased properly. I can see *what* you're doing. I guess the real question is *why* you're doing it in the parking lot. At night. Alone."

I kept my attention on the task at hand. "Because I just got them this afternoon. I haven't had a chance to put them on yet, and the forecast says it might start snowing any minute."

His eyes narrowed, and it was obvious he was going to start connecting dots I wasn't too keen on him connecting. "You just got those this afternoon?"

"Yeah, what of it?" Something gave, and the old wiper blade slipped off. I got the new one on, then dropped the old one onto the hood and moved to the other side just as soft snow began to fall.

Noah was standing where I needed to be, so I nudged him with my hip, and he took a step to the side.

"Where did you get them?" he asked in an interrogative tone I'd grown to know too well.

I looked up with a defiant glare. "What difference does it make?"

"It's just that there's a car parts store outside the city limits, and a certain someone with ties to a woman you're looking for happens to work there."

Turning away from him, I started tugging on the wiper. "I could have bought these at Walmart for all you know, Noah."

"But you didn't get them at Walmart. You got them at Emerson Auto Parts. Where Jake works."

I ignored him and continued to jerk on the windshield wiper, trying to slide it off the metal bar, but it seemed to be jammed in. Then again, this was my first attempt at changing my own wiper blades with only a short YouTube primer a few minutes ago, so I could have been doing it wrong.

Noah reached around me for the blade, trying to move me to the side.

"Stop!" I dug in my heels and turned to glare at him. "I don't need you to save me, Noah. I'm perfectly capable of taking care of myself."

An indignant look covered his face as he released the wiper. "Is that what you think I'm doing?"

I propped my hands on my hips. "Isn't it?"

We were close, inches apart, and a hint of his shampoo wafted in the air. He smelled good, and he looked good too. Up close with the glow of the streetlights behind him and snow falling around him, he looked like an angel—a guardian angel. But no matter how good he looked and smelled, he was still the same hot mess he had been hours ago. And so was I.

"Maybe I'm just being neighborly."

His voice had a husky tone that Margarete never used when borrowing things, so I wasn't buying the neighborly act. "You're giving me very mixed signals."

He took a step back and ran a hand over his head. "I just want to help you, Maddie."

"And while I appreciate that, I'm not some damsel in distress. *But,*" I added, "while we aren't neighbors, if you're doing it to be friendly, then you have to let me help you too. Otherwise, it's just a handout, and I don't need or want charity."

His gaze narrowed with suspicion. "You want to help *me*?"

I knew this was a terrible idea, yet I couldn't seem to help myself. "Sure, why not? Don't you want a friend?"

He squared his shoulders. "I have Lance."

"But we can all use more than one friend." I said, tilting my head to the side. "Besides, my friends in this town consist of my aunt with dementia, my sixty-year-old neighbor, and Chrissy, who acts like she wants to kill me and grind me into the coffee beans half the time."

One side of his mouth lifted into an amused smirk. "That sounds oddly specific."

I shrugged. "Threats may have been made, so if I up and disappear, maybe skip the coffee here for a while."

"Thanks for the heads-up."

"See?" I asked. "That's what friends do. So what do you say? Can we be friends? Because I don't think I'm going to be able to get this wiper blade off on my own."

He laughed, a rich sound that warmed my insides, making me second-guess this friend idea when his face softened like that. But he wasn't interested in starting something with me, and I definitely shouldn't be interested in him. So if friends were all I could get, then I'd make do, because there was no denying that Noah had a hold on me, and I didn't want to let go.

He gently moved me to the side and grabbed the windshield wiper. "Go inside. It's cold out here, and this is a one-person job."

Part of me wanted to protest, but if I stuck around, I suspected he'd start asking questions about my trip to a certain auto shop. "If you pop the trunk, I'll carry in one of the mats."

He dropped the wiper blade and pulled out his car keys. The trunk lid popped open, but by the time I'd wrestled one of the mats out of the back, he'd already finished with the wiper.

"Show-off," I grumbled.

He laughed again. "You should let me get this. You're not wearing a coat."

He was right. The wind was biting through the loose weave of my heavy cardigan, but at least I had my mother's scarf wrapped around my neck. I hadn't been able to find my coat before leaving the house, so I'd grabbed my sweater from the coat rack. I suspected Aunt Deidre had hidden it in an attempt to make me stay home.

"You're not wearing one either," I said. He had on the same sport coat and dress shirt he'd worn earlier. Which meant he hadn't been home yet.

"I'm used to standing out in the weather. You're used to library stacks. Go inside."

I got the mat out. The end landed on the ground, but I hefted it up. "I'm good."

He easily grabbed two more mats, closed the trunk, and followed me. I banged on the back door.

Petra opened it, and a huge smile spread across her face when she saw Noah. "Detective Langley! You came back!"

"Maddie needed mats, and I enjoyed myself so much, I decided to stick around for tonight's lesson too."

She hustled us inside, saying, "Oh dear. I hope the snow doesn't keep the women away."

We all knew it would. Southern Tennessee got so little snow there weren't many plows. The temperature was several degrees above freezing, and the roads were clear, but I was still surprised when five women showed up, probably because they were hoping to see Noah. Chrissy, on the other hand, had called to say there was no way she was coming in to work for free in the middle of a raging snowstorm. I was pretty sure Petra didn't bother pointing out that they were only flurries.

The class flew by, and when we finished, Petra took a photo of all of us—Noah included—lamenting that the entire class wasn't there for the picture. She told everyone to get in line for a free drink while she went into the back, printed off the photos, and grabbed their gift cards. Since she'd already sent the teenage workers home, I was the only barista available, so I got to work.

The women lined up at the counter, while Noah stood at the back of the line. I took two orders, then started on the drinks. One of the women, Roxie, turned to face Noah. "Detective Langley, should we be worried about all these break-ins?"

A reassuring smile spread across his face. "Be sure to lock your doors, and if you have security cameras, post a sign that they're on the premises. The signs alone are a huge deterrent to theft."

"Do you think we should get a security system?" Marissa asked, looking worried.

"Honestly," he said, turning to face her, "it wouldn't hurt. I have one in my own home, and so does Maddie." He nodded toward me.

My brows lifted in surprise. I hadn't told him I'd gotten one installed, and I hadn't told Lance either.

The women talked amongst themselves while I finished the first two drinks and started on the third, but then Diane said, "Jennifer Gibbs said her house is still a crime scene, but Val's house was released right away. What was the difference?"

Noah's lips pressed into a grim line. "I'm not at liberty to say."

"So *should* we be worried, Noah?" Marissa asked, grabbing his arm.

Noah? I couldn't deny the zip of jealousy that raced through me. Jealousy I had no right to. Marissa was married, and I knew Noah was no home-wrecker.

He gave her a reassuring look. "Like I said, lock your doors, install a security system, and post a sign. Maybe even post a sign before you get the system. I can't stress enough how much of a deterrent that can be."

"I heard the thieves left something behind at Jennifer's house," Diane said.

"You mean like their tools?" Roxie asked with a frown.

"No," Diane said. "Dirty photos." She leaned closer and lowered her voice. "Of his you-know-what."

I couldn't stifle a gasp as I lifted my gaze to Noah.

His jaw clenched with irritation. "Where did you hear that?"

"From Nadine, whose cousin is friends with a guy who plays golf with a guy whose wife is best friends with a police officer's wife."

"Is it true?" one of the quieter women asked. "Did he leave dirty photos?"

"I can't confirm or deny anything," Noah said. "But take gossip like that with a grain of salt, ladies." His mouth tightened. "I think I'll get those mats out to the car while there's a break in the snow."

The women watched him walk over to the mats, then kept their gazes on his butt as he leaned over to fold them up. When he headed toward the back, one of them sighed.

"Will you be offering another class, Maddie?" Roxie asked. "I'm worried I'm going to forget everything."

"I'm still trying to figure out what's next. But we have your email addresses, so we'll email all y'all once we have it figured out."

"Will Noah be helping you?" Diane asked in a dreamy tone.

My gut churned with irritation. "I'm not privy to Detective Langley's schedule."

By the time I started making the last drink, Noah still hadn't come back in. (He wasn't fooling me with how long he was taking to carry the mats out to the car.) As I was finishing, Petra came out with the certificates, photos, and gift cards. She passed them out and encouraged everyone to head home before the temperature dipped and the snow started to stick to the road. But the women hung around for several long seconds, staring at the backroom while clutching their drinks.

A few moments later, Noah came out, and the women swarmed him, telling him how much they'd enjoyed him helping with the class. One of them asked if he offered private lessons, to which he offered a curt no. He ushered them to the front door, telling them they needed to get home and drive safe. Then he picked up the last two mats and turned to Petra and me. "Are you ladies ready to go? You need to get home too."

"I'll be ready in just a moment," Petra said, heading into the back. "Let me get my stuff."

"Let me make your drink, Noah." I walked back over to the espresso machine and started making an Americano.

"Maddie, you don't need to do that. You really do need to get home."

"I suspect you've got a long night ahead of you, so this will help. Besides," I smiled up at him, "I owe you for helping me with both the wiper and the mats." And my grumpy attitude when he first showed up, but I kept that part to myself. "Also," I added, "I have front-wheel drive. I drove in Nashville in the snow. I'll be fine."

"How'd you know I'd be doing paperwork?" he asked, leaning against the counter.

"Because you haven't been home. You have a case involving someone who's leaving pornographic photos at people's houses, and you said you'd be too tied up with it to bring the mats tonight—even though you came anyway."

The corners of his mouth twitched. "Maybe we should get you a job at the Cockamamie Police Department."

"No thanks," I said with a chuckle. "I don't think I'd look

good in a bulletproof vest and that tool belt I've seen the officers wear."

His grin transformed his face. "I'm not going to comment on that because no matter how I answer, I suspect it's going to get me into trouble."

"Fair enough," I conceded. "So tell me how you knew I got a security system."

He turned serious. "I'm not spying on you, if that's what you think. I was checking alarm permits with the city for this case and saw yours."

A wave of fear washed through me. "Did they really leave something pornographic?"

His eyes shuttered. "You know I can't answer that, Maddie."

"Half the town will think it's true by tomorrow morning."

He grunted his displeasure.

I added water to his drink, put the lid on, and handed it to him. "Here you go. This should keep you up for another couple hours."

"Thanks." He cast a glance at the back, then lowered his voice. "You went out to Emerson Auto Parts, didn't you?"

I didn't see the point of denying it, and I didn't want to lie. Besides, I really *did* want to tell him what I'd found. I'd just been caught in a weird adversarial attitude earlier. "Lots of people go to Emerson Auto Parts. I saw two other customers shopping while I was there."

"Maddie..." he said with a groan.

"He had no idea why I was there," I said reassuringly. "I didn't ask anything about Amy."

He pinned me with an intense stare.

"I didn't, Noah. I swear. I went in and bought some wind-shield wipers and an air freshener for my car. I found out he has a cousin who recently became single." Now, onto the next part that was sure to flip him out. "Oh, and Boomer drives a blue pickup truck." I tugged my phone out of my back pocket. "Here's a photo of the license plate."

He took the phone from me and scowled as he looked at the photo. "How did you get this?"

"I stopped by Amy's house, and it was parked in the driveway."

"You stopped by Amy's house?" he asked, his voice rising. "Did you talk to Boomer, Maddie?"

I gave him a defiant look. "Yes, I did. But here's where it gets weird. He said she never came home Monday night."

He stared at me for a moment, and I could see his curiosity overpowering his anger. "Mrs. Johnson said she saw Amy leave Tuesday morning."

"Barbara told me the same thing—"

"*You talked to the neighbor?*"

"Of course I talked to the neighbor. And I'm sure you know by now that sometimes people are scared to tell the police everything, which was the case with Barbara Johnson." I paused, giving him time to comment, but although his pinched eyes suggested he wasn't happy, he remained silent. "Anyway, Barbara said she was *certain* it was Tuesday morning. She admitted that she didn't tell you the entire truth." I lifted my brow to make my point. "Barbara actually *talked* to Amy. Amy told her she was leaving Boomer and even though she didn't say where she was going, Barbara thought she was headed back to Georgia. She said Amy said something about her cousin."

His face was neutral. "Why didn't she tell me that?"

"Barbara said she called the sheriff's department after she saw a nasty fight between Boomer and his previous girlfriend a couple of years ago, and the sheriff's department not only didn't do anything about it, but they did next to nothing when Boomer slashed Barbara's tires in retaliation. They claimed Barbara couldn't prove he'd done it. She said she decided she was done getting involved."

Noah's eyes turned stormy as he processed what I'd said. "Did she tell you anything else?"

"Barbara said Amy's face looked rough when she saw her yesterday morning."

He was silent for a couple of seconds. "Did you learn anything else from Mrs. Johnson or Boomer?"

"No," I said with a sigh.

Noah released a sigh of his own. "If Boomer really did beat her as badly as Mrs. Johnson said, he may be lying to avoid culpability." He tilted his head to the side. "Which would only be an issue if Amy tried to press charges, but it sounds like she just wanted to get away from him. I suspect she's hiding out in Georgia somewhere, and he'll never see her again. He'll move on to the next girlfriend, and he'll probably end up beating her worse."

I frowned. Amy was the second girlfriend he'd beaten—that I knew of. I had no doubt he'd beat the next one too.

Noah gave me a suspicious look. "If you didn't ask about Amy, what made Jake volunteer that his cousin is single?"

I shrugged. "People like to tell me things."

His gaze pierced mine. "*Maddie.*"

I wasn't going to tell him about Jake coming on to me, and I sure as hell wasn't going to tell him Jake wanted me to meet him at Cock on the Walk Friday night. "He has no idea who I am. I paid cash, and he never even saw my car leave. It was perfectly safe."

He drew in a deep breath, then slowly released it. But he didn't look remotely relaxed. "I know you're determined to find Amy, but my gut tells me Jake and Boomer are dangerous. We already know Boomer beats his girlfriends, so it's not outside the realm of possibility that Jake would be rough with women too. Stay away from them."

"I'm not going back to the auto parts store, Noah. Stop worrying."

"Ready to go!" Petra called out from the back.

Relief flooded through me. Saved by my boss. "I'm ready too. Let's go."

I made sure the front door was locked, grabbed my sweater and purse, and looped my scarf around my neck. I headed for the back door, shutting off the lights as I went, Noah on my heels.

We all filed outside and waited while Petra locked the back door. The snow was starting to cover the hoods of our cars, but it was already cleared from my windshield and Petra's. I could see fresh scrape marks, so now I knew what had taken Noah so long to come back inside.

Petra made a beeline to her car, got in, and didn't wait for her engine to warm up. She pulled out before Noah had even walked me to my car.

I reached for the handle, not surprised when he said in a low tone, "Maddie, promise me that you'll stay away from Jake and Boomer."

I looked up at him, my heart starting to beat faster. "Barbara Johnson said Amy left the asshole. Why would I talk to them again?"

Worry filled his eyes. "But *you* haven't spoken to her, and knowing you, you won't stop looking for her until you do." There was an intimacy in his voice that suggested this wasn't just an officer of the law trying to protect a citizen. He was making a personal entreaty.

"I just want to make sure she's safe," I said softly.

He started to lift a hand to my face, then let it drop to my neck. He gave my scarf a small tug. "I know, and I love that about you, but please stay away from Jake and Boomer."

"Okay," I said. "I will."

His shoulders relaxed. "Thank you."

Something in my chest tightened, and I didn't say anything for several seconds while I looked deep into his eyes. The electricity sparking between us made me hyperaware of everything about him. He broke the moment by opening my car door. "Be safe driving home."

"You too, Noah." I got in and started my engine, letting it warm as he walked around to his car.

As I pulled out of the lot, I could see him in my rearview mirror, still standing next to his car as he watched me drive away.

Chapter Fourteen

Maddie

Since I didn't work at the coffee shop on Thursday mornings, I usually ran Uber pickups. Today had the potential to be a good day. The overnight snow had left a light dusting on the ground, and the temperature was hovering around freezing. I wasn't worried about driving, but there was a chance some of the older citizens in town would be hesitant to go out.

While I waited for Linda to arrive to watch Aunt Deidre, I spread salt over the front walk, part of the driveway, and out the back door in case the temperature took a dip and my aunt decided to go outside. Then I turned on my car to heat it and defrost the windshield and back window. It didn't help the side windows, though, so I pulled out my scraper and got to work.

Aunt Deidre stood on the porch, wrapped in her house coat and house slippers, watching me as she fussed with the end of one of her sleeves. "You're gonna catch your death of cold, Maddie!"

I laughed and said, "I like the cold." Truthfully, I preferred it—at least compared to a one-hundred-degree day with seventy-percent humidity. "You're the one we need to worry about."

"I never took you for a damn Yankee," she said in disgust and without a hint of teasing.

I stopped scraping and stared after her in shock, a lump forming in my throat. The Aunt Deidre I'd known for thirty-four years would never have talked to me like that. I'd been warned there was a possibility her personality would change. Shoot, I'd seen her talk to her caretaker in the most hateful tone. But she'd never turned like this on me before.

"When are you going to get our Christmas tree?" she called out in a harsh tone. "Albert would have already gotten it by now. Then again, you were always so irresponsible."

My mouth dropped open. She had never once accused me of being irresponsible. If anything, it had been the opposite—she always said I took on too much. I drew in a shaky breath, then said, "I'll get a tree this weekend. I promise."

She pursed her lips as though she didn't believe it, then turned and went inside.

I continued to scrape, my heart hurting. I kept telling myself not to take it personally, but it was hard to see the woman who had become my protector change so drastically.

I'd just started cleaning the passenger window when my phone rang in my coat pocket. I scrambled to pull it out before it went to voicemail and smiled when I saw Mallory's name on the screen.

"Hey, Mal," I said, propping the phone between my shoulder and my ear as I continued to scrape. "What's up?"

"How would you like some company this weekend?"

I barely restrained my excitement. "Really?"

"Yeah, I feel a cold coming on, and I'm going to call in sick tomorrow." To punctuate her statement, she coughed.

"You *do* know that at some point your boss is going to figure out that all these colds you conveniently get hit you on Thursday or Friday." Mallory worked in corporate for an insurance company, and she'd actually liked her job before her boss had taken over her previous boss's position a year ago. Now she hated it and looked for any excuse to stay out of the office.

She snorted. "Not likely. Donna is too worried about getting sick to notice any pattern. Hey," she said as though something had just occurred to her, "maybe I can pin my illnesses on the Tuesday staff meetings in the conference room and make a case for doing them over Zoom instead."

I rolled my eyes and laughed. "Well, in that case, Godspeed. Are you coming down tonight?"

"This afternoon. I'm going to try to get my work done early and head out by three. I'm putting my suitcase in my car so I can take off straight from work."

"I have to work tomorrow."

"That's okay," she said. "I'll work remotely so I can still get paid. Either at Cabbage Rose House, or maybe I'll head over to your coffee shop."

"That would be awesome!"

Aunt Deidre's nurse, Linda, pulled up in front of the house.

"Hey, Mal, Linda's here. I need to let you go so I can talk to her, but I can call you back in about ten minutes."

"No need. I wanted to give you a head's up before I showed up at your front door."

"You can help me get a Christmas tree. Aunt Deidre is wanting to put one up, but she wants a real one, and you know how big she likes them."

"There's a dirty joke in there that I'm refraining from making, but only because we're talking about Aunt Deidre."

I laughed again, grateful Mallory was coming down. I was lonelier than I cared to admit, and she always lifted my spirits. "Be careful driving down. I'll have a bottle of Moscato chilled and waiting for you."

"You're the best."

She hung up just as Linda started walking up the salted part of the driveway.

"Good morning, Maddie," she said good-naturedly. "You should try to get that garage cleaned out so you won't have to scrape your car windows in the morning."

"That seems like a huge undertaking," I said, feeling exhausted at the thought. While my Uncle Albert hadn't been a hoarder, he had packed a lot of equipment he hadn't used in years in the detached garage over the last few decades.

"You could hire one of those companies to haul all the junk away," she said with a smile.

"Which takes money." Money I didn't have. Steve and I had used one of those places to clean out the junk left behind in his flip house, and it had cost nearly a thousand dollars.

She frowned. "So maybe you do little by little. You know what they say about eating an elephant—one bite at a time."

I laughed. "I'll keep it in mind."

"There's always your aunt's money. When you eventually sell the house, you'll have to clean it out anyway. Might as well start doing it now before Deidre needs more extensive care and they take what's left of her money."

She had a point, and I wondered if I should be fixing up other things around the house too. It was also a bitter reminder of what had just happened a few moments ago.

She started to walk past me, but I said, "Linda, before you go in, I wanted to..." What? Tattle on my aunt? I took a breath. "I know Aunt Deidre has been unkind to you in the past, but this morning, she was ugly to me." I made a face. "It's not the first time, and I'm not sure why I'm telling you. I guess I'm just warning you in case—"

Before I could finish, Linda reached for me and wrapped me up in a hug. "I'm so sorry, Maddie."

Part of me wanted to pull away—Linda wasn't really my

friend—but I found myself sinking into her embrace. After a few moments, she released me and stared at me with warm eyes. "It's only going to get harder."

"I know. She seems to be getting worse faster than I expected."

She nodded. "It's likely because she lost her anchor when your uncle died, but I also suspect she was in worse shape than you realized when you moved back. I wouldn't be surprised if she and Albert purposefully hid the progression of her condition."

I suspected she was right. "In any case," I said, trying not to let it get me down, "she's in a mood. Sorry."

A smile lit up her face. "Honey, that's my job. I can handle it. But..." She seemed hesitant to continue.

"Go on," I encouraged.

She made a face, then said, "You should start giving consideration to where she'll go when she needs more care." She patted my arm. "I'm not saying she needs to go anytime soon, but it would be good to have a plan for when the inevitable happens. Perhaps you should start booking some tours and considering your options." A grim smile lifted the corners of her mouth. "Then you won't feel like you're scrambling to come up with a decision when the time comes." She gave me another pat. "It won't make initiating that decision any easier, but it will be less of a burden if you have a plan to follow."

I nodded, then wiped a tear from my face. "Yeah. I suppose you're right."

"I can make a list of places for you to consider. And you might want to bring a friend to help you with the process. A sounding board."

"Thanks, Linda. That's a great idea." Maybe I could ask Mallory to help me. "I'm not sure what I'd do without you."

Her smile brightened. "I'm just doin' my job. Now you run along, and I'll make sure your aunt is taken care of."

After I snuck inside to get my purse and a fresh thermal mug of coffee, I fired up the Uber app and marked myself available. I only had to wait a few minutes before I got a request from a residence a half mile away from a woman named Patsy. No waiting today.

Patsy was waiting for me on her front porch, an older woman bundled up in a pink knee-length dress coat, a dress, and black pumps. A black cat brushed against her leg but dashed into the bushes as I pulled up to the curb. A gray cat in the hedges batted at it.

I left my car running, then hurried up the walkway to her porch. "Let me help you, Miss Patsy."

"Well, aren't you a dear?" she said, her voice crackly with age. As I got closer and saw the deep wrinkles on her face, I realized she was likely older than I'd first thought. Maybe even in her eighties.

I offered her my arm, and after she hooked hers around my elbow, I slowly led her down the steps and path to the car. When I opened the back door, she got in, beaming. "I haven't had service like this since my Harry was younger."

"Is Harry your son?" I asked.

"Oh, no. Harry was my husband," she said with a wave of her hand, then reached for her seatbelt. "He's been dead for twenty years now."

"I'm sorry for your loss," I said. "My aunt lost her husband a few months ago, and I doubt she'll ever really get over it."

"Who's your aunt, dear?" she asked, looking up at me with interest.

"Deidre Saunders. My uncle was Albert."

Her eyes lit up with recognition. "Oh, I know Deidre from

the women's club, and Harry and I were invited to some of their dinner parties." She sobered. "You must be Andrea's girl."

"Yes, ma'am," I said, shutting the door and walking around to the driver's seat. Why had I gone and mentioned my aunt? I should have known better by now.

I got inside and looked at the map on my phone, realizing I hadn't paid attention to her destination when I'd accepted her ride.

"Bob's Market?" I asked.

She made a face. "I much preferred the Piggly Wiggly, but after that whole mess with Peter McIntire…" She tsked. "Well, I can't bring myself to shop there anymore."

Peter McIntire had been arrested for the murder of the man I'd driven to his death. He'd killed Martin Schroeder to cover up his side hustle of selling black market goods. His father, who'd run the store before retiring, had taken over again while Peter was in jail awaiting his trial, but I wasn't sure it would survive the scandal.

"Same," I said, then regretted it, hoping she wouldn't connect the dots that I had helped get Peter arrested.

But if she realized, she let it slide. "I usually shop on Wednesday, but I had to move my hair appointment from Tuesday to yesterday. I figured I'd do my shopping today, but then it snowed. Harry didn't like me driving in the snow."

"That's why I'm around," I said, smiling at her in the rearview mirror. "I can drive you where you need to go."

"Can you wait for me while I'm in the store?" she asked.

I was about to tell her the app didn't work like that, but I realized I'd been presented with an opportunity. I mean, I was going to be there anyway, and if I could just get one more person to confirm they suspected Amy had run away to Georgia, then maybe I could let it go. "Sure," I said. "You know, I have a little bit of shopping of my own, so I'll just make myself unavailable and drive you home when you're done."

"You're a dear," she said, reaching forward and patting my shoulder. "What's your name?"

"Maddie."

"Oh, that's right. Short for Madelyn, isn't it? Such a pretty name. You should go by that, dear."

I grinned. "I'll take it under consideration."

The parking lot of the grocery store was fairly empty, so I found a spot close to the door and walked Miss Patsy inside, making sure to make myself unavailable on the app. After I helped Miss Patsy get a cart and pointed her toward the produce section, I started wandering the aisles, looking for an available employee.

I found a young woman stocking cans in the soup aisle, so I headed over to her, crossing my fingers that she'd have helpful information about Amy.

"Hi," I said, stopping next to her. "I'm Maddie Baker. I'm friends with Amy Davis."

She looked up at me from her squatted position, a can of bean soup in her hand. Wrinkling her nose, she said, "That's a bald-faced lie. Amy ain't got no friends."

"We weren't best friends or anything," I said, taken aback, "but she asked me for help, so I think that meant she considered me a friend."

"You're the woman with the self-defense class, right? The one asking questions with the police detective the other night."

"Yeah," I admitted.

Her upper lip curled. "You ain't no friend."

"But I'm still worried about her," I said insistently. "She was supposed to meet me on Tuesday morning, but she didn't show. I think she's in danger, and I want to help her."

"Sounds like you already did," the young woman said, turning back to the cans. "You taught her self-defense."

"Only one night of lessons," I said, feeling like I was being judged. "And I think you know why she wanted those lessons, as well as the private lessons she asked me to give her."

She glanced over her shoulder at me, and the look on her face said she either didn't believe me or didn't care.

"Look, all I want to do is make sure she's safe. Have you talked to her since she left Deja Brew on Monday at about eight?"

"Nope." But she'd hesitated before answering.

"Do you know anything about her family in Georgia? We think she might have gone back home."

She laughed. "She ain't got no family in Georgia to go back to. Her grandmother raised her after her daddy went to prison and her momma ODed. She moved here with Boomer because her grandmother died in August, and the landlord kicked her out."

My stomach sank. "You're sure there's no one else she could have run to? What about a cousin?"

The woman turned to look up at me in disgust. "Girl, if she had a place like that to run to, don't you think she'd have gone sooner? She was trapped with Boomer and his good-for-nothing cousin. She wanted out, but Boomer took her paycheck and barely doled out any cash to her."

Air stuck in my lungs, and I started to feel light-headed. "Her neighbor said she put her suitcase and a bag in her car before she left Tuesday morning. Where could she have gone?"

"Beats me. I doubt she had enough gas money to make it to Georgia, even if she wanted to go there, which I highly doubt. She wasn't any happier there. If she really left, she probably found some other poor sucker to take her in."

"You don't like Amy?" I asked in surprise.

"I don't dislike her," she said with a shrug. "She just reminds me too much of my mom, both of them lettin' men run roughshod over 'em and never standin' up for themselves."

"Did you ever think that maybe she needed a friend?" I asked bitterly.

She stood up, looking me in the eye. "Women like my momma and Amy always choose the man over the friend, or even their own daughter. *Always.* They can't help themselves." She squatted again. "Like I said, Amy didn't have no friends. Boomer wouldn't let her."

"Do you happen to know her grandmother's name?"

She shook her head with a look of disgust. "What difference does it make? She's dead. I have work to do, and if my manager sees me talkin' to you, I'm liable to get in trouble."

"Sorry," I said. "Thanks for your help."

Her snort didn't sound like *you're welcome.*

Dejected, I grabbed a cart, deciding I could pick up a few things for Mallory's visit. I headed to the wine section and saw Miss Patsy in a middle aisle, which meant she was probably about halfway done. After I picked up a couple bottles of Moscato and a Pinot Grigio, I found the chip aisle and grabbed several bags of the store-brand versions of the kinds Mallory liked. She'd pitch a fit and likely go buy the name-brand bags herself, but I'd missed some work a few weeks ago with the whole Peter McIntire fiasco and needed to buy Christmas presents. I was flat broke.

I was tempted to buy more groceries, but I didn't plan on going home, which meant I couldn't get anything refrigerated. Besides, it was bad enough I'd be Ubering with wine bottles rolling around in my trunk. I didn't need multiple bags of groceries in the mix.

Only two cashiers were checking out customers, so I chose

the shortest line, not surprised to see an older woman buying a gallon of milk, a loaf of bread, and a few other items.

"You're lucky we had any milk and bread left," said the cashier, a woman who looked about my age. "I heard we had a run of people snatching them up last night."

The older woman nodded. "I'm preparing for the big snowstorm."

The cashier chuckled. "I thought *last night* was the snowstorm."

"But there's still snow on the ground," the older woman said. "And I was too busy watchin' my program last night to leave the house."

"Were you watching the *Jeopardy* championship?" the cashier asked. "I heard that one guy had won over a hundred thousand dollars!" Then she grinned. "But *your* total is eighteen-fifty-two."

"Oh, no," the older woman said as she removed a twenty-dollar bill from her wallet. "I was watching a *Magic Mike* marathon." She shook her head with a wistful look. "That boy sure does have some washboard abs."

The cashier burst out laughing as she took the money and dug out the change. "Go get 'em, Loretta!"

The older woman made a growling sound and took her money before snatching up her bags and walking toward the exit.

I put my wine and chips on the conveyor belt.

The cashier looked over my items and winked. Her name tag read *Nina*. "Having a *Magic Mike* watch party of your own?"

I laughed. "I wish...although if my best friend finds a *Magic Mike* marathon, she'll likely turn it on," I added, "She's visiting from Nashville this weekend."

"Oh!" she exclaimed. "Fun!"

"Say," I said, deciding to give this a shot. "I'm sort of friends with Amy Davis, and I know she works here—"

"*Worked* here," she said. "Past tense. They fired her this morning."

I cringed. I understood why the manager had fired her, but it still felt wrong.

"I'm really worried about her."

Nina leaned closer. "There are lots of rumors flying around about her going back to Georgia, but I'm not buying it. She didn't have anyone to go back to. That asshole was all she had."

Which was what the woman I'd just talked to had said. The manager had told Noah that Amber and Gloria were Amy's closest friends here. Had I talked to Amber a few minutes ago? She hadn't worn a nametag.

"Did she ever mention her boyfriend by name?" I asked.

"No. It was like he was a big secret. Half of us didn't believe he was real until the asshole showed up and threatened one of the guys who works here for looking at her funny. But I've heard that she dropped his name once—Boomer. That's all I know about him other than that he liked to use her as a punching bag."

That made me think the employee I'd talked to earlier was Amber. She'd known Boomer and Jake's names, something no one else had known.

"Amy's neighbor said Amy told her she was leaving Boomer. The neighbor thinks she went back to Georgia."

Nina shook her head. "I just don't see that happening."

"If you don't think Amy went back to Georgia, what do you think happened to her?"

Her eyes darkened. "I think that good-for-nothing boyfriend did something to her. I heard a policeman was asking about her a couple nights ago."

"Detective Langley. He's a friend of mine. He knew I was worried about Amy because she didn't show up to meet me

Tuesday morning, so he agreed to look into it. But no one's officially reported her missing, so he couldn't do much."

"I'm not surprised," she said in disgust. "If some rich girl were missing, they'd be all over it, but a poor girl datin' a piece of scum?" She shook her head. "Nobody gives a shit about someone like that."

"*I* give a shit," I said.

"But what can *you* do about it?" she asked. "Amy's probably buried in a shallow grave somewhere, and nobody cares except for you and me."

A cold chill washed through me. Nina had just voiced my biggest fear.

"There you are," Miss Patsy's voice cracked behind me. "I was worried you'd left." She leaned over into her cart and started to set the items on the belt, one by one.

I left my bags at the end and walked over to help her. She was so unbalanced, she looked like she was about to fall into the cart, and as slow as she was moving, it might take all day if I didn't help. As I grabbed her items, I realized at least half of her purchase comprised bags of dog and cat food, but she'd also bought several cans of tuna, a loaf of bread, and some canned soups, vegetables, and peaches. After the cashier rang up everything and gave her the total, Miss Patsy dug around in her purse and pulled out several bills and coins, counting them out. She was fourteen dollars short.

Looking embarrassed, Miss Patsy said, "Let's put the peaches and tuna back. How much is it then?"

She was putting her own food back, and there was little of that to begin with. She was putting her animals' needs above her own. There was absolutely no way I was letting this poor woman starve.

"Don't put anything back," I said, pulling out my own cash and handing it to Nina.

Miss Patsy's face flushed. "I can't let you do that."

"I'm just paying it forward," I said. "The person in front of me paid for part of my groceries just a few minutes ago. Fifteen dollars' worth. Right?" I sent Nina a pleading look, silently asking her to back me up.

"That's right," Nina said, printing up the receipt.

Tears filled Miss Patsy's eyes. "I don't know what to say. Thank you."

"There's nothing *to* say," I insisted in a no-nonsense tone. "You just pay it forward yourself sometime." In fact, I suspected she already had. I doubted she had enough animals in her house to consume all the pet food she'd purchased. I'd seen those cats slinking around her bushes. She was probably feeding strays.

I loaded her bags and mine into my cart, and we walked out to my car. After placing our packages into my trunk, I drove her home and purposely left my driving app off. There was no way I could charge her now.

Some Uber driver I'd turned out to be.

Still, I didn't have any regrets as I carried the heavy bags of dog food up to her house.

After I took everything inside and set the bags on her kitchen table, I went back to my car, opened the Uber app, and found my next ride less than a minute later. Someone just outside town wanted to go to Benton's Diner downtown.

I headed that way, listening to the radio as I drove, but my mind was on Aunt Deidre. How long would I be able to keep her in her home? Cabbage Rose House had been Uncle Albert's grandparents' home, and he and Aunt Deidre had moved in with his grandparents right after their wedding. Aunt Deidre loved her house. It would destroy her to leave. But I also had to make sure she was safe.

I'd schedule some tours next week.

About fifteen minutes later, I arrived at the neighborhood

for my Uber pickup. The older neighborhood was just on the edge of town, but based on what I saw as I drove past the houses by the entrance and turned down a side street, the residents seemed to take good care of their homes. I was halfway down the street when I noticed a garage door opening a few houses ahead. A white van pulled out. It didn't stop at the end of the driveway before turning onto the street toward me, swinging wide, and hitting the front of my car.

"Hey!" I shouted even though my windows were closed. "What are you doing?"

I put my car in park and started to open my door to get out and exchange information, but the driver, a redheaded man with a scruffy beard, backed up, flipped me off, swung around me, and sped toward the entrance of the neighborhood.

I jumped out and turned to get a look at his license plate, but the van was already too far away for me to see it.

Damn it.

I walked around the front of my car. While the bumper was smashed in and the hood had a deep dent, it looked like it was still drivable. But the asshole had just driven off without giving me his insurance information, and now I'd be stuck paying for an expensive car repair I couldn't afford.

Fuck that.

He'd just pulled out of the garage of the house next to me, so I could see if someone at the house had his contact information. If that didn't work, at least I had an address to turn over to the police. In fact, the garage door was still open, so the odds were good someone was at home.

Except...his behavior was odd for a homeowner in this neighborhood.

And that's when it hit me. This could be the home invasion guy Noah was looking for.

I jumped back into my car, pulled into the driveway, then

backed up and sped after the van. As I drove, I grabbed my phone and called Noah.

"Maddie," he said when he answered. "Can I call you back? I'm in the middle of something right now."

I drove through the stop sign at the end of the street and turned left. I could see the van turning left on the county road heading out of town. "I think I just saw a van leaving the scene of a break-in."

"*What?*"

"You said you were investigating some break-ins, right? I just saw a white van pull headfirst out of a garage and leave the door open. Do you think it might be related?"

"Where did you see it?" he asked, his tone urgent.

I made a rolling stop at the entrance to the neighborhood and turned left. "The Orchard subdivision. Off Cherry Street. Do you know it?"

"Yeah, there was a break-in over there last week. How long ago was this?"

"I told you. I *just* saw it." The van was about a hundred feet away in front of me. I stepped on the gas. "The van just turned onto Cherry, heading out of town."

"Did you happen to get a license plate number?"

"No. But I got a look at the driver. He has red hair and a bushy beard." Then I added, "The van was plain, with no writing that I could see. There's also paint from his van on the front of my car, although I'm not sure what good that will do you."

"*What?*"

"The asshole pulled out of the driveway and didn't look where he was going. He hit me."

"What are you doing in the Orchard subdivision?"

That ticked me off. "I'm picking up an Uber passenger, not that it's any business of yours, *Detective Langley*." Crap. My

Uber passenger was waiting for me, and if they were watching the app, they'd see me driving away.

What was my plan here? Follow the van to the thieves' secret lair? Get the license plate number?

"Sorry," he grunted. "You're right. Do you remember the address the van pulled out of? Are you still there? Do you need a tow truck?"

I made a face as I drove over the speed limit to gain on the van. "My car's drivable, so I don't need to be towed, and I don't know the number, but it was on Apple Blossom Drive. The garage door's still up."

"Are you still in the neighborhood picking up your passenger? Can you drive back to the house and wait for me or an officer to arrive? We need to get your statement."

I hesitated. "I already left the neighborhood."

"What aren't you telling me, Maddie?"

"Why are you asking me that?" I was almost close enough to read the license plate number. I pressed on the gas, shooting well over the speed limit.

"Maddie, where *are* you?"

"Get ready to write something down."

"What?"

The letters and numbers on the plate came into view. "BFG 2468, Hamilton County."

"Jesus Christ, Maddie. *Did you follow him?*"

"Did you get it?" I asked insistently.

"BFG 2468, Hamilton County," he spat out grudgingly. "If you're following him, *stop.* These guys are *dangerous,* Maddie."

"The asshole hit my car and didn't give me his insurance information. I'm done with men screwing me over, and I'm going to make this one pay."

"Maddie..." He sounded apologetic, but then his hard

resolve returned. "You got the license number, so turn around, and let me handle it."

"There's no place to turn around. It's all just country roads with gravel shoulders and fields."

"Fuck," he grunted under his breath, then added, "if he turns off, do *not* follow him."

"I won't," I said in exasperation. "I was just trying to get the plate number. And you're welcome, by the way. I'll turn off on the next road, okay?"

"You stay on the line with me until you're headed back to the house," he said, sounding slightly out of breath. "Lance and I are on the way."

"I plan on turning around," I said in exasperation. "I'm not trying to make a citizen's arrest here."

"I'll meet you at the scene of your accident," he spit out. "Once you turn around, go back *there*."

"Fine," I said shorter than I'd intended. None of this was his fault, and he had just cause to be concerned. Still, I was pissed about my car. I couldn't afford a new car. Even a used one.

It wasn't fair, but I knew firsthand that life wasn't fair. It didn't make me any less bitter about it.

"Don't hang up," Noah barked. "You stay on the line with me until you've turned around and made sure he doesn't follow you."

I snorted. "Why in the world would he follow me?" But I knew it was a stupid question even as it fell out of my mouth. Sure, I'd followed him to get his license number, but the guy was likely a burglar. It was doubtful his insurance was going to pay to fix my car when he hit me during his getaway. This wasn't the smartest thing I'd ever done. I guess I'd just gotten caught up in my irritation.

"*Maddie.*"

"There's a deserted gas station up ahead." I flipped on my

turn signal and started slowing down. "I'm turning around there."

"What's the van doing?"

"It's driving, Noah, for God's sake," I said, growing more irrationally angry by the minute. Logically, I knew I was mad at myself—for following that stupid van *and* for calling Noah like it was the most natural thing in the world, and if I were honest with myself, a small part of me did it to help him. Okay, maybe more than a small part.

I started to slow down to make my turn. "You *do* realize it's suspicious when I turn around. He can still see me." Then again, he'd hit me, and I'd sped after him. It already looked suspicious.

"Do it anyway."

I pulled into the parking lot. "I'm turning around now, and the van is continuing down the road. Happy?"

"No. I would be happier if you hadn't followed the van in the first place."

"I'm hanging up now."

"Go back to the house and wait for us," Noah said, his voice tight. "That's Detective Langley ordering you, not Noah. We need to get your statement."

"Fine." I pressed the end button on my screen.

Chapter Fifteen

Noah

"Noah," Lance said, shaking his head. "She's not in danger. You can slow down."

"She followed him. Why the fuck would she follow him?"

Lance sat back in his seat. "She was trying to get the license plate number, and she succeeded."

"And the plate turned out to be stolen, so she risked her life for fucking nothing."

"It could still be useful. It's too early to tell."

We were silent for several seconds before I asked, "Why would she do something so dangerous? I realize he hit her car, but sane people don't follow hit-and-run drivers. She's from Nashville, for fuck's sake. She's heard of road rage."

"Sure, the van hit her, but the fact that she called you and told you about the break-in means she was also doing it to help *you*. Take it as a sign that you still have a chance with her, despite treating her like shit."

"She could have gotten herself killed, Lance. I'm not going through that again."

He didn't respond immediately. Instead, he considered my

words for a long beat before asking, "Are you talking about what happened in Memphis?"

I didn't answer. It was obvious enough.

"You can talk to me about it," he said gently. "It might be a good idea to tell me, since we're partners."

"There's not much to tell," I said in a tight voice. "I can get you the report, if you want."

"I've read the report. I want to hear about it from you."

"That's gonna take a few drinks."

"Good thing my mother owns a bar."

I shook my head, then shot him a grim smile. "I'll tell you sometime. I swear. Just not today."

"You have to ream Maddie first?"

"Something like that." It was hard to admit to myself, let alone to Lance, how terrified I'd been during that phone call. I'd avoided a relationship with her in part to protect her from my life as a cop, but then she'd gone and followed a perp on her own.

I wasn't sure how to handle it.

When we arrived, her smashed car was parked in front of a brick raised ranch. The front driver's side was crushed, but it was obviously still drivable. Two police cars were parked against the curb on either end of her car. She was standing next to the street, talking to one of the officers.

I pulled up to the curb across the street and hopped out, heading straight for Maddie while resisting the urge to take her in my arms to reassure myself that she was okay.

She studied me for a moment but didn't say anything. Her dark glare said it all. She was still pissed, which I didn't understand. *I* wasn't the one who'd been foolish enough to drive after potential danger.

I gave her a sharp nod, then turned to the uniformed officer. "Has anyone been inside?"

"No, we just contacted the homeowners, who gave us permission to check it out, but we decided to wait for you and Lance."

I nodded again, then turned my attention to Maddie. "Give your statement to Officer Hicks. If I'm not back out by the time you finish, wait for me."

The look in her eyes made me brace myself for her protest, but she bit out, "Fine."

I wasn't sure whether to trust her answer, but now that I'd seen for myself that she was safe, I had more pressing issues—like what we were going to find in the house. Lance and I headed for the still-open garage, pulling on gloves as we strode inside.

Tension gripped the back of my neck as we walked into the house. The door opened to a neat and clean kitchen with no signs of ransacking and no photos.

"No Polaroid," Lance said. "That's a relief. But Maddie's description of the driver matches the one the neighbor gave you yesterday."

"Maybe it wasn't the driver who left the pics," I said, taking cautious steps into the living room. "We know he likely had help. Maybe it was the guy who was in back, out of view." There was an empty spot on a TV console on a wall across from the sofa. "Looks like they took a TV."

"Nothing crazy in here," Lance said as he scanned the room.

"Let's check out the rest of the house."

We made our way down a hall off the living room and found a hall bath, two bedrooms, and a home office. The kids' rooms were ransacked, and if there had been a computer on the desk in the office, it was now gone.

"No master bedroom?" Lance asked, confused.

"It must be on the other side of the house."

Retracing our steps, we headed back to the kitchen and

found a small hallway with a door at the end. We pushed through it to reveal a bed strewn with women's clothes.

"Shit," Lance muttered under his breath.

"Yeah," I said with a sigh as we walked farther into the room.

Sure enough, there was a Polaroid on the bed, and this time it was a full-on dick pic. Even worse, he had a pair of women's panties wrapped around his penis, his hand in a firm grip.

"Jesus," Lance groaned.

"Let's check out the bathroom."

He followed me through the doorway, stopping in his tracks as soon as he crossed the threshold. A pink lipstick heart had been drawn on the mirror like in the last house, but this time, a woman's photograph was attached to the bit of mirror inside it.

I took a step closer, my heart starting to race as I took a closer look. It wasn't a candid snap—it looked like it had been taken by a professional. "We need to find out where he got this photo. If he got it here, we need to see if there's an empty frame. Maybe he left prints this time."

"You think he'd be that stupid?" Lance asked. "There weren't any prints at the last scene."

"We can only hope."

We headed back outside, but I was already calling the forensics team to come work their magic. Maddie wasn't outside when I walked out, and panic washed through me. Had she already left even though I told her not to?

"She's in Hicks's car," Lance said in a tone low enough that the other officer in the front yard couldn't hear. "It's cold out here. He must have taken her to his car to keep her warm."

"Yeah," I said, trying to sound nonchalant. "Makes sense."

"I know you're worried about her. There's some sick pervert breaking into houses, and she followed him."

"I'd be worried about anyone who followed this creep."

"But Maddie's not just anyone."

"Stop," I said with a groan. "I don't have time to make this personal."

Lance's brow furrowed, and he looked like he was about to say something before shaking his head in disgust. "I'm going to see if she gave Hicks anything more than we already have. If not, I'll tell her she's free to go." He gave me a cocky look. "Unless you can think of some reason to keep her here."

"Nope," I said, my heart in my throat. "She's free to go."

"Great." He turned on his heels and walked over to the patrol car, whistling a catchy tune.

Asshole.

I didn't have time to worry about Maddie. I needed to focus on this sick bastard and arrest him before his behavior escalated even more.

Chapter Sixteen

Maddie

I'd just finished giving Officer Hicks my statement when a knock rapped on my window. I jumped, then felt foolish when I realized it was Lance.

He opened the door and squatted next to me. "You get her statement, Hicks?"

"Yep. I just finished."

Lance looked over his notes, then gave me a warm smile. "Then you're free to go, Maddie."

"Was the house broken into?"

"I can't talk about the case, but if we have any more questions about what you saw, we'll be in touch."

Lance took a step back to give me space to get out of the car. As I shut the door, I shot a glance at Noah, who was on the phone and seemed to be purposely trying not to look at me. I turned my attention back to Lance. "You really can't tell me if there was a break-in?"

"I'm sure you'll hear about it in the local news."

Or the gossip network. I hadn't intentionally sought out gossip since being back to Cockamamie, mostly because I knew plenty of it was about *me*, but I wasn't above using it if necessary.

"Fine," I said, then darted a glare at Noah.

"He was pissed because he was scared for you."

I knew he was right, but I felt some residual anger.

"Maybe next time don't purposely follow the bad guys."

I lifted a brow. "So they *were* bad guys."

"*Alleged* bad guys," he corrected, struggling to suppress a grin. "Even more so since the guy hit you and ran off. But in the future, you should presume anyone suspicious is a bad guy and take the proper precautions."

"While I hope you catch the bad guys so they stop stealing people's stuff, I highly doubt he'll pay for my car repairs."

He shifted his weight and shoved his hands into his pockets. "I have a cousin who does bodywork. How about I talk to him and see if he can give you the family discount?"

"You don't have to do that, Lance. The last thing I want is charity."

"It's not charity, Maddie. It's one friend helping another."

I pushed out a sigh. "Okay. Send me his name and number, because there's no way I can do Uber pickups with a crunched-up car."

I got into my car and cast a glance back at the front yard. Noah wasn't on his phone anymore, and his gaze was firmly on me. Lance walked up to him and started talking. Noah ripped his gaze away from me to focus on his partner.

And just like that, he'd dismissed me. Again.

I knew he was doing his job, and of course, that took precedence, but I'd expected Noah to confront me or even comfort me. Instead, he'd completely ignored me and asked Lance to do his dirty work. Again.

Why was I so surprised?

I drove out of the neighborhood, unsure what to do for the rest of my day. Maybe look for another job? I'd struck out the last time I'd tried doing that, but it occurred to me that I might be able to get some seasonal work since Christmas was coming up. It would at least help toward my car repairs.

I was heading back to town when my phone rang. Deja Brew's name appeared on the screen.

"Petra?" I asked when I answered.

"Yeah," she said. "Is there any chance you could come in and work? Cynthia didn't come in today because of the snow, and we're struggling."

I glanced at the clock. It was nearly eleven. "Of course." I had nothing else to do, and I wasn't going to make any money Ubering. "Why didn't you ask me to come in sooner?"

"We thought it would be slow today with the snow and all, but it's turned out to be the opposite. Everyone and his brother are in here getting hot drinks."

"Sure, I'll be right there." Even at eight dollars an hour, it was more than I'd made so far today. Miss Patsy hadn't tipped me, so I'd made a whopping $3.52 and had probably used at least a gallon of gas, which meant I was in the hole, especially after my car accident.

I was starting to give serious thought to selling photos of my feet on Only Fans. The upside was that I could write off pedicures as a business expense.

Deja Brew was bustling when I walked behind the counter from the back. Petra was taking orders, and Chrissy was making drinks. Chrissy shot me a dark look, which wasn't all that unusual, but her mood seemed even bleaker than usual.

"Where do you want me?" I asked as I tied my apron.

"Take over the register," Petra said as she handed a customer back his credit card. "I'll head to the back and make sandwiches."

I jumped into work. I took a few orders at the register, helped Chrissy catch up, then took more. Thankfully, after several months of working together, we were like a well-oiled machine.

"I told her to call you sooner," Chrissy grumbled. "But would she listen to me? No."

"I'm sure she had her reasons," I said in a hushed tone.

She rolled her eyes. "You mean other than she's cheap?"

That too, but it felt disloyal to say so. Petra had always bent over backward to accommodate my schedule around my aunt's caregiver's hours.

The crowd continued through lunch, with lots of orders for breakfast sandwiches, yogurt, and cheese boxes. I wondered what was up until one of the customers explained the diner was closed due to the weather. The coffee shop was one of the only places to get lunch downtown.

Around two, we finally got a breather. Chrissy took a break, leaving me alone at the front counter. I'd taken a few orders and was handing a macchiato to a woman when a familiar male voice said, "Hey, Maddie."

For a moment, I felt a disconnect. The man attached to that voice certainly didn't belong in Cockamamie, let alone Deja Brew.

I slowly turned to face Steve, my mouth hanging open in shock.

He laughed. "Based on the look on your face, I'm the last person you expected to see."

My shock gave way to anger. "Why are you here? Because you could have just mailed a check, you know."

"Oh, come on, Maddie," he said good-naturedly, holding his hands out at his sides. "Surely, you're a *little* happy to see me."

"About as happy as I would be to find out I had genital warts." My eyes narrowed, then I repeated, "Why are you here?"

"I just wanted to see you."

"You drove two-and-a-half hours to see me?" I shook my head in disgust. "Not buying it. What do you *really* want?"

His face softened. "I wanted to see you, Maddie. Truly. When do you get off work?"

I scowled. "Why?"

"I want to have dinner with you tonight."

I propped a hand on my hip. "*Why?*"

He took a step closer. "Look, I know things didn't end well for us—"

"You think?"

"—and I know I wasn't the best boyfriend—"

"Understatement."

"—but I've done a lot of soul searching...and...well..." His eyes turned pleading. "Just have dinner with me, okay? I'll explain it all then." His face brightened as though I'd already agreed. "What's the best place to eat around here?"

"Cock on the Walk," Chrissy said from behind me. "Best burgers in the county."

Steve scrunched up his nose. "I was thinking something like steak."

"They have steak too. You can't beat the price," Chrissy said, now standing beside me. She placed a hand on my shoulder. "Maddie here will meet you there, say eight o'clock?"

What was she up to? She had no idea who I was talking to. And why was she encouraging us to go to the biker bar?

Steve pursed his lips as though considering it.

I groaned in frustration. No matter how much I resented him, I couldn't send him out there when I had no intention of showing up. I didn't want to be responsible for someone else's murder.

Guess he'd caught me on a good day.

"I'm not meeting you for dinner, Steve, and even if I wanted to—which I don't—I can't leave my aunt. I've been gone for three nights in a row, and I can't ask Margarete to watch her again."

Chrissy held up a finger. "I have an idea," she said in a bright tone that sounded alien coming from her. "How about you have dinner at Maddie's tonight?"

Steve's eyes lit up. "Will you make your world-famous lasagna?"

Chrissy turned to me, her brow shooting up. "You've been holding out on me, Madelyn. World-famous lasagna? Why haven't you shared that with your Cockamamie friends? It's about time we changed that."

"Did someone say lasagna?" Petra asked, coming out of the back. "I love lasagna."

"There you have it!" Chrissy said enthusiastically. "It's a dinner party at Maddie's house."

Steve looked just as steamrolled as I felt.

I shook my head. "I don't—"

"Have time to make lasagna?" Chrissy asked with a bright smile. "No worries. You'll be getting off soon, and we can set dinner for seven-thirty." She turned to Steve. "Does that work for you?"

"It works for me," Petra said.

Steve shifted his gaze to me, but I was too shocked by this turn of events to protest. "Yeah, I guess..."

"So it's a date." Chrissy lifted her hand and wiggled her fingers. "Toodle-loo."

Steve took a few steps back before turning and making a beeline for the door.

"What the hell was that?" I demanded, turning to face Chrissy.

"Look, the guy obviously wants something from you, and it's in your best interest to find out what that might be."

"In the middle of *a dinner party*?"

Her grin turned evil. "I have my ways. Besides, you're too much of a pushover. At first, I was trying to ditch him for you, but then I came to my senses and realized there's power in knowledge. We'll pump him for information tonight, because I also realized you need someone else around to make sure you don't give the guy your car or the deed to your aunt's house."

"I wouldn't do that," I protested. "I left the guy, didn't I?" Besides, there's no way he'd want my car now, but I kept the accident to myself. I didn't feel like getting into it.

Chrissy rolled her eyes. "Sure, after your uncle died and you were forced into it."

I frowned, but she had a point. I *had* let him walk all over me, but I'd wised up in the past few months. Besides, I hadn't just walked into a terrible relationship. Steve had been nothing but charming in the beginning. Things had gotten progressively worse over time. It was like being a frog slowly boiled in a pot. I'd needed to escape the situation to see how truly bad it had gotten, and now that I was at this vantage point, there was no way I was giving him anything. Still, having him over to a dinner party was a disaster waiting to happen. Not to mention, I didn't want to encourage him. "My friend Mallory is coming this afternoon. The timing sucks."

"The more the merrier," Chrissy said with a smile so wide I saw more of her teeth than I'd ever seen before. "I look forward to meeting her."

I put both hands on my hips. "Who are you, and what have you done with Chrissy? She'd never say something like that, let alone want to go to a dinner party."

"It's not just a dinner party," Chrissy said with a maniacal gleam in her eyes. "It's a roast."

There she was.

Chapter Seventeen

Maddie

It was so busy that I didn't get off work until four, but during the last couple hours of my shift, I'd realized I was too tired to go through the drama of Chrissy—and Mallory—because who was I kidding? She'd be all over this plan—roasting my ex over lasagna and a cheap merlot. I couldn't risk the chance the whole thing would cast a pall over my lasagna, because, to be honest, my lasagna was one of the last good things in my life.

So when I got off work, I sent Steve a text.

> Change of plans. Meet me at Lucky's Tavern at 4:30.

I wasn't sure why I'd picked Lucky's. Maybe because it had been empty when I'd met Noah there the day before, and I didn't want witnesses if I tossed a drink in Steve's smug face.

> Address?

Still the same helpless Steve. I nearly looked it up to send it to him, then realized I was already falling into a familiar pattern. Maybe Chrissy was right.

> Look it up. That's what Google's for.

I sent a quick text telling Mallory that I'd gotten hung up, and I'd be forever grateful if she made a grocery store run to get the ingredients for lasagna, salad, and garlic bread. Because while I was in the process of ditching Steve, having a dinner wasn't a terrible idea. It would now be a ladies' night in that included Aunt Deidre.

I only hoped she was feeling up to it.

> Going all out to greet me? I can't say I'm disappointed.

> We're having a dinner party at 7:30. I'll explain later.

> Color me intrigued. ;)

Grateful that was dealt with, I headed over to the tavern, now berating myself for having suggested Lucky's. What if Noah was there? But then I got pissed. So what if he *was* there? It was none of his business what I did. *Still,* I didn't exactly want him hearing my business with my ex. It comforted me a little to think he was probably still tied up with his robbery case.

I pulled into Lucky's parking lot at four-fifteen and breathed a sigh of relief when I didn't see Noah's car in the parking lot. One potential bad situation averted.

When I walked in, a man in a business suit was sitting at the bar, nursing a drink. He glanced up at me, then returned his attention to his glass. Matilda was behind the bar, and she smiled when she saw me.

"Maddie! Glad you came back. What can I get you?"

I knew I should ask for water, but I was nervous. Steve was lazy, so for him to make the trek to Cockamamie on a weekday—with snow on the ground—I knew something was up.

I stood in front of the bar, eyeing the wall of alcohol bottles behind her. "Um...can I get a whiskey sour, please?"

She cocked an eyebrow, but said without judgment, "Coming right up."

I stood there, shifting my weight as I waited.

"You meeting Noah here?" she asked innocently as she started to make my drink, but I could tell it was more than idle curiosity.

"No, someone else."

She lifted her eyebrow again. "Oh?"

So Matilda was the nosy type. I gave her a tight smile. "A friend."

She made a face that suggested whoever I met was no business of hers, but I knew better. Was she curious out of boredom, or for Noah's sake? I guessed the latter.

Quit thinking about Noah!

She finished making the drink and placed it in front of me. "Do you want to start a tab?"

"No, I won't be staying long." I placed a ten-dollar bill on the counter. Ten dollars I couldn't really spare. *Damn, Steve.* "Does this cover it?"

She looked even more intrigued. "The drink's only eight dollars, so I'd say so."

"Keep the change." I carried the drink over to a booth and sat so I was facing the door, taking off my scarf and coat and setting them on the seat beside me. I wanted plenty of warning before Steve joined me. I didn't have to wait long. He strolled in through the door, looking the same as he had a few hours ago. He lifted his hand in a cocky half-wave when he saw me, then walked over to the bar and ordered a bourbon. He had on expensive jeans, a deep blue crewneck sweater, and a dark gray jacket. His hair was perfectly styled. He looked good, and he knew it.

His gaze was on me the whole time, and he was giving me that same damn cocky smile that used to drive me crazy in a good way. Now it made me want to gag.

He handed Matilda some cash, his gaze still on me. Matilda gave him a dark look as he headed in my direction.

"You're looking good, Maddie," he said as he slipped into the seat across from me.

I took a sip of my half-finished drink, then set it down. I was dressed in jeans and a partially faded black turtleneck sweater. My hair was pulled back into a ponytail, and I was only wearing mascara. He was full of shit. "Let's skip the pleasantries and get to why this conversation couldn't take place over text."

He sat back in his seat, studying me through narrowed eyes. "You've changed."

I pushed out an exhausted groan. "Get to the point, Steve."

He took a sip of his drink, holding the glass near the top with his pinky finger sticking out, showing off his gold and onyx ring. He'd started holding cocktail glasses that way about a year ago. I'd found it annoying then, and now it irritated the snot out of me. Now I could see it for what it was—a pathetic attempt to look classy. I was embarrassed it had taken me so long to see what an asshole he truly was. Then again, he hadn't always been that way, or if he had, he'd hidden it for a few years.

He set his glass down before reaching across the table to rest his hand over mine. "I've missed you, Maddie."

I jerked my hand away. "Is this some pathetic attempt to get me back?"

He flashed a cheesy smile. "Let's hope it's not *that* pathetic."

I drew in a deep breath, then started to get out of the seat, but he reached over and grabbed my wrist. I tried to pull away from him, but his hold tightened.

"Jesus, Maddie," he said in frustration. "You always run at the first sign of trouble. Will you just grow up and listen?"

My jaw dropped, and it took me a second to regain composure. I jerked again, but he tightened his grip on my wrist.

"Let me make this perfectly clear," I said through gritted teeth, livid. "Unless you're here with a check for fifteen thousand dollars plus interest, then we have *nothing* to talk about."

"You can't write a check for fifteen thousand dollars plus interest, Maddie," he smirked. "This is why you need me. To handle all your finances."

"You mean like you handled my finances by taking my savings for that stupid flip house? I know you sold it, so give me what you owe me." I tried to jerk free again, but he pressed my arm against the table.

"We were good together, Maddie. You *have* to know that. I miss you. Come home."

He honestly thought holding me here against my will was the way to win me back? Had he lost his mind? Obviously he had, because he seemed to have forgotten the reason I'd moved here in the first place. "And what am I supposed to do about Aunt Deidre?"

He gave me an awkward grimace. "Come on, Mads. We both know she was just an excuse. You were frustrated that I wouldn't propose, and you used that situation to force my hand. Well played." He reached into his pocket with his free hand, then set a ring box on the table.

I stopped tugging, in shock. How long had I waited for a proposal from him? The last three of the five years we were together. Tears stung my eyes. Three months ago, I'd been so desperate to have a family that I would have said yes and been grateful he'd asked.

Now? Realizing what an idiot I'd been sent a fresh wave of embarrassment through my veins, but Steve mistook my tears of shame for joy.

"Ah, don't cry, baby," he said, his smug grin back. "I'll make it up to you with a huge wedding." He opened the box, and my jaw dropped again when I saw a round solitaire diamond ring. It had to be at least two carats. "I was thinking we could get married in January."

"*January?* As in *one month* from now?"

"I don't want to wait. I want to prove how much I want you."

What the hell was happening? The fact that he was deluded was a given, and I needed him to come to terms with reality. "Moving in with Aunt Deidre wasn't some kind of desperate ploy to force you to propose, Steve. That was me *actually* leaving you to take care of my aunt."

Steve was so busy admiring the diamond in the ring box it bought me the distraction I needed to grab my purse and coat and slide out of the booth. But he quickly realized what was happening and jumped to his feet, blocking my path. "Maddie, wait."

I tried to duck around him, but he snaked out an arm to stop me. "I know this wasn't the fancy proposal you probably wanted." He grimaced as he took a quick glance around the tavern. "I mean, I admit that a rundown bar is pretty tacky, but I *did* want to take you out for a nice dinner. You're the one who changed the plans."

My blood boiled. For one thing, Lucky's wasn't a dive by any stretch of the imagination. For another, leave it to him to blame me for his own lack of planning.

"I'm just saying," he continued, "I know I've gotten a few things wrong, but I'm serious, Maddie. Let's get married."

The way he was casually tossing out *let's get married* hurt more than it should have. In the past, he'd come up with every excuse under the sun to put off an engagement, and now he was acting like getting married was no more consequential than heading over to Deja Brew for a cup of coffee.

I wasn't wasting another breath on this asshole.

I tried to go around him again, but he grabbed my arm and stopped me, his fingers digging into my arm to hold me in place.

I was about to knee him in the groin, then twist his arm around his back and force him to his knees, when I heard a familiar male voice say in a very threatening tone, "Take your hand off her *now*."

Noah was standing several feet behind Steve, his face contorted in barely controlled rage.

Steve dropped his arm and turned to face Noah, irritation filling his eyes. "This is a private conversation, so *fuck off*."

Noah reached into his coat pocket and then flashed his badge. "*This* makes it my business."

Steve lifted his hands into the air. "Everything's cool, Officer. Just a lovers' quarrel."

Noah's gaze drifted to mine. The anger was still on his face, but his expression was tinged with astonishment, likely from Steve's declaration.

I didn't say a word. I just slung my purse over my shoulder and charged for the door, not bothering to put on my coat.

I was already across the parking lot and about to get into my car when I heard Noah call out, "Maddie. Wait."

He jogged over to me as I stood between the open door and the car. "Do you want to press charges?" he asked when he reached me.

"For what?" I asked in disbelief. "Blocking my path?"

"He grabbed you and held you against your will." His gaze dropped to my reddened wrist.

I shook my head. "I could have handled it, Noah. I didn't need you to save me."

He started to say something, then stopped. "Who is that guy?"

"No one you need to worry about."

He made a quick glance over his shoulder toward the bar before looking back at me. "Are you *seeing* him?"

My anger raced to the surface. "That's none of your fucking business, Noah Langley. You've made it perfectly clear you don't want anything between us." I got into my car and slammed the door shut. After I turned on the engine, I put the car in drive and pulled out past him.

When I reached the street and switched on my turn signal, I noticed that he was still standing where I'd left him, watching me drive away.

Tears flowed down my cheeks, anger and humiliation bleeding together. The worst part was that I wasn't crying over Steve, or the five years of my life I'd spent on that loser. Or even that I'd never see my lost savings again.

No, stupid me was crying over the fact Noah Langley didn't want me. Because I still wanted him.

Badly.

Chapter Eighteen

Noah

I felt like dog shit on someone's shoe.

But I couldn't sulk over Maddie. I needed to get back inside and figure out who the fuck had just manhandled her and put the fear of God into him.

Five minutes ago, I'd been on my way to Lucky's when Matilda had called.

"How close are you?" she'd asked in a tight voice. Lance had already called ahead to tell her we were dropping by for something to eat. He'd even given her our order so it would be ready when we got there. We'd skipped lunch working on the case, and we were both starving. Lance had an errand to run, so I'd dropped him off at his car, with the plan to meet at his mom's place.

Her tone had instantly caught my attention. "A couple minutes. Why?"

"There's some guy here grabbing your girl's arm and keeping her from leaving the table."

"*Maddie?*"

"How many girls you got?" she'd spat in disgust. "Never

mind. I already know the answer to that, but if you're not interested, I'll take care of it myself."

I'd never seen Matilda in action, but I'd heard stories of her breaking up out-of-control bar fights and tossing guys out by twisting their ears. I had no doubt she could handle it, but this was Maddie, and I felt an overwhelming need to protect her myself. "I'm about a minute away, so I'll take care of it unless it looks like he's going to hurt her. In that case, pull out your Louisville slugger." (Aka the baseball bat she kept under the bar.)

"Got it."

I wasn't sure what to expect when I walked in, but I was shocked by what I saw: Maddie with tears in her eyes while a man had her arm pinned. I'd seen her stand up to thugs and fight like hell to escape, but she'd looked more vulnerable in this guy's grip than I'd ever seen her before.

An inexplicable need to hurt the man who had been the cause of bringing her to tears overcame me, but I'd choked it back in at that moment to make sure she was okay. Then she'd stormed out, so I'd told the asshole to stay inside unless he wanted to be arrested for evading the police and chased her outside.

Of course, she'd wanted nothing to do with me. How could I blame her after the way I'd been treating her? Showing an interest in her, then putting distance between us. Ghosting her, just like she'd claimed. Lance was right—I'd treated her like shit.

All I knew was that when she drove off, I felt worse than when I'd walked in and found her at that guy's mercy.

And now I felt an overwhelming need to make that asshole pay for treating her badly.

I'd be lying if I said some of my need for vengeance didn't come from my own guilt for being just another jerkwad in her life.

When I walked back inside, he was sitting in the booth, playing with a black velvet ring box as he sipped his drink. A gold ring flashed on his pinky finger, which he had extended like he was some rich playboy. I balled my fist at my side to keep from punching the smug grin off his face.

"What's your name and your relationship to the woman you were manhandling?" I asked as I approached his table.

He looked up at me, his mouth lifting into a smirk. "I'm Steve Campbell, and that woman is my fiancée."

I did a double take. This was the guy she'd dumped before moving back to Cockamamie? She was seeing him again? They were *engaged*? I hadn't noticed a ring on her finger, but then again, he had a ring box on the table. "Fiancée or not, you can't treat women like that in this town."

He released a sarcastic laugh. "Like what, Officer? Couples aren't allowed to have disagreements? What is this place? Pleasantville?"

I resisted the urge to grind my teeth. "You and I both know you were holding her against her will in that booth. Try it again, and I'll have you arrested and charged with false imprisonment."

He lifted his hands in surrender, but the gleam in his eyes made it clear he wasn't taking this seriously. "You don't need to worry, Officer. Maddie's just a bit spirited, if you know what I mean. But I assure you, it won't happen again."

"Detective. Detective Langley," I said in a dry tone, trying to ignore the "spirited" jab. From his tone and attitude, he must have realized I had a personal investment in her, and he was definitely poking at my wounds.

Amusement washed over his face. "My bad, *Detective* Langley." Campbell turned to face Matilda, who was standing behind the bar, watching the whole encounter with disdain in her eyes. "You serve food in this place?"

"Only the best burgers in town," a guy sitting at the bar called out.

Campbell curled his upper lip. "I was looking for steak."

"Then you'll have to head over to Cock on the Walk," Lance said, walking toward me with his hands in his coat pockets. I wasn't sure how long he'd been here or how much he'd witnessed, but obviously enough to give Campbell attitude. "I hear they have a pretty good steak. I suspect it's more your kind of place."

Campbell eyed Lance up and down, then glanced over at me. "I'm starting to get the impression that I'm not welcome here."

"Whatever gave you that idea?" Matilda called out sarcastically.

The asshole finished his drink and dropped the glass on the table with a loud thud. He grabbed his coat and stood. "I hope there's another place in town that doesn't serve watered-down drinks."

Matilda's jaw firmed as her face reddened.

"How many drinks have you had there, son?" Lance asked even though it was apparent Campbell was older than him. "Maybe we should give you a breathalyzer before we let you behind the wheel of a car."

Campbell lifted his chin with a gleam in his eye. "Careful, or I might have to report you for harassment." He leaned over the table, snatched up the ring box, and stuck it in his pocket. "I'll be in town for a while, working out some issues with my fiancée. Maddie can be stubborn sometimes, but she ultimately always sees things my way. All that to say, I suspect I might see you again, *Detective*." He gave me a nod. "Have a good night." Then he strutted past me and Lance and out the door.

As soon as the door shut behind him, Lance turned to me. "What was that all about?"

Some of the tension in my shoulders relaxed, but I was still on edge. "I'm not quite sure."

"You boys sit down," Matilda called to us. "I've got your food ready in the back."

I moved over to the booth Campbell had vacated and noticed something green lying on the floor under the table. I sat down on the seat and leaned down to pick it up, realizing it was Maddie's scarf.

Lance sat down opposite me and looked grim. "Did that guy actually claim to be *Maddie Baker's* fiancé?"

"Yep. When I showed up, he had hold of her arm and was blocking her from leaving."

"And she didn't let her inner ninja loose on him?" he asked with a half laugh.

"No," I said, my gut churning. "She looked like a deer caught in headlights."

Lance's smile fell. "That doesn't sound like Maddie."

"I know." And that was what worried me.

He folded his hands on the table. "Okay, so who is that guy? Really?"

"I'm pretty sure he's Maddie's ex, the guy she left in Nashville when she moved in with her aunt."

"And now he wants her back?"

Pain stabbed me in the chest. "Yeah, sounds like it." I looked him in the eye. "Your mom called to tell me that a guy was holding her in the booth. When I got here, they were standing. I followed her out to the parking lot to make sure she was okay, but she was pissed and left."

He was silent for several seconds, tapping his finger on the table. I was about to tell him to spit out whatever it was he wasn't saying when Matilda came out with our plates. "Hope you boys still have an appetite after that nonsense."

"Thanks, Mom," Lance said, picking up his fork and digging in. "You're the best."

She ruffled his head, beaming. "You only say that because I feed you."

He grinned. "And you give awesome hugs too."

She threw her arms around him and squeezed him tightly. "I'll get you boys something to drink," she said as she released him. "The usual?"

"Yep," Lance said, and I nodded.

"Kiss ass," I mumbled as I reached for my fork. She headed back to the kitchen.

Lance laughed. "Hey, she *is* the best. No point in keeping that a secret." Then he shoveled a fork full of mashed potatoes into his mouth.

I took a bite too, albeit much smaller, mulling over Steve Campbell's reasons for being in Cockamamie. Obviously, he'd tried to propose, but why *now?*

"You look a little worried," Lance said good-naturedly.

"You decided to stop shoveling food in your mouth long enough to come up for air?" I asked.

"Maddie's a smart woman. She has to see what a weasel he is. Hell, she left him, didn't she?"

I kept my gaze on my plate. "Yeah. Besides, it's none of my business who she sees or doesn't see." I glanced up at him to make my point. "She told me so in the parking lot before she peeled out of here."

He laughed. "Can you blame her?"

"No." And there was the rub.

I'd been telling myself for nearly a month that I was doing us both a favor, saving us from potential heartbreak. I couldn't give her what she needed, and even though I'd only known Maddie a short time, I knew she deserved nothing less than the best.

All of that was still true, but while I was no good for her, neither was Steve Campbell.

Matilda brought our drinks out, then crossed her arms over her chest and pointed her gaze at me. "So what are you gonna do about that weasel trying to propose to your girl?"

"What?" Lance asked, lowering a forkful of green beans back to his plate. "He proposed to her *here?*"

"Try is the operative word," Matilda said, keeping her dark glare on me.

"I'm gonna need to know what happened," Lance said.

Matilda held my gaze. "I'll tell y'all, but Noah has to ask me himself."

I looked down. "It's none of my business."

"It's not an officer of the law's business when a citizen is accosted in public?" she scoffed.

My gaze jerked back up. "Accosted?"

She puffed out her chest. "He had her by the wrist and wouldn't let her out of the booth. Then he pinned her arm to the table and pulled out a big ass ring. Tried to convince her to get married in January. Wanted it to be some big fancy affair."

"January?" I asked despite myself. "How was he going to pull it off that quickly?"

A grin stretched across Lance's face. "Since when did you become an expert on weddings?"

"My sister, you dumbass," I grunted. "She needed a full year." Then it hit me who was standing next to me, and I cringed. "Sorry, Matilda. I shouldn't insult your son like that in front of you."

She shrugged. "He *is* a dumbass if he thinks you can pull off a fancy wedding in a month."

"If he couldn't afford to give Maddie back her fifteen thousand last month, then how can he afford a big wedding now?" The answer struck me. "He sold his flip house."

"He had a flip house?" Lance asked.

"Yeah, he took Maddie's savings and sunk it in the house. It's part of the reason she's so cash strapped."

His eyes lit up. "You know a lot about her finances for not having a personal relationship with her."

"We spent some time together when I spent the night at her house."

He exaggeratedly waggled his brows.

"Stop. You and I both know I was protecting her from the men who tried to kidnap her."

He didn't say anything, but his smirk remained firmly in place.

Growling, I turned back to Matilda. "Anything else we should know?"

"He seemed pretty desperate to get back with her. It's suspicious as hell." Her eyes narrowed. "I'd watch out for that one."

"Thanks," I mumbled, turning my attention back to my plate.

She headed back to the kitchen, shaking her head and muttering to herself that men were fools.

We ate in silence before Lance finally said, "So what *are* you going to do about it?"

"About what?" I asked, refusing to look up.

"Maddie."

"There's nothing *to* do," I said, spearing some green beans with my fork. "She's a grown woman who can do as she pleases."

"You really want that weasel sniffing around her?"

I started to tell him the truth—hell no—then stopped myself. "She told me it's none of my business, so I have to respect her line in the sand."

"You and I both know how you can make it your business," he said.

I had a string of obscenities ready to unleash on him when my phone vibrated in my pocket. I pulled it out and saw "Deputy Taylor" on the screen. He was my contact in the sheriff's department, and I'd called him the day before about Amy Davis. Did he have new information?

"Detective Langley," I said when I answered.

Lance gave me a worried look.

"Hey, Noah," Taylor said. "This is Deputy Brent Taylor. I'm calling about that missing woman you're looking for."

"Yeah? Did you find her?"

He hesitated. "How soon can you get out to Wallace Road and County Road 21?"

I reached for my wallet with my free hand, ready to toss some cash on the table for my meal. "We'll be there in fifteen minutes."

Chapter Nineteen

Noah

You know we're supposed to be working *our* case," Lance said in the passenger seat of my car as I pulled out of the parking lot.

"And we will. We're just taking a short break."

"By checking out a potential crime scene in the Wayfare County Sheriff's jurisdiction?"

My jaw set. "I told Maddie I'd find her, and I plan to see this through."

He lifted his hands in surrender. "Okay, I agree that you need to tell Maddie what they found, but you didn't necessarily need to go to the crime scene yourself."

I shot him a disapproving stare. "First of all, this is a professional courtesy to Brent. He asked me to come, and second, you were gung-ho about looking for her after Maddie talked to you in the diner."

Lance grimaced, looking slightly embarrassed. "And I *do* want to find her. But the chief's riding our asses about the break-ins, and if we solve this in a timely manner, he said he'd look into bumping me up to detective."

I didn't hide my surprise. "Wow. That's great news, Lance! You definitely deserve it. Why didn't you tell me sooner?"

"I didn't want to put any pressure on you to get this case solved. But I'm worried he'll get pissed if he hears about us working with the sheriff's office on an unrelated case."

"I'll take full responsibility for getting sidetracked," I said firmly. "Besides, Cockamamie PD doesn't exactly have a great reputation with the Wayfare Sheriff's Department, and I'm trying to change that. It took me months to convince Brent I wasn't like the other assholes before me." I cast a glance at him. "And I'll be sure to put in a good word for you with the chief. I'd love to officially make you my partner."

He grinned. "You just need me around to ride your ass."

"Maybe," I said with a half shrug. Truth was, I considered him one of my only friends here in Cockamamie, and I liked working with him. He had the makings of a great detective, and I'd do everything in my power to help him officially become a detective.

"So Deputy Taylor didn't say anything about *why* he wants us to come to his crime scene?"

"He didn't even confirm that it *was* a crime scene. He just asked if I was still looking for Amy Davis, then told me to come to Wallace Road and County Road 21. But he must have found something significant. Otherwise, he would have just told me over the phone."

Whatever it turned out to be would likely be bad. How would Maddie handle it if Amy was dead?

"Well, you owe me a dinner," Lance grumbled. "I barely touched mine before you dragged me out of there."

"You wolfed down half your dinner within thirty seconds of the plate hitting the table," I countered. "But if you're a good boy at the crime scene, I'll take you out for ice cream later."

Lance released a hearty laugh. "I know you're just being an asshole, but I'm gonna hold you to it."

We both stopped talking as we approached the intersection. Multiple sheriff's cars were parked on both sides of the road. I'd expected a house or structure of some kind, but the area was heavily wooded. The blue and red lights from the four sheriff's patrol cars on the scene bounced off the trees, creating an eerie glow in the overcast sky. A light layer of snow covered the ground, and a group of deputies stood at the side of the road next to a grouping of trees covered in yellow crime scene tape.

I parked behind the deputies' cars, and Lance and I got out without saying a word. Since it looked like whatever Brent wanted me to see was in the woods, I popped open my trunk to get out my work boots. Resting my butt on the edge of the open trunk, I tugged off my dress shoes, then pulled on a pair of rubber boots. Lance did the same. He'd tossed his boots into my car after learning where we were headed.

Once we'd donned appropriate footwear, we walked over to the group of deputies, and I flashed my badge. "Detective Langley with the Cockamamie Police Department, and this is Officer Forrester. Deputy Taylor gave me a call asking me to come out."

The deputy who seemed to be running the log-in sheet nodded. "We've been expecting you, Detective Langley." He handed me the clipboard and pen. "We're still waiting on the crime scene team to arrive."

After Lance and I signed in, the deputy lifted the yellow tape. "The car's down the embankment and to the side. You can head down that trail on the right, then cut over to the left at the bottom." He pointed to a path covered in footprints between the thick pine trees. It ran parallel to an eight-foot-wide service road or private drive that led down the slightly sloped hill. The road seemed to curve to the left at the bottom.

Car? Had Amy's car run off the road?

I slipped under the tape first, followed by Lance, and then we started down the path.

Dread swamped me as a cold sheen of sweat broke out on the back of my neck. I expected to find Amy Davis's dead body at the bottom of this embankment, but something else was setting off my defenses. I just didn't know what.

The pine trees were so thick that the car hadn't been visible from the road, but as we reached the bottom of the slope, we could see the back of a silver-colored car with its hood wrapped around a tree trunk. The service road was covered in snow, with no visible tire tracks, but a set of footprints ran up and down the middle of it, made after the snow stopped. From the size and tread, it looked like they'd been left by a man's athletic shoes. Probably the person who'd seen something suspicious and gone down the road to investigate.

Deputy Brent Taylor was standing next to the open driver's door with another deputy. He spotted me and gave me a grim look that confirmed the worst. "Noah."

"Hey, Brent," I said as Lance and I moved closer. "This is my partner, Lance Forrester."

The slightly older-looking man behind Brent gave a half wave. He didn't look as happy to see us. "Tripp Donahue."

Brent nodded. "Sorry we're meeting under these circumstances, and thanks for coming out so quickly. I know you said you were looking into this unofficially, but I figured you'd be interested in checking out the scene. Or, at the very least, you might be able to give me some insight."

"Did she drive off the road and hit a tree?" Lance asked as he made a wide path around to look at the front of the car.

"That's what someone wants us to think," Brent said.

My brow shot up.

"We're waiting for forensics to show up," he said, motioning inside the car. "But have a look for yourself."

Making sure I didn't step on any footprints, I inched closer and peered inside. My stomach dropped at the sight of the woman strapped to the seat with her seatbelt. Her head was slumped slightly. Even though her face was pale and covered in cuts and bruises, she looked a lot like the photo of Amy the grocery store manager had given me.

"Her injuries don't look like they came from this accident," Brent said. "There's no fresh blood from her wounds. No visible blood inside the car."

I studied the steering wheel and dashboard, confirming the lack of blood. "I heard her boyfriend beat her up pretty badly on Monday night. Her neighbor saw her with facial injuries before she left the house on Tuesday morning around nine-thirty. Amy told the neighbor she was leaving her boyfriend. The neighbor thought she might be going to Georgia."

"She never made it out of the county," Detective Donahue grunted, stating the obvious.

Lance tilted his head as he studied the front of the car. "The dent in the hood isn't deep enough if she really drove off the road and hit a tree, not to mention she would have turned a corner down here. Seems more likely she'd just hit a tree before the road turns." He looked up at me. "Detective Donahue's right. Someone staged this."

Brent gave a curt nod. "They wanted it to look like she died in a car accident."

"Someone not very bright," Lance muttered, shoving his hands in his pockets.

"Obviously it was before the snowfall last night," Brent said. "No tire tracks in the snow. Our guess is someone drove her car down the road and around the curve, then hit a tree, but they couldn't have been going very fast."

"I'm guessing twenty-five miles an hour," Lance said. "More likely less." He shrugged. "I've worked enough traffic accidents to know."

I stood upright and turned to face both men. "Seeing how today's Thursday, it sounds like it happened sometime between Tuesday morning and last night."

Brent pursed his lips. "So if this really wasn't an accident, which I'm waiting on forensics to confirm, that means someone intercepted her after she left home on Tuesday."

"I don't see an apparent cause of death," I said. "No signs of blood on her clothes, and she's not wearing a coat."

"Take another look," Brent said. "You'll probably need some light to see it."

The light was dim, so I pulled a Maglite out of my pocket and shined it inside the car. I pointed it at her feet and worked my way up her body, taking in her untied athletic shoes. Her heels weren't in the shoes, and the backs were folded down. "Looks like she put her shoes on in a hurry." I glanced back at Brent. "Or maybe someone else put them on to make it look like she was wearing shoes. But if that's the case, they were in a hurry themselves."

"My thought too," he said.

She was wearing jeans that had smears of something dark on the front of her zipper. "Is that blood on her jeans?"

It wasn't much, but it didn't look like it had come from a wound on her abdomen. It was either from wounds on her hands, or if someone else had dressed her, blood on their hands.

"Looks like it to me," Brent said. "Of course, we'll need forensics to confirm."

I nodded, taking in her pale blue sweater lacking any visible blood. Her eyes were closed, but now that I had better light, I could see the imprints of fingers on her neck.

"Strangulation." I stood upright. "Shit."

"Why would someone stage an accident when it's obvious she was strangled?" Lance asked in disbelief.

"If this was staged right after her murder, the murderer may not have noticed the markings," I said. "When the body doesn't have blood flowing through it, it can take longer for bruises to show." I turned to Brent. "How sure are you that it's Amy Davis?"

Brent's mouth pressed into a thin line. "Her purse was in the passenger seat, and we found her wallet. Obviously, we'll wait for an official ID before announcing it to the public. It doesn't look like robbery was a motive. We found $22 in her wallet. I'm hoping you might have a list of possible suspects from your own investigation."

I rubbed the back of my neck. "Obviously my investigation wasn't official. As I mentioned yesterday, she only fell on my radar because she was supposed to meet a self-defense instructor on Tuesday morning at ten and never showed. Amy had appeared scared and anxious at the class and had asked the instructor to give her a private lesson in getting out of chokeholds."

"So the strangulation marks might be from before she disappeared?" Detective Donahue asked.

I shrugged and glanced over at him. "Possibly. I guess that's for the ME to decide, but I do know that Amy wore a turtleneck to the class on Monday."

Brent turned speculative. "You checked into the instructor? Seems kind of odd he was supposed to give her a lesson in breaking out of a chokehold, only for his student to end up murdered the same way. Think he might have motive?"

I gave him a grim smile. "*She* was the one who brought it to Lance's attention. I happened to walk in and hear the story. She was worried when Amy didn't show for her lesson. Trust me, Maddie Baker didn't have anything to do with Amy Davis's disappearance or potential murder. She continued looking into it when I had to stop." Then I added, "One more thing. Maddie got a phone call around two on Tuesday morning. No one said anything, but she could hear breathing, and then the call ended. Once I got a copy of Amy's employment information from Bob's Market, we compared the phone number to the call Maddie received, and the numbers matched."

Brent's partner finally spoke up. "Why would Ms. Davis call her self-defense instructor in the middle of the night? Were they friends?"

"We have no idea why Amy called her," I admitted. "Maddie had never met her before Monday night."

Brent's face pulled into a frown. "Why does the name Maddie Baker sound familiar?"

Detective Donahue released a short laugh. "She was part of that big murder investigation in Cockamamie a month ago. She Ubered a guy to his murder."

Brent's eyes widened. "Oh." Then his gaze turned speculative.

"Why would Maddie Baker contact *you*?" Donahue asked. "Wasn't she a person of interest in your case?"

"We cleared her name as soon as evidence indicated she was innocent. She trusts us," Lance said in brisk tone. "She knew we would take her concerns seriously."

Brent turned to study the dead woman in the car, then sighed. "Well, looks like she had reason to be worried."

Chapter Twenty

Maddie

By the time I pulled into the driveway at home, I'd calmed down some, which was good because Mallory was parking her car at the curb in front of the house.

I got out and headed toward her. She was already grabbing a large suitcase and a duffel bag out of her backseat.

"That's a lot of luggage for a weekend," I said.

She shouldered one of the bags and handed me the other. "You know me. I'm a chronic over-packer. Besides, this is Tennessee. It's cold today, but it could be seventy tomorrow. I had to be prepared."

I took the bag and released a short laugh. "There are these things called weather apps. You can look up the forecast, you know."

"Where's the fun in that?" she asked, then reached into the back and grabbed another bag.

I narrowed my eyes but didn't say anything. Mallory was right; she was a chronic over-packer, but usually not this much, even for a long weekend.

"Something interesting happened today," I said, grabbing

the other bag from her. "You'll never guess who dropped by the coffee shop earlier."

Her blue eyes darkened. "Detective Asshat? Did he come to his senses and try to win you over? Not that I'm condoning giving him a chance. But surely he's realized what an idiot he was for ghosting you."

"Nooo...not him." I still hadn't told her about the way he'd been helping me. Actually, it struck me that she'd never met him in person. Her distaste was purely from what I'd told her. "Think bigger asshat."

She stopped in her tracks. "I'm stumped."

"Steve."

She gave me a blank stare. "Steve? I've never heard you mention a Steve here in Cockamamie."

"Steve Campbell. My ex-boyfriend?" I snorted in disbelief. "You just called me about him a couple days ago."

She gave a short shake of her head. "Wait. *Your* Steve? He came all the way down *here*? What the hell?"

A shudder ran through me. "He's not *my* Steve, but he sure *wants* to be."

Mallory dropped her suitcase on the damp grass. "What does that mean? Tell me *everything*."

I glanced around. "Out here?"

"You and I both know that once we walk inside, we'll be dealing with Aunt Deidre, and I suspect you don't want her knowing about any of this. So spill."

"Let's sit on the porch. This might take a couple minutes."

I headed up the steps and dumped Mallory's luggage by the door before taking a seat on the porch swing.

She dropped her bags, then sat beside me. "I want to hear everything."

"First, I haven't told you that Steve actually *called* me yesterday."

"What did he want?"

"I'm not sure because I didn't give him a chance to tell me. I asked him where my money was, told him to mail it to me, then hung up."

She stared at me for a long second, obviously trying to process it. "So he came to the coffee shop to give you your money?"

"No, he said he wanted to take me out to dinner tonight, but I told him to meet me at a tavern instead. Turns out he not only wants to get back together, but he wants to get *married*. He had a ring and everything."

She stared at me in shock. "He *proposed?*"

"If you want to call *hey, let's get married* a proposal."

Her gaze turned serious. "How big was the ring?"

"Mallory!"

She made a face. "It's a legit question."

I sighed. "It was big, but he's up to something. He's in a huge hurry. Get this. He not only wants to get married in January, but he wants it to be a big wedding."

"What? I think I'm having an aneurysm." She winged her hands out from her head in a "mind blown" gesture. "This is *crazy!*"

"I *know!*"

She stared at me for several seconds before she asked, "What did you say?"

"I told him to take his ring and shove it, of course. I was so embarrassed that I put up with his bullshit for so long. There's no way I'd ever go back to him. But as you can only guess, he didn't take my rejection well."

"I bet," she said with a snort.

"I'm sure that's not the end of it. You remember how persistent he was when we first started dating."

"He was relentless." She sat back and pushed off the floor-boards, making the chair swing. "So what are you going to do?"

"Keep turning him down," I said. "And if he becomes too persistent, I'll file a restraining order."

"Good plan. Any word on that missing woman from your class?"

I told her what I'd learned from Amy's neighbor, Barbara, and the women at the grocery store.

"Do you really think she went to Georgia?" Mallory asked.

I twisted my mouth. "I don't know. I'd like to think she got away and is safe, but if so, why didn't she call me and cancel our meeting?"

"Oh, I don't know," Mallory said sarcastically. "Maybe she was too busy trying to escape the monster who was strangling her?"

She had a point.

"Look," she said, placing a hand on my arm. "I know you want a nice, neat answer, but sometimes we don't get those. Just like we may never know why Steve is suddenly so desperate to get married."

I pushed out a frustrated breath. "I know. Look at my mother's murder."

She whacked her forehead with the palm of her hand. "Jeez, Mads. Sorry. You must think I'm a first-class bitch to have forgotten."

I gave her a tight smile. "It's okay. Really." I wished more than anything that I could forget, but it was always there—a fresh scab waiting to be picked off by the most innocuous things.

"It's not okay, but you're too nice to admit it," she said. "But I have a good feeling about Amy. Be thankful she got away from her abusive asshole of a boyfriend. So many women don't."

"Yeah, you're right." I leaned my cheek onto her shoulder. "You have no idea how much I hate not having you around. I miss our weekly wine nights and shopping and just hanging out."

"Well..." She pulled free and looked me in the eye. "How would you like me being closer?"

I stared at her in confusion. "I know you hate your job. Are you thinking about moving to Chattanooga?"

She made a face. "Closer."

I studied her, and then it hit me. "You lost your job."

"More like quit, but yeah. I'm no longer gainfully employed."

"Which is why you brought all the luggage. You're staying here for a while?"

"If you're open to it," she said in a rush. "But I know you have extra rooms, and I'll pull my weight. I promise."

I threw my arms around her and squeezed tight. "Of course, Mallory! You're welcome to stay as long as you want."

"Thanks, Mads, because I couldn't take another minute with that tyrant boss."

I released her and sat back. "Do you have any idea what you want to do?"

"I called a headhunter on the way down. I want to look for a position that'll let me work remotely." She clasped my hand. "I want to stay here with you and help with Aunt Deidre."

My mouth dropped open. "Oh, Mallory... I can't let you do that."

"I want to. I miss you, Mads." She squeezed my hand. "Terribly. And Aunt Deidre's like family to me too."

I squeezed back. "I've missed you too. But she's worse than the last time you saw her. I may have to put her in a facility sooner than expected."

"I'm sorry," she said softly. "But I'm here now. I'll help you through it."

"Screw men," I said with a laugh. "We'll just live together like a couple of old spinsters."

She laughed. "If we give up men entirely, people will think we're a lesbian couple."

"There are worse things," I said with a sigh. "Too bad I don't swing that way."

"Yeah, same. I love you, Mads, but not enough to give up men."

"Fair." My inability to stop thinking about Noah was proof I wasn't ready to give them up either. I got to my feet. "Let's get inside. We have to get ready for our dinner party."

She gave me a cheesy smile. "You're hosting a dinner party for me?"

"Long story," I said with a laugh, "but if you like, we'll say it's for you."

"The groceries are still in the back of my car," she said. "Let's get my luggage inside. I'll get the groceries, and we can get started."

I got to my feet. "Oh, I almost forgot. There are a couple of nicely chilled bottles of wine in the back of my car. We can kill a bottle while we make dinner, then we'll be ready to entertain."

A mischievous glint filled Mallory's eyes. "You know me too well."

Chapter Twenty-One

Maddie

To Maddie and her amazing lasagna!" Petra called out, holding up her glass of wine. The other four people at the dining room table held up their glasses too.

"You haven't even tasted it yet," I protested.

"I don't need to," Petra said. "It smells divine."

"Whatever," Chrissy muttered, then gulped down a generous portion of her wine. "Let's eat already."

She hadn't been thrilled when I'd broken the news that Steve wasn't coming, but she hadn't been pissed enough to leave. "No sense wasting a good lasagna," she'd said.

I sat at the head of the table. Chrissy and Petra were on one side of the table, while Margarete and Mallory sat on the other. Inviting Margarete had been a must. Aunt Deidre was at the other end, opposite me.

The day had gotten off to a rocky start for my aunt, but things had turned around after her afternoon nap. She'd recognized Mallory earlier and had seemed excited not only at the prospect of my friend staying indefinitely but also the dinner party.

She'd hung out in the kitchen with me and Mallory while

we made dinner and helped put the salad together. Then she'd greeted Chrissy and Petra with obvious delight, and she and Chrissy had really hit it off.

I cut a hunk out of the lasagna in the middle of the table and started serving it to everyone while they passed around the salad and garlic bread.

We'd just started to eat when the doorbell rang.

I started to get up, but Margarete waved her hand. "Sit down and enjoy your friends. I'll get it."

I had no idea who it could be, yet I wasn't surprised when I heard Margarete call out, "You can't just barge in here!"

I turned to face the living room as Steve rounded the corner from the entryway.

"It looks like you started without me."

Mallory started choking on a sip of her wine, but Chrissy's eyes lit up with glee. She got up from her seat, saying, "Steve, let me get you a place setting. Pull over that chair in the corner, and sit between me and Petra." She moved her chair closer to me, then bolted to the kitchen.

"What are you doing here?" I demanded.

He started to slip off his coat. "I'm here for dinner," he said as though my question was the stupidest thing he'd ever heard. "It smells delicious."

"It tastes even better," Petra said, then shoveled another bite into her mouth.

Margarete appeared behind him and mouthed, *He just pushed his way in.*

"It's okay," I said. It wasn't okay that he was here, and I was still on the fence about kicking him out, but Chrissy looked so excited, I decided to let her have her fun.

She'd owe me.

He tossed his coat onto the sofa, grabbed the extra chair in the corner, and carried it over to the table.

"Here we go," Chrissy said cheerfully as she walked out of the kitchen, carrying a plate, silverware, and a wine glass. Steve sat down, and Chrissy arranged everything in front of him. "Wine, Steve?"

Mallory's mouth parted in shock. She'd just met Chrissy, but she'd heard enough from me to know how out of character this was for her. Besides, there was nothing sweet about her appearance, from her usual perpetual scowl (which seemed to evaporate the moment Steve walked in) to her multiple piercings and short dark hair that gave her a goth look.

Steve's mouth puckered as he studied the label on the wine bottle. "I keep telling you to stop buying the cheap stuff, Mads," he said in a disapproving tone.

I gave him some side eye. "That's all I could afford, *Steve*."

"It's delicious," Petra said, holding up her wine glass. "No matter how much it cost."

Steve leaned toward me. "She has to say that, Mads. You should really be serving your guests something better. That's why you need me. To help you with these things."

Aunt Deidre's mouth pinched as she glared at him.

Mallory fisted her hands on the table. "We all know you're a wine snob, Steve, and if Maddie is so notorious for choosing cheap wine, why didn't you bring something you found to be more acceptable instead of trying to embarrass her? It's customary to bring a hostess gift, you know."

He lifted his hands in surrender. "You're right. You're right. But I was in such a hurry to see Maddie that I figured I'd gift her and the rest of you lovely ladies with my presence." A huge smile broke out across his face.

"So Steve," Chrissy said, picking up the spatula and scooping a piece of lasagna onto his plate. "Tell us about yourself."

His face brightened. Talking about himself was his favorite

topic. "Well, I was born and raised in Nashville. My father manages a few country music stars." He winked at her. "I'd name a few of them, but I signed a confidentiality agreement."

"He manages groups you've never heard of, with the exception of Colt and Maggie," I said dryly. "But he only managed them for a few months before they wised up and fired him."

"Now, Maddie," Steve said, like I was a disobedient yet amusing toddler. "No need to be so dramatic."

"No," I said, "you seem to have that covered."

Mallory choked out a laugh, and Aunt Deidre grinned. Poor Margarete looked guilty for having let Steve in, and Petra was too busy scarfing down lasagna to pay attention to the conversation.

Chrissy rested her chin on her fist, watching him with rapt attention. "Tell me more. What is it that makes you so special, Steve?"

He looked taken aback. "I...uh..."

"It's obvious you're special, but *why*? Break it down for me, Steve."

Steve started to squirm, then picked up his fork and dug into his slice of lasagna. "Enough about me. Let me hear about you lovely ladies." He looked over the table at Margarete. "How are you doing, Deidre? Maddie tells me you've had some health problems."

Margarete's mouth dropped open.

"That's not Aunt Deidre," I said in disgust.

His brows lifted, then he turned to my aunt at the end of the table. "My apologies. You look different than the last time I saw you."

"She looks exactly the same," I said.

He looked down at his plate and took another bite of lasagna. "Your lasagna is as perfect as ever," he said.

"What's your favorite food, Steve?" Chrissy asked.

His grin returned. "That's an easy one. Maddie's lasagna."

Petra put her fork on her plate and scooped out another piece. "It's my new favorite too."

"What do you do with your free time?" Chrissy asked.

He looked uncomfortable. "I'm a bit of a workaholic. I don't have much free time."

"Everybody loves a hard worker," she said. "What are you so busy doing?"

"This and that," he said, then lifted his gaze to me. "I got a new job, Mads."

"Is it flipping houses?" Mallory asked, "because I don't think that's your strong suit." She gave him a pointed look. "Speaking of flipped houses, where's Maddie's money?"

He set down his fork. "Funny you should mention that..." He started to reach into his jeans pocket.

"Don't you dare pull out that engagement ring and try to propose again," I snarled.

"That's the thing, Mads. I really *do* want to marry you, and once we're married, your money will be my money, so there'll be no need for me to give you a check."

"Cash works," Chrissy said, looking innocent.

He laughed and tapped her nose. "You're so cute."

I was hoping to see Chrissy bite off one of his fingers, but it didn't happen. Instead, she just batted her eyelashes and smiled at him like it was a compliment.

What was she up to?

"But seriously, Steve," she said. "What's your new job?"

His eyes lit up. "Client support for a PR firm in Nashville."

"And what exactly does that mean?" she pressed.

"I was just getting ready to ask the same thing," Mallory said.

I was curious myself, but I didn't want to encourage him.

"Well," he said, reaching for his wine glass. He gave it a sniff and wrinkled his nose, but took a sip anyway. "I work with high-end clients for my firm."

"But what exactly does that *mean?*" Chrissy asked.

"I might pick them up from the airport or take them to a record studio."

"Oh," Chrissy said, getting excited as she took a sip of her wine. "So you're just like an Uber."

"What?" he asked in horror. "I'm *nothing* like an Uber."

"Is there something wrong with Uber?" Chrissy asked. "Because Maddie drives for Uber, so it kind of sounds like you're insinuating there's something wrong with Maddie."

His eyes widened. "You drive an Uber?"

"Not right now," I said. "Someone hit my car today, so I can't pick up Uber customers until I get it fixed, which is why I really need that fifteen thousand dollars."

"Plus interest," Mallory added.

"I want to know more about this job," Chrissy said, her voice as sweet as honey. "What else do you do?"

"Well, you know, the usual PR stuff."

"No," she said, her voice still soft but insistent. "I don't know. That's why I'm asking."

"Why aren't you at the bank anymore?" I asked, deciding to get to the heart of it.

"Because I decided to move on to bigger and better things," he said, stabbing a forkful of salad.

"By driving people around like a chauffeur?" Chrissy asked innocently. She batted her eyelids for effect.

Damn, she was good.

If I didn't know her, I'd never guess she was setting him up for some kind of kill. Presuming that was what she was doing. I supposed I should have stopped her, but Steve had always been the master of manipulation. It was nice to see the tables turned.

"No, not like a chauffeur," he grunted, showing the first signs of irritation.

"But you said you drive people around," she protested, sounding confused.

"That's only one part of my job."

"So what are the others?"

"Arranging for clients to meet with media to promote new releases."

"So you work with authors?" she asked.

Her questions were coming rapid fire, and he looked flustered.

"No, I live in Nashville," he ground out. "I work with music artists."

"You mean, like country singers?"

He flashed a smile. "Well, that's what Nashville is known for."

"What's the name of your firm?"

"Serendipity PR," he said, looking confident again.

Chrissy rested her chin on her hand again, staring at him like he was a Greek god. "Don't they represent Hallmark movie stars and Kids Bop singers?"

"What do you know about Serendipity?" he asked harshly. "You're a barista at a coffee shop in a Podunk town."

"It's Cockamamie," Aunt Deidre said.

He turned to her in surprise. "What?"

"The town's name is Cockamamie. Not Podunk."

He started to say something, then must have thought better of it. Instead, he drew in a deep breath and let it out. "I'm sorry. I must be tired. I apologize for my sudden outburst of rudeness."

"Sudden?" Mallory challenged.

Steve gave her a weak smile but bit his tongue.

"Let's all enjoy our meal," Aunt Deidre said, sounding tired. "I'm really looking forward to the cheesecake Mallory made."

Mallory had bought it, something Aunt Deidre knew. For a moment, I thought her dementia was rearing its head, but then she gave Mallory a wink. She'd seen her put the cake on a serving plate and had presumed she wanted to pass it off as her own.

"Yes," I said. "That sounds like a great idea."

But it wasn't, because a silence that soon became uncomfortable had descended on the table. The only two people who seemed immune were Petra, who was working on her third helping of lasagna, and Chrissy, who just smiled like that creepy guy from *The Shining* as she finished off the food on her plate.

When it was clean, she said, "Boy, I'm ready for that cheesecake.'

"Want to help me get it ready in the kitchen?" Mallory asked.

"There's nothing I love more than helping my hostess," she said sweetly.

Honestly, she was starting to freak me out.

"I'll start a pot of coffee," Mallory said as the two of them headed into the kitchen.

Steve lifted his gaze to watch them, and I realized he was watching Chrissy's jeans-clad butt as she walked away.

Seriously?

I picked up my wine glass and finished it off. "So Steve, I'm curious about why you really left the bank. You claimed to be on the fast track to superstardom, so I can't see you voluntarily leaving that."

He glanced over at Aunt Deidre and Margarete. "I think that's something we should discuss in private."

Margarete pushed back her chair. "Deidre and I were just getting ready to clear the table in preparation for dessert, isn't that right, Deidre?"

"Yes," she said, getting up too and grabbing her plate. "Nothing like a fresh table to enjoy your dessert."

Margarete grabbed several plates, and she and Deidre disappeared into the kitchen too.

Steve cast a glance at Petra, but she was focused on savoring her newest slice of lasagna.

"So?" I asked. "Why did you leave?"

He kept looking at Petra.

"She's not paying attention to anything we're saying, so go on."

He shrugged, and his weak grin was back. "I just didn't see a future there."

"Why did they fire you?"

His head jutted back as he released a gasp of outrage. "I wasn't fired."

"Then why did you really leave?"

His face turned red. "Like I said—"

I pulled out my phone, opened up my contacts, and after a short search, I pressed a name and put the call on speaker.

Steve went still, and his eyes widened. "What are you doing?"

"Fact checking," I said, mimicking Chrissy's sweet demeanor. The phone rang several times before a woman answered. "Hello?"

"Hey, Nancy, it's Maddie Baker."

"Maddie! Oh, my gosh! I've been thinking about you! I never got a chance to tell you goodbye. Steve said you left him and went to live with your new boyfriend in Timbuktu."

Steve looked like he wanted to grab the phone out of my hand. Nancy was one of his old coworkers. We'd met at a holiday party and had hit it off so much we'd exchanged numbers and gone out to lunch a few times. I hadn't talked to her since a few months before I'd left Nashville.

"More like my elderly aunt in Cockamamie, but I can see how he'd get confused."

Nancy chuckled. "I've missed you, girl."

"Yeah, sorry I left town without giving you warning. It all happened fast, and once I made the decision, I had a lot of loose ends to tie up. I missed you in the mess."

"Don't you worry," she said. "I forgive you. Leaving Steve was the smartest thing you ever did." She laughed. "You know, a few things came to light after you left."

"That's enough," Steve forced out, looking livid. He started to get up and reached for my phone, but Chrissy was suddenly standing next to me on the opposite side of the table from Steve with a butcher knife in her hand. "Sit your ass down, Steve, and keep your mouth shut."

His eyes widened at the sight of the knife, and the blood fled from his face as he lowered his butt to his seat.

Mallory appeared next to her and pushed the lasagna dish closer to Petra before setting the cheesecake on the table in front of Chrissy, making it a grand gesture. I presumed it was to show that Chrissy had a legitimate reason to be flashing a knife.

I'd testify to it in a court of law if it came to it.

"Is Steve *there*?" Nancy asked.

"Yes," I said. "He's sitting in front of me, telling me that he left the bank for bigger and better things, all while trying to convince me to marry him. His story smells like shit from a mile away, so I figured I'd go to someone who could break it down. What do you know?"

She laughed. "How much time do you have?"

Chrissy resumed her seat next to Steve, still holding the knife. "Plenty," she said.

Mallory sat down too.

"Well, soon after you left," Nancy said, sounding like she

was enjoying every minute of this, "Steve started acting strangely. Like he couldn't believe you'd actually left him."

Steve clenched his jaw. "I missed you, Maddie. I've told you that," he ground out.

"But about a month ago," Nancy said, "he began taking lengthy lunch breaks. He was coming in late and leaving early. And when he was in his office, his mind wasn't on his job."

"I was upset over losing Maddie," he said, looking furious. "Besides, you were always jealous of me, Nancy."

"Yeah, right," she said with a dismissive laugh. "*In any case,* our boss decided to call Steve out on his performance. Only when he went to Steve's office to talk to him, he caught him in a performance of his own." She paused. "Despite the fact we have a very strict policy regarding no sexual fraternization with the clients, Steve was screwing a client on his desk."

"The boss's desk?" Chrissy asked hopefully.

"No, Steve's desk," Nancy said.

Disappointment washed over Chrissy's face.

Nancy laughed. "But as mad as our boss got, it might as well have been. Turned out, it was our boss's client. Steve was trying to poach her."

"In more ways than one," Mallory said dryly.

"Our boss lost his shit," Nancy continued. "He fired him on the spot. We all thought our boss was going to have a stroke. They could hear him shouting two floors down."

Chrissy turned to Steve and began twirling the knife in her hand. "How long had this been going on? Did you cheat on Maddie?"

Steve jumped out of his chair, grabbed his coat, and ran out the front door.

Chrissy and Mallory began to laugh.

"What happened?" Nancy asked.

"Steve just left," I said, still in shock.

"And I'm pretty sure he left a crap stain on the seat," Chrissy said, turning back to the table and slicing into the cheesecake.

"I have a stain remover for things like that," Margarete said nonchalantly as she entered the dining room and took a seat next to Mallory.

I was still stuck on the fact that Steve would risk his job like that. His job had always been so important to him.

"For what it's worth," Nancy said, "I'd bet money that he didn't start anything with the client until about a month after you left. I don't think he cheated on you."

"It doesn't matter," I said. "I left him. I don't care if he cheated on me or not."

Mallory pinned me with a gaze that said *liar*.

"So he's working at Serendipity PR now," I said, pulling myself together. "He said he works on client accounts."

"So we heard," Nancy said. "We were all kinds of surprised for a couple of reasons. For one, we thought he'd be working on the numbers side of things, but Tony heard he's their PR liaison."

"What's that?" I asked.

"You know, the person who runs errands, drives people back and forth."

"I *knew* he was a chauffeur," Chrissy said.

"You said you were surprised for a couple reasons," I said. "What was the other?"

"Serendipity has a morality clause. They insist on impeccable reputations and morals in their employees. After the way Steve left the bank, we couldn't believe he met their criteria."

"Well, he showed up in Cockamamie today," I said, "super eager to get married next month. I haven't talked to him since I told him I was leaving, so this is totally out of the blue. Plus, the way he's going about it…he's up to something. I just can't figure out what."

"If I hear anything on my end, I'll be sure to let you know," she said, then hesitated before adding, "Maddie, if I'd suspected Steve was doing anything unscrupulous when you were with him, I would have told you."

"Thanks, Nancy. I appreciate that."

"I hope you're happy, Maddie. You deserve someone better than Steve."

"Thanks," I said, glancing around the table. Mallory and Margarete were offering me expressions of support. Chrissy looked happier than I'd ever seen her, and while Petra was still focused on finishing her last slice of lasagna, she gave me a thumbs up. "I'm actually pretty lucky to have landed where I am. I'm much happier here than I was with Steve."

"Good. You take care, Maddie, and the next time you're in Nashville, let's grab drinks."

"I'd like that."

I hung up, and we all exchanged looks, still processing what we'd just discovered.

Aunt Deidre sat down in her chair and glanced around at everyone. "What did I miss?"

Chrissy shook her head, grinning from ear to ear. "Where do we start?"

Chapter Twenty-Two

Maddie

Everyone stayed for another hour, rehashing the dinner and the phone call while we ate dessert. Then we speculated on why Steve suddenly seemed so eager to marry me, but we couldn't come up with anything solid.

"It has something to do with his job," I said. "I just don't know what."

Petra, who hadn't seemed to be listening to a word over dinner, said, "Men like Steve don't always need a reason for what they do. They just get a wild hair up their butts, and once they're determined to do something, they become relentless. My ex was just like that."

I stared at her in shock.

"What? Sometimes you hear the best stuff when no one thinks you're listening."

Good to know for future reference.

Everyone helped clear the table, but I shooed them away when they offered to do dishes. "Go on home. I've got this."

After everyone left, Mallory announced that she was going to take Aunt Deidre upstairs and help her get ready for bed. I protested that she didn't have to, but she said, "I told you I'm here to help. Besides, I've already promised to read a chapter of *Wuthering Heights* to Aunt Deidre after she's in bed."

"Thanks, Mallory," I said, tears burning my eyes. "Sometimes this all feels so overwhelming."

"Girl, you've got this. I'm just here to help." She gave me a quick hug, then linked arms with my aunt. "I haven't read *Wuthering Heights* since college. I can't wait to dig in."

I headed into the kitchen to start cleaning up, and a few minutes later, I heard the water turn on upstairs for Deidre's shower. I had just started loading everything into the dishwasher when I heard a knock at the front door.

It was after nine o'clock. Who on earth could be dropping by so late?

Then it hit me.

Crap. It had to be Steve.

He'd waited to come back until everyone else had left so I wouldn't have backup. I considered not answering, but then he'd start incessantly ringing the doorbell and disturb Aunt Deidre. I'd just answer the door and tell him off. If he didn't leave peacefully, I'd call the police and have him arrested for trespassing.

I dried my hands with a kitchen towel as I made my way to the front door, squaring my shoulders, but when I opened the door, Noah stood on the porch.

"Oh. Noah."

He was wearing his dress coat, but his cheeks and nose were red like he'd been outside for a while, and his hair looked windblown. He was holding my scarf in both hands in front of his chest.

Crap. I hadn't even realized I was missing it.

He lifted it slightly. "You left this at Lucky's this afternoon. I found it under the table."

"Oh." I must have left it behind when I'd stormed out.

That damn Steve.

"Thank you for bringing it by," I said as I reached for it.

"Yeah, no problem," he said, shifting his weight. "I know it's late, but that's not the only reason I came by. Can I come in?" he asked with a worried look in his eyes. "I would have waited to come tomorrow, but this seemed pressing."

I steeled my back, remembering that I was pissed at him. I should turn him away, but he *had* brought my scarf back to me.

His face softened. "Maddie, I know I'm not your favorite person right now, but this is important. Please. I don't want to do this on your porch."

Something was off, although I didn't know what, so I found myself backing up and letting him walk past me.

"Is your aunt still up?" he asked, heading into the living room.

"No, she's upstairs in bed. My friend Mallory is in town and is reading to her. What's up?"

He gestured to the sofa. "Let's have a seat."

"You're scaring me, Noah." I hadn't realized it until the words came out of my mouth. I didn't understand *why* he was scaring me, only that something about him was off. "Are you okay?"

He gave me a soft smile as we sat down. He took my hand in his. "I'm fine." He grimaced. "Actually, in the spirit of honesty, I'm not fine. I'm still the messed-up guy you met last month, but I'm not here about me." He squeezed my hand. "I'm here about Amy."

"Amy?" Would he have come by this late if he'd verified she was safe? No, he would have called or sent a text. I felt lightheaded, but I said insistently, "No. She's in Georgia."

Tenderness filled his eyes. "No, Maddie. You were right to keep pursuing it. She didn't make it to Georgia. Amy is dead."

I slowly shook my head as tears filled my eyes. "No."

He pulled me into a tight hug. "I'm so sorry, Maddie. I wished there'd been a better outcome."

"No," I said more forcefully, pulling away from him. "How could this happen?"

"We don't have an official cause of death yet, but..." He stopped, worry pinching his mouth.

"But what?"

"It looks like she was strangled."

A sob broke loose, but I covered my mouth with my hand and darted a glance at the staircase in the entryway. Thankfully, the water was still running upstairs. I didn't want Mallory or Aunt Deidre to hear me. I needed to deal with this alone.

"Come on," he said, helping me to my feet. "Let's go into the kitchen, and I'll make you a cup of tea."

I let him lead me by the hand. Gently, he helped me sit in a chair at the kitchen table. He'd been in my kitchen several times now, and he knew it would offer more privacy than the living room. I was grateful for that.

I hated that I wanted him here right now, but I couldn't bring myself to turn him away. After all, we'd started this together—it only felt fitting for us to be together at the end of it.

He walked over to the kettle and started to fill it with water.

"You know how to make tea?" I asked with a laugh through my tears.

"I've learned."

"How long has she been..." I swallowed, then started again. "How long has she been dead?"

"We're not sure," he said, turning off the water and turning on the kettle. "The autopsy is scheduled for tomorrow, but we know that she most likely died before the snow fell."

"How do you know that?"

He gave me a grim look. "I can't tell you yet. Technically, I shouldn't be telling you anything, but Deputy Taylor plans to contact you in the morning to get your statement. He agreed to let me break the news tonight." He paused. "I wanted you to hear it from me."

Fresh tears stung my eyes, quickly followed by guilt. I should have tried harder to get her to talk to me on Monday night. I should have convinced her not to go home. I should have brought her home with me. Anything to keep her safe.

I'd had the chance to save her, and instead, I'd let her walk out the door to her death.

Noah walked over and pulled out the chair from the other side of the table. He placed it next to mine and sat down. "I'm sorry, Maddie. If I'd..." His face fell.

"You did everything you could," I said through my tears. "You went above and beyond what you were supposed to do."

"I took this seriously, Maddie. It's important to me that you know that."

"I know you did. Thank you for being the type of cop who would." During my mother's murder investigation, I'd learned there were two types of cops in Cockamamie—the ones who genuinely wanted to help people, and the ones who got a power trip along with their badge. Noah was rare in this town, and I knew it. Cockamamie needed him.

He held my gaze, and I found myself getting lost in his deep blue eyes. It was funny how he could be cold to me, yet he was always there when I really needed him.

"This isn't your fault, Maddie."

My gaze dropped to my lap.

He placed his finger beneath my chin and lifted my face so our eyes met again. "This isn't your fault."

More tears fell. "I should have stopped her, Noah. I should have—"

He slowly shook his head. "No. You did everything you

could have too. You couldn't force her to do whatever it is you think she should have."

"She's dead," I said, releasing a sob. "She was alive in my class, and now she's dead."

He wiped tears from my cheek with his thumb. "I know. I'm sorry."

I was the last person to have seen Martin Schroeder alive, but he'd been a sleazeball, so while his death had bothered me, it hadn't *devastated* me. Not like this.

Other than her murderer, I was the last person to have seen my mother alive too. How many people could say they'd had that experience with three people?

I was the harbinger of death.

"What's going on in your head, Maddie?"

I gave him a weak smile. "I'm bad luck."

He frowned in confusion. "What?"

"Never mind. It's nothing." I drew in a deep breath. "I'm glad you were the one to tell me about Amy. I'm not sure how I would have handled hearing this from a stranger." I swiped at my tears. "I know we've been hot and cold lately, but you really were here for me tonight, and I want you to know how much I appreciate it. Thank you."

Shaking his head, he said softly, "Don't thank me. I owed you this."

We locked gazes again, the tension between us palpable. His hand was cradling my face, and I leaned into his touch, resisting the urge to close the distance between us and kiss him. He may have helped me again, and I knew we both felt the crazy chemistry between us, but he still didn't want anything to happen. I needed to respect his wishes.

Friends. We could only be friends.

But Noah looked like he wasn't so sure he was committed to

his plan anymore. His finger stroked the line of my jaw as he stared at my lips, leaning closer.

Noah was going to kiss me. Was I going to let him?

I didn't have to make that decision because the kettle began to whistle. He jolted backward as though he'd been caught shoplifting and jumped out of his seat.

Saved by the whistle.

"Umm..." he said with his back to me as he flipped the kettle off. "Are the teabags and mugs in the same place?"

"Yeah."

He opened the correct cabinet like he belonged here, pulling out two mugs and teabags. He poured hot water into the mugs, put spoons in each cup, then carried them over to the table and sat down, scooting the chair a few inches away from me.

I knew it was better this way, but I was still disappointed.

The best way to handle this was to ignore what had almost happened. Honestly, I would have preferred to confront him, but I wasn't sure I could handle more hard truths tonight.

"Steve had an affair with a client," I said as I grabbed the bottle of honey from the other end of the table.

Why had I confessed that?

"Is that why you broke up with him?" he asked, his voice tight.

"Um...no." I squeezed honey into my mug, then set the bottle on the table. "I found out tonight when he crashed my dinner party. In fact, I'm pretty sure it started after I left. He was spouting a lot of nonsense about his new job, but he refused to tell me why he'd left his old one. I called one of his old coworkers, and she told me that he had been fired for trying to poach their boss's client by sleeping with her."

"The man's a fucking idiot."

I couldn't stop my grin. "True." I slowly stirred my tea.

"You're not really engaged to him, are you?" he asked cautiously.

"God, no," I scoffed. "The man's delusional. I have no idea why he suddenly wants to get married, and quickly at that, but I want no part of it."

His eyes darkened. "Is he harassing you?"

My heart skipped a beat at his protectiveness, but I reminded myself that while he was great at being a protector, the moment the danger was gone, so was he.

Still, right now, I couldn't bring myself to be annoyed at him.

What did that say about me?

"So have they arrested Boomer yet?" I asked, setting my spoon on the table and picking up my mug.

"I think they were bringing him in for questioning and looking for evidence. While a lot of people saw Amy with bruises, based on what I've heard, Amy never admitted he was the one who'd hit her. What about you? Did the neighbor tell you she'd admitted it to her?"

"No," I said with a sigh, then realized where this was heading. "He's not going to get away with it, is he?"

"No. Deputy Taylor will find who is responsible."

I stared at him in shock. "Does that mean you don't think Boomer did it?"

"It means the sheriff's department plans to look at all the facts, collect evidence, and make a decision based on the information they gather. It's never good to presume someone's guilty, Maddie."

"But it's so obvious," I protested in irritation.

"Even so," he said slowly, picking up his mug and blowing across the surface. "Deputy Taylor seems like a thorough investigator, so he'll gather enough evidence to make it an airtight case. No matter how bad it looks, unless there's enough evidence to persuade a jury to convict him, it doesn't mean shit."

"Yeah," I said. "That makes sense." I picked up my mug and blew on it too. My mind was going back to the night I'd met Amy, running through our conversation. I couldn't stop trying to figure out what I could have done differently.

"You can't change the past," he said gently. "It's a pointless exercise."

"I just feel so guilty," I said, my voice breaking.

"I know, and I wish I could convince you that you have nothing to feel guilty about. Most abused women don't go around broadcasting that they're being abused. Amy may have asked you for help, but I sincerely doubt she would have confided in you after class, no matter what you said. Yeah, I think she was headed in the right direction, but it would have taken time." He reached across the table and covered my hand with his. "There's absolutely nothing you could have done differently, short of following her home and marching into her house, vowing to protect her." A wry smile twisted his lips. "And if you'd tried that, you might be sitting in the county jail for stalking, trespassing, and intimidation."

"But Amy might still be alive," I pointed out, then shook my head. "Don't worry. I'd never do something like that."

"No, but you pursued a van as it was leaving the scene of a hit and run *and* a break-in," he said dryly.

"That was different," I muttered, then took a sip of my tea.

His expression became more pointed. "Maybe, maybe not. But I need you to promise to let the sheriff's department handle this case from here on out."

"Why wouldn't I let them handle it?"

"I can think of a number of reasons, the biggest being that you don't think they're going to arrest Boomer, so you might try looking for evidence yourself."

I started to protest, then stopped. I could see why he might think that. I'd done some digging on my own with Amy after Noah had stopped, but this was an official investigation now, and if I tried to pry into things, I might screw it up. That was the last thing I wanted.

"I promise," I said sincerely. "I'm going to leave it to the sheriff's department."

Relief flooded his face. "Thank you."

"Trust me. I want this guy arrested and convicted just as much as you do. I wouldn't do anything to jeopardize that."

We sat in silence for several seconds, Noah staring into his tea with the look of a haunted man.

"You were there," I said as the realization hit me. "You saw her body."

His gaze lifted, and he cleared his throat. "Uh...yeah." He ran his free hand over his head and set his mug down.

"How are you sleeping at night?" I asked.

Surprise filled his eyes.

"You told me you don't sleep well. Has that gotten better?"

He grimaced, looking embarrassed. "No."

"Do the victims you see haunt you?"

He released a wry snort and sat back in his chair. "Some more than others." Drawing in a breath, he sat up taller, then leaned over the table, resting his weight on his forearms. "Some of the victims were killed in the middle of doing something questionable. It doesn't justify their deaths, but people like to find blame. Me included sometimes, if I'm being honest. But it's the people who were at the wrong place at the wrong time that haunt me. Or victims of long-term abuse, like Amy. I suspect she lived a hard life and did the best she could with the hand she was dealt." He tapped his finger on the table. "But she could never catch a break, and there are plenty of others out there just like her. Kids who got the raw end of the deal." He swallowed again, his Adam's apple bobbing. "Those are the ones who stay with me."

"I'm sorry," I said softly. "It has to be hard to see people at the most tragic moments of their lives. Or the fallout."

"Especially when I tried my damnedest to help them," he said in a broken voice.

I knew he wasn't talking in general terms. I suspected he was talking about the case in Memphis that had brought him to Cockamamie—the one that had nearly gotten him killed with a bullet wound to the chest.

"You can't change the past, Noah," I said softly, throwing his words back at him. "A wise man told me it's a pointless exercise."

He turned his head toward me and smiled, but then his expression turned serious, and his eyes darkened. "You have a way of making the heaviness lighter."

"Good," I said. "Because you do the same for me."

He held my gaze and seemed to be considering something before he said, "I like you, Maddie. A lot. You know I've been staying away from you because I'm messed up. I think it's time I explained why."

Chapter Twenty-Three

Maddie

I covered my hand with his.

He drew in a shaky breath, then offered me a weak smile, looking more than a little lost, so I decided to help him out.

"Tell me about your father."

His eyes widened in surprise.

"You told me a few weeks back that he thought your life was one mistake after another. That must be hard."

"It would be if I cared what he thought," he grunted, his jaw tight.

"You don't care?"

"I only care because of how it affects my mother and my sister, my mother particularly. She bears the brunt of his ill temper."

I wasn't sure I believed that he didn't care, but then I remembered that when we were discussing Amy's abuse, he talked about abused women as though he had experience in the matter. "Does your father hurt your mother?" I asked carefully.

He released a bitter laugh. "Not in the way you're probably thinking. He's hard to live with, even more so when he's upset with me. He blames her for a lot of my mistakes. He was barely around when I was a kid, so she pretty much raised me and my sister as a single mom. He thinks she was too lenient and babied me too much."

"Why wasn't he around?"

"He was too busy working." He grimaced. "He's a retired lieutenant with the Memphis Police Department. Your typical workaholic."

"Kind of like you?"

His gaze turned pensive. "Yeah. I suppose I'm still trying to prove I'm not a fuck-up. Even though I don't really care what he thinks, and he's not paying attention anyway."

"It's hard to ignore the voices in our heads," I said, leaning forward. "I have my own, although the voice in my head isn't my mother's. It's my own."

I stopped, hesitant to continue. Was I really going to tell him this? He was sharing things about himself. If we had any chance at something between us, didn't I owe it to him to share my own trauma? Still, it wasn't lost on me that I'd never shared any of this with Steve and had only hinted at it with Mallory.

"My mom was a doer," I said with a sad smile. "She volunteered for a lot of projects and organizations. She was president of the Women's Club, and when she was in charge, it truly was a service organization. She was an amazing schoolteacher, always there for her students, helping them outside of class, and not just with their schoolwork, but their personal lives too." I paused, swallowing the lump in my throat. "Sometimes it felt like she was there for everyone but me."

Noah flipped my hand over and interweaved his fingers with mine. I bit my lip and looked up at him, taking in the empathy and encouragement in his eyes.

"When I was a kid, some part of me knew she was an amazing woman. Now that I'm older, I can see how hard it was for her to raise me on her own—how difficult it must have been for her to balance work, motherhood, and her altruism. When I was a kid, she'd take me with her to the food pantry or the Thanksgiving dinners she helped organize for low-income and homeless people. The toy drives for needy kids. But once I hit my teen years, I started to notice how different my friends' moms were. They were bringing them shopping and to get their nails done, but my mother was packing up backpacks for foster kids." A tear slipped down my cheek, and I wiped it away. "Aunt Deidre was the one who took me shopping for clothes and helped me figure out hairstyles. She was the one I talked to about boys. My mother found a lot of those things to be frivolous, and I knew she was disappointed I wasn't more like her. Around the time I was fifteen and sixteen, I started to become jealous of the things she devoted her time to, because in my mind, they were more important to her than I was."

His thumb stroked the back of my hand.

"I knew I was being selfish. She was a good person. Hell, the whole town thought of her as a saint, but I felt abandoned. It seemed like whenever she was presented with the choice of me or helping others, she chose the latter. But in my head, a little voice told me that if I was good enough, worthy enough, she'd choose me instead."

"Maddie..."

I shook my head. "I know better now, but the voice is still there. I have to fight it back into the corners of my mind, and I suspect you have to do the same with your father's voice."

He cradled my hand in his and gave me a soft smile. "Yeah. I do."

"I don't know what mistakes you've made, other than ghosting me a month ago," I said with a tearful laugh, "but I know you're a good person too."

His smile spread wider before slipping away. "That's a lot to deal with for a kid."

I shrugged. "Any more so than what you dealt with as a kid?"

"At least I had my mother. She was a buffer."

"And I had Aunt Deidre." I glanced at the ceiling over my head. "I owe her for so much more than just taking me in after my mother died. She's always been there for me. I want to return the favor." I drew in a breath. "So what other mistakes does your father think you've made?"

He pulled his hand free. "He made no secret of the fact he thinks I'm a fool for breaking up with my old girlfriend, Monica."

I felt a twinge of jealousy. "She's the one you told me about? The woman you broke up with a year and a half ago because she wanted to get married and you didn't?"

"Yeah." He ran a hand through his hair. "We'd been together for years, and Monica was a planner." He released a shaky laugh. "We'd only been together for a year before she started dropping hints about getting married. After seeing my parents' poor excuse for a marriage, I knew I didn't want that, but I told her there was no hurry. Things were good between us."

My heart lurched. This story was uncomfortably similar to my own.

"I was a workaholic like my dad, but at least I recognized it. I knew there was no way I could commit to raising a family with my work situation. I vowed never to do to my kids what my father did to my sister and me. I told Monica how I felt, but she insisted I'd change my mind. A couple of years went by, and I now realize that we started living separate lives. She hated hearing about my job, and I didn't like bringing it home, so we had less and less to talk about."

"What about mutual hobbies?"

He shook his head. "She liked shopping and fashion. She even had a small Instagram following for clothing and makeup. She asked me to be in some of her posts, saying the other women's boyfriends helped, but I never agreed to be photographed or videoed. Didn't seem like a good idea, considering my job."

"I can see that."

He glanced down at the table. "In any case, after a couple of years, people started hounding us about getting married, and she was leading the pack. She told me we either got engaged, or we were done."

"So you broke up?"

He pursed his lips, then said, "It was ridiculously easy. Like I said, we'd grown apart. I *did* love her, but I guess not enough to give her what she wanted."

"And your father didn't approve?"

"No. He said I'd been lucky to find a woman who didn't nag me about my job, which my mother had supposedly done, although I never remembered her doing that. He thought I'd made a huge mistake. Still does."

"What about your mother?"

"I think she understood, but she wasn't vocal about it. And my sister, Leah...she's married with kids of her own. Eight-year-old twins. She loves her life and can't understand why I don't want marriage and kids too."

"Do you think you really don't want a family? Or did you just not want that with Monica?" I asked, my heart in my throat.

His eyes turned glassy as he studied me. "Honestly, Maddie. I'm not sure anymore.'

I nodded. "That's fair." It gave me a small glimmer of hope, though.

"It didn't help that she resented all the time I spent with

Caleb, especially since I'd told her I didn't want kids of my own." A wry smile lifted the corners of his mouth. "My father *definitely* didn't understand my relationship with Caleb."

I studied him for a moment, sensing this was important. "Who's Caleb?"

"A kid I mentored. I was his Big Brother."

He was silent for several seconds, and I could see he was wrestling with what to tell me. While I wanted to know everything, I wouldn't press. I only hoped that sharing my heart with him would encourage him to do the same.

Finally, he said, "A lot of my cases involved young men who were missing father figures in their lives." His voice was rough with emotion. "I was idealistic enough to think I could help change that, so I joined the Big Brother organization and was assigned to a thirteen-year-old boy named Caleb."

That surprised me. For a man who thought he didn't want kids, it seemed strange that he'd volunteer to mentor a boy. I could understand why it had confused Monica.

"Caleb's mother had gone to prison for drug possession, and his father was AWOL. His grandmother couldn't take him in, so he went into foster care. He was scared and hurting when I met him, and he hated my guts," Noah said with a wry grin and a faraway look in his eyes. "At first, I only saw him once a month, but I realized that wasn't enough time to form a bond with him, so I started seeing him weekly."

"What did Monica think about that?"

"I was already mentoring him when we started going out, and at first, she thought it was sweet, but she grew to resent the time I spent with him. Honestly, I understood that, but I told her that he needed me."

"I'm sure he did."

"After Caleb realized I wasn't going anywhere, he began to trust me. I helped him navigate his emotions after being shuffled from foster home to foster home, along with the new schools that came with them. The system really sucks for kids like him. He wasn't an aggressive boy, and he was small for his age. He dealt with a lot of shit. Shit no kid that young should have to deal with."

"How long were you his Big Brother?"

Pain filled his eyes. "Officially for five years." He paused. "His mother got out of prison when he was seventeen, and they let him live with her for a short time...until about two months after she got out. She started using again. Caleb tried to hide it, but she got busted for possession with intent to sell, and back to foster care he went. Only he was nearly eighteen by then, and no one wanted him. I asked Monica about letting him live with us until he turned eighteen, but she wouldn't hear of it. I knew he wanted to live with me, and I felt like I had let him down. It really killed me since Monica and I broke up shortly after."

"It wasn't your fault, Noah."

He didn't answer for a few seconds. "When he graduated and got kicked out of the system, I helped him find an apartment. I paid for the furniture and home goods we found for him in thrift stores. I taught him how to pay bills. He was doing good. Really good. Until he wasn't."

"What happened?" I asked in a whisper.

"He started using, but he hid it from me really well. There was a string of robberies around his neighborhood. They weren't on my radar until a convenience store owner was murdered during one of the robberies." He swallowed hard. "I was assigned the case. One of the witnesses reported a kid who matched Caleb's description, but I refused to believe it could be him."

"It's hard to think the people we care about could do anything bad," I said, my heart breaking for him.

His face hardened. "But I was a homicide detective. I was supposed to be impartial."

"Not when you love someone, Noah," I said gently.

His face twisted into a look of self-derision. "I think Caleb knew we were closing in on him. One night, he asked me to come over to his apartment, but my dog had been sick, and I needed to get home to check on him. I knew Caleb wanted me to invite him over, but with the investigation...I just didn't think it was a good idea."

"Your dog?"

"Sergeant. He was an English bulldog," he said, his voice breaking.

I didn't miss the *was*.

"I had gotten home by eight and was in bed around ten," he said quietly. "I was woken up a couple of hours later by a loud noise in the living room. I grabbed my service weapon and went to investigate. Sarge hadn't been in bed with me, and I found him whimpering in the living room, covered in blood. Caleb was there, holding a handgun, and he was strung out on oxy. He was furious with me. He said he'd shot Sarge because I loved my dog more than I did him. He said he knew I was about to arrest him for murder, but if I really cared about him, I'd protect him. I couldn't believe what he was saying. He admitted to the robberies and murdering the convenience store owner. He asked me if I was going to get rid of evidence that tied the cases to him. After a moment of shock, I told him I'd help him find a good lawyer but wouldn't cover up the truth for him. Then he lifted his gun and shot me."

"Oh, Noah," I gasped.

"But I got in a couple of shots too. I survived. Caleb didn't. Neither did Sarge. In a matter of a few seconds, I lost two people I loved."

I leaned over and wrapped my arms around him. "I'm so, so sorry."

He let me hold him for several seconds, then pulled away. I sat back to look at him.

"It took me a long time to recover physically, and emotional-ly…" He paused and held my gaze. "I'll be honest, Maddie. It's been seven months, and I'm still not good."

"How could you be? You don't just recover from something like that."

"I thought about giving up being a cop, but it's all I know. So I started looking at job postings, saw something for here, and applied. It damn near broke my mother and sister's hearts when I moved, but I have to admit, it's easier to breathe this far from the air my father breathes."

"I can see that. I'm sure he thinks you brought everything on yourself."

A wry smile lit up his eyes even though they were still filled with grief. "So you've met him?"

"No, but I know the type."

His smile fell, and his gaze held mine with an intensity that made him the center of my universe. Everything else faded away.

"Maddie, I need to ask you something."

"Okay," I said, forcing myself to focus on his words.

"Do you want marriage and kids?"

My heart broke, because I had an idea where this was going. "Yeah, I do."

Resignation filled his eyes. "I suspected, but I had to confirm it."

"Did you ever think that maybe you don't *not* want kids? That maybe you just weren't ready?" I asked quietly. "You helped Caleb."

Bitterness filled his eyes. "I *failed* Caleb."

"Did you, though? You can help people, but in the end, they make their own choices. Caleb made his."

"It broke my heart to lose him like that. I couldn't grieve him because I was so angry. Still am. He killed Sarge. He nearly killed me. After everything we'd been through..." He swallowed a sob. "I'm not sure I can open myself up to that kind of hurt again."

"I know it ended badly, but what about the five years before that? Were they good?"

He drew in a sharp breath, then nodded. "For the most part. But it's hard to remember them without the ending. Being with my sister's kids helps. My niece and nephew are amazing." His shoulders relaxed a bit. "I love them. They're funny as hell and both smart as a whip."

"So maybe it's not that you don't want kids. Maybe it's that you've convinced yourself you'd be a terrible father."

"I had a very poor example of what a father should be," he said, sounding exhausted. "And I failed Caleb in the end. I can't do that to another kid."

"I think the deck was stacked against Caleb from day one, and he was lucky to have you for five-plus years. At least you gave him some happiness during that time. Imagine what his life would've been like without you in it. Do you think he would have been as happy?"

Closing his eyes, he said, "I honestly don't know."

"I think you do. It's just hard to admit it."

"I..." He swallowed. "I have never wanted anyone as much as I want you. You fill me with a sense of peace I've never experienced, but I'd only hurt you if I follow through on what *I* want. You deserve better than that. I don't want to be another asshole in your life."

I started to protest but stopped. I wanted him too. So much so it hurt, but he was right. Whatever we had between us couldn't last if we didn't want the same things. He was telling me that he didn't want a family, and even though I suspected his stance was more complicated than that, I had to take him at his word.

"No," I said with a resigned laugh. "You're not an asshole. You're anything but."

"I've tried to stay away, Maddie, but I just can't..." His voice trailed off. "I said I wanted to be friends with you, but I don't think I can see you and not want to..." He drew in a breath. "It won't work."

"I know," I said softly.

He stared at his mug for a few seconds, then slid his chair back and got to his feet. "I think I should go before I do something I regret."

I stood too, knowing this was likely my last chance to see if kissing him was as amazing as I thought it would be. I knew I'd likely regret it later, but I'd regret it more if I didn't.

I wrapped my hands around the back of his neck and raised up on my tiptoes, pressing my lips to his.

He stiffened, but I licked his lower lip like I'd wanted to moments ago. He groaned and then wrapped an arm around my lower back and parted my lips with his tongue, kissing me in a frenzy of passion and need.

I hung onto him as he took over, his free hand sinking into the hair at the back of my head, angling it so he had better access.

A fire swept through me as our tongues tangled. I'd never felt like this with a man before, and yet it wasn't nearly enough. I needed more. I needed to feel him skin to skin. I needed him inside me.

But just as quickly as the kiss started, Noah pulled himself away, breathing heavily as he stared at me with a mixture of lust and dismay.

"I'm sorry," he said, taking another step back.

"Why?" I countered. "I'm the one who kissed *you*. I'm not sorry."

"We crossed a line, Maddie," he said, sounding sad. "Now that I've kissed you..." He shook his head and bolted for the door.

In just a matter of seconds, I'd experienced the single best kiss of my entire life, then lost the man who'd given it to me.

I knew I should regret it, but I didn't. I'd needed to know if it would be magical with him, yet now that I knew, the loss was that much greater.

What I *did* regret was that I'd selfishly hurt Noah to find out.

More guilt to add to my ever-growing pile.

Chapter Twenty-Four

Noah

Any word from forensics about either of the last two break-ins?" I asked Lance, shifting in my desk chair to relieve the pressure on my ass from sitting so long. I'd spent half the night awake and come in early. I suspected there wasn't enough caffeine in the state, let alone the police station, to keep me alert.

He kept his gaze glued to the computer monitor on his desk. "You asked that ten minutes ago, and nothing's changed. Are you okay?"

"Yeah," I said absently. "I didn't sleep well last night."

"How'd Maddie take the news?"

I shot him a wry look. "I'm surprised you waited a couple of hours to ask me."

He turned to look at me. "I was hoping you'd volunteer the information, but then I realized I was expecting the impossible."

"Sorry," I said, draining my coffee cup. "I'm not on top of my game today."

"Yeah, I noticed. Does this lack of sleep have anything to do with Maddie?"

I froze. "Why do you ask?" Had he somehow found out that

I'd kissed her? Jesus, kiss was an understatement. I'd devoured her. But then I realized the obvious—he was asking about how she'd taken the news about Amy's murder. "Sorry, like I said. I'm off my game." I shook my head. "She was upset, of course. She feels like she could have saved her if she'd gotten her to talk, or whatever she figures she could have done."

"That sucks."

"I expected as much. She had questions about the case, but I couldn't share any details. She wanted to know if Amy's boyfriend had been arrested. I told her Brent was still building his case." I tilted my head. "That pissed her off, but I assured her that Brent would put together an airtight case. Then I made her promise she wouldn't look into it anymore."

"How'd she take *that*?" he asked with a chuckle.

"Better than I expected," I admitted.

"*Something* happened," he said, studying me. "You're acting stranger than usual. Did you two have another fight?"

"No," I said, grabbing my cup and standing. "I'm going to get another coffee. Want me to get one for you?"

He glanced down at his half-empty cup, then back up at me. "I got this like ten minutes ago, not to mention I got to the station at six, and this is my third cup. Why are you acting so weird?"

"I'm not acting weird. I'm just tired." I headed for the coffee maker, images of Maddie filling my head.

Part of me was pissed that she'd kissed me. I'd been ready to walk away from her. While I'd spent the last month suspecting the chemistry between us would combust with contact, I'd been willing to leave it at that.

Then she'd kissed me. She'd not only confirmed my suspicions, but now she was all I could think about.

And I couldn't fucking have her.

Still, part of me was grateful to have at least gotten one kiss.

I'd spent a good deal of the rest of the night thinking about what could have happened if I hadn't come to my senses. She'd been willing—more than willing. Would she have stopped me if I'd tried to fuck her right there in her kitchen? Because as amazing as that kiss was, it wasn't enough. If I could have had her at least once before I truly walked away, maybe then I'd have been satiated enough to leave her alone.

But even if I had taken it further, I hoped the rational part of me would have stopped at some point. Maddie deserved better than to have a quick fuck on a counter while her aunt and best friend were upstairs. She deserved someone who would give her everything she wanted and more.

It hurt like hell that I couldn't be the man to do it.

Yet, her words kept running through my head. What if she was right? What if I hadn't wanted marriage because Monica hadn't been the right person, even if everyone else had thought so? I was still hung up on having kids, and Caleb's death had only confirmed that I'd be a terrible father. Look how I'd failed him. Even more so than my father had failed me. But I also hadn't been Caleb's father. Part of me resented Monica for not allowing me to be his foster father, but I was equally, if not more so, to blame. I should have known then that she and I weren't going to work. Would it have made a difference if he'd lived with me? Why hadn't I considered fostering him sooner?

Was I questioning truths I'd believed for years because I wanted a shot with Maddie or because I was beginning to consider those beliefs had been built upon unsound ground?

I carried my coffee back to my desk and started to sit down, but Lance looked up at me with excitement in his eyes. "Move your chair over here. I found something."

"Really?"

He'd spent the last few hours studying video footage from businesses and homes along the county road Maddie had seen the white van travel down. We'd hoped that we could figure out where they'd gone, but the road was sparsely populated, and not many people had security cameras facing it. It was like searching for the proverbial needle in a haystack.

"Look here," he said, pointing to an image on the screen. "Not only did Maddie get the van's white paint on her Ford Focus, but the van now has Maddie's gray paint on it. See?"

I saw the dark splotch and what looked like a dent in the grainy still image. "It'll help differentiate this van from any other random white van if this video ever goes to a jury trial," I said. "That is, if we can get a video of it from this angle."

"Glad you mentioned that," Lance said, clicking his mouse at the bottom of the screen. "Here's another photo of the van heading east on Wallace Road about ten minutes after Maddie called you with the license number."

"You got an address on that?" I asked.

"Yep. But there's more."

"Hot damn," I said, getting excited. "Show me."

Lance had three photos, all showing the van heading down Wallace Road, traveling east. Then he pulled up a video showing the road and hit play. "Check this out. No van." A blue sedan passed the camera, heading west, then Lance fast-forwarded the video. Nothing came down the road for the next three minutes. "This is the timeframe we should have seen the van if it had continued at the same speed. I checked a full half hour of video after it should have passed—no van."

"It turned off somewhere."

"Yep."

I gave him an appreciative grin. "You got a map pulled up to see where it could have turned off?"

"Not yet. I was too excited about this and wanted to show you. That was my next step."

"Let's get a printed map and plot this out in the conference room," I said, rolling my chair back to my desk.

I grabbed a map, a marker, and a highlighter, and Lance brought his laptop. It only took us a few minutes to plot out the locations the van had been seen and the location of the home with the video camera that hadn't captured it.

"So between here and here," I said, drawing a circle around the location. "It looks like it's about a half mile from point to point, and there are only two minor roads it could have turned down."

Lance rested his hands on the counter to stare at the map. "I called in a favor to get the sheriff's department to send me this footage. Want me to call in another to see if we can get some from the side roads?"

"Not yet," I said, folding up the map. "We're going out there to look around ourselves."

I filled my thermal mug with fresh coffee, and we headed out to Wallace Road. About ten minutes after leaving the city limits, we drove past the location where Amy's car had been found. There was still crime tape up, but only one sheriff's car was parked on the side of the road.

"Have you heard anything from Brent?" Lance asked.

"No," I said with a frown. "Last I heard, they went out to Amy's last-known residence, but Boomer wasn't home when they stopped by to question him. Neither was the next-door neighbor. Brent planned to go back and talk to the neighbor today and also question Maddie this morning."

His brow knitted. "Was she okay with that?"

"Sure," I said. "Why wouldn't she be?"

"Um..." he said in a tone that suggested he thought I was an idiot. "Maybe because things didn't go so well when we questioned her about Martin Schroeder."

I scowled. "This is different."

"Is it?"

"She's not a person of interest this time."

"Still...maybe you should check on her."

"I'm the last person she wants to talk to."

Maybe not completely true, but I needed to stay away from her anyway.

Why had she kissed me? I'd spent a good portion of the night obsessing over that. At first, I wondered if she'd done it to manipulate me into seeing things her way, but I knew in my gut that wasn't true. If anything, it had felt like a kiss goodbye. What had been a sweet kiss ended with me practically attacking her. Then I'd abruptly stopped and walked out on her *again*. Instead of discussing it like a fucking adult, I'd run away.

Jesus, I was messed up.

But I'd warned her, hadn't I?

Like that's an excuse.

Lance's face lit up with a smug smile. "So you *did* piss her off."

"How close are we to the house that didn't capture the van on video?" I asked, reminding him we weren't on a joy ride to discuss our feelings.

He glanced at the map and then the GPS on my phone. "It's just up ahead. Now answer the question. Did you piss her off?"

"It wasn't a question the first time," I said, getting annoyed. "And, no, I didn't piss her off."

"Then why are you so convinced she doesn't want to hear from you?"

"Christ, you're nosy as shit," I grunted.

"That's the house," he said, pointing to the left up ahead. There were trees on the south side of the road and fields to the north. No other houses except that one. "And I wouldn't consider it being nosy. I'd call it me being a concerned friend."

He glanced out the window as we approached the house. "Okay, keep your eyes peeled."

I dropped my speed. "We're looking for the van but once we turn onto a side street, watch out for security and doorbell cameras on any houses or business you see."

"Thanks for the reminder, Dad," he joked.

Yeah, I was stating the obvious, but I was also trying to get him to stop talking about Maddie.

"The first street is up ahead. Do you want to go north or south?" I asked.

"You're asking me? North."

I switched on my turn signal and turned left. We drove a short distance, then past a house that didn't look like it had a security doorbell. We continued on for another few miles, slowing down in front of every house and striking out.

"How far do you want to go?" Lance asked.

"At least a few more miles, or until we find a place with a security camera."

He nodded and stared out the window.

We drove for another minute before we saw an abandoned-looking house up ahead with a dilapidated outbuilding next to it. I slowed down as we approached, then hit the brakes and backed up, stopping in the middle of the road. Not that it mattered. There was no one on either side.

"That's the van."

The back end of a white van was sticking out from behind the outbuilding.

"It's *outside*?" Lance asked. "You know what that means, don't you?"

"Yep. We don't need a search warrant to look around and see if it's our van." I pulled into the mostly dirt gravel driveway and parked. We both got out and glanced around the place. The property truly looked deserted, but I kept my guard up anyway.

"Hello?" I called out. "Detective Langley from the Cocka-mamie Police Department. Is anyone here?"

Silence.

I walked up to the front door of the ranch home and knocked on a screen door that was mostly frame and very little screen. It was hanging crooked by a single hinge. "Anyone home?"

After several seconds of no one answering, Lance said, "Looks like we're in the clear."

"We need to make sure we don't even step a toe inside any buildings on the property," I said, tense. "I'd hate to fucking blow it at this point."

The outbuilding looked like it had been a garage for an RV, but part of the roof was caved in on the street side. I gave the building a wide berth, and Lance followed suit as we made our way to the back and around the vehicle. The van had been pulled completely behind the building, but whoever had parked it hadn't realized that it could be seen from an angle on the road. The interior was blackened, and it smelled of smoke. Someone had set it on fire, but it hadn't totally burned up. The driver's front end was smashed in, and I thought I could see some smears of gray paint, but it could have been soot from the fire. Forensics would have to confirm it.

I pulled my phone from my coat pocket and took several photos. "We'll coordinate with the sheriff's department about getting a search warrant to get access to the van and the rest of the property. I'll contact Brent and ask him to suggest a liaison since he's busy with Amy's murder case."

"I'll find out who owns the property," Lance said.

"Good idea. I suspect they dumped it here, but we can only hope they dumped it on a property with ties to them."

Only I doubted we'd get that lucky.

Chapter Twenty-Five

Maddie

I'd barely started my shift at the coffee shop when a man in a brown sports coat and jeans walked in. It wasn't uncommon for businessmen in suits and jackets to come into the shop, but this man had a confident air that made him stand apart from everyone else. I was sure it didn't hurt that he was very attractive. Something about him reminded me of Noah, which sent a spike of sorrow through my heart.

I'd probably never see him again after my stunt last night, but I kept trying to tell myself it was for the best. He was right, after all—unless Noah did some soul searching and decided whether he'd come to the conclusion to remain childless for the right reasons, it would be better to stay away from each other.

It made perfect sense, so why did it hurt so much?

Several people were in line ahead of the man. He waited patiently while he glanced around the room, his eyes always returning to me. I knew I should be creeped out, but I didn't get a menacing vibe from him. More like he was studying me and liked what he saw. When he finally approached the counter, he gave me a friendly smile. "Maddie Baker?"

How did he know my name? Then again, I was sort of infa-

"

mous in Cockamamie for a variety of reasons. Also, my first name was on my nametag. "That's me."

His smile broadened. "I'm Detective Brent Taylor with the Wayfare County Sheriff's Department. Could you spare a few moments to talk?" He didn't say why he was here, but I knew. My stomach twisted with anxiety.

I glanced over at Chrissy, who didn't look very pleased.

"She's in the middle of her shift," she said, piercing him with a dark look. Her protective switch had been flipped. "Can it wait?"

"It can..." he admitted sheepishly, "but it would be helpful to my case if you could spare a few minutes now."

My stomach now began to churn. "Do I have to go to the sheriff's headquarters?" I had absolutely nothing to do with Amy's death, but I still felt apprehensive about talking to the detective. Call it lingering trauma from the investigation following my mother's murder.

He shook his head, still looking friendly. "No, nothing like that. I just want to ask you a few questions about Amy Davis and her attendance at your self-defense class."

"Sure," I said, wringing my hands. Then realizing what I was doing, I stopped. "But let me get you a drink first. On the house."

He gave me a dubious look.

"We do it for all law enforcement officers," Chrissy grunted. "So don't think you're special."

To my surprise, he laughed. "Well, in that case, I'll take an almond milk latte."

Chrissy tilted her head as if appraising him, then turned to me. "I like him better than Detective Americano."

Rolling my eyes, I shook my head and motioned to him. "Wait for me at a table. I'll get my manager to come out and cover for me."

Petra readily agreed once I told her I needed to talk to Detective Taylor about Amy's disappearance. Her death still hadn't made the news *or* the gossip circuit, so I didn't feel comfortable announcing that part yet. Besides, I hated thinking about it. It made me cold inside to think she might have been dead the entire time we were looking for her.

Why hadn't I just shown her how to escape a chokehold the night she'd asked? What if I could have saved her?

I felt like I was going to throw up.

By the time I'd walked out from the back, Chrissy had finished Detective Taylor's drink. I picked it up from the counter and carried it over to where he was sitting, a two-person table by the window. I noticed the nearest occupied table was a couple of tables away.

I took the seat opposite him and placed his coffee in front of him. "Thanks," he said, taking a sip. He looked down at my empty hands. "Have you had so much coffee working here that you're sick of it?" It could have sounded condescending coming from someone else, but his tone was good-natured and friendly. I suspected Detective Taylor was a charmer who didn't have much trouble sweet-talking people into spilling what they knew.

I'd have to keep that in mind.

"I doubt me being tired of coffee is possible," I said, folding my hands on the table. "But I've already had two cups today, so I think I'll wait until this afternoon for my next caffeine boost." I drew in a breath, mentally preparing myself. "What would you like to know?"

He sat back, keeping his hand on his cup, which sat on the table. His brow furrowed. "You look like you expect me to arrest you."

"The last time I was questioned by police, I was a person of interest in a murder, and the time before that, I was treated like dog crap, so forgive me if I'm apprehensive." My words had more bite than I'd intended, but I supposed it was better for him to know what he was getting himself into.

"What happened the time before that?" he asked, his interest piqued. Again, it seemed like a friendly question, not that he thought I was guilty of hiding deep, dark secrets.

"My mother's murder." Then I added, "It was a long time ago, and water under the bridge."

A faraway look filled his eyes. "Maddie Baker... Wait. Your mother was Andrea Baker. A schoolteacher found murdered in her classroom. The whole area was shaken up for years."

"That's right," I said, steeling my back. "And the Cockamamie Police weren't all that kind to me. I guess it's fair to warn you that I have a strong aversion to talking to police, but I want to help...I..."

"I understand, Ms. Baker," he said, leaning forward, his face softening with concern. "You aren't a suspect in any way, but based on what Detective Langley told me, you're the first person to have noticed Ms. Davis was missing. Anything you can tell me about what you know will help."

He had kind eyes, and I found myself relaxing. I wasn't sure I could totally trust him, but I hadn't been able to help Amy while she was alive. The least I could do was help find her killer.

I told him everything I knew, from talking to Amy after class to the middle-of-the-night phone call, her being a no-show to our meeting the next morning, along with the conversations I'd had with Lance and Noah, her neighbor, the people she'd worked with, and even Boomer. Detective Taylor took notes and asked questions, making me feel more comfortable than I'd ever felt in a police interview. The only thing I kept to myself was my visit to Emerson Auto Parts. Nothing came of it, and I didn't want him to think I was an interfering idiot.

"Thank you," he said, closing his notebook. "I may have some follow-up questions later, but this is very helpful."

"I take it you haven't made an arrest yet," I said.

He flashed me a grim smile. "Still building a case." He hesitated, then said, "Your mother's case was never solved."

"True."

"They ever have any suspects?"

"They refused to tell me much back then, and supposedly the case file is now missing."

Surprise filled his eyes. "Missing?"

"So I've been told." I cast a glance toward the counter. There were three people in line, and two more walking in. "I really should get back to work."

"Of course." He hesitated, then said, "Actually, I'm intrigued about your self-defense class. Would you be willing to tell me about it sometime?"

"Sure," I said, "but I'm not sure what there is to tell. We finished our final night of lessons a couple of days ago."

"Are you planning to offer them again?"

"I'm considering it." I checked on Petra, who was talking to a customer, then turned back to Detective Taylor and lowered my voice as well. "We gave the lessons here at the coffee shop for free, but Ken Park at the dojo down the street suggested I could offer them at his place."

"For a cut of your profits," Detective Taylor said, then leaned closer and lowered his voice as well. "I might be able to help. Let's talk. Maybe over lunch? I'd suggest grabbing coffee, but I figured you might want to go somewhere other than where you work."

"Good point."

"How about tomorrow?"

I blinked in surprise. "Don't you have a murder case to work on?"

"I still take lunch breaks."

I was pretty sure Noah hadn't taken lunch breaks during his

investigation of Martin Schroeder's murder, but I wasn't sure how things were done. And he *did* have to eat. Still...

Oh, my word. *Was he asking me out?*

"Um...tomorrow won't work. I have a friend in town, and we need to cut down a Christmas tree and figure out how to bring it home with my tiny Ford Focus."

His face brightened. "I have a truck. I could help you out."

I gave him a skeptical look. "During your lunch break?"

He shrugged. "Sure."

I scooted my chair back and stood, trying to sort through my feelings about this. It felt like cheating on Noah, which was ridiculous. We'd never even gone out. "I'll have to talk to my friend."

He stood too and fished a business card out of his pocket. "Sorry. I guess it seems odd that I'd just volunteer something like that, but I'd like to get to know you better, Maddie. And friends help friends." He handed me the card. "Just think about it. I'd be happy to help you. With the self-defense classes too. No strings attached."

I took his card and looked it over. *Detective Brent Taylor, Wayfare County Sheriff's Department.* "Thanks. I'll consider it." Because, like it or not, I really *didn't* have a way to bring the tree home, but wasn't finding evidence to arrest Amy's murderer more pressing?

"Are you planning to arrest Boomer?" I asked with a bit more antagonism than the situation warranted.

He turned wary. "As I mentioned, we haven't made any arrests yet, but I suspect we will soon."

"You know, it's funny. I don't even know his last name."

"Jackson 'Boomer' Garfield is his name, and I'm not at liberty to discuss much about the case." Still, he didn't seem upset that I'd asked.

"Yeah," I said. "I don't suppose you can, but I hope you arrest him ASAP."

He gave me a conspiratorial look. "Trust me. If things keep going well, this will be wrapped up soon."

"I'll be in touch," I said, then left him to go back to work, slightly disturbed that he'd tried to pick me up while questioning me about a murder investigation, yet I had to admit I was also flattered and a little intrigued. Detective Taylor was a good-looking man, and Noah had made it *very* clear there was no future for us. Maybe the best thing to do to get over him was to go out with somebody else.

Chapter Twenty-Six

Noah

Since Brent was busy with the Amy Davis murder investigation, he'd handed the abandoned van case over to Scott Preston, an older detective in his fifties from the sheriff's department. After I'd filled Detective Preston in, he was more than happy to request a search warrant for the van. Then he drove out to meet us at the property while we waited at the end of the driveway. The warrant came through a few minutes after he arrived.

The property search had shown that the property was two years delinquent on taxes. Given the state of the place, it had likely been abandoned, but Preston followed protocol and knocked on the front door to serve the warrant. As expected, no one answered. Donning gloves, we headed over to the van and opened the front driver's door. The stench of burnt chemicals rolled out of the vehicle, making us cough and gag.

"Gotta love it when the idiots try to destroy the evidence," Preston muttered.

"Sometimes it's all too effective," I said as I opened the back doors.

More fumes poured out, but I covered my face with my hand and peered inside.

The interior was mostly burned up. The back was melted plastic and metal, but parts of the dashboard were intact. There was no backseat, and the two front seats had been reduced to melted vinyl and metal frames.

"The van was stolen from Chattanooga, which matches with the Hamilton County on the plates," Preston said. "You think the burglars are from out of town, or locals who are stealing out-of-town vehicles to commit their crimes?"

"We can't say for certain," I said, "but if I had to guess, I'd say local. The homeowners of six of the eight robberies are members of the same church. But it's a large church, so it might just be a coincidence."

"When's the crime team expected to arrive?" Lance asked.

"They ain't," Preston said, leaning into the van. "They've been stretched thin with the latest surge of bigger cases the last few months, and since these are just robberies, no need to waste them on this."

Lance glanced over at me in surprise.

I smothered my irritation. "I realize crime scene resources aren't routinely used for B&Es," I said carefully, "but the perpetrators have taken a disturbing turn in the last two cases."

Detective Preston poked around under the front seat with a ballpoint pen. "I know you're some big fancy city detective, Langley, but this ain't the big fancy city. It's probably a bunch of teens goofin' off."

My shoulders stiffened. "Except two witnesses have seen the driver, who appeared to be a full-grown man in his thirties or early forties."

He backed out of the van and turned to face me, puffing out his barrel chest. "Wayfare County has its fair share of crime, but it ain't no Memphis. You can't be lookin' for evil around every corner, Langley."

"With all due respect," Lance said, his voice tight and controlled, "he's not looking for evil. We found it in the form of Polaroid photos."

Preston chuckled. "And I'm tellin' you, it's a bunch of kids. And yeah, I heard that your witnesses say the driver was older, but kids look older these days." He started to take off his gloves. "There ain't nothin' here. I'll call to have it impounded."

"We'd like to look through it ourselves," I said.

"Knock yourselves out. In fact, I'll leave you two to stick around and wait for the tow truck," he said, starting to walk away. "Guess the Cockamamie PD has more resources to waste than Wayfare County."

I watched him walk around the building, my anger growing.

"Why'd he seem so eager to come out here and help us, only to blow us off like that?" Lance asked in a low voice.

"Good question," I said, keeping my gaze on the street. "Probably to school us on wasting county resources."

"But he was so quick to get a warrant," he said in confusion.

"He had no reason *not* to ask for the warrant. The license plate matched a van seen leaving the scene of a crime. But he's right. Simple B&Es don't typically get a full forensics workup. There are generally too many of them."

"But he knows they aren't simple B&Es," he protested.

I frowned. "Like I said, I think he's trying to prove a point. I've heard rumors the sheriff is in poor health. Maybe Preston wants to run for sheriff in the next election. Could be part of him trying to look fiscally responsible."

"Fuck me," he grunted.

"Yeah," I said with a sigh. "But we're not done yet. We'll search the van as best we can, then we'll wait for the impound tow truck and seal the van ourselves. After we get back to the station, we'll petition to have the wreckage claimed under our jurisdiction so we can get a forensics team to look at it. We'll just hope the chain of custody doesn't get screwed up along the way."

The van was parked next to the outbuilding, but there was enough space for us to open the sliding cargo door. The inside was full of soot, but we gowned up and looked around as best we could while we waited. In the end, our search revealed nothing—not that I was surprised. They'd likely cleaned out anything that would tie it to them. The fire had been an effort to destroy forensics evidence, and if Preston had his way, it had been a wasted effort.

The impound truck arrived about twenty minutes later. We sealed up the doors and windows with tape that would show us if it had been opened, then watched the driver hook up the van, load it onto his flatbed, and head for the road.

I pushed out a frustrated sigh, ready to head back to my car, when something square and white caught my eye on the ground underneath where the van had been.

Putting on another pair of gloves, I walked over and leaned closer. It was a matchbook. The cover was white, and the outline of a black rooster was printed in the center. The cover was too fresh and stiff to have been outside before the van was stowed here. Which meant the burglars had likely dropped it.

"Lance, get an evidence bag."

He was standing several feet from the building, watching the impound truck turn out onto the street. "You found something?" he asked in surprise.

"Maybe."

He pulled a bag from the kit we'd carried back and held it open.

I started to put it inside, then flipped open the cover and

saw two matches were missing, and the name George was written in block letters on the inside cover.

"Think they used this to start the fire?" Lance asked.

"Maybe, but who uses matches anymore?"

"I've heard rumors that Cock on the Walk gives out matchbooks, but I've never seen one."

I glanced up at him in surprise.

He studied the matchbook in my hand. "But do you think these guys would burn the inside of the van to cover their tracks and then be careless enough to leave the matchbook behind?"

"I've seen stranger things happen, but I suspect it was a mistake. Know of any Georges that hang out at Cock on the Walk?"

"No, but Dukas might."

Mike Dukas was Cockamamie's only narcotics detective. Since the city didn't have enough money to keep him full time, he also worked with the Wayfare Sheriff's Department. He was familiar with a lot of characters who hung out at Cock on the Walk, including members of the Brawlers, a group that was responsible for most of the drug distribution in the county.

"Call him."

Lance pulled out his phone and placed the call, putting it on speaker. Once Dukas answered, Lance explained that we were working several B&E cases and had just located a van tied to the last two break-ins. "Do you know anyone named George who's working with the Brawlers?" he asked.

"Nope. A lot of those guys go by nicknames, but I know most of their given names. Don't know of any Georges."

Lance shot me a frustrated look, then asked, "Do you know anything about matchbooks given out at Cock on the Walk? We found a matchbook near the van. The matchbook's white with the outline of a rooster in black. I've heard rumors that Cock on the Walk gives them out."

"Can't see the Brawlers getting mixed up in break-ins," Dukas said. "For one thing, they don't need to. Drug business is pretty lucrative. They don't need to mess with the hassle of fencing stolen goods. Besides, I can't see them letting someone in their organization do something as low level as break-ins, because if they get caught, the DA's sure to give them a sweet deal to squeal on their buddies."

"That makes sense," Lance said. "What about the matchbooks? Have you heard about them?"

"I have, but they're fairly new, and I haven't seen any myself. I'd love a pic if you could send one."

"Sure," Lance said. "Do you know anything about how they give them out?"

"Like I said, they're new, but I think they're handed out by the owner of the place, not the Brawlers themselves."

"I thought the owner was a Brawler," Lance said in confusion.

"Rumor has it he's no longer in the group, but he's still friendly with them."

"Is that even possible?" Lance asked.

"Time will tell," Dukas said.

"Mike, this is Noah Langley," I said, leaning closer. "There are plenty of other questionable characters who hang out at Cock on the Walk. The burglars might not be part of the Brawlers. Do you know any of the others?"

"A few," he said, "but I don't know of anyone named George. If I hear anything, I'll be sure to let you two know."

"Thanks, Mike," I said, then Lance hung up.

We stared at each other for several seconds. I was still processing everything and trying to figure out what to do next.

Lance finally made a face. "Do you want to go out there and ask around?"

"You think anyone at that place would share information with a couple of cops?" I asked sarcastically.

He snorted. "So we've still got nothing to work with."

"Not quite. These guys have to be doing *something* with the stolen goods, and even though the pawnshop owners claim they aren't bringing the stolen items there, we could ask if anyone named George has been making inquiries. And we can check with pawn shops in Lynchburg and Chattanooga."

"Which will take forever," Lance groaned.

"Welcome to the glamorous life of a police detective."

"It still beats working traffic."

Some days, I wondered.

Chapter Twenty-Seven

Maddie

When I got off work, I saw I'd missed a text from Mallory.

> We need eggs. I'd go get them myself, but Linda went home early, and I promised Aunt Deidre we'd make a bourbon cake.

I had so many questions, including why she hadn't asked for bourbon. I knew for a fact Aunt Deidre didn't have any in the house. Trust me, I'd looked through Aunt Deidre's limited alcohol inventory.

> No problem

I texted back even though the thought made me grit my teeth.

> I'll pick some up on the way home.

While I didn't mind picking up the eggs, I *did* dread going to Bob's Market. I wasn't sure if word had gotten out about

Amy's murder, and I really didn't want to lie to her coworkers, even if it was a lie of omission. At the same time, I couldn't bring myself to go back to Piggly Wiggly.

As soon as I got there, I hustled into the store and headed straight for the dairy department to find the eggs. I was perusing the selections when I heard a woman ask next to me, "Are you that woman who runs the self-defense class? The one looking for Amy?"

I turned to face her, trying to hide my guilt. She looked young, probably early to mid-twenties. She had long, dishwater blond hair pulled back in a ponytail. Her face was pale, but I suspected it was from genetics and lack of sun, not because she was scared or sick. She was wearing jeans and a thick tan cardigan over a forest-green T-shirt with the Bob's Market logo on the front. Her name tag was partially covered with her sweater, but the first few letters were "AMB."

Was this Amber, the other cashier the night manager had said was Amy's friend?

"Yeah," I said with a warm smile. "I'm Maddie."

She twisted her fingers in front of her stomach in a nervous gesture. "I take it you haven't found her yet?"

I turned back to the refrigerated case and leaned over to grab a carton of eggs. I hated lying, and I couldn't look her in the eyes while I did it. "No. I haven't found her." Not a lie, but not the full truth either.

"I know something that might help you find her."

I stood upright and turned to face her again. "I think the sheriff's department is involved now. You should really talk to the detective in charge, Brent Taylor. I can give you his number, if you'd like. He gave me his card."

She vigorously shook her head, anger covering her face. "No. I'm not talking to no police or sheriff. That's why I'm talking to *you*. Do you want me to tell you or not?"

"Yes," I said. "If you know something, they need to know. I *will* tell Detective Taylor that I found something."

She looked terrified, and I was sure I'd blown it by admitting I'd tell the police. Still, I had to protect the investigation, but I wouldn't tell her any other lies. I felt guilty enough.

Finally, she said, "You won't tell them where you heard it?"

"No. I promise," I said earnestly. "I'll keep your name out of it." Not that I even knew her full name.

Amber glanced around, but we were the only two people in this section. Nevertheless, she pulled her sweater tighter to completely cover her nametag, then leaned in close and lowered her voice. "Amy was savin' up to leave that lowlife Boomer."

"She was holding back money from her paycheck?"

She released a bitter laugh. "Hell no. That asshole took her paychecks and deposited them into his account. She was getting her money from someplace else."

"Where?"

"I don't know, but I think she had some kind of side hustle goin' on. She said she had a couple thousand dollars saved up so she could leave him."

A couple *thousand?* "And you have no idea what she was doing?" I asked in shock.

She shook her head again. "Nope. But I doubt it was legal, if you know what I mean."

"What makes you say that?"

"For one thing, she didn't talk about where she got it, and the one time she did, she made it sound like it was top secret—and not just from that asshole who beat her."

"And you really have no idea what she was doing?" I asked.

"Nope, but I *do* remember her meeting someone out back once."

"Did you see who she met?"

"Some guy, I think, but I couldn't make out what he looked like."

"Not even if he was young or old? Tall or short? Thin or heavy?"

She pierced me with a dark expression. "Look, I saw his boots and jeans. I suppose she could have been meeting a woman, but most women I know don't wear boots like that and don't have such big feet. Or deep, booming voices."

"How is it you saw the guy's boots and jeans and not the rest of his body?"

"Amy had the door open to the dumpster corral, and they were standing on the other side. All I saw was their feet, but I heard their voices. Hers and a man's."

"Did you hear what they were saying?"

"Not most of it. They were speaking too low. I *did* hear Amy say that she didn't have what they needed, but she'd try to find out something by the next day."

"And you don't know what they needed?"

"Nope. That's pretty much all I heard."

"Do you happen to remember when this happened?" I asked.

She made a face. "About a week ago?"

"And when was it that she told you she had the money saved up?"

Her mouth twisted to the side as she considered it. "Last week, I think. After I saw her with that guy."

"Did you ask her about meeting the guy out back?"

"Hell, no," she said in disgust. "I figured it was none of my damn business." Then she added, "But I got the impression it wasn't the first time she'd met with him. While she worked the register some, she mostly stocked shelves. It would have been easy for her to slip out the back door to meet him."

"Do you think she was selling drugs?"

She barked a short laugh. "Hell, no. Amy hated the stuff. Said her cousin ODed on oxy. There's no way she'd sell drugs, even if it was to help herself."

This could shed new light on the murder case. I needed to tell Noah right away. Then I tripped on the thought because it wasn't Noah I needed to call—it was Detective Taylor. There was a slight problem, though. Noah and Lance were used to me coming up with unverifiable information. What would Detective Taylor think when I refused to name my source? Would he assume I'd done something to Amy and was trying to cover my tracks?

I gave Amber a pleading look. "You're sure I can't persuade you to tell the police?"

"No way," she said, taking a step back. "And if you say I'm the one who told you, I'll deny it until I'm blue in the face."

"Okay," I assured her, lifting my hands in surrender. "I won't tell them I heard this from you. I promise. But I *do* have to tell them. This could be important."

She frowned but didn't protest.

Then something else hit me—Amber was acting like Amy was in trouble, but for all she knew, she was back in Atlanta, safely away. I felt like a bitch for not setting her straight. At the same time... "If Amy was planning to run away, why are you so worried about her?" I blurted.

"She said she'd let me know when she was ready to run," she said, her voice breaking. "She promised to let me know when she got away. I've tried calling, though, and her phone goes straight to voicemail. I suppose she probably changed phones to hide from Boomer, and I guess she could have found the chance to leave and did, but something about all of this doesn't feel right. You know?"

"Yeah," I said. "I know." I paused, then asked, "Did Amy intend to go back to Georgia?"

"Hell, no," she said in disgust. "She said there was nothing for her there."

"Do you know where she was planning to go?"

"Nashville," she said with a bitter laugh. "Thought she could get a job in country music, not as a singer, but something behind the scenes." She shook her head. "That girl was a dreamer." She turned and walked away, still shaking her head.

I needed to get this information to Detective Taylor as soon as possible, but I couldn't call him while I was inside the store. I needed to get out of there.

In my haste, I briefly considered putting the eggs back and just heading for the exit. Then I threw that idea out. Mallory wasn't serious about many things, but cake easily made her top three. If I went home without the eggs, Detective Taylor might be investigating *my* murder, and Mallory would be the lead suspect.

I headed to the front to check out, thankful when I only had to wait a few seconds for the customer in front of me to finish her purchase before Gloria, the cashier I'd met the first night, could ring me up.

"Heard anything about Amy?" she asked with a worried look.

I swallowed, trying not to show any guilt, as I swiped my debit card and punched in my PIN. "Detective Langley had to work on another case, and I haven't seen anything on the news."

"I've got a bad feeling about all this," she said, taking the receipt from the register and handing it to me. "A really bad feeling."

"Me too," I said as I took it, refusing to meet her gaze. My mind drifted to Amy as I hurried out of the store. Noah hadn't told me where or how they'd found her. Only that she'd been strangled. Had Boomer drawn out her death? Or had someone else killed her? The mystery person she'd been helping...

I clicked my key fob and got inside my car, then turned it on to warm up while I regained my composure. I couldn't start crying before I called Detective Taylor. He might consider it a sign of guilt. It was bad enough I was calling him with secret information. I drew in a deep breath, then placed the call.

"Detective Brent Taylor," he answered in a brisk voice.

"Detective Taylor," I said hesitantly, still worried about how he'd react to my information. "This is Maddie Baker. We spoke this morning."

"Maddie," he said in surprise. "I wasn't expecting to hear from you so soon. Did you decide to take me up on my offer to help get your Christmas tree home?"

"No," I said. "Actually, I'm calling about the case."

"Amy Davis's murder?"

"Yeah, I just found out something that might be helpful to your investigation."

"Is it about Jackson Garfield? Because we arrested him an hour ago and then put out a press release about his arrest and Ms. Davis's murder."

"Oh," I said, now wondering how receptive he'd be to my information. "It's not about Boomer, actually. It's more about Amy herself." I paused. "Amy was saving money to leave Boomer, and it wasn't coming from her paychecks."

"Where did you hear that?"

"Someone who doesn't want to talk to the police or a deputy."

He was silent for a moment. "So it's hearsay."

"I suppose..."

"Do you have any names or information about where Amy was getting the money?"

"No."

"Did the person who told you this know how she was getting the money?"

"They thought she was working for someone, but they didn't know what she was doing. They insisted Amy wasn't selling drugs, though."

He hesitated. "And this person is adamant about not talking to me or anyone in law enforcement about it?"

"Yeah."

"Do you have anything else I can use? Names?"

"The only other thing I know is that Amy met some guy outside the delivery entrance of the grocery store a couple of weeks ago. My source didn't see his face."

"Did your source hear any part of the conversation?"

"They spoke too low for my source to hear most of it, but they *did* hear Amy say she didn't have what they wanted, then she promised she'd try to find out about it. Or something like that."

"No mention of what it pertained to?"

"No."

He was silent again, but when he spoke, he sounded resigned. "I doubt the prosecutor could use your testimony at trial, and even if she did, it doesn't sound like there's much to go on. Unless you have something else?"

"No, that's it."

"I think we have enough evidence to convict Garfield, but if we need more, I might follow up with you. Is that okay?"

"Yeah, of course. Whatever I can do to help."

"Which leads me to ask..." he hesitated. "Are you investigating this case on your own, Ms. Baker?"

His professionalism was back, and I was suddenly uncomfortable. "I assure you, Detective Taylor, I did not seek this information out. The person who approached me knew I'd been asking about Amy and volunteered what they knew. I tried to get them to talk to you, but they refused."

"It's okay, Maddie," he said, sounding apologetic. "But I *had* to ask."

"Yeah. I get that." And I really did. Still, I hated feeling like I'd done something wrong.

"Thanks for the information," he said, his voice kinder, like he knew he'd thrown us off balance and was trying to repair things. "I'll be sure to let you know if I need to take an official statement."

"Okay."

He hesitated again. "I hope you know that my offer to help with your Christmas tree still stands. Now that this case is wrapped up, I'll definitely be free to help."

"Oh," I said, taken by surprise. "I still haven't had a chance to talk to Mallory."

"Well, when you do, feel free to text or call me."

"Yeah," I said. "Okay."

I hung up and set my phone on the console. I couldn't help thinking that Noah and Lance would have looked into the information that I'd just given Detective Taylor, even if it seemed superfluous. Boomer was an abusive asshole, and if he'd discovered Amy was planning to leave him, then he could have gotten violent enough to kill her. But what if it hadn't been him at all? What if the mysterious man had killed her because she hadn't gotten whatever it was he wanted? It wasn't outside the realm of possibility. Shouldn't Detective Taylor be looking into it?

I considered calling Lance to get his opinion, but it felt a lot like tattling, and besides, what could he do about it? Amy's murder wasn't his or Noah's case.

I'd have to let it go.

A knock rapped on the passenger window, and I shrieked, jumping in my seat.

Steve's face appeared, and he grinned in delight. "Didn't mean to scare you, Mads," he said, his voice muffled by the glass.

That was bullshit, and we both knew it.

"Go away," I said, putting my foot on the brake and shifting the car into drive.

"I can follow you home, and we'll have this conversation in your front yard," Steve said. "Or we can have it here in the privacy of your car. Which do you prefer?"

It really wasn't much of a choice. I put the car back in park and clicked the unlock button.

The passenger door opened, and Steve climbed in.

"I miss you, Mads."

"It only took you three months to figure that out?" I said snidely. "I haven't heard a single word from you since I left. Why the sudden turn around?"

"I told you," he said, putting his hand on my forearm. "I missed you." I shook him off, but he continued as though he hadn't noticed. "Look, we both know I'm a stubborn guy, and I didn't want to admit to myself that I couldn't live without you." He turned in his seat to face me. "Didn't you say I needed to be more vulnerable? Well, this is me being vulnerable, Mads. I need you."

"And you want to marry me next month?" I asked, keeping my tone neutral.

"Yes!" He looked excited. "I even picked the date and the venue. I put down deposits and everything."

"I haven't even agreed to marry you, Steve," I said in disbelief. "Why in God's name would you do that?"

He turned solemn. "To prove to you how serious I am. They're non-refundable, Mads. That's pretty damn serious."

For him, yeah, but this still stunk of freshly sprayed skunk.

"What if I don't want to get married next month?" I asked, still keeping my voice neutral. I needed to know what he was up to, and being confrontational wouldn't work. "I've always wanted to get married in the spring."

His face froze, and his eyes darted to the side, but he quickly recovered. "If I had known you wanted to get married in the spring, I would have checked their availability for then. But can't you appreciate that I took the initiative not only to set the date but also to put down deposits?" he asked, sounding irritated. "I went to a lot of effort for you. You could show a little gratitude."

Where had he gotten the money to put down deposits? And then I knew.

"You used the profit from your flip house to put down deposits for a wedding I never agreed to?" I demanded. "You hadn't even asked me to marry you, Steve! You can't just presume I want to marry you next month!"

"For fuck's sake, Maddie," he groaned. "It was supposed to be an awesome surprise. You've been harping about getting engaged for at least two years. Can't you be happy?"

"I broke up with you!" I shouted in disbelief.

"Yeah, because I hadn't proposed, but I was working on it when you left, Maddie." He pulled the ring box out of his pocket and set it on the console. "I had the ring and everything!"

I narrowed my eyes. "You're telling me that you had the ring when I moved out, but you didn't bother to tell me?" When he hesitated, I added, "I'd like to see the receipt."

He eyed me like I was a misbehaving child. "I never took you to be so materialistic."

"I don't want to see the price, you fool. I want to see the purchase date."

"Now, Maddie..." he said in a tone that was all too familiar. He'd used it a million times when he wanted to get his way and tried to make me feel like I was being unreasonable. I'd been stupid enough to fall for it before, but I saw right through him this time.

"No," I said firmly. "I'm not falling for that shit anymore.

For a man who'd supposedly bought an engagement ring, you weren't all that upset when I left."

"That's because I thought you were bluffing and would be back."

"I put my furniture in storage," I said dryly.

"You always did like to prove a point." He didn't sound judgmental, just matter of fact.

"That goes to show you never really knew me at all," I said. "I'm not marrying you, Steve. We're done, which means there's nothing to talk about, so get out of my car, and take your ring with you."

His face hardened. "We're getting married, Maddie. The sooner you get on board with the plan, the easier it will be." Something in his voice sounded ominous.

My blood ran cold. "What the hell does that mean?"

"It means I'm not taking no for an answer," he repeated sternly. "I will go to extreme measures if necessary." He held my gaze with a look of desperation. "I'm *that* serious."

What the hell? Why was he so adamant about this, and what did he plan to do if—*when*—I refused him?

"We're *not* getting married," I said through gritted teeth, then grabbed my phone from the console and held it up. "I just got off the phone with a Wayfare County sheriff's detective. If you don't get out of my car right now, I'll call him back and have you arrested for harassment."

He looked at the phone as though he wanted to snatch it out of my hand, but instead he drew in a deep breath, his face relaxing. "I'm sorry I got so intense just now, but I've realized what a fool I've been, and I'm desperate to get you back. I need you. You're my everything. I just want you to marry me so I can spend the rest of my life proving it to you."

"Well, moving away from you proved to *me* that I don't need or want you. *At all.* In fact, the only thing I want from you is the money I loaned you for your flip house, so if you don't have a cashier's check or cash for fifteen thousand dollars—you can have the damn interest—then get out of my car."

"I'm not giving up, Maddie," he said with a cold edge to his voice. "I'll win you back." Then before I could answer, he snatched the ring box and got out.

I didn't waste any time pulling out of the space, but as I left, I could see him standing in the middle of the parking lot, watching me.

In all the time I'd been with Steve, he'd annoyed the hell out of me and pissed me off, but I'd never been scared of him.

Until now.

Chapter Twenty-Eight

Maddie

Mallory and Aunt Deidre were waiting for me in the kitchen when I got home.

"Cake time," Mallory said, pulling out ingredients for the cake.

Aunt Deidre accepted the eggs from me with a smile, and I went upstairs to change, still feeling unsettled.

I didn't like that Detective Taylor wasn't doing anything with the information I'd gotten for him. And I knew Steve was up to something. It was hard to admit I couldn't do anything to resolve either situation, other than call Lance—which I still wasn't willing to do—or file a restraining order against Steve, something I actually wasn't opposed to doing.

After changing into yoga pants and a long-sleeved T-shirt, I headed back downstairs and grabbed a bottle of wine from the fridge.

Mallory, who was measuring a cup of flour, gave me the side eye. "Had to deal with too many highly caffeinated customers today?"

"Nope. I ran into Steve."

She turned to me, her eyes wide with surprise. "He came by the coffee shop again?"

"Who's Steve?" Aunt Deidre asked. She was sitting at the kitchen table, cracking eggs into a bowl. From the looks of the open carton, she'd already cracked more than half.

"How many eggs do you need for the cake?" I asked.

"Two," Mallory said, looking over at the table. "Oh shit."

Setting the wine bottle down, I walked over and took two eggs out of the carton.

"I need those," Aunt Deidre said, her eyes flashing with anger. "We're making a cake."

"I know," I said. "I was the one who picked up the eggs for you. But I think you can spare these two."

"We need them all," she insisted.

"We're good, Aunt Deidre," Mallory said, holding up her tablet. "I just checked the recipe, and we can let Maddie have two."

Aunt Deidre frowned as though she thought we were pulling a fast one on her but said nothing as she picked up another egg. So far, she had a mixing bowl full of eggs. I hated to waste them, so when she was finished, I'd cover the bowl with plastic wrap and use them for scrambled eggs tomorrow.

I set the two eggs on the counter next to Mallory's other ingredients.

"She was good earlier, Mads," she said under her breath. "I swear. In fact, she's the one who suggested making a cake."

"A bourbon cake?" I asked skeptically.

"That was my idea, but she agreed to it." She frowned. "Then again, I should have questioned why she thought it was a good idea."

"It *was* a good idea. I love bourbon cake, but I didn't think Aunt Deidre had any bourbon."

"She didn't. I brought some with me from Nashville." She

snuck a glance at the kitchen table, then back to me. "She wasn't like this earlier. I swear."

"I know. It comes and goes," I said with a sigh. "There's no rhyme or reason to it, although it tends to be worse when she's overly tired."

"She took a nap," Mallory insisted. "When she woke up, she said she wanted to make a cake, and we looked up the recipe together." She picked up a whisk and began whisking the dry ingredients in a ceramic bowl. "But we can talk about that later. When and where did you see Steve?"

"I saw him in the grocery store parking lot. I'd gotten into my car and made a call to Detective Taylor, and a few seconds after I hung up, he knocked on my passenger window."

"Jeez!" she exclaimed. "Stalker much? He must have been watching you!"

"Yeah, I guess," I said absently. Why hadn't I thought of that? It couldn't be a coincidence that he'd run into me in that particular place at that particular moment. He must have followed me to the grocery store. Had he watched me leave the coffee shop? A cold chill ran down my back.

"So what did he want?"

I tried to put a lid on my growing anxiety. "Same old, same old. Insisting we get married but falling back on his gaslighting, saying I'd always wanted to get married, so he didn't understand why I wasn't more grateful he'd put down deposits."

She stopped whisking and swiveled at the waist to face me. "Wait. He put down deposits?"

"Non-refundable. With money he made from selling the flip house."

Her eyes narrowed. "What is he up to?"

"I have no idea, but he's creeping me out. Oh!" I added. "Get this. He claims he had an engagement ring when I moved out, but he didn't say anything because he thought I was pulling one of my 'typical' stunts." I used air quotes to emphasize the word.

"What the hell does *that* mean?" she whispered as she turned her gaze on Aunt Deidre, who was now adding all the eggshells to the egg mixture. "Should we stop her?"

I frowned. "No. She's in a mood. I think stopping her would only make it worse."

Mallory placed a hand on my shoulder. "I'm sorry, Mads."

Tears stung my eyes. "Yeah, me too."

"Wait. You said you'd just gotten off the phone with Detective Taylor. Who's that?"

I told her about the sheriff's deputy, giving him my statement, and his offer to help with the Christmas tree.

"Is he cute?"

I rolled my eyes. "Focus, Mallory."

"Girl, you can give him information about a murder case and still *look* at him. I presume you weren't in a confessional."

"We were at the coffee shop."

She waggled her eyebrows. "So no confessional."

"A woman is dead, Mal."

"But *you're* very much alive. If you talked to him this morning, why did you call him this afternoon? To take him up on his offer?"

"No. One of Amy's old friends at the grocery store told me that Amy had been saving up to leave Boomer. She thinks she had some sort of side hustle, and the friend said she had a couple thousand dollars saved up."

"What the hell was she doing?" Mallory asked as she cracked one of the eggs into a small bowl.

"I don't know," I admitted. "Unless she was stripping at the new club outside of town."

She made a face as she considered it. "I hear you can make good money stripping." She glanced down at her body. "If I hit the gym and lay off desserts for a few weeks, maybe I'll go audition."

"Be serious, Mal."

"I *am* being serious," she said as she put butter and sugar into a bowl, then turned on Aunt Deidre's old free-standing mixer.

The sound of the motor filled the room.

While I tried not to think about Mallory stripping, my thoughts turned to Amy. Could she have been working at the strip club? It seemed like Boomer was too controlling for that to be a possibility, but she had days off from the grocery store, and if Boomer had a job, she would have been alone during the day.

I shouldn't be thinking about this at all. Detective Taylor said he'd arrested Boomer, so that was that.

Right?

But I couldn't help thinking there was more to all this, and no one was looking into it. I couldn't get involved in a police investigation...

But I *could* offer my condolences to Amy's neighbor.

The last time we spoke, Miss Barbara hadn't known Amy was dead. According to Detective Taylor, that information had now been released to the public, so I wouldn't be sharing anything confidential. And while I was offering my sympathy, I could ask if she knew about Amy's part-time job.

"I have to go out for a bit," I said abruptly, just as Mallory turned off the mixer.

"What? Where?" Mallory asked in dismay.

"I need to go talk to Amy's neighbor, Miss Barbara. I have to see if she knew about Amy's side hustle."

She frowned as she studied me. "Is that a good idea?"

"Probably not, but I don't plan to ask right away," I said. "I'll bring her some flowers and then figure out a natural way to work it into the conversation."

"Still...isn't hunky Detective Taylor supposed to be handling it?"

"I never said he was hunky, and yes, I think he should be handling it, but he isn't." When she didn't say anything, I added, "It's not dangerous, Mallory. I'm going to offer my condolences to an older woman who thought her abused neighbor had escaped. She's bound to be upset."

She made a face. "Well, if you say so..."

"You don't approve."

Shrugging, she added the eggs to the butter and sugar mixture. "I guess I'm just thinking about the last time you looked into a murder. You were nearly kidnapped by a bunch of goons, and then you *were* kidnapped and nearly murdered by that stupid grocer. Maybe you should leave it to the professionals."

She was right, of course. I needed to let Detective Taylor handle it, but it still felt wrong to do nothing and even more so to go to Lance. There wasn't a thing he could do about it, but that might change if I had more proof.

Mallory studied me for a long moment, then rolled her eyes. "Go."

"What?"

"You're right. It's just a neighbor, and even if you don't ask her about how Amy was making money, it'd be a nice gesture to bring her flowers. She probably is upset. Aunt Deidre and I will finish the cake while you're gone."

Aunt Deidre was currently mixing the eggs and eggshells with a wooden spoon.

"Go," Mallory said. "Then you'll be back in time to help make dinner."

I glanced longingly at the still-unopened bottle of wine on the counter.

"Go," she said again, giving my arm a slight shove. "We'll

open that when you get back, but right now, I need you to find out what Amy was doing to make that much money. If it's not stripping, I might be interested."

"Mallory!"

"What?" she asked innocently, holding out her free hand, a spatula still in the other. "The world doesn't stop when people die, and Mastercard likes it when I make regular payments."

Living with her was going to keep me on my toes.

Chapter Twenty-Nine

Maddie

After a quick stop at a florist to pick up a mixed bouquet, I headed out to Miss Barbara's house. Since the purpose of this trip was to see Miss Barbara, I parked directly in her driveway.

When she opened the door, her eyes widened in shock. I supposed finding me on the front porch with a flower bouquet was the last thing she expected.

"I just heard about Amy," I fudged. "I wanted to come by and say how sorry I am."

Miss Barbara's face crumpled, and she backed up as she held the door wider. "Oh, it's horrible. Come on in."

I walked past her into the living room, noticing a talk show on the large TV, but the volume had been muted. "I'm sorry if I interrupted your show."

"Oh, no," she said with a wave of her hand. "They don't have any good guests on today, just some rapper who loves to curse and someone from that reality show, *Darling Investigations*. Would you like some tea?"

"No, I don't plan to stay long," I said, handing her the flowers before I slipped off my coat. "I wanted to give you these.

I'm just so devastated that Amy didn't get away to Georgia like you'd hoped."

Miss Barbara took the bouquet and sniffed a daisy. "It's such awful news, but these flowers are sure to put a bit of a smile on my face. Amy so loved flowers. Did I tell you how she planted chrysanthemums after she moved in?"

"You did," I said somberly.

She made a face and shook her head. "Sorry. It's just that I keep thinking about the poor dear. It's good to have someone to talk to about her. I'm glad you came. I'm sure everyone at the grocery store must be torn up about it."

It took me a moment to remember she thought I'd worked with Amy. "News about her death hadn't hit the store when I left an hour or so ago," I said, which was the truth. "I didn't find out until after I left."

She walked into the kitchen, and I followed her. Grabbing a vase out of a cabinet, she began filling it with water.

"I was just thinking about her smile," Miss Barbara said, resting her hand on the counter as she stared out the window over the sink. "Such a sweet spirit." The vase began to overflow, and she pulled it out from under the water, shaking her head. She turned to face me as she set the vase on the counter and turned off the water. "I knew something was up when I saw the sheriff's cars pull up into Boomer's driveway earlier today. You know, they dragged him out of the house in handcuffs."

"When did that happen?" I asked. When I gave my interview this morning, Boomer still hadn't been arrested. "Doesn't Boomer usually work on weekdays?"

She slipped the plastic sleeve off the flower stems. "He does, but he didn't go in today. But he sure was wailing when they hauled him off." She shook her head in disgust, then put the flowers in the vase. "Sobbing that he didn't kill her and they needed to find the person who did. Blubbering that he loved her, and he'd kill the person who hurt her and other such nonsense."

"So he acted like he was surprised?"

Picking up the vase, she started for the living room. "Puttin' on a good act, if you ask me," she said with a snort.

"Was his cousin home?" I asked as I followed her.

She set the vase on the coffee table, then sat in the recliner, gesturing for me to take a seat on the sofa. "Nope. Just Boomer. I only knew he was home because his truck was in the driveway, and it had been there since the middle of the night. I hadn't seen hide nor hair of him all day, not that that's unusual. When he's home, he usually holes up in the house."

"He was gone last night?" I asked as I settled on the sofa, putting my coat next to me.

"Yep. He came home from work, then left around six. Didn't come home until about two-thirty in the morning. Jake didn't come home at all."

"You were up late enough to see him come home?" I asked in surprise.

"Couldn't sleep," she said, pinching her lips together. "I just kept thinking about Amy."

We were silent for a moment, so I decided to broach the real reason I was there. "Do you know if Amy had another part-time job?"

Surprise filled her eyes, then she laughed bitterly. "How on earth could she have had another job? Boomer watched her like a hawk. He knew her schedule at the store. He wouldn't have approved of her workin' somewhere else." Her face turned thoughtful, and she tilted her head. "You're not askin' out of curiosity. You *know* something."

I needed to be careful about what I said. "She told one of the cashiers at the store that she had several thousand dollars saved up to leave Boomer. Do you think she was working some-where else on her downtime?"

She stared at me in disbelief. "I don't see how that's possible. Like I said, Boomer watched her every move."

"Maybe she was doing something at the store," I said. "She was seen meeting some guy a couple of weeks ago out by the delivery entrance. I guess she could have been selling drugs or something?"

Her nose scrunched up. "Drugs? I don't see Amy selling drugs. She told me that her cousin had died from an overdose. She hated the things. I don't see her selling 'em to someone else."

That matched what Amber had told me.

"So what else could she have been doing to make money?"

"She *wasn't* making any money," Miss Barbara said as though I was silly to consider it. "I think she would have mentioned it to me if she had been. She knew how worried I was about her. And there's no way she would have taken my money the morning she left if she had that kind of money in the bank. She knew how tight things were for me." She shook her head. "I don't know where that cashier got that idea, but she was wrong."

"She seemed pretty certain," I said.

Miss Barbara chewed on her lower lip. "She must have been mistaken. I would have known. And if she was working some-where else, seems like the police would be looking into it. They wouldn't have arrested Boomer for her murder. They searched that house for over an hour after they arrested him. Seems like they would have found something."

Or maybe they *did* find something, and that's why Detective Taylor hadn't seemed too interested in my information. Actual proof would be better than my hearsay. I suddenly felt a lot better about the whole thing.

"Yeah," I said, grabbing my coat. "You're probably right. I should get home." I stood and started to slip my coat back on. "I just wanted to tell you how sorry I am about Amy."

Miss Barbara got up from the chair. "You were so sweet to bring the flowers. Such a dear. And that stuff about Amy working another job…" She paused. "Maybe I was too quick to dismiss it. Did you happen to notify the sheriff's department?"

"I talked to the detective investigating her murder," I said, "but he didn't seem interested."

"Oh, really?" she asked in surprise. "Why on earth not?"

"I'm hoping he found evidence of where she was working when they searched the house."

A fierce look filled her eyes. "Why don't I give him a call? He might be more likely to look into it if two of us are pressing him, and I can be very persuasive. I'll call him as soon as you walk out the door."

"Thank you. Miss Barbara," I said in relief. "Can you let me know how it goes?"

"I will, but it might not be until tomorrow," she said, worry in her eyes. "I'd call you tonight, but I'll be heading out to Connie's sixtieth birthday party right after I get off the phone. Do you have plans tomorrow?"

"I'm probably going out to the Christmas tree farm early afternoon, but I'll have my phone with me. I think if *you* call too, Detective Taylor might take this more seriously."

"The important thing is justice for Amy." She pulled a tissue from her pocket and dabbed at her nose. "That poor girl never stood a chance."

I gave her a hug, then walked out the door. As I headed to my car, I cast a glance over at Amy's house, surprised there wasn't any crime scene tape on the door or around the house. Then again, Miss Barbara had seen Amy leave the house on

Tuesday morning, so she likely hadn't been killed there. Boomer must have been waiting down the road and intercepted her.

It wasn't up to me to figure out the logistics. I was sure Detective Taylor was competent and had been thorough in his investigation before arresting Amy's boyfriend. Mallory was right. I had to let this go and let the professionals handle it from here on out.

When I got back to the house, I was hit with the delicious smell of the bourbon cake. I slipped off my coat, hung it on the coat tree, then cut through the living room to the kitchen.

Aunt Deidre was perched on the edge of the sofa, working on a jigsaw puzzle on the coffee table. She didn't glance up when I walked past her. I gave her a long look as I started through the dining room, which was why I was greeted with a surprise when I glanced up.

A bouquet sat in the middle of the dining room table—a huge arrangement of white tulips, calla lilies, eucalyptus, pinecones, and other greenery shoved into a crystal vase I didn't recognize. The whole thing must have cost a fortune.

"Aww..." Mallory said sarcastically, leaning against the doorway to the kitchen. "You found the flowers. They're so small they're hard to spot. It's like a *Where's Waldo?* game."

I snorted. "Did your boss send them to try to win you back?"

She released a short laugh. "Uh, *no*. She has no idea where I am, and even if she did, she's more likely to dance around a pentagram and give thanks to Beelzebub or whoever she prays to." Her brow rose playfully. "They're for you."

"Me? Who on earth sent me..." But then I knew.

Dammit.

I snatched the card from the bouquet and read the hand-written message.

I'm sorry, Mads. Truly, I am. I love you, and the thought of living without you is so unbearable it made me crazy. Please forgive me and say yes. We'll be so happy together.

Love, Steve

I looked up at Mallory. "I take it you read the card."

"Well, of course," she said as though it was the most ridiculous question she'd ever heard. "You're not falling for his bullshit, are you?"

I groaned. "Please..."

"Don't *please* me," she said bluntly. "Last summer, you would have eaten this shit up."

That was embarrassing because it was true. "Blame it on inertia. I had to have some reason to propel me out of that relationship, and I found it with Aunt Deidre. I can't go back to Nashville, and he's not moving here."

"You can go back when Aunt Deidre's no longer able to live at home." She cast a glance toward the living room and lowered her voice. "Honestly, Maddie, I think that's going to happen sooner than either one of us had planned."

I swallowed the lump forming in my throat. "I know."

"Which means you'll be free to move back to Nashville. You could come visit her on weekends."

"I can't leave her," I said, starting to get pissed. "Even if she goes into a home, I'll still stay here to take care of her."

"I don't see why you couldn't move back. Honestly, Mads. She's worse than when I was here a month ago, and if she keeps declining at this rate, she won't know if you were last with her the day before or the month before. That is, if she knows you at all."

She was right, but I couldn't bring myself to verbally acknowledge it.

"All I'm saying," she continued, "is that you won't be stuck here. Which means you *could* go back to Nashville."

And *back to Steve* was unsaid but implied. She was testing me.

My back straightened. "Even if I go back to Nashville, I'm not going back to Steve, Mallory. I always knew he was a narcissist, but I swear he seems worse than he was before."

"Maybe," she said, "but I think you just didn't notice the changes. He got worse little by little, so it was hard to see how bad it had gotten." She gave me a pleading look. "Don't go back to him, okay? No matter what he promises."

I cringed. "I'm humiliated that you think I would go back to him at all, which tells me what an idiot I was." I lifted my chin. "You don't need to worry. I won't be going back to him, and if he keeps popping up out of nowhere, I'll file a restraining order."

She waggled her eyebrows. "And maybe you can get one of those handsome men in law enforcement to be your bodyguard."

I groaned. "Mallory..."

"Just sayin'," she said, pushing away from the doorjamb. "Now let's go finish off that bottle of wine you were about to open earlier."

"Finish?"

"I may have started without you. And speaking of alcohol, how do you feel about having bourbon cake for dinner?"

"We *do* have leftover lasagna, you know," I said in a dry tone.

"I know, but it feels like a boozy kind of night."

I couldn't argue with that.

Chapter Thirty

Noah

Lance sat across from me in our usual booth at Lucky's. It was seven o'clock on a Friday night, and we were drinking beer and eating chicken wings. Things could be worse, but they could also have been a hell of a lot better.

Lance finished tapping on his phone, then set it down. "Brent's on his way over."

"Brent Taylor?" I asked in surprise.

"How many Brents do you know here?"

"He's the only one, I guess."

"Exactly."

I narrowed my eyes. "But what are *you* doing texting him, and why is he coming over?"

"Because I invited him to come celebrate the arrest of Amy's murderer. This way, we can get some details, and maybe his good luck will rub off on us."

I *did* want the details, for curiosity's sake. Maddie would want to know more too, but I wouldn't be the one telling her. No, I'd walked out of her life for good last night. A fact I'd need to remind myself of frequently, in all likelihood.

Maddie Baker was no longer my concern nor my responsibility. I needed to let her go.

I needed to focus on my own damn case.

After the van was hauled away, we'd arranged for the crime lab to go through the wreckage and check for fingerprints. But that was bound to take a few days or more, which meant we were at a standstill. We'd gone around to the local pawn shops and asked if the name George rang any bells and struck out at every location. No luck from our calls to the pawn shops in Lynchburg either. Which meant the only thing we could do was wait for the burglars to strike again. Something that didn't sit right with me.

"At least they haven't hit another house yet," Lance said as though reading my mind. Which probably wasn't all that hard, actually. These robbery cases were pretty much all either one of us were thinking about right now. That is, when I wasn't thinking about Maddie.

"True. They might be stealing another van to use." I picked up a wing. "We should check whether any vans have been stolen in Chattanooga or Lynchburg in the last twenty-four hours, then run a BOLO if anything pops up that would work for their jobs."

"Good idea," he said. "I'll run something when we leave here."

I pinned him with a dark gaze. "You're on your second beer. You think you'll be up for that?"

"I'll get on it first thing in the morning then."

"I'll do it tonight," I said. "I'm only planning to have the one beer."

"Suit yourself," he said with a grin, then picked up another wing.

We were both mid-bite when Brent walked in and headed to our table.

I dropped my wing on my plate, picked up a paper towel, and wiped my hands as I got to my feet.

"Brent, glad you could drop by," I said, then lifted my greasy hand. "I'd offer my hand to shake, but..."

He laughed. "Hey, I'd say we've moved past handshakes and onto bro hugs, but I'm going to pass in this case. And because the information you gave me on the Amy Davis case helped speed up the process, I planned to buy you a beer in thanks. What are you drinking?"

I shook my head. "I'm sticking to one beer tonight. I'm going to do some work after I leave."

"A workaholic, huh?" he asked good-naturedly. "No wonder you're so damn good." He pointed to the bar. "I'm going to grab a drink of my own." He glanced over at Lance. "What are you having?"

"I'll get it," Lance said as he climbed out of his seat.

"I planned to buy you one too," Brent said.

Lance shook his head. "The first drink is on me as a celebration of closing your case so quickly."

"Don't let him fool you," I said dryly. "His mom owns the place."

A grin spread across Brent's face. "I think we need to become better friends, my man."

Lance grinned back. "That can be arranged."

They headed over to the bar together, and I couldn't help glancing at my phone. Did Maddie know about the arrest? Should I tell her? Or have Lance do it? She deserved to know. She *was* the first person to have worried about Amy and reported her missing.

Lance and Brent were back in under a minute, and Brent slid in next to Lance on his bench seat, both of them holding mugs of beer.

"Hey," I said, "Lance, you should text Maddie to let her know that Boomer was arrested."

"Maddie Baker?" Brent asked, then took a sip. "She already knows."

"How do you know?" I asked, my tone not quite as neutral as I'd meant it to be.

Lance gave me an odd look, but if Brent noticed, he didn't let on. "I talked to her this afternoon. I told her then."

"When you interviewed her?" I asked.

He took another pull, set down his mug, and reached for a wing in the basket. "No. I interviewed her this morning. She called me a little after three to say she'd heard that Amy Davis had saved up a couple thousand dollars to leave Boomer. She thought she might have had a second job somewhere."

My jaw clenched. "How in God's name did she find *that* out?"

"No idea," Brent said, taking a bite of the wing. "But I told her I'd let her know if I needed to take her statement about it."

"Why wait?" Lance asked.

"Because she wouldn't give her source," Brent said. "Which means it's worthless."

"She has a way of getting information and refusing to say where she got it," I said, remembering how she'd tried to protect the homeless man who'd witnessed Martin Schroeder's murder.

"It was good to have confirmation, though," he said. "We found a little over two thousand dollars stuffed up under the driver's seat of Amy Davis's car."

Lance's jaw dropped. "Say what?"

"Yep. We know she wasn't making that kind of bank at the grocery store because we can see that her paychecks were deposited in Jackson Garfield's bank account, and most of the money went to purchases made with a debit card. Jackson

Garfield's debit card. So that left us baffled about where she got the money."

"But you arrested Garfield for her murder," Lance said.

"And we still think he did it. The autopsy showed that she was not only strangled but also raped. Looks like she was redressed postmortem. Garfield told one of his coworkers that if Ms. Davis ever left him, he'd strangle her. Another guy overheard it. During his interview, Garfield denied saying it, but he changed his tune when we told him we'd spoken to two witnesses. Said he was joking. That, plus his history of domestic violence, and we're sure we have the right guy."

"What about the money?" I asked.

"We'll look into it," he said, wiping his hand on a paper towel. "It's highly doubtful she obtained it by legal means, but there was no evidence of where she might have gotten it in the things she left behind at the house." He leaned his head closer. "But here's an interesting tidbit—Garfield reported a break-in at the house on Monday night."

"Monday night?" I asked, sure I'd heard wrong.

"Yep. A deputy went out and took a report. Garfield claims a TV was missing, but it doesn't look like much else was taken. Place just got ransacked."

I gave Lance a questioning look. "Ransacked? Anything else out of the ordinary?"

"I talked to the deputy who took the report. He said there were clothes everywhere in the bedrooms, but he didn't think that was out of the ordinary. He said it looked like they lived like pigs."

"Maddie said Amy kept the house clean," I countered. "And she was last seen on Tuesday morning, which means she would still have been living there on Monday night."

Brent narrowed his gaze on me. "You don't say."

"As you know, we're working a string of burglaries," I said.

"Up until Tuesday, the burglars were neat and tidy. Break in, take the shit, and leave. Other than the missing items and a broken back door, you would never have known they were there."

"And what happened on Tuesday?" Brent asked, turning serious as he put down his wing.

"The burglarized house on Tuesday morning was trashed, and a Polaroid photo of the man groping his dick through his underwear was left on the master bedroom bed. On top of a pile of women's underwear. He drew a heart on the bathroom mirror."

Brent wiped his hands on a paper towel before digging his phone out of his pocket. "I'm calling Duane now. He was the responding deputy. We'll get the story straight from him." He dialed a number, then looked around. We were alone in our corner, so he put the phone on speaker and set it in the middle of the table.

"Pittman," a man said when he answered.

"Hey, Duane, this is Brent. I'm on speaker with Detective Noah Langley from the Cockamamie PD and his partner, Officer Lance Forrester. They've been working a string of burglaries, and they think the one on Harrington Road Monday night might fit with their perp's MO."

"The one with the guy you arrested for murdering his girlfriend? Do they think those robberies are tied to her murder?"

Lance gave me a wide-eyed stare.

"No," I said. "I don't think so." I ran over the cases in my head. The first case to escalate was on Tuesday, after Maddie talked to Amy in class, but before Amy had left her house that morning. "Amy was last seen on Tuesday morning by a neighbor, leaving her house."

"Garfield swears Ms. Davis didn't come home on Monday night," Brent said, "but the neighbor and her friend both say they saw her leave on Tuesday morning. Ms. Johnson said she spoke to her, and her friend verified that she passed her car as it was pulling out of the driveway."

"This is Officer Forrester," Lance said, leaning toward the phone. "What time did you show up at the Garfield house on Monday night?"

"About six-thirty," Pittman said. "The homeowner said he came home and found the place trashed."

"And how long did you stay?" Lance asked.

"About an hour, tops. I wrote down the inventory of what was missing—which wasn't much. A couple of TVs and an iPad. I took a few photos, then left."

"So you were gone by seven-thirty?" Lance asked.

"Let me look at the report to be sure." He paused for a long moment, then said, "I left at 7:37."

"And who was there?" Lance asked. "One or both Garfield cousins?"

"Jackson Garfield placed the 911 call," he said, "and his cousin Jake Garfield showed up sometime after I got there. About halfway through."

"So around seven," I said.

"Yeah, I guess so."

"Amy was at the self-defense class at seven," Lance said. "She wouldn't have come home until after eight."

"Do you remember anything peculiar?" I asked. "Any Polaroids left behind by the burglars or hearts drawn on the mirror?"

Pittman laughed. "Are your burglars stupid enough to leave photos behind?"

"They're not showing their faces, if you know what I mean."

"Oh, shit."

I shifted in my seat. "Brent said that you mentioned there were clothes everywhere. Did you notice anything unusual about Amy's clothes? In the last two break-ins, the female home-owner's underwear was left piled in the middle of the bed."

He was silent for a moment. "I don't remember seeing any women's underwear. They might have been there, but I don't remember. And I know I didn't take any photos of the beds. Sorry."

"Yeah, no problem. It wasn't an issue in our previous burglaries, and without the photo on top of them, we likely wouldn't have thought much of it either," I said. "But thanks, this is helpful."

"You think it was the same crew hitting your houses?" Pittman asked.

"I don't know," I admitted. "It doesn't totally fit the pattern, but I'm not willing to rule it out."

"I can send over what I have on the case tomorrow, if you want."

"Yeah," I said. "That would be great."

"If you need anything else, feel free to let me know," he said, then hung up.

"You're building bridges, Noah," Brent said thoughtfully, as he picked up his phone and put it back in his pocket. "Most deputies think Cockamamie PD is synonymous with horse shit, but word's gotten out about you. Pittman was more than willing to work with you because of it."

"I never got the fighting between departments thing," I said, shrugging it off. "We're here to serve the community, and criminals often don't pay attention to jurisdiction lines. It only makes sense to have a friendly relationship with neighboring forces. It makes it easier to work together."

Brent sat back in his seat. "Speaking of friendly..." He glanced at Lance, then back at me. "You two seemed to have gotten pretty friendly with Maddie Baker during the Schroeder murder case."

A knot formed between my shoulder blades, but I tried to play it cool. "What makes you say that?"

"She called you two when she was worried about Amy Davis. And you wanted to be the one to tell her Ms. Davis had been murdered." He paused. "You just seem on friendlier terms than most witnesses from cases."

"You're right," Lance said, "Noah and Maddie really—"

"We're friends," I said.

A hopeful look filled Brent's eyes. "So there's nothing between you? Because I got the feeling that maybe..."

"Nope," I said. "Nothing."

His eyes lit up. "So you won't mind if I ask her out?"

It was hard to breathe, but I forced a smile. I needed to let her go, and what better way to do that than to help her find someone else? "Go for it. She's an amazing woman." Then I added, "Just know she's got a lot on her plate, so she needs a stand-up guy, Brent."

Lance gave me a look of disbelief, but quickly wiped it off his face. "We think the world of Maddie, so be forewarned. If you break her heart, I'll be forced to break your face."

Brent laughed. "Let's not get ahead of ourselves. I'm just trying to get her to let me haul a Christmas tree home from the tree farm for her."

"She needs help getting a Christmas tree home?" I asked, then remembered I wasn't supposed to care about things like that anymore.

Was I really going to stand back and give him my blessing to take her out?

Yeah. I was. Because Maddie deserved someone who would be good to her, and I was pretty sure Brent filled the bill.

"I changed my mind," I said as I got out of my seat, ignoring the hopeful look in Lance's eyes. "I think I need another beer after all."

Lance's face fell, and I had the sinking feeling he was disappointed in me.

I headed off the bar, really needing that second beer. Honestly, I suspected I was going to need more than one more. But there likely wasn't enough beer in the world to make any of this okay.

That was just too fucking bad.

Chapter Thirty-One

Maddie

"Why won't you call him?" Mallory pleaded as we pulled into the Christmas tree farm parking lot the next afternoon. "You said he was cute."

"Doesn't calling a man to help us haul our Christmas tree home detract from us being strong, independent women?"

"Trust me, if you knew a woman with a pickup truck, I'd be open to calling her too. But you don't, and you also need a distraction from Detective Asshat."

I groaned. After Aunt Deidre went to bed last night, and Mallory and I were halfway through our second bottle of wine, I'd told her about my conversation with Noah. Everything, including our hot kiss, but I'd also told her that we were done.

Not that anything had ever really happened in the first place.

"You need to get back up on that saddle, Mads," she'd said, which I might have taken more seriously if she hadn't spilled some of her wine into her lap.

The gravel parking lot was full of trucks, vans, and a few cars, making it obvious that most people had come prepared to take home a tree.

I pulled into a space and turned off the car.

"Detective *Langley*," I said, giving Mallory a hard stare, "didn't do anything wrong. He never promised me anything, and he was honest about what he wants and doesn't want. He could have slept with me for a few months before breaking it to me, but he knew it was important to me to have a family and didn't want to hurt me later. Honestly, I wish more men would be so up front. And besides," I added, "I was the one who kissed *him*."

"I guess," she grumbled.

"And sure, if the right guy came along, I'd be open to going out with him, but Detective Taylor offered to bring home my tree at the end of a police interview. Not exactly great timing."

"Okay," she conceded. "So his timing was off..."

"Drop it, Mal. Let's just go pick out a tree, strap it to the top of my car, and head home."

"You're a fun killer, you know that?" she demanded, pulling a stocking cap on her head before she opened the door.

I got out and wrapped my scarf tighter around my neck. It was unusually cold for southern Tennessee, but Aunt Deidre had mentioned the tree again at breakfast this morning. "Not a short squatty tree," she'd said adamantly. "Something that nearly reaches the ceiling."

Given that the main floor had twelve-foot ceilings, that was going to be a challenge.

Still, it wasn't like it was her dementia making the request. She'd always had full, tall trees. I couldn't let her down this year. Not when it would be the first holiday she'd be spending without Uncle Albert in decades. I was determined to give her the best Christmas ever, which meant I'd get her a ten-foot tree, even if I had to go to Chattanooga to do it.

Mallory and I started walking toward the small grouping of

cut trees. "Um, Mads, I don't think they have a big enough tree for Aunt Deidre's wishes."

She was right. Most of them looked like they were six feet or below.

"Crap," I muttered under my breath. "Let's go ask."

There were a few people examining the prechopped trees, but most people seemed to be renting axes and saws, then heading up the hill to a grove of pine trees.

"There's a guy who looks like he works here," Mallory said, pointing to a man in a brown work jacket and jeans. His back was to us, but he was putting a tree on top of a family's car. "Let's ask him."

"Yeah," I said absently. I could see there really weren't any cut trees that would meet our criteria, but I'd never chopped down a tree before, and I was pretty certain Mallory hadn't either. Even if we somehow managed to cut down a tree, we'd have to drag it back here to pay for it, not to mention get it on top of my car.

This seemed impossible.

"Excuse me," I heard Mallory say behind me. "Do you have any precut ten-foot trees?"

"Sure don't," a familiar male voice said, but I couldn't quite place it. "We don't have many precut trees that size, but when we do, they go quick. If you're really wanting a ten-footer, I'd suggest you head up to quadrant four. There's some nice big ones out there."

"Chop it down ourselves?" Mallory asked in disgust.

I turned around to join the conversation, stopping in my tracks when I saw she was talking to Jake Garfield.

Oh. Shit.

He narrowed his eyes when he saw me, as though trying to place me, then his eyes widened with recognition. "Oh. It's you." He turned to Mallory. "You're the cousin, right?"

"What?" Mallory asked in confusion.

"Sorry we never showed last night," Jake said, scrubbing the top of his head. "My own cousin...well, let's just say he had something he couldn't get out of."

More like some*place* he couldn't get out of, like the Wayfare County Jail.

"Do you know him?" Mallory asked me, looking hopeful, but I cut her off before she could ask more.

"We just met a few days ago at the auto parts store, and he invited the two of us to meet him and his cousin at Cock on the Walk last night." I held her gaze to make sure she knew not to question me in front of him. Then I turned back to Jake. "We didn't make it ourselves. We had an issue pop up with our aunt."

"Sorry to hear that," he said. "And now you're cutting down a tree?"

"We'd hoped it would already be cut," I said. "I'm surprised to see you working here. You're pulling two jobs?" Honestly, he didn't seem the type.

He gestured to the woods behind him. "My buddy's family bought the place, and I help out on weekends." He grinned. "Cash, under the table. Know what I mean?"

"Smart," I said. "So what happened with your cousin?"

Jake looked uncomfortable, stroking his beard and glancing down at the ground. "He ran into a bit of legal trouble, but he's sure to get out of it soon. We're coming up with an alibi for him."

Alibi? Mallory mouthed at me with wide eyes.

"That really sucks," I said, ignoring her. "Are you gonna have any trouble coming up with one?"

"Maybe? I mean, he was installing garage doors all day, but he didn't have his phone with him, so they can't track his location for most of the day. But his deliveries were all on time."

"So you're saying he didn't do what they accused him of doing," I said with a sly smile.

Mallory gave me a look that suggested I'd lost my mind. I supposed I had. But Jake was freely talking about Boomer, and I wanted his take on the situation.

He made a face. "Honestly, Boomer can be a mean son-of-a-bitch, but he really needed that job. I can't see him risking it by doing something as unhinged as what they accused him of. He'd be sure to get fired, and he really likes his job."

Mallory's eyes had opened so wide, I thought her eyeballs might be in danger of falling out of her head. Boomer wasn't that common of a name, and she was no fool. She'd connected the dots.

Me? I was trying not to choke on Jake's insinuation that Boomer was capable of murdering his girlfriend, but likely wouldn't have during work hours for fear of losing his job.

"Well," I said graciously. "I hope he gets out of his legal trouble soon."

"You and me both, but just because he's tied up doesn't mean you and me can't go out," he said with a sleezy grin. "No need for the cousins now."

"I don't know," I said. "I'm kind of busy with the holidays and all."

"Yeah, sure. You're here for a tree," he said, glancing up the hill. "Like I said earlier, your best bet for a nice ten-footer is to head up to quadrant four. I can get you a map and loan you a hatchet and a saw."

"Thanks," I said.

He headed to a shed and reached for the tools on the wall.

"Have you lost your mind?" Mallory hissed in my ear. "We can't stay here!"

"Why not?" I said grumpily. "We need a tree, and this is the only place in town to get one as big as Aunt Deidre wants."

"Maddie, his cousin is a murderer!" she whisper-shouted.

An older man walking past us shot us a strange look, and I grabbed her arm. "Mallory, keep your voice down. And it's not like *Jake* murdered anyone."

"The saying guilty by association was created for a reason, Maddie!"

"I'm staying," I said, digging my feet in, literally. "I'm not leaving without a tree, so are you with me or not?"

"It's kind of hard to say yes when the cousin of a murderer is walking toward us with an ax."

She had a point. Still, Jake wasn't stupid enough to murder anyone in front of witnesses, was he? Besides, Mallory was being silly. He had absolutely no reason to murder us.

Jake approached with a hatchet and small bow saw in one hand and a piece of paper in the other. Unless he planned on asking us to sign a consent form for our murder, I was fairly sure we were safe.

"I'm gonna need a driver's license to hold while you use the tools," he said.

I glanced at Mallory, who shot daggers at me.

She had a point. We might be staying, but I still wasn't ready to let him know who I was.

Offering him an apologetic smile, I said, "I'm sorry, I don't have one to give you."

He nodded, understanding filling his eyes. "You lost it, huh?"

"Something like that."

A grin spread across his face. "No worries, sweet thing, I understand. I just got my license back a few months ago. Gotta watch out for them Cockamamie cops, you know? They like to sit and wait for God-fearing citizens to leave bars and arrest 'em for DUIs."

Mallory started to protest, but I grabbed her arm to quiet her.

"You seem trustworthy to me," Jake said. "So I'm gonna let you just borrow the tools without the license. I made sure the hatchet's extra sharp." He winked as he handed it over.

I carefully took both the hatchet and saw from him. "Thanks."

"And here's a map to help you find quadrant four." He handed it to Mallory. "It's a hike up the hill, but it's pretty quiet up there. Not many people chop down the big ones. I'd go up and help you," he said, giving me another sleazy grin, "but I gotta stick around down here for a bit longer. But if you want to wait…" The insinuation was clear.

I made a face and took a step backward. "Thanks for the offer, but we need to get back to our aunt."

"I get it," he said. "Since I'm dealing with my own family issues."

"Yeah," I said, "dealing with such serious charges can't be easy."

He stared at me for a second, then said, "Yeah. I'll see you when you get back."

"Can't wait," Mallory said under her breath, as she turned to walk to the edge of the woods. We stopped to look at the hand-drawn map.

"How many miles away is this quadrant four?" Mallory asked.

"I don't think it's drawn to scale," I said, handing her the hatchet so I could get a better look at the map. I noticed all six sections were identified by lines topped with small triangles that looked like flags, so I gazed up the hill. Sure enough, there were several poles with small colored flags. The closer ones had numbers. I showed them to Mallory.

"Well, if that section to our left is two," she said, pointing, then raised her hand higher, "four would be above it."

"Okay, let's get going."

She glanced down at her two-inch ankle boots. "I didn't exactly wear the appropriate footwear for hiking."

"It's not hiking, Mal. It's more like walking through trees."

"Aka, *hiking*."

"Do you want to wait in the car?"

She crossed her arms over her chest while looking up the hill. "Give me a moment. I'm thinking."

I linked my arm with hers. "Come on. Let's go. Think of how happy Aunt Deidre will be."

"That's not fair."

"And it could be the last Christmas she remembers."

She gave me a dirty look. "That's *really* not fair."

"Tell you what," I said. "If we can't manage it ourselves, we can call Detective Taylor to come help."

Her face brightened. "Great! So why don't we call him now?"

"Because I want to at least *try* to do it ourselves." I highly suspected we'd be calling him, but I wasn't ready to admit defeat just yet.

"Fine," she grumbled, "but I'm telling you right now that I don't plan on dragging a tree down a mountain."

I gave her a tug. "Come on."

We found a path between the trees and started weaving up the hill. It wasn't a mountain, but it wasn't a small jut of earth either. By the time we reached the fourth quadrant, the trees were taller. There were plenty of stumps next to the path, and the remaining trees were misshapen. We'd have to keep walking to find something good.

I said as much, and she replied, "Wait," leaning over her legs and gulping air. "I'm obviously out of shape." She took in several more deep breaths before lifting her head to look down the hill. "Can we call Detective Hunky now?"

"Not yet," I said. "The hard part's done. Now we just have to chop down the tree, then drag it down the hill. The tree farm people will take over from there."

The expression on her face turned murderous. "You think the rest is easy? Come on, Mads. Quit being stubborn, and *call him*."

"We're strong, independent women who don't need men," I said cheerfully.

Her eyes narrowed. "I feel that it's only fair to warn you that if I had that ax right now, I'd throw it at you."

"Duly noted," I said in my cheerful tone. "Note to self: Don't let Mallory have the ax. But for the record, we can at least find the tree before we ask him to come. Now let's go."

We started walking horizontally along the tree line, stopping occasionally to check out a tree.

"Did you happen to bring a tape measure?" Mallory asked.

"No," I scoffed. "I'll just have you stand next to the tree and figure it out from there. I mean, you're five-five, so we want a little less than double your height, right?"

Her lip curled, and I could have sworn I heard her growl.

We continued until I found a tree that was the perfect shape and looked about ten feet tall.

"This is the one!" I announced. "It's perfect."

"Are you sure it's tall enough?" she asked dryly.

It was my turn to give her a dirty look.

She eyed it up and down, then walked around the base to examine the shape before she grudgingly admitted, "Fine. It's a good tree."

"Great! Let's chop it down."

"You know this is bad for the environment, right? Global

warming and all that shit. We need trees to recycle carbon dioxide."

I gave her a piercing look. "Perhaps you should have made that argument *before* we hiked up a mountain."

She pointed her finger at me. "Ah-ha! You *admitted* we hiked!"

"Fine," I groaned. "We hiked. Now stand to the side before I chop a tree down on you."

"Only if you buy me a new pair of boots if these are ruined."

"Fine," I repeated with more bite. "Now move aside before I kill you with a tree."

"*Please*...it's going to take you more than two seconds to chop that thing down."

She was right. After ten minutes and an initial notching with the hatchet before I used the saw, all I had was two very sore arms and a bunch of gouges in the tree trunk. Oh, and the saw was stuck.

"I'm not giving up," I grunted, sweat dripping down my forehead. I swiped it with the back of my hand.

She propped a hand on my foot, a disapproving look on her face. "*Now* can we call Detective—"

A loud crack filled the air, and something thunked into the tree behind us.

That sound was all too familiar.

Mallory stared at me, her jaw gaping, her eyes wide. I dove for her, tackling her to the ground just as another crack rang out. I didn't hear the bullet hit a tree, so I was hoping it had whizzed past us.

"Someone's *shooting at us?*" she screeched underneath me.

"Shh!"

"I can't shush when we're being shot at!"

I was pretty sure the gunshots were coming from the top of

the hill, so I got behind the tree next to ours and dragged Mallory behind me.

"It's that damn Jake!" Mallory whisper-shouted. "I told you he was going to murder us!"

"We don't know for sure it's him," I said, digging my phone out of my pocket and calling 911, worried she was right. But why?

"911, what's your emergency?" a woman answered.

"I'm at Christmas Tree Lane," I said breathlessly, "in quadrant four. I was chopping down a tree, and someone is shooting at me and my friend."

"Are you sure they're shooting at you?" she asked. "Christmas Tree Lane is close to a lot of private woods, and it's still deer season, not to mention raccoon and grouse."

Another shot rang out, and the tree to our right splintered.

Mallory released a shriek.

"No," I said, my voice shaking. "I'm really stinking sure a bullet hit the tree next to us."

"You can say fucking," Mallory said, gripping my coat sleeve. "If ever there was time for the word 'fucking,' it's *now*."

"Can you please send someone to help us?" I begged. "We're trapped behind a pine tree, and I have no idea if they're coming toward us or waiting us out."

"We're sending a unit now, ma'am," the woman said. "I can see that we just got another call that a person was seen on the top of the hill at Christmas Tree Lane, pointing a gun toward some trees."

"He's pointing it toward *us*!" I whisper-shouted.

"You need to send someone now!" Mallory demanded, snatching the phone from my hand, and shouting into the phone.

"Mallory!" I hissed as I tried to grab the phone from her hand, but it flew into the air.

Another gunshot sounded, followed by the sound of cracking glass.

"He shot my phone!" I said in disbelief.

"Do you know how good his aim must be if he managed to shoot your phone?" Mallory asked.

Holy shit, she was right.

"So what do we do now?" she asked. "Try to outrun him?"

"After he hit my phone? No. We wait for the sheriff to show up."

I only hoped we didn't have to wait long.

Chapter Thirty-Two

Noah

I was spending a rare Saturday afternoon at home, getting ready to watch a University of Tennessee football game on TV, when my phone rang. Lance's name appeared on the screen.

"Have you been listening to the scanner?" he asked, his voice tight.

I sat up in my chair. "No. I'm at home about to watch the UT game. Was there another break-in?"

"No. There's an active shooter at Christmas Tree Lane."

My heart slammed into my ribcage.

"Wasn't Maddie going out there today?" Lance asked, his voice tight.

I leaned forward, running a hand over my head. "Yeah, that's what Brent said. Maybe you should call her."

"I already did, Noah. It went straight to voicemail."

"That's county," I said, trying to catch my breath, but I was already out of my chair. "Not our jurisdiction. Try Brent. I'll call Maddie's home number."

"Let me know what you find out."

I hung up, pacing as I called Maddie's landline.

"Cabbage Rose House," a woman answered.

I recognized her voice. "Margarete? It's Noah."

"Detective Langley," she said, sounding pleased. "How lovely to hear from you."

"Is Maddie there? I *really* need to speak to her."

"Maddie and her friend Mallory are out for the afternoon. Did you try her cell?"

"Where did they go?" I asked. "This is important, Margarete."

"Nowhere dangerous," she said in confusion. "They went to get Deidre her Christmas tree."

"At Christmas Tree Lane?"

"Well, of course. They didn't want to drive to Lynchburg."

An overwhelming wave of fear swept over me, but I kept it together. "When she gets home, can you please have her call me? And if she refuses, can *you* do it? It's important."

"Should I be worried?" she asked, her voice tight.

"No, just let me know the moment she gets home."

I hung up, but I was already at my back door, shoving my feet into my shoes and grabbing my coat. Then I backtracked, ran to the gun safe in my room, and pulled out my service Glock before I headed out the back door and jumped into my car.

I called Lance as I backed out of the driveway. "Maddie's not home. She and her friend Mallory went out to Christmas Tree Lane to chop down a tree. I'm heading out there right now."

"I'm already on my way," Lance said. "I'll meet you there."

Chapter Thirty-Three

Maddie

I wasn't sure how long it had been since we'd first been shot at, but I was guessing it was no more than a minute. We hadn't heard any more shots after my phone was taken out in the not-so-fun game of skeet. I should have been relieved, but I was terrified the gunman was coming for us.

"Why aren't people screaming?" Mallory whispered. "Someone called 911 to report a gunman, so why aren't people screaming bloody murder?"

"I don't know," I admitted, wondering the same thing. "But the 911 operator said it's hunting season, and we're close to the woods where people hunt. Maybe they thought the gunshots were from a hunter."

"So do you think he's gone? He hasn't shot at us for a bit."

"I don't know," I said. "I'm going to see if he's still there."

Her eyes flew wide. "How are you going to—"

Before she could finish, I tore my scarf from my neck and tossed it up into the gap in the trees next to us.

Another gun blast went off.

"Fuck me," Mallory muttered under her breath.

Staying behind the tree, I tried to peer up between the

branches but could barely make out the tree above us. There had to be at least ten or more rows to the top.

"We can't just sit here," I said. I still hadn't heard sirens, and there was nothing to keep the gunman from coming down to get us. In fact, I wasn't sure why he hadn't tried already.

"You think we should run?" she asked in disbelief.

"I think *I* should run," I said. "He's probably here for me."

"*You?* Why you?"

"I don't know," I groaned. "Process of elimination? The only person who could want to murder you is your boss, and you already said she doesn't know where you went."

She shuddered. "Yeah, you're probably right."

"*I've* been asking questions about Amy. It makes sense he's after me."

She smacked my arm. "I *told* you it was Jake!" she whisper-shouted. "He followed us up the hill and is trying to kill us!"

"Maybe, but why would he go to the top of the hill to shoot us when it would be easier to shoot us from below?"

"I don't know!" she whisper-shouted. "Do I *look* like a criminal mastermind to you?"

"Does *Jake?*" I asked in disbelief.

She lifted her hands in defeat. "Maybe he was worried we'd roll down the hill and tackle him."

A branch snapped above us, and Mallory released a small squeak.

I put my hand over her mouth and mouthed, *I'm running that way.* I pointed away from the shed below us.

She shook her head wildly.

I nodded yes, terrified we were running out of time. Leaning into her ear, I whispered, "Give me five seconds. Then you run toward the other quadrant. Head down to the shed."

She shook her head again.

I gave her a quick hug, then grabbed a small rock under the

tree, throwing it up the hill toward the next tree line. It hit a tree branch, and a gunshot went off. I bolted for the tree I'd partially cut down.

No gunshot.

I dug around under the tree and found another rock, throwing it up the hill and hitting another tree before I darted for shelter. Another gunshot rang out, hitting the tree above me.

It was working, but I could hear more tree branches breaking overhead, so I took off running toward quadrant six and away from the shed. I cut down to the line of trees below me.

A gunshot went off, but it hit a tree above me, which meant the shooter didn't have a clear shot at me.

I kept running, hoping Mallory had gotten away to safety.

As I darted to the next tree line beneath me, I finally heard sirens in the distance. Maybe that would scare the gunman away.

Another bullet hit a tree closer to me.

Or maybe not.

I kept zigzagging, running down the hill between trees, and we were starting to hit the more populated section of shorter trees with families dressed in holiday attire out chopping down their Christmas trees. When they saw me running—and heard the gunshots following me—they took off running too.

I started running horizontally, trying to move away from the families.

People were now screaming—which must have made Mallory happy—as they fled toward the parking lot and the tool shed.

The sirens were closer now, and as I ran between trees, I could see deputy cars pulling into the parking lot. I started angling toward the far corner of the quadrant, down to the parking lot, but the trees were sparser here, making me vulnerable. Several more shots rang out, one narrowly missing me.

A dark sedan sped to the far corner of the lot. It skidded to a halt, facing the trees. The driver got out, crouched behind the driver's door, and pointed a handgun out from behind it. A male voice shouted, "Get down on the ground!"

I wasn't sure if he was talking to me, but he was pointing a gun in my direction, so I dove to the ground toward a nearby tree, hoping to God I could trust the officer. I covered my head as gunshots rang out from both directions.

The shots stopped, but I kept my head buried, terrified to move, since it had sounded like the bullets had whizzed near me.

Footsteps pounded the ground, coming toward me from the parking lot. Someone kneeled beside me, and a familiar voice said, "It's okay. You're safe." Gentle hands pulled me off the ground, and as I got to my feet, I found myself staring into the concerned gaze of Detective Brent Taylor.

His eyes widened in surprise. "Maddie!" He took a moment, then gave me a wry smile. "I guess you needed help at the Christmas tree lot after all."

Chapter Thirty-Four

Maddie

I let him help me to my feet, then turned toward the sound of shouting in the woods. At least half a dozen deputies were running toward the forest.

Detective Taylor wrapped an arm around my back and guided me down the hill toward his car. "Let's get you out of the line of fire."

I didn't argue with him, just let him usher me to the passenger side of his car. Then he hurried over to his side. More deputies were running into the woods as he backed up and drove over to the tool shack.

"What happened?" he asked, casting a worried glance at me.

"Mallory and I were chopping down a tree, and someone started shooting at us."

"Just you two? No one else?"

I shook my head, starting to shake as my adrenaline crashed.

"Do you know why they would shoot at you?" he asked.

"No, but it might be Jake Garfield." I gasped, covering my mouth with my hand. "Oh my word. *Mallory!* I have to make sure she's safe! The last time I saw her was when I was trying to lead the gunman away from her."

"You did *what*?"

"I figured he was after me, not Mallory. I owed it to her, especially since she didn't want to hike up the hill, and she wanted to leave after we ran into Jake."

"You know Jake Garfield?"

"It's a long story."

"A long story I want to know more about, but first I think we should focus on finding your friend."

Several people were huddled together behind the tool shack, and more were in a group at the back of the parking lot. Sheriff's cars blocked the exit, and several more were in the parking lot, their lights flashing.

Mallory was in the group behind the shed. As soon as Detective Taylor pulled his car to a halt, I opened the door and raced toward her. Detective Taylor shouted after me, but I ignored him.

"Mallory!"

She turned to me, relief washing over her face. "Maddie!"

I practically threw myself at her, pulling her into a bear hug when I reached her. "Are you okay?"

"I'm the one who should be asking *you*!" she cried out, holding me at arm's length and looking me over. "I was scared to death! Are you okay? Did he shoot you?"

"I'm okay," I said, watching as Detective Taylor approached us. "Detective Taylor showed up and scared him off."

Mallory stopped in her tracks. "*That's* Detective Taylor?"

I turned to look at him, seeing him with new eyes. Sure, I'd thought he was good looking before, but honestly, that was selling him short. He was tall, with thick dark hair and dark brown eyes. He was the walking definition of tall, dark, and handsome, and it didn't hurt that his jeans clung to his hips, and the dark blue jacket framed his broad shoulders. He walked with a confidence that caught me off guard. But I couldn't help comparing him to Noah.

Noah doesn't want you, you fool.

That wasn't exactly true. He wanted me. He just didn't want the same future I did.

Still, comparing anyone to Noah was pointless. Noah wasn't an option. But that didn't mean I was ready to date someone else.

"Mallory, I presume?" Detective Taylor asked her.

She seemed surprised he knew who she was. "Yeah…"

"Good to see that you're safe. Maddie was worried about you." His gaze scanned the group of a dozen people, including several children. A few of the women and children were crying. "Is everyone okay? Anyone hurt?"

Everyone began speaking at once, but I got the impression no one was hurt other than a woman with a twisted ankle. Everyone had just been terrified, with the exception of one man who was pissed at his wife for making him leave his concealed handgun at home.

"Did you catch the bastard?" one of the men asked, his hands fisted at his sides.

"There are deputies out after the shooter now," Detective Taylor assured him.

He glanced up the hill in the direction the gunman had run. "I think it's safe enough to get you all to the back of the lot, behind the deputies' patrol cars. You ready to move?"

After they all affirmed that they were, Detective Taylor rounded us up and steered us toward the larger group. He followed behind, walking backward with his gun drawn. His gaze scanned the hill, looking for threats.

"Where's Jake?" I asked Mallory under my breath.

"You think I'd be standing at the shack if Jake had been

there?" she demanded. "He wasn't around when I got there. And before you start worrying," she continued, "I don't think anyone else got hurt. The people I was with think there was only one gunman, and he followed you."

"You didn't see Jake Garfield leave?" Detective Taylor asked, obviously paying attention to our conversation even though he wasn't looking at us.

"No," Mallory said, glancing over her shoulder at him. "I bet he left soon after we headed up the hill. He left to *shoot* at us."

Several people in our group gasped in shock.

"The shooter is someone who works here?" a woman asked in horror.

"We haven't IDed the shooter," Detective Taylor said, darting a glance over his shoulder to see how close we were to the deputy cars. "Did anyone get a good enough glimpse of them to give a description?"

A murmur of nos spread through the group. "Not close up, anyway," a woman said. "We could only see a dark figure on the hill."

Detective Taylor led us to the other side of the deputies's cars and told everyone to stick around so they could give statements, then helped the woman with the sprained ankle to a waiting ambulance.

My legs began to shake. I pulled away from Mallory and walked over to the drainage ditch next to the road, then quickly sat down before I fell over, and rested my face in my hands.

A few moments later, Detective Taylor kneeled next to me and put a hand on my shoulder. "Maddie, are you okay?"

"Yeah," I said, my face still in my hands. "I just need a moment to catch my breath."

"You wait here. I'm going to see if they caught the gunman. Then I'll be back to ask you a few questions."

"It won't take long for me to answer," I said, looking up at him. "I never saw the person. I only knew we were being shot at."

"I never saw him either," Mallory said, sitting next to me and starting to rub my back.

I held the detective's gaze. "But *you* did, didn't you?"

A hard look filled his eyes. "I got a look at him, but not a good one. He was wearing dark jeans and a dark hoodie that covered his face."

"So you can't know for certain that it was Jake?" Mallory asked.

"No," he said. "But I'm sure the deputies have caught whoever it was."

He walked away to check on them, but when he came back about five minutes later, he looked grim.

"He got away," I said, feeling defeated.

"They lost him in the woods. But we've got air support coming in to look for him, as well as deputies stationed at all access points. He's got to come out of the woods at some point, and we'll catch him when he does." He looked down at me. "Other than Jake, is there anyone who could possibly want to kill you?"

"Yeah," Mallory said with a huff. "Possibly her ex-boyfriend."

I spun to look at her. "*What?*"

"Come on, Mads. He's acting weird as fuck."

"Language," a woman snapped. Two small children stood in front of her, and she'd covered their ears—well, one on either side—with her hands.

"Sorry," Mallory said apologetically, then turned back to me. "But that doesn't make it any less true."

"Weird how?" Detective Taylor asked, his jaw set.

Mallory got to her feet. "Maddie left him at the end of August and moved here from Nashville to take care of her aunt.

He let her go without a fuss, then dropped into town a few days ago and instantly proposed. Like out of nowhere."

Detective Taylor turned to me. "I take it you turned him down since you think he might be trying to kill you."

I stood and held up my hands. "*I* never said I thought he was trying to kill me. That was all Mallory."

She propped her hands on her hips in frustration. "You *know* he came on super strong and made some weird statements about getting you back *no matter what*."

"Small problem with that theory," I said sarcastically. "He can't get me back if I'm *dead*."

"No," Detective Taylor said, "but if he believes you truly won't go back to him, then he might want to make sure that if he can't have you, no one can."

I stared at him in disbelief. "No. Steve's a lot of things, but he's not a murderer."

"*Attempted* murderer," Detective Taylor said. "I think we should head down to the station, and you can tell me more about Steve and why you think Jake Garfield might want to murder you."

"I don't think either one of them tried to murder me," I insisted.

I really didn't want to go to the sheriff's station, but I knew it was better than talking here, and it seemed too complicated to discuss all of this in his car. "Okay," I said. "Let's go."

Chapter Thirty-Five

Noah

I raced through town and out to Christmas Tree Lane. When I arrived, I pulled onto the side of the road, parking behind a long line of sheriff's patrol cars. I jumped out and raced for the parking lot, where a group of people had gathered, surrounded by several deputies.

A deputy tried to block me from entering the parking lot, but I held up my badge. "Detective Noah Langley with the Cockamamie Police."

The deputy waved me through. "Last I heard, the gunman was still at large."

"How many casualties?" I asked.

"I haven't heard."

I jogged past him, moving toward the crowd. "Maddie!" I called out. "Maddie Baker!'

I got a lot of odd looks, but one woman pushed her way toward me.

"You're looking for Maddie?"

"Yes," I said. "Is she here?"

She narrowed her eyes as she glared up at me. "Who's asking?"

I pulled out my badge. "Detective Noah Langley." I stuffed it back in my pocket, then asked more insistently, "Is she here?"

She pursed her lips and looked me up and down. "Okay. I get it now."

"I'm sorry," I said. "Do you know Maddie?"

She gave me a sassy look. "I know her better than just about anyone else."

I felt myself relaxing and couldn't help but smile a bit. "You must be Mallory." If she wasn't freaking out, then Maddie must be okay.

"And you're Detective Americano or Detective Asshat."

I grimaced. "I'm not sure who you're comparing me to, but I'm hoping I'm Detective Americano." At least, that was what Chrissy called me.

"Oh, no," she said, waving her hand in dismissal. "You misunderstood. You're *both*. The one I prefer changes depending on my mood."

Seeing how she was Maddie's best friend, I supposed I deserved that. I glanced around, still not seeing Maddie. "Where is she, Mallory?"

She lifted her chin. "Detective Taylor has it under control."

"She's with Detective Taylor?"

"Oh, so you're *slowwww*," she said, drawing out the word. "Yes, Maddie is in Detective Taylor's *very* capable hands."

"Why is she with him?" That asshole didn't waste any time, but then again, he'd mentioned helping her with her tree. But Mallory was here, so it couldn't be a date...right?

"Jealous, much?" she asked flippantly.

I was, but I wasn't about to admit it. "Look," I said in frustration. "I'm just trying to make sure she's okay. I realize she's with Detective Taylor, but where exactly are they?"

"The sheriff's station."

My breath stuck in my chest for a moment. "Is she in trouble?"

"Only if you consider getting shot at as trouble."

Shit. So she *was* the target. I drew in a deep breath. "Look. I'm going to need you to tell me exactly what happened."

"What *didn't* happen?" she exclaimed in exasperation. "When we got here, they didn't have any precut ten-foot trees, and Aunt Deidre *insisted* the tree had to nearly touch the ceiling, so Maddie decided we needed to chop one down, despite the fact I begged her to call that hot detective who offered his services. But it turned out Boomer's cousin Jake is working here. I wanted to leave, since I didn't feel like getting murdered today, but Maddie insisted that he's not a murderer just because his cousin might be. But then we got to the top of the mountain—"

My gaze darted to the tall hill, ignoring her comment about the hot detective even though it stuck in my craw.

"Okay," she said grudgingly, "it's a hill. But it sure as hell wasn't easy in these boots." She pointed to her muddy feet. "In any case, Maddie got her tree halfway cut down, and the next thing we knew, someone started shooting at us."

"Randomly shooting?"

"No, I mean shooting at *us*. Or more accurately, at Maddie. She got this crazy idea that she could save me if she took off on her own, and sure enough, the shooter followed her all the way down the friggin' hill."

"What in the hell was she doing running down the hill?" I demanded.

"She was sure the shooter was going to come down and get us since he kept missing from the top, and the sheriff's department hadn't shown up yet. She didn't want to wait for him to come get her. Anyway, after she took off, I ran down to the shed, and sure as shit, Jake wasn't down here."

"Did you see the shooter?"

"No, and Maddie didn't either. We couldn't see him when he was at the top, and she said she never looked back when she was running down. Then Detective Taylor drove up like a badass, and he started shooting at the guy. The guy got away, though, and the deputies ran after him in the woods. They didn't get him."

I narrowed my eyes. "So why is Maddie at the sheriff's station?"

"Because Detective Hunky is trying to figure out who might have it in for her. So far, the suspects are Jake and Steve."

I ignored her nickname for Brent and focused on her second suspect. "Her *ex* Steve?"

"One and the same. He's turned out to be a stalker who refuses to take no for an answer. He even put down non-refundable deposits for their nonexistent January wedding."

I scowled. I'd definitely be looking into Steve some more. But then I realized that, while Maddie was gone, Mallory was still here. "Do you have a ride home?"

My question caught her by surprise. "Look at you being gallant and all. You actually earned a few brownie points for that. But don't worry. I have Maddie's car keys."

I pulled a card from my pocket and handed it to her. "If you need me for anything—even if it's just a ride—call me."

She took it and looked it over, then stuck it in her pocket instead of spitting on it and stomping it into the ground. "Thanks, Detective Asshat." While still a dig, the name carried more appreciation than it had before.

I left her and headed toward the woods, up into where multiple deputies had gathered. They'd already started setting up a perimeter with evidence tape. When I reached the deputy running the crime sheet log, I flashed my badge, signed in, and looked for the detective in charge.

Brent's partner, Tripp Donahue, was standing next to a pine

tree that had a bow saw jammed into it. "Hey, Noah," Tripp said as he looked up. "What brings you out here?"

"I heard about the shooting and headed over." I glanced around. "I don't see Brent."

"He's over at the station interviewing the intended victim."

"So you don't think this was random?"

"Nope, which I guess is a good thing since we don't have a would-be mass shooting on our hands, but not so good for the intended victim."

"And no idea who did it yet?" I asked.

"That's what Brent's hoping to find out."

There were already evidence labels planted on the ground. One was next to a forest-green scarf I immediately recognized as Maddie's.

I felt like I was going to throw up.

I took a couple of breaths through my mouth, and my stomach settled. "The shooter was up at the top of the hill?"

"According to eyewitnesses," he said. "I've got a couple deputies up there looking for shell casings as we speak."

I let my gaze drift back to the top of the hill as I tried to piece this together. Who in the hell wanted Maddie dead?

He shot me a speculative look. "You think this might be tied to your break-ins?"

I started to say no, then stopped.

Maddie had followed the van.

What if this wasn't tied to Steve or Jake—which had seemed like a stretch in the first place—but *was* tied to the break-ins? What if the burglars had somehow gotten her license number too and had come after her?

The only question was why? She was no further threat to them. Could it be for revenge?

"So you think it *could* be related," Tripp said. "I've seen that look on Brent's face when he starts putting something together."

I told him about Maddie's run-in with the van.

"You really think they'd try to shoot her for revenge?" he asked, his brow furrowed. "And in such a public place? Why not shoot her outside her house when she's walking out to get in her car?"

"I don't know," I admitted. "It's unlikely, but it's a theory, and theories are all we have to go on right now. *Still,* whoever's breaking in is starting to become unhinged. They were forced to dump the van after Maddie followed them, which had to be an inconvenience. If they have anger issues, they might have wanted to take out their frustration on the person who caused their inconvenience."

"We need to tell Brent," Tripp said.

"I'm headed to the sheriff's station now," I said, then started down the hill.

"Thanks for the lead," Tripp called after me. I lifted a hand in acknowledgment.

But as I headed toward the path, a flash of green caught my eye. Maddie's scarf. It would kill her to know her mom's scarf would be put in an evidence bag, and who knew for how long. Maybe it wouldn't be pertinent to the case. I'd be sure to let Brent know how important it was to her.

When I reached the bottom of the hill, Lance was walking toward me with his hands stuffed in his pockets.

He greeted me with a grim smile. "I knew you'd want to go up there and check things out."

"Yeah," I said. "I expected you to get here before me."

"I got delayed, but I talked to Maddie's friend, Mallory. She told me what happened and also that Maddie's at the sheriff's station giving a statement. Have you checked on her?'

"I'm sure Brent's got it covered."

He frowned. "So you're really going to give her up?"

He'd tried to talk to me about her after Brent left Lucky's

last night, but I'd shut down the conversation. Obviously, *he* wasn't giving up.

"She wants a family, Lance," I said with a lump in my throat. "Just like I expected, and we both know I don't. Starting something with her when we both know there's no happy ending...well, she deserves better."

Lance looked like he wanted to say something, but stopped. Finally, he said, "I'm sorry."

"Yeah, me too, but I don't plan to start braiding your hair and talking about my feelings, so let's drop it. We have more important things to worry about. Like the fact that I'm starting to wonder if the shooting is tied to our break-ins."

Lance's eyes narrowed. "What makes you say that?"

I told him my working theory. "I'm not saying it's them, but while Maddie's ex seemed like a dick, I can't see him killing her for not marrying him."

"I don't know," Lance said, looking unconvinced. "I've worked enough domestic violence cases to know that spurned men can lash out, and Maddie's ex sounds entitled. I'm sure he doesn't take rejection well."

"But to gun her down at a Christmas tree farm? Seems unlikely."

"Mallory also mentioned Jake was here. That seems like a stretch."

"I don't know," I said, rubbing my temple. A tension headache was already forming. "Maddie went into the auto parts store a few days ago. He might have recognized her."

"He *did* recognize her," Lance confirmed. "Mallory said he knew her and had invited Maddie and 'her cousin'"—he used air quotes—"to Cock on the Walk last night. He apologized for not showing."

Alarm raced through my head. "Jesus, they didn't go, did they?"

"No. That was the first Mallory had heard of it. Jake told them he didn't go because his cousin was having some legal issues. Mallory said everything seemed okay until Maddie sympathized with him and said it had to be tough seeing his cousin facing serious charges. Jake looked surprised but didn't say anything. Mallory didn't think much of it at the time, but she said when she got to running everything over after the shooting, she realized that Maddie had kept everything vague during the conversation. Maybe the fact she knew Boomer's charges were serious freaked him out."

"Well, fuck. What if he thought she had something to do with getting his cousin arrested? Did they take him to the station for questioning?"

"No," Lance said slowly. "He disappeared. One of the tree farm customers saw him walking toward the woods before the shooting started."

"Shit," I grunted.

"They have an APB out for him now."

I nodded. "Maybe we should see if Brent and Tripp want our help."

"Actually," Lance said, "we have a lead of our own, which is why you got here quicker than I did. I got a hit on a minivan that was stolen from Lynchburg. It was spotted in downtown Cockamamie earlier today."

My brow furrowed. "Someone took down the license number in Cockamamie? Why?"

"The trophy shop owner said the van was parked in his lot. He has a sign that says customer parking only, and he didn't have any customers, so he took down the plate number. He was about to call a tow truck, but a guy with a red beard got in and left, ignoring the owner as he shouted that the driver needed to wait for the police. The store owner called the non-emergency number, and an officer went out and took a report, which included the license plate number of the stolen van." He held my gaze. "I think the store owner saw our guy."

My eyes widened. "We need to get back to Cockamamie and interview him. This might be the break we need."

I'd call Brent on the way back to town.

Chapter Thirty-Six

Noah

Since Lance and I had driven separately, we both drove our cars downtown and parked in the lot that said *For Craigmore's Trophy Shop Parking Only.*

"This is bound to piss him off," Lance said when he got out. "Two of us parking out here."

I glanced around the eight-lane lot. We were the only two vehicles parked there. "Yeah, all of his customers will struggle to find parking places."

I headed toward the sidewalk in front of the store.

"Did you reach Brent?" Lance asked as he fell into step beside me.

"No," I said with a frown. "They told me he was busy in an interview. I left a message for him to call us ASAP after he talks to Maddie, but no word yet."

"He's probably giving Maddie his full attention," Lance said. "I'll bet she's nervous and needs a bit of soothing."

Picturing what he was insinuating made me feel murderous. "Are you *purposely* trying to be a dick, or does it just come naturally?"

He grinned and held out his hands in an *aw shucks* move. "It's a gift."

Why was he still riding my ass on this? Letting her go was the honorable thing to do. She deserved everything she wanted. After all the shit she'd been through, fate owed it to her. So why was Lance being such an asshole?

Now wasn't the time to think about it. We had a burglar with sexual predator tendencies to catch.

I pushed open the shop door, ignoring the tinkle of the bell as we entered. An older man stood behind the counter.

"What are you doing in here?" he asked somewhat belligerently.

No wonder the place was dead.

I pulled out my badge and flashed it at him. "I'm Detective Noah Langley, and this is Officer Lance Forrester. Are you Harold Craigmore?"

His chin lifted. "That's me."

"We're here about the van parked illegally in your lot this morning."

Irritation filled his eyes. "It's about time someone took me seriously about these loiterers. It's bad enough when homeless people congregate there, but when lazy assholes start parking in my lot just to jog down to the coffee shop, well, I have to draw the line."

"Is this a recurring problem?" I asked.

"Do you consider every day recurring?" he asked in a tone that insinuated I was an idiot.

Lance ignored him and asked, "How do you know they're going to the coffee shop?"

"Because they return with a cup of coffee that says Deja Brew in their hands?"

"Fair enough," Lance said good-naturedly.

A new fear hit me. "Did the man who parked here this morning come back with a cup of coffee in his hand?"

"No," the owner said. I allowed myself a moment of relief before he added, "But I don't know why he didn't. I saw him park, and then I went out the front door and watched him. He ducked into the coffee shop, but when he came out a few minutes later, he didn't have a cup. He hadn't been in there long enough to drink one, unless he gulped it down. But who gulps steaming hot coffee?"

"I take it he didn't come inside your shop?" I asked.

"Of course not," he said in disgust. "He went straight back to his van, just like I knew he would. I'd already gotten the license number and had the tow truck on standby in case he didn't come inside my store. But when I told him to wait because I was calling the police, he just cursed me out and took off."

"Can you describe the van?" Lance asked.

"It was a minivan," he said in frustration. "Not a new one, but not a rust bucket either. It was red, a dull red. I don't know what make and model."

Lance pulled out his phone and tapped on the screen a few times. "Did it look like this?" He held the phone out for Mr. Craigmore to study.

"That's it," he agreed with a sharp nod.

Lance nodded in my direction. It matched the description of the stolen van.

"What time did this happen?" I asked.

"It's on the damn police report the other officer took earlier," Mr. Craigmore grumped.

"We don't happen to have it with us," I said, forcing patience. "Take your best guess."

"Not long after we opened, but before lunch. Maybe eleven."

"Eleven," I repeated. Lance had called me around 1:45. Plenty of time for the perp to look for Maddie at the coffee shop, discover she wasn't there, then find her at the Christmas tree farm. But how had he known where to look for her?

"Thank you, Mr. Craigmore," I said. "You've been very helpful." I gave Lance a significant look, then headed for the door.

"*I've* been helpful?" the older man called out. "*You're* supposed to help *me*! Are you going to arrest this man? We need to send a message!"

Lance followed me out the door, then muttered "Friendly dude" once we were on the sidewalk.

Rather than respond, I started walking toward Deja Brew, worry beating into my mind.

"You think he was at Deja Brew looking for Maddie?" Lance asked, quickly catching up.

"That's what I'm hoping to find out." I walked into the shop and recognized the people behind the counter as part of the weekend crew. There were a few customers in line, but I cut around them and walked right up to the barista, Henry, a guy in his twenties.

"How's it hangin', Detective Langley? You want your usual today?" he asked cheerfully.

"Hey," a woman sneered to the cashier. "He cut in line!"

I held up my hands. "I'm not here for coffee. I'm here on official business."

"You're here on a police matter?" Henry asked. "Totally cool!"

"I need to know if a man with red hair was in here late morning—say, eleven o'clock or so."

Henry frowned and turned to the teenage girl behind the register. "Amanda? Do you remember a redheaded guy coming in this morning?"

"There were a couple," she said as she swiped the credit card of the woman who'd protested me cutting in front of her.

"Did anyone ask for Maddie?" I asked.

"The Maddie who works weekdays?" Henry asked, then shook his head. "No one asked *me*. Amanda?"

She shook her head too. "Nope. But now that I think of it, a guy came in late morning acting pretty strange. He never got in line, just looked around, stared behind the counter for a few minutes, then took off. He kind of gave me the creeps."

"How old do you think he looked?" I asked.

"I don't know," she said, leaning over the counter. "Old, I guess. At least in his thirties."

Lance coughed to cover a laugh.

"What was he wearing?"

"Jeans and a hoody. Both dark."

"What color was his hair?"

She made a face. "It was hard to tell. He was in a dark spot in the room, by the table with the napkins and creamers. But he had a really thick beard. He was in the shadows, so I'm not sure what color it was."

"Anything else you can remember about him?" I asked.

"Not really," she said. "I thought it was weird he didn't get in line, or even sit at a table. He just stood there and stared at us, but I thought maybe he was waiting for someone in line."

I took a card from my jacket pocket and handed it to her. "If you remember anything else, you can reach me at that number."

She took the card and looked it over. "Sure thing, Detective Langley. But are you sure you don't want your usual?"

"I think you should get your usual," Lance said, giving me a significant look. "And I'll get something too. It could be a long day and night."

"Sure thing!" Amanda said, grabbing a large paper cup and writing my order on the side. "And what can I get your friend?"

I started to tell her he didn't deserve anything, but my phone rang in my pocket, and when I pulled it out, Brent's name was on the screen. "I have to take this."

I took the call as I walked out the front door, grunting, "Any leads on the shooter?"

Brent chuckled. "Don't waste any time on greetings, huh? I can appreciate that. And no. Nothing. I hear you showed up at the crime scene."

"There might be a connection to our burglary cases." I reminded him about Maddie chasing the van, then told him how a man matching the description of the driver had exited a stolen van and come into the coffee shop where Maddie worked, acting odd.

"You think they're related?" he asked.

"Seems suspicious," I said. "We're chasing him down, anyway, so it's worth looking into. We've got an APB out for the stolen red Nissan Quest."

"I've sent some deputies out to track down Steve Campbell, Maddie's ex. We're going to ask him a few questions, and we also have some deputies looking for Jake Garfield."

"What's your gut on Garfield?" I asked.

"I talked to him after I arrested his cousin. The guy's an ass, but I just can't figure out what motive he'd have to kill Maddie. Even if she possibly alerted him to the fact she might know more about Boomer than she'd let on. It's still not grounds for murder."

"Yeah," I said. "I was thinking the same thing."

"Let me know if you find out anything new about the burglary driver."

"Will do," I said. "Are you done questioning Maddie?"

"Yeah, honestly, she didn't have much to give me. We sent her home."

"*Alone?*"

"Her friend Mallory picked her up."

"You're not posting a deputy outside her house?"

"We don't have the budget. Plus, she's in Cockamamie's city limits. You and Lance might be working with the sheriff's department, but there are still quite a few Cockamamie officers who'd think we were stepping on toes if we didn't honor jurisdiction."

"So that's a no."

"I plan on going over after I get off to check on her. I told her and her friend to stay home, keep the doors locked, and call 911 if they saw any trouble. That's the best I can do," he said, sounding apologetic.

"Yeah," I said grudgingly. "I get it." And I did, but I still couldn't accept it. I hated to think of her in danger, holed up in the same house people had tried to kidnap her from no more than a month ago.

I hung up and seconds later, Lance walked out carrying two cups of coffee.

"You're lucky I was feeling generous and brought you your drink," Lance said with a grin. "Find out anything?"

"Brent finished questioning Maddie and sent her home with Mallory. No deputy stationed outside the house."

He frowned. "I hate to say I'm not surprised."

"I plan to see if the chief will pony up to post someone outside tonight, but in the meantime, I think you should go check on her."

"Me?"

"Yeah. I'm too busy to go over, but we need to make sure she's okay. Plus, she called *you* when all of this started with Amy. Not me. You need to be the one to go."

He started to protest, but stopped and asked, "What exactly are you too busy doing?"

"After I call the chief? I'll find some surveillance video on

Main Street. Someone picked this guy up on their video feed, and I'm going to get an image to ID him."

Chapter Thirty-Seven

Maddie

I don't know how we're going to walk into that house without a Christmas tree," I said as I parked in my driveway. I was still freaked out that someone had tried to kill me, but if I let myself dwell on it, I'd have a complete breakdown.

"Um, you were just shot at," Mallory countered. "A Christmas tree should be the last thing on your mind."

"We can't tell her someone was shooting at us," I countered. "We don't want to freak her out."

"True. Two freaked-out women is plenty. So why don't we tell her the tree lot was closed for... I don't know." She shrugged. "The toilet overflowed?"

"They have porta potties."

She gave me a pointed stare. "But does *she* know that?"

"Good point."

It didn't matter. Aunt Deidre thought I'd ordered a tree and that Mallory and I had gone to see why delivery had been held up. Now I had no idea when or where we'd get a tree.

This day really sucked.

Maybe Margarete was right. Maybe I should have just ordered an artificial tree and sprayed it with pine scent.

"Come on," I said. I opened my car door, but hesitated, terrified that someone was about to start shooting at me again. Still, I couldn't stay in my car all day. "Let's get this over with."

Only when we went inside, Margarete was playing solitaire on the coffee table, on top of Aunt Deidre's puzzle.

She glanced up, looking relieved. "I take it you didn't get a tree?"

I grimaced. "There was a little mishap at the tree farm."

"Oh, trust me, I heard all about it," she said, keeping her gaze on her cards while putting a three of clubs on a stack. "*Everyone's* heard all about it."

"What exactly did you hear?" Mallory asked.

"Only that there was a shootout at the Christmas tree farm, and pretty much every sheriff's deputy in the county showed up, and a few Cockamamie police officers too."

Mallory released a short laugh. "That sounds about right."

So she didn't know the full story, or at least the part that involved me. I decided not to worry her.

I wrapped my arms around myself, glancing around for any new floral arrangements. "Did Steve happen to drop by while we were gone?" I asked.

"Nope. It was just the two of us." She shot a glance into the dining room. "He certainly has good taste in flowers."

I held back a retching sound.

"I think this situation calls for some popcorn and really bad rom coms," Mallory said. "I'll pop the corn, and you pick the movie."

I'd have preferred to go upstairs and take a nap, but I suspected I'd only have nightmares. Besides, I didn't feel like being alone. "Margarete, do you want to join us?" I asked.

"Thank you, girls, but no. I have plans with my kids tonight. They're making me dinner."

I sat down next to her and took her hand. "Thanks for staying with Aunt Deidre. I don't know what I'd do without you."

Her mouth tipped down. "You know I'm happy to help, Maddie." But I could tell she was leaving something unsaid. Probably that it wouldn't be long before Aunt Deidre would be too much for either of us to handle.

Margarete left soon after that, and Mallory came out with popcorn and iced tea. We curled up under blankets and started watching a movie so cheesy it made us laugh for all the wrong reasons. I'd started to forget about our nightmare afternoon when a knock landed at the front door.

"I'll get it," Mallory said, jumping to her feet and rushing into the entryway. She grabbed a long umbrella from the coat tree and lifted it as though it were a bat. Seemed to me the pointed end would work better for self-defense, but I wasn't all that worried that someone dangerous might be at the door. I couldn't see a potential murderer knocking and asking for permission to come in.

Mallory opened the door, and I could hear Lance say, "Hey, I just dropped by to check on you guys."

"Come on in," she said as she opened the door wider. "Make yourself comfortable."

Lance walked through the door, shut it, then headed into the living room. He sat in the chair next to the sofa, leaving his coat on. He wasn't wearing his uniform, just jeans and a blue Henley. His warm brown eyes studied me with a sympathetic expression. "How are you doing, Maddie?"

"I've been better, but I've definitely been worse. How'd you find out?"

He grinned. "The question should be, how could I *not* find

out?" He turned serious and leaned forward, resting his elbows on his thighs. "Do you have any idea who could have been shooting at you?"

I pulled my blanket closer. "The only person I can think of is Jake. I told Deputy Taylor about Steve, but I can't see him doing anything like that."

"We're worried that the robbery driver might also be a suspect. That he may have gotten your plate number somehow."

"Oh."

"We don't know for certain that he was the gunman who shot at you today, but we have reason to believe he was at the coffee shop this morning, looking for you."

Mallory's face paled. "What? How did he know to go to Christmas Tree Lane?"

"We're not sure," Lance said. "We're still investigating." He turned his focus on me. "Maddie, have you noticed anything unusual since you followed that van?"

"You mean more unusual than my ex-boyfriend showing up declaring we're getting married in a month?"

"Yeah," he said with a grimace. "I heard about that. Anything else? Any other suspicious people showing up at the coffee shop? Did you pick up any unusual Uber riders?"

"I haven't picked up an Uber client since the accident on Wednesday."

"Okay," he said. "Anything else?"

I pursed my lips. "I talked to someone in the grocery store about Amy yesterday. But no one saw us." I held up my hand. "And before you accuse me of looking into what happened, I was just there getting eggs. *She* came up to *me*, volunteering the information, but she was adamant that I couldn't share her name."

"And this is the person who told you that Amy had been saving up money from a part-time job?"

"Yeah," I said in surprise. "How'd—"

"Brent Taylor."

"Oh, good. I was worried he was blowing me off, since I didn't have much else to tell him."

"No," he said carefully. "He took it seriously. But you're sure no one else overheard you?"

"I don't think so."

He looked like he was about to say something else, but his phone rang. He pulled it out of his coat pocket and answered. "Hey, Noah."

Noah. My heart raced. Was he calling to check on me? I had to admit I was disappointed he wasn't the one to come over.

Lance listened for a few moments, then said, "Yeah, I'm about done here. I'll meet you there." He hung up and stuffed the phone back into his pocket. Turning to me, he said, "If you think of anything else, give me a call, okay?"

"Yeah," I said with a soft smile. "We appreciate you coming to check on us, but we're okay."

He turned serious. "There's a potential murderer on the loose who tried to kill you a few hours ago. I doubt they're going to stop with their attempt at the Christmas tree farm. The sheriff's budget doesn't have enough money to cover a deputy to watch over the house, but Noah's working on getting the Cockamamie PD to spring for an officer to camp outside tonight. In the meantime, stay in here, don't open the door for anyone, and call 911 if you think anything's the least bit off. Dispatch will send out an officer to check it out and make sure you're safe."

My blood ran cold. "Thanks, Lance."

Mallory followed him to the door, and they both went outside. She was gone for over a minute before she came back inside. I nearly accused her of talking about me behind my back, but the expression on her face told me that they'd had more interesting things to discuss.

Was there a potential relationship there?

"I think you should tap that," I said with a grin.

Her eyes flew wide. "Maddie!"

Her reaction caught me by surprise. This wasn't just a crush. She was *really* interested.

"What?" I said with a laugh. "At least one of us should have a love life."

"You could have one with Detective Hunky. He's definitely interested."

"My love life is the last thing on my mind. Right now, I'm just trying to stay alive." And I'd prefer a love life with Noah, but it looked like that would never happen.

Chapter Thirty-Eight

Noah

After dropping by to check on Maddie, Lance walked into the station with eagerness in his step. "I want to see the images you found."

"I have a good image from the diner cameras. The guy fits the descriptions we got from Craigmore and Amanda at the coffee shop, as well as the witness statements from the burglaries."

"Got an ID on him yet?" Lance asked as he shook off his coat and tossed it over the back of his chair.

"No, but the minivan's owner has surveillance cameras set up outside his house. He sent me footage from two nights ago, when the van was stolen. Have a look."

Lance stood behind me as I loaded up the video and hit play. The van was parked in a driveway, and a man stepped into view, heading right up to the driver's door. It was unlocked, so he opened it, and the van backed out of the driveway about five seconds later.

I glanced back at Lance. "The owner accidently left the key fob in the car."

Lance pulled a face. "*That's* an expensive mistake. I wonder how many attempts the perp made before he found a van that he could steal."

"We just might find out. I've put in a request to get footage from nearby houses. If nothing else, I want to see if we can discover the vehicle that took him there. Maybe it's connected to him. Or his accomplice."

Lance shifted his weight. "Unless he and his buddy stole a car to drive up to Lynchburg. I'll see if any abandoned cars were found in the area."

We both got to work, energized to have a more solid lead. Brent called a few hours later, before we'd made any solid progress.

"We brought in Steve Campbell, and I'm about to question him. Thought you and Lance might like to watch, since you're friends with Maddie."

I was already out of my seat, grabbing my coat off the back of my chair. "We're on our way."

Taking my cue, Lance was pulling his coat on before I'd hung up. "Another lead?"

"We're about to watch Brent hand Steve Campbell his ass."

A grin spread across his face. "Sounds like a good time."

Yes, it did.

When we arrived at the sheriff's station, a deputy led us back to Brent's desk. He saw us, took a gulp from a coffee mug, then got up from his chair.

"We've got him stewing in an interview room," he said as we approached. "Honestly, I'm surprised he hasn't asked for a lawyer."

"Does he know why he's here?" I asked.

"The deputies said he protested when they picked him up,

but he didn't ask why he was being brought in. He just claimed he was innocent."

Lance shot me a look.

"That sounds incriminating," I said.

"Let's go see what he has to say." An eager look filled Brent's eyes as he straightened his jacket. He led us down a dim hallway and pointed to a room with a plate affixed beside the door reading Observation Room #2. "You can watch in there."

We went into the small, dark room that contained several waiting-room-style chairs. Lance took a seat, but I remained standing as I stared through the one-way glass. The small room on the other side had white walls, and Campbell sat on the far side of a metal table in a flimsy-looking chair. Two sturdier chairs were still empty on the opposite side. He had on jeans and a black turtleneck. Dark clothes. I could make out a pair of athletic shoes on his feet. His hand clenched and unclenched on the tabletop, and his eyes were dark with anger.

He was alone for another couple of minutes before Brent walked through the door with two disposable coffee cups.

"Sorry to keep you waiting, Mr. Campbell," Brent said good-naturedly. "I had a few things to tie up before I could get to you. I'm sure you know how it is."

"Actually," Campbell snapped, "*I don't.* I've been here for nearly an hour, and I'm not sure why I was brought here in the first place."

Brent settled into a chair opposite Campbell and handed him one of the cups. "It's not as good as they make at Deja Brew, but it's not too shabby either."

Brent had thrown out a link to Maddie, but Campbell didn't respond. Instead, he reached for the cup and took a sip, then made a face and set it down. "The sooner Maddie and I get out of this hick town and back to civilization, the better."

"Maddie," Brent said, tilting his head. "That your girlfriend?"

Campbell narrowed his eyes. "Fiancée."

"Congratulations," Brent said enthusiastically. "When's the big day?"

"January 15th," Campbell said, starting to relax just a little.

"What brings you and Maddie to Cockamamie?"

He pushed out a beleaguered sigh. "Maddie has been taking care of her ailing aunt. I'm here to bring her home."

"So Maddie's been in town for a while."

"A few months."

"The separation must have been hard," Brent said sympathetically.

Steve leaned away from the table, growing more comfortable. "Long distance only makes you appreciate what you have."

"Yeah, I can see how that might be so," Brent said. "Still, distance has been known to put stress on a couple. How would you describe your relationship with Maddie?"

Campbell rested a forearm on the table. "We're good. Solid."

"Why the hell does he think he's in here?" Lance asked me. "He's acting like Brent has no idea what he's been up to."

I leaned my shoulder into the window frame. "He seems like a classic narcissist, which means his version of the truth is the real one as far as he's concerned."

Brent was continuing his interrogation. "And how would *Maddie* describe your relationship?"

Campbell shrugged. "Oh, you know women..."

"Not really," Brent said. "I was raised in a house full of boys and haven't had a girlfriend in a while. Explain it to me."

He shrugged. "You know. Sometimes they get a mind of their own."

"Funny how human beings like to think for themselves," Brent said without missing a beat, his tone still friendly.

I had to admit, I liked how he was handling this.

Campbell made a face. "Now come on," he groaned. "You know that's not what I meant."

"Actually, Steve," Brent said, his voice tight, "I think that *is* what you meant. You said you didn't know why we brought you in today. Are you sure about that?"

A smug smile spread across Campbell's face. "Look, I admit that I've been coming on pretty strong with Maddie. I think it might have scared her, but she wants to get married." He leaned closer, looking earnest. "Trust me. She begged me to marry her for a couple of years. She's just trying to make me sweat."

I wanted to jump through the glass and punch the smug fucker in the face.

"Funny," Brent said, scooting his chair away from the table and crossing his legs. "When I spoke to Maddie a few hours ago, she said that you proposed, but she turned you down. Said she wasn't interested at all. The way I read things, I doubt she'd even consider you her boyfriend."

"What?" Campbell said, looking incredulous. He rolled his eyes. "Look, she's upset with me, and I understand that, but she'll come around. She always does. She's just trying to make a point."

Brent turned back to the table. "Exactly. She's trying to let you know that she's done with you. *For good.*"

"I know Maddie," Campbell said dismissively. "She'll change her mind."

"What if she doesn't?"

"She will," Campbell scoffed. "This is all just a test to see if I'm serious."

"I'd say *she's* serious," Brent said slowly. "She's not interested in your proposal, and she wants you to leave her alone. In fact, she's filled out the paperwork to file a restraining order against you."

That was news to me, and a quick look at Lance suggested it was news to him too. Was Brent bluffing?

Fury filled Campbell's eyes, but then he closed them and took a deep, steadying breath. When he opened them, he was the epitome of calm again. "I'll just talk to her," Campbell said with a smile. "Clear all this up."

"*Actually*," Brent drawled again, "a restraining order means you *can't* talk to her. You can't even be within fifty feet of her."

Campbell balled his hands on the table. "She wouldn't."

Brent lifted his shoulders into an *aw shucks* shrug. "She already did."

Campbell's face reddened as he shot a glance toward the door.

"I'm sure that has to throw a wrench in your January wedding plans."

No response.

"What were you doing this afternoon, Steve?" Brent asked in a breezy tone.

Steve's head jerked up to face him. "What?"

"This afternoon. What were you doing? Say around one-thirty? Two o'clock?"

Campbell's jaw set. "I was in my motel room."

"Got anyone who can back that up?"

Campbell sat up straighter. "Why?" He glanced around the room. "Am I being charged with some kind of crime?"

"That depends," Brent said. "Can anyone vouch that you were at the motel around that time?"

Steve slammed both hands on the table. "Are you *serious*?"

"The deputies found you in your motel room around four. Have you left it today?"

"I went out for breakfast."

"Did you happen to go to the coffee shop to look for Maddie?"

"No," he said firmly. "Maddie doesn't work there on the weekends."

"And how do you know that?"

"She's my girlfriend." He gave Brent a look of disgust. "See? Boyfriends know things like that. Which proves I *am* her boyfriend."

Brent slid his hand into his pants pocket and pulled out his phone. "And if we call Maddie and ask her, will she confirm that she told you?" He tapped on the screen, then showed it to Campbell. "Got her number pulled up right here. So let me make this clear..." His voice hardened for the first time. "If I find out you're lying to me, the rest of our talk is going to go a whole lot differently than it has up until this point."

Steve's face paled.

"So let me ask you one more time," Brent said, his voice tight. "How did you find out about Maddie's schedule?"

Campbell held up his hands. "Okay. Okay. I went to Deja Brew a couple of nights ago and asked about her. They told me she only works on weekdays."

Brent smiled at him like he was a star pupil. "See? That wasn't so hard."

Campbell grunted.

"When was the last time you saw Maddie?"

"Yesterday. I saw her in the grocery store parking lot."

"And how did you know to find her there?"

Campbell grunted again and turned away.

"Come on, Steve. I'm going to find out one way or another. How did you know to find her there?"

"I was in the parking lot behind her coffee shop, waiting for her to get off work so I could talk to her, but then she got in her car too fast and left. I had no choice but to follow her to the store."

"And you waited for her to come out so you could talk to her?"

"Exactly," Campbell said.

"Why didn't you talk to her immediately after she came out?"

"It took me a minute to get out of my car."

"Or maybe you could see she was on the phone?" Brent suggested.

Campbell gave a half-shrug. "It would have been rude to interrupt."

Lance snorted. "Since when does he worry about being rude?"

Campbell was pissing me off. "He doesn't give a shit about Maddie."

"Then you tried to convince her to marry you?" Brent asked.

"Look," Campbell said, spreading out his hands, "I'm no quitter. When I know what I want, I go after it, and I want Maddie."

My temper started to rise, but if Brent was pissed, he didn't let on. "But Maddie still said no."

"Like I said, she just needs more convincing."

"Did you threaten her?"

"What?" he asked in outrage. "No. Of course not!"

"You didn't say something to the effect of you going to extreme measures to make her marry you?"

Campbell chuckled and rolled his eyes. "Maddie's always been overly sensitive. I realized that I upset her and sent her flowers to apologize."

Brent nodded and tapped the table with his finger, giving

Campbell a few moments to stew. Then he straightened in his seat. "Did you see her today?" He held up a finger. "No lying."

Campbell grimaced, then pushed out a sigh. "I drove by her house."

"Drove by, or camped out and watched it?"

He shifted in his seat, hesitating. "I may have parked across the street and watched the house for a bit."

"See?" Brent said in a placating tone. "That wasn't so hard. And it makes me trust you more." He rested his forearms on the table. "So you parked outside Maddie's house. When was that?"

Campbell drew in a deep breath, stalling. "Around noon?"

"And you didn't go by the coffee shop this morning?"

"I went there to get coffee, yeah."

"But earlier you said you didn't," Brent pointed out.

"You asked if I'd gone by asking about Maddie. I didn't ask about her. I got my chai latte and sat at a table for a while to read the paper."

Smart ass.

"Okay," Brent said. "You went by Maddie's house, but she said she hadn't seen you today. Why were you there, and how long did you stay?"

"I was going to ask her to get lunch with me, but I wasn't sure that was a good idea. Then she and Mallory—her best friend—came outside, got in Maddie's car, and left."

"So it sounds like you were outside Maddie's house for more than a *bit.*"

Steve tilted his head from side to side, making a face. "Okay, so it might have been more like an hour, but it's a public street. I wasn't doing anything wrong."

"And what did you do when Maddie left in her car?"

Campbell didn't answer.

"You followed her, right?"

He still didn't answer.

"Steve?"

He glanced down at the floor. "Yeah."

"And then what happened?" Brent prodded. When Campbell didn't answer, Brent said, "You followed her to the Christmas tree farm."

Campbell hung his head, then looked up. "Hey, it's a free country. I can drive wherever I'd like."

"Do you own any firearms, Steve?"

"*What?*"

"It's a yes or no question."

"Yeah," he said, flustered. "Doesn't every God-fearing man in Tennessee?"

"Well, I don't know about that," Brent said, back to his laid-back tone. "Right now, I'm more interested in what *you* own, Steve."

"I...uh...I have a Glock and a Sig."

Handguns that could potentially have serious firepower. I felt like I was going to be sick.

"Any long guns?" Brent asked.

"Um...yeah. A Remington rifle."

"Twelve gauge, am I right?" Brent asked.

Campbell's face lost even more color. "Yeah. Why are you asking?"

"Did you happen to bring any guns with you to Cockamamie, Steve?" Brent asked in his friendly tone.

"Uh..." Steve gulped.

"Don't lie to me, Steve," Brent cajoled. "I'd really hate it if you lied to me."

"I brought one," he said, still not meeting his gaze.

"Which one?"

He swallowed hard, his Adam's apple bobbing. Then his

eyes widened, as though it was just occurring to him that he might be in serious trouble. "What's going on here? Why are you asking about guns?"

"Which gun did you bring to Cockamamie, Steve?" Brent asked, his voice a little sharper.

Campbell's gaze darted around the room. Terror filled his eyes, but then his mouth suddenly dropped open, and he jumped to his feet. "Maddie! Is Maddie okay?"

"You tell me, Steve," Brent said, looking up at him. "How good of a shot are you?"

Campbell stumbled backward. "*What?*"

"Which gun did you bring to Cockamamie?" Brent repeated.

"The Remington."

"And where is that gun now?"

Campbell's eyes widened in fear. "It was stolen out of my motel room. I swear!"

"Did you report the theft?"

Campbell didn't answer for a few moments, but then he squeaked out, "I'd like to call my lawyer."

"Dammit," I grunted, stepping away from the window. "Brent was so close to breaking him. So fucking close."

"He didn't do it," Lance said, his hands folded over his chest.

I turned to face him. "What makes you say that?"

"Just a gut feeling. And if you could get past your concern for Maddie, I think you'd feel it too."

I rested my hand against the wall and closed my eyes, running over the interview. Maybe Lance was right. Maybe I'd wanted to believe Steve was guilty because I wanted Maddie to be out of danger. That and because he was an asshole. But Lance was right. My gut told me this wasn't our guy.

We said as much to Brent when he popped into the observation room to discuss the interview, and he was less than thrilled to hear it.

"Come on," he said, pointing to Campbell, who was still sitting at the table, his head hanging in defeat. "He brought a twelve-gauge to town, and it was conveniently stolen? Who just carries a rifle around?"

"Test him for gun residue," I said with a sigh. "I bet you twenty bucks it'll come back clean."

"He could have showered," Brent said. "Plus, we found twelve-gauge rifle casings at the scene, Noah. He's our guy."

I shook my head. "We both know twelve-gauge bullets are a dime a dozen. Most rifles use that caliber." I released a frustrated breath. "Trust me, I wish to God I believed Steve Campbell was the shooter, but my money's still on the van driver."

Brent put his hand on his hip and stared down at the ground. Finally, he looked up. "Well, I'm holding him for now and getting a search warrant for his motel room and car. If nothing else, I can try booking him on stalking charges until we get more evidence to firm up the attempted murder charge. If you can prove someone else did it, you won't hurt my feelings, but I'm holding him for now."

"Fine by me," I said. "A couple days in a jail cell will do him some good, and this way we know he won't be harassing Maddie."

Brent nodded. "I'll tell Maddie..." He eyed me carefully. "Unless you and Lance want to break the news."

"No, you go ahead," I said, waving my hand even though it went against every instinct inside me. But if I wasn't going to pursue something with her, I needed to let her go. Even in this. Otherwise, I was giving her mixed signals. "I'm sure she'll be glad to hear he's in custody."

I pulled my phone from my pocket and checked my

messages. Five more videos had been sent to my inbox. "Besides, I've got some video footage to go through."

"Ditto," Lance said, getting to his feet. "Thanks for letting us watch the interview."

"No problem. Teamwork."

Chapter Thirty-Nine

Maddie

I was worried about how Aunt Deidre would react when she woke up from her nap and realized we still didn't have a tree, but she seemed to have forgotten all about it. We were just finishing dinner when my new phone rang with Detective Taylor's number. Mallory had run to the phone store right before they closed to get me a new one. Thankfully, my phone had been backed up on my laptop, and I could restore my contacts and photos.

"Good news, Maddie," Taylor said after I answered. "We made an arrest."

"You did?" I asked in surprise, as I got up from the table. "Who?"

"It's rude to leave the dinner table unexcused," Aunt Deidre called after me, but I ignored her and walked into the kitchen.

"Your ex-boyfriend, Steve," he said.

"Steve?" I asked incredulously.

"He pretty much admitted to stalking you, so we're holding him for that while we search his motel room and car. But we *do* have some compelling evidence that he was the person who shot at you."

"That just doesn't make any sense," I said.

"You said he's been insistent that you marry him next month. Did he ever give you a reason for that?"

"No. Did you ask him?"

"We didn't get around to that before he asked for an attorney. I'm waiting for the warrant to do the searches, but I hear he's calling an attorney from Nashville, so I doubt I'll get another chance to speak to him until tomorrow."

"I don't know," I said. "Steve's a lot of things, but I'm not sure he's capable of murder." Especially killing me.

"Sometimes people surprise you," he said. "We are investigating some other leads, which means you should still be on guard, but there's a good chance Steve is our man."

"Thanks for the update, Detective Taylor. I appreciate it."

"Of course," he said. "No problem. Be sure to turn on your security alarm and try to get some sleep tonight."

"Thanks."

I hung up and turned around to go back to the table, but Mallory was right behind me.

"Well?" she demanded impatiently.

"Detective Taylor thinks Steve might have been the one who shot at us. They've arrested him, and they're getting a search warrant for his motel room and his car."

Her mouth dropped open as if on a hinge. "Really?"

"Yeah," I said, leaning my butt against the counter in front of the sink. "But I can't bring myself to believe it. He just doesn't have much of a motive. The van driver seems more likely."

"You know who might know if he had a motive?" Mallory asked. "Nancy."

I crossed my arms over my chest. "We talked to Nancy the other night. Wouldn't she have told us then?"

"We won't know until we call her." She snatched my phone

from my hand and started to search my recent calls. I let her make the call on speaker because I was curious too.

When Nancy answered, Mallory responded, "Hey, Nancy. This is Mallory and Maddie. We have a few follow-up questions about Steve."

"Hey, Nancy," I added, leaning closer to Mallory and the phone. "Sorry we're bothering you on a Saturday night."

"Are you kidding? My Saturday night could use a little excitement. Besides, I did a little more digging into Steve's new job at Serendipity. I planned to call you about it tomorrow."

Mallory shot me an *oh shit* look.

"And what did you find?" I asked.

"You're not going to believe this," Nancy said with excitement in her voice. "I have a friend who has a friend who works at Serendipity. She said Steve told the big boss that he's getting married in January, and get this, he actually invited him to the wedding."

"Why on earth would he do that?" I asked.

"Apparently, marriage is an unofficial requirement for employees in high positions. Something about family values and morals, as though some married asshole is more legit than a single person. Anyway, if Steve wants to advance in the company, he needs to get married."

"But why would he invite his boss to our wedding?" I asked.

"To impress him, I'm sure," Nancy said. "Rumor has it that Steve planned a pretty elaborate event. My friend thinks it's Steve's attempt to make an impression." She gasped, then said, "Oh crap. Hey, I need to go. My dog just projectile vomited all over the wall and my new wool rug."

"Thanks, Nancy," I said, but she'd already hung up.

I stared at Mallory. "He's going to be humiliated when I don't show up for our wedding. What's he going to do *then*?"

"He must be crapping his pants," Mallory said with a laugh,

"because you've made it pretty clear you're not—" She gasped. "Oh. My. God."

"What?" I asked.

"That's his motive to kill you," she said, looking terrified.

"You can't be serious," I said in disbelief. "You think he would kill me to spare himself the humiliation?"

"You have to admit that it would solve his problem," Mallory said in a rush. "If his fiancée dies, he has a legitimate reason to call off the wedding and save face. We all know he'd play the sympathy card to his boss and everyone else. Poor Steve. The love of his life murdered the month before their wedding. He'd play that role to the hilt. *And* he might get all of his deposits back."

"I don't believe it," I said, but I wasn't as confident as I'd been before. "He wouldn't go that far."

"He's desperate, Mads," Mallory said softly.

I swallowed the lump in my throat. "I need to tell Detective Taylor."

With shaky fingers, I called the detective back, telling him everything, and then gave him Nancy's name and number so he could call her himself.

After I hung up, we went back out to the dining room, but Aunt Deidre had already finished her dinner and was out in the living room, working on her puzzle.

I'd lost my appetite, so I started cleaning up, and Mallory joined me. To my relief, she didn't bring up the Steve situation, and we loaded the dishwasher in silence.

After we got Aunt Deidre ready for bed and tucked in for the night, we went back downstairs, and Mallory opened a bottle of wine. We sat on the sofa, sipping our wine in silence until the buzz of Mallory's phone interrupted us.

She looked at the screen, then answered the text with a soft smile on her face.

"Who was that?" I asked.

Glancing up with a grin, she stuffed her phone back into her pocket. "A certain handsome police officer."

"Oh?" I asked with an answering smile, happy to have something positive to focus on. I could see that Lance and Mallory could be good together.

"He said Noah's request for an officer to park out front was denied. Long story short: Lance is coming by to sleep on our sofa."

"Is that what the cool kids are calling it now," I teased, pointedly ignoring the part about Noah.

"I'm not sleeping with him, Mads," she said in exasperation, then grinned. "At least not tonight. He said he's worried about us."

I could have protested. Steve had been arrested, after all, and Detective Taylor thought he was the shooter. I still wasn't sold on the idea that he was a potential murderer, though, and I wasn't above letting an officer with a loaded gun stand between any potential bad guys and me and the people I loved. Especially if Lance was the one protecting us.

But it reminded me of when Noah stayed to protect me a month ago. We'd slept in the same bed, and although nothing had happened—we didn't even kiss—we'd shared an intimacy deeper than sex. We'd started baring our hearts, something neither of us found easy, yet somehow it was easier with each other.

I really sucked with men.

"Tell Lance I said thank you," I said, getting to my feet. "I'm exhausted, so I think I'm going to bed."

She started to protest, then got up and pulled me into a hug. "It's going to be okay, Mads. I promise."

"I'm glad you're here."

"I'm glad I am too, although I wish I'd waited in the car at the Christmas tree farm."

"That's fair," I said with a chuckle.

I started up the stairs and heard the knock on the door behind me, followed by a murmur of voices as Mallory greeted Lance at the door. When I hit the top stair, I turned and gave him a wave. My heart warmed as I watched them move into the living room. They already looked so comfortable with each other, so in sync.

Mallory deserved to be happy, but I couldn't help but wonder when it would be my turn.

Chapter Forty

Noah

I woke early on Sunday morning and headed into work. More videos from the neighborhood of the missing van had hit my inbox—they were coming in a few at a time—and I was starting to piece together a timeline of when and where the suspect had canvassed the neighborhood. He'd tried at least five vans before finding one he could take. After yet another batch showed up, I finally found the vehicle that had dropped him off. One of the videos clearly showed a silver sedan pulling up to a curb, followed by a shadowy figure hopping out and heading to the right of the camera.

The car pulled away too quickly for me to see the driver or the license plate, so I pulled up another video I'd already reviewed, one from farther down the street. I rewound it several minutes until the back of the silver car came into view, but the license plate was too grainy to read.

Maybe I'd see it in another video.

I'd already printed up a satellite map of the neighborhood and marked the houses that had submitted footage. I'd just pulled up another video to see if I could get a better look at the car when my phone rang. I wasn't sure what to think when I saw my sergeant's number.

"Detective Langley," I answered.

"Noah, we've got another break-in." He paused. "This one has a murder victim."

"Shit," I growled, shutting down my computer. "Send me the address. I'm on my way."

I called Lance as I rushed out to the car.

Multiple police cars were parked in front of the house in a neighborhood near downtown Cockamamie. Lance's car was already parked across the street. He was standing next to two officers just outside a taped-off perimeter around the house. I recognized one of them, Neil Erikson, and he looked like he was struggling to keep it together.

A man and two kids stood down the street in a huddle, all of them crying, and a wave of dread washed over me as I walked up to the officers. "What have we got?"

"Um..." Neil took a breath. "Lindy Fleming stayed home from church today because she wasn't feeling well, so her husband took the two kids to the early service and Sunday school without her. A boy and a girl, ages five and seven. He left around seven forty-five." He swallowed, and I could tell he was working his way up to it. "When they got back from church a little after ten, the husband found the garage door open. He said he'd been running late before he left, so he figured he might have forgotten to close it. But when he got inside..." He stopped and swallowed hard.

I put a firm hand on his shoulder, already dreading what he was about to tell me. "It's okay, Neil. Tell me what you know."

He swallowed again. "He and the kids went inside through

the garage door, and Mr. Fleming went to the bedroom to check on his wife, and…" His voice cracked.

"He found her on the bed," said the other officer, looking only slightly less distressed. "She was naked, and she'd been strangled."

I considered asking how he knew she'd been strangled but decided to wait and see for myself.

"Did the kids see her?" Lance asked, sounding concerned.

"No," the other officer said. "They were in the kitchen."

"Did the suspects take anything?" I asked. "Was it a break-in gone wrong?"

Neil's eyes clouded over. "Maybe. Other than the murder, it's like the other break-ins. Forced entry through the back door and took the usual. TVs. Computers. Jewelry. Then they left through the garage."

Goddammit. I knew in my gut it was building to this, and I hadn't done enough to prevent it. Other than a map tracking the movements of a car thief in a city fifty miles away, all I had was a bunch of nothing.

I clenched my jaw. "I want every available officer canvassing this neighborhood, asking if anyone saw anything and if they have any surveillance video. We're going to find these bastards and make sure they never see the fucking light of day again. Got it?"

Both officers nodded, looking more settled now that they had something tangible to do that could help us catch the murderer.

I looked over at Lance. "You ready?'

"Not really, but yeah."

Lance and I grabbed coveralls, booties, and gloves out of the trunk of my car and put them on in silence. I was dreading what we would find, and I'm sure Lance was too. I knew he'd spent the night at Maddie's, and I nearly asked him how she was, but I was already worried about a connection between her and the killer. I wasn't a superstitious man, but I felt too raw to mention her name here.

The kitchen had dishes in the sink and a glass on the counter. No Polaroid. We walked into the living room and saw the empty spot where the TV should have been.

"No sign of a struggle," Lance said in a hushed voice.

"I noticed that," I said, echoing his tone.

We continued down the hall leading to the bedrooms, pausing to look into each room. The kids' rooms were trashed enough that it was impossible to tell what had been taken. We'd have to get a list from Mr. Fleming later.

The door to the room at the end stood ajar. I led the way, pausing in the doorway when I saw the victim on the bed.

I'd seen death more times than I could count, but it still felt like a sucker punch to the gut. Particularly in instances like this, where I knew it had been both violent and drawn out.

I stepped inside the room so Lance could enter too.

"Jesus," Lance groaned, then drew in a deep breath.

"Yeah."

We both took in the sight of the naked woman sprawled out on the bed, her hands tied to the bedposts. Her eyes were open, staring at the ceiling in frozen horror. I knew she'd haunt me at night for some time to come.

"Forensics is on the way," Lance said in almost a whisper.

I nodded but didn't say a word as I crept closer, wanting to see why Neil had thought she'd been strangled. I leaned over the bed to get a better look at her neck, seeing the bruising on her throat. Multiple fingerprints were visible.

I gave myself a moment to experience the anger and horror of seeing this woman like this, then I mentally shut it down. Lindy Fleming didn't need me to mourn for her. She needed me to seek justice.

I cleared my throat. "No one comes in this room unless they're essential to the case. No gawkers. She deserves privacy and respect."

Lance didn't answer, and I glanced over at him. He was staring at the victim's face. He must have realized I'd addressed him, because he startled and then met my gaze. "Sorry. It was hard seeing Amy's body, but she was clothed. This is the first time I've seen..." His voice sounded choked.

"This is why I do what I do," I said. "To lock up the animals who do shit like this."

And I'd find this animal if it was the last thing I did.

Chapter Forty-One

Maddie

When I woke, sunlight was streaming in through my windows. Startled, I sat up in bed and checked my phone.

10:03.

I hadn't slept that late since moving to Cockamamie. Shoot, I hadn't slept that late in years.

Aunt Deidre.

I jumped out of bed so quickly, I got tangled in the sheets and nearly fell on my face, but I disengaged myself and dashed out of my room. Just as I'd feared, Aunt Deidre's room was empty, so I bolted down the stairs, sounding like a herd of elephants. I raced around the corner, through the living room and dining room, and into the kitchen—where I found Mallory and my aunt sitting at the kitchen table with coffee mugs.

"What's the hurry?" Aunt Deidre asked with a laugh.

So it was a good day. Relief cascaded through me. Her mental status was such a rollercoaster, and there was no guarantee she'd be herself in a few hours, but I planned to enjoy every moment I could.

"I was afraid I'd miss breakfast." I turned my gaze on Mallory. "Why didn't you wake me?"

"Because you needed the sleep, and I've been listening to Aunt Deidre tell embarrassing stories about you as a kid."

I put my hand on my chest to slow down my rapid heartbeat from my run downstairs.

"There's coffee in the pot," Mallory said. "Grab a cup, and feel free to listen as long as you don't interrupt."

Aunt Deidre studied me for a moment. "Looks like Maddie's already had a cup too many."

I forced a laugh. "Very funny. So what's for breakfast?"

"Lance made some pancakes before he left," Mallory said. "We saved you a couple."

I winged up my brow and shot her a grin. "Oh, really?"

"It's not like that."

"Then how did Lance get here early enough to make us breakfast?" Aunt Deidre teased.

Mallory's face lit up. She must have remembered we were keeping all the danger from my aunt, because she said, "There was no funny business. Scout's honor. He came over last night to hang out, and we both fell asleep on the sofa watching a *Star Wars* marathon."

"I didn't think you liked *Star Wars*," I teased as I poured myself some coffee.

"Maybe I just needed the right person to explain it to me."

So Lance was a *Star Wars* nerd. Mallory must really like him because she'd always declared the *Star Wars* franchise too commercialized.

I found two pancakes on a plate by the stove, so I popped them into the microwave. After I doctored them up and sat down, I listened to Aunt Deidre tell a few stories about my youth, only occasionally protesting what she had said.

After I finished my breakfast, Aunt Deidre turned wistful.

"What is it, Aunt D?" Mallory asked, covering her hand with hers.

"I was just thinking how nice it would be to go to church."

Mallory and I exchanged a surprised look. My aunt was so with it, she even knew what day it was.

I glanced at the clock on the wall. "What time does service start?"

"There are several," she said. "If we hurry, we can make the eleven o'clock."

"Let's do it," I said, getting to my feet. If that's what she wanted, I'd make it happen.

Making it by eleven seemed like a stretch—it was already 10:40—but Mallory and I helped my aunt upstairs and then went to our rooms to change. I hadn't even brushed my teeth yet, so it was nearly eleven by the time I joined them downstairs.

To my surprise, Mallory had brought a dress appropriate for church, and Aunt Deidre was wearing one of her favorite dresses and a low pair of heels. She tended to be unbalanced these days, so I offered her my arm and led her out to my car. Of course she was attentive enough that she noticed the damage it had sustained from the crash.

"It's nothing," I said. "Someone hit me in the parking lot at work, and of course they drove off without leaving their information."

"People these days," she muttered in disgust.

We got to the church a few minutes late, but everyone was standing and singing a hymn, so it wasn't too disruptive. Multiple people waved to Aunt Deidre from their pews as we made our way to an open spot closer to the front.

I'd taken my aunt to church a few times after moving home, but her condition had worsened enough that I'd started to worry about bringing her out. The joy on her face made me feel guilty, and I swore to myself that I'd start paying more attention to how she was doing so I could give her more of the experiences she loved while she could still handle it. I wasn't sure how many good days she had left.

Since Mallory was an atheist and often mocked organized religion, I'd expected a few eye rolls, but she participated in the hymns with enough gusto to make Aunt Deidre send her several looks of approval.

The service was drawing to a close, with everyone singing a hymn for the offering, when a deacon approached the minister on the altar and whispered in his ear. The minister looked stricken. He turned to whisper something back, and then the deacon went to speak to a few men in the front row.

I wasn't the only one to have noticed. Half of the congregation stopped singing. The choir started to sing louder to encourage everyone to join back in, but then the minister stood and walked to the pulpit, signaling for the choir to stop.

He drew a breath, looking close to tears, and then said, "Brothers and sisters, I've just received word that a tragedy has struck a family in our congregation."

A murmur went through the crowd, and Aunt Deidre, who was sitting between Mallory and me, grabbed both of our hands and squeezed them.

The minister cleared his throat. "Lindy Fleming was murdered in her home this morning while her family was here at church."

People cried out in distress, and some started to sob.

"Let us pray for the Fleming family." We bowed our heads, and the minister started a prayer for the family, the congregation, and the town, asking God to help the authorities mete out justice for her death.

Blood was pounding in my ears. I was only half listening, my mind caught on what he'd said. Had this been done by the same man who'd hit my car? I knew the thieves had left disgusting photos in at least one of the homes. But leaving photos and murdering someone were two entirely different things.

What if this meant Noah's initial hunch was right, and the burglars had tried to kill me yesterday? At the same time, that didn't seem to fit. If they'd decided to kill me, wouldn't they have followed their pattern—break in and kill me in my home?

The congregation sang several songs, including "It Is Well with My Soul," but I struggled to sing the words. It wasn't well with my soul. None of this was.

The minister dismissed us, but we struggled to make it down the aisle to the exit. Everyone had gathered in groups to talk about Lindy Fleming's murder and speculate on what could have happened.

"Everyone who was burglarized was a member of this church," one woman said to a group in the back of the church. "And now they've killed Lindy."

"That's not true," someone else said. "I know the Middletons, and they don't go here."

"Well, everyone else belongs to the church," the first woman sniped.

No one argued with her, and I wondered if it was true.

Aunt Deidre looked distressed and had started to shake, so Mallory and I took each of her arms and started pushing our way through the crowd to get her outside. I wanted to kick myself for not getting her out of here sooner. The gossiping and the horror...it had been like this when my mother was killed, and being on this side of it was soul crushing. We had to get out of here, not just for Aunt Deidre, but for me too.

We'd made it to the main hall, about ten feet from the exit, when I overheard a man telling his friends, "Elijah said she was strangled."

I stopped in my tracks, nausea roiling through me.

No. Please, God, no.

Stumbling a step, I let go of Aunt Deidre and turned to the man. "Are you sure she was strangled?"

He shot me a glare. "I think the man who found his wife naked on her bed would know. He called me himself."

I drew in a sharp breath and took a step back, another wave of nausea hitting me, even harder this time.

"Mads," Mallory asked with pleading eyes. "Let's just go, okay?"

Amy had been strangled. How often were people strangled? I'd learned in self-defense classes that strangulation isn't like you see in movies or TV. It takes a few minutes to squeeze the life out of someone. It takes a special kind of sociopath to watch the life drain from someone's eyes. That's why it was the kind of crime so often linked to domestic violence—to killing someone you knew.

My mother had been strangled.

The room started to spin, and black dots filled my peripheral vision, but I forced myself to get a grip. I wasn't doing anyone any good if I passed out in the church foyer. I could only imagine how much more it would upset Aunt Deidre.

"Maddie!" Mallory said, getting irritated. Aunt Deidre was making moaning sounds, and multiple people were staring at the both of us.

I took Aunt Deidre's arm, and we made it outside into the sunshine. The temperature was warmer today, so I didn't feel so bad about Aunt Deidre's coat hanging open.

My mind was a storm of thoughts, worries, and *memories*. It wanted to dwell on the past, on the horrors that my mother had faced, but I forced it to leap back to the future.

Boomer had beaten Amy, so him strangling her seemed to

fit, but there was no way he could have killed Lindy Fleming. He was currently in the Wayfare County jail.

But what about his cousin?

I pulled out my phone to call Detective Taylor.

"Maddie?" Mallory asked in dismay. "Who are you calling?"

"I'm checking in with Detective Taylor. Can you take Aunt Deidre to the car? I'll be with you guys in a minute."

She looked worried but agreed, taking my keys so they could get in.

When Detective Taylor answered, I barely gave him a chance to answer before I asked, "Have you found Jake Garfield?"

"What?" he asked, caught off guard. "No. Not yet."

"Do you think he could be involved with the break-ins in Cockamamie?"

"What? Uh..." he stammered, then seemed to regain his senses. "Where's this coming from, Maddie?"

"I took my aunt to church today, and at the end of the service, the minister announced that a woman in the congregation was murdered this morning while her family was at church. Someone who spoke to her husband said she'd been strangled. Just like Amy Davis. That's not very common, Detective Taylor. It happens most frequently with domestic violence victims. So what if Jake killed Amy, not Boomer, and then he murdered that woman this morning?" I knew I sounded hysterical, but all I could think about was someone squeezing the life out of those women, just like someone had squeezed the life out of my mother. What was to stop the murderer from doing it again?

"Okay," he said softly. "Take a deep breath. That's all great speculation. I'll take your theory to Detective Langley."

"Okay," I said, feeling another headache coming on.

"Where are you now?"

I looked up at the stone building. "I'm standing outside the Baptist church."

"Go home. Lock your doors, but I'm guessing this murderer isn't the same person who tried to shoot you. Killers usually stick to the same MO."

I'd had the same thought, but it didn't make me feel much better.

"Thanks," I said. I wasn't sure he was taking this seriously enough, but then again, I'd worried he wouldn't follow up on my information about Amy's extra job. Lance had confirmed that he had looked into it.

I hung up and found Mallory behind the driver's wheel and Aunt Deidre in the passenger seat.

"Snooze, you lose," Mallory said with a wicked grin, but I saw the strain in her eyes. She was as freaked out as I was, but she was trying to lighten the mood for my aunt.

I was starting to wonder if maybe I should move back to Nashville after all. There were good residential care homes up there—probably better than here—and even though Nashville had its share of crime, this all felt much closer to home.

I'd consider it later. I was too distraught to make a decision right now.

Chapter Forty-Two

Noah

"What a fucking shit show," Lance groaned when we walked out of the house a couple of hours later, stripping off our protective gear.

He wasn't wrong. Word about the murder had gotten out, and the street was literally packed with people. Some claimed to have come to comfort Mr. Fleming, but most were there to gawk.

The medical examiner, Dr. Dave Mueller, said he'd have to wait until the autopsy to make it official, but Lindy Fleming's time of death fit within the time period when Mr. Fleming was at church. He agreed that it appeared she'd been strangled, but he couldn't definitively declare it the cause of death until he performed the autopsy the next day. After observing external abrasions in her vaginal area, he also thought it likely she'd been raped.

"Just like Amy Davis," Lance said.

I hadn't missed that either. "We need to get someone to watch Maddie's house." A guy tied to these crimes had been seen going to her place of work for the sole purpose of observing the people there, and now someone had been brutally murdered. She was in danger.

"On it," Lance said, already pulling out his phone to make the call.

But as we started walking down the driveway, Brent and his partner, Tripp, were walking up.

"Did you call them?" Lance asked.

"They asked me to come take a look at the Amy Davis scene, and then I dropped by their crime scene yesterday," I said. "I invited them to check it out, since it might be tied to their case." I gave them a nod of greeting, which the crime log officer noticed and let them sign the sheet.

"I thought you were at the Christmas tree lot because you were terrified something had happened to Maddie," Lance said in a smug tone.

That too, but I wasn't about to advertise it.

After Brent and Tripp finished signing in, they met us in the middle of the driveway, taking in the crowd on both sides of the street.

"Looks like you have a different kind of chaos going on than we did yesterday," Tripp said with a grim look.

"Yeah," I said. "Apparently, the family's pastor announced what happened at church this morning."

Tripp grimaced. "Jesus."

"In more ways than one."

"You said your victim was strangled," Brent said, not looking happy about it.

"And likely raped," I said, speaking quietly so the onlookers wouldn't hear.

Brent grunted. "Dammit."

"We just learned that part, which makes this case even more like yours." I gestured to the house. "Do you want to check out the crime scene? The medical examiner is about to load the body for transport, but you can still take a look."

Brent gave a sharp nod. "Wouldn't hurt to see if there are any connections beyond the obvious to the Amy Davis case."

"I didn't notice anything," I said, "but I welcome fresh pairs of eyes."

"I'm going to check with the sergeant and see if the officers made any progress canvassing the neighborhood," Lance said, obviously none too eager to go back inside.

"Good idea," I said. "The sooner we can view any surveillance video, the better."

Since Lance and I had already stripped off our protective outer layer, I suited back up with the sheriff's detectives before we all headed in.

"This scene fits with our other robbery cases," I said as we entered the house. "Forced rear entry"—I pointed to the busted-in back door—"exit through the garage door. TVs, electronics, and jewelry taken. Just like I mentioned to Brent Friday night."

"I wasn't privy to this conversation," Tripp grunted. "Fill me in."

"In the first robberies, the houses were left neat, but that changed last Tuesday. The place was trashed, and we found the photo and a lipstick heart drawn on the mirror."

"Do you have a theory why things changed?" Tripp asked.

"No. But the next break-in occurred two days later—the perp was escalating. Usually there were more than two days in between robberies. That's the one where Maddie saw the getaway van, and it hit the front of her car. She followed it to get the license number."

"And you're concerned they might have IDed Ms. Baker," Tripp said.

"Yeah. And, as you know, they ditched the van outside city

limits. They stole another in Lynchburg on Thursday night, a red Nissan Quest. I've been piecing together surveillance footage from the neighborhood, trying to get a license number on the gray sedan that dropped the guy off, but no luck so far. The car thief's appearance fits two eyewitness descriptions from the last couple of break-ins—a white guy in his late thirties with a bushy red beard. We've got the van theft on video."

"So you have an image of him?" Brent asked.

"We do. That one was okay, but we got a better one yesterday afternoon. That same Nissan Quest was parked in the Craigmore Trophy lot on Main Street in Cockamamie. The license plate matches the police report, and the guy meets the description of who the witnesses saw in the van after the robberies."

"Including Ms. Baker?" Tripp asked.

I nodded. "It gets worse. The suspect was seen walking from the lot down to the Deja Brew Coffee shop where Maddie works. The cashier said he didn't buy anything, just stood in the back by the door and watched the counter for a bit before leaving. The trophy shop owner said he was in Deja Brew for about ten minutes."

Brent's brow shot up. "He was looking for Maddie?"

"That's what we think. He didn't ask about her, just looked around, then left."

"Have you got someone watching Maddie now?" he asked, concerned.

"Lance spent last night on her sofa. After we realized this situation was tied to the same suspects, we sent an officer over to sit outside her house."

"Good," he said in relief. "Still, it doesn't fit the attempt on her life yesterday. Why shoot at her instead of breaking into her house and strangling her like the others?"

I shuddered inwardly at his bluntness. "I've been wondering

the same thing. I agree, it doesn't fit the MO, but we figured better to be safe than sorry."

"Agreed."

I led them back to the bedroom, where Dr. Mueller was writing something on a clipboard. The body still hadn't been moved.

"Dr. Mueller, can you hold up moving the body for a few minutes?" I asked.

He looked up and nodded to the two detectives. "Detectives Taylor and Donahue. I wondered if I'd see you here. I see we're thinking the same thing."

"You see a connection to Amy Davis's murder?" Tripp asked.

"Obviously I can't say for certain, but we don't get many strangulations in these parts, do we?" Dr. Mueller asked. "Got any theories?"

"If Amy was murdered Monday night," Tripp said, "I'd say that killing her set something loose in him—or *them*—and they've escalated since. Boomer Garfield *did* claim that Amy didn't come home on Monday night."

"So let's say Jake Garfield *did* kill her Monday night," Brent continued. "Last Tuesday and Wednesday, he got off on the thrill of masturbating with the homeowner's underwear. But today, it wasn't enough, and he had to reenact what he did to Amy."

"There's a problem with that theory," Dr. Mueller said. "While Amy Davis was likely raped before her death—probably up to twenty-four hours before—I put her time of death to be late morning or early afternoon on Tuesday."

"There are a few other problems too," I said. "We have two witnesses who say they saw Amy on Tuesday morning, even if we ignore her estimated time of death. So Jake Garfield didn't kill her before the first instance of escalation. Second, how do you account for the Garfield home being burglarized? And three, Ms. Fleming usually goes to church. If they targeted this house, they likely expected it to be unoccupied."

"Which means it could have been a crime of opportunity," Tripp said. "She was here, so he took advantage of it."

"Yeah," I said. "Maybe he would have worked his way up to this, but he advanced sooner because the opportunity was there."

"And we know the two witnesses saw Amy and not someone pretending to be her," Brent said. "The neighbor actually spoke to her and saw that her face had been beaten. Boomer admits Amy was friendly with the neighbor, so she did know who Amy was. She would have known if it wasn't her."

"Sure, but she still could have been raped the night before," Tripp said. "Boomer Garfield beat her after she came home on Monday night, so it stands to reason he could have raped her too. He's obviously an abuser. The grocery store staff said they'd seen evidence of it before."

I added, "And Maddie said Amy asked her to teach her some self-defense moves to break out of a chokehold. That, along with her habit of wearing turtlenecks, suggests he made a habit of strangling her. Maybe he didn't mean to kill her. He was just trying to exert his dominance and lost control."

"Which would fit with all of it," Brent said, getting excited about this theory. "He raped and beat her on Monday night. That spurred her to actually leave him the next morning, but he'd already figured out she was leaving, so he ambushed her somewhere down the road. He beat her and killed her."

"Two huge problems," I pointed out. "Why would Boomer rob his own house? And two, Boomer's currently in the county lockup. There's no way he could have killed Lindy Fleming today."

"Fuck," Tripp grunted.

"Which is why Jake Garfield makes more sense," Brent said solemnly. "*He* could have killed Amy. Maybe Amy was part of the operation and was helping fence the stolen goods. Jake's still at large, so he could have committed the murder this morning too. They're cousins. They live together. It's not outside of reason for them to work together on this."

"But that still doesn't explain why the Garfield residence was broken into," I said. "Why would they rob themselves? To throw us off if we caught up to them?"

"Maybe," Tripp said, a faraway look in his eyes. "But Boomer Garfield was the one to report it. Not Jake."

"So what if Jake's behind the robberies and Boomer is clueless?" I asked. "Jake could have committed the break-in on Tuesday. He wasn't at work when I went by to ask him questions about Amy. And he apparently makes deliveries for his job. He could have left for long enough to burglarize a home before going back to work."

Tripp's mouth twisted to the side as he considered it.

"Jake was at the Christmas tree farm," Brent said. "And he has a beard."

"But it's not red," I countered.

"There's always temporary hair dye. He might consider it enough of a disguise," Tripp said.

"But Maddie's seen both Jake and the man in the van. She never said he was the same guy," I said.

"The red beard may have thrown her," Tripp said. "We should show her the stills of the guy in your videos. Can you get them for us?"

"Yeah," I said. "Sure."

Brent pursed his lips, then pulled out his phone. "I'm getting another warrant for the Garfield residence."

"Didn't you get one to search the house when you arrested Boomer?" I asked.

"Yeah, but that was before another murder and an attempted murder. Want to come take a look with us?"

"You know it."

Chapter Forty-Three

Maddie

Aunt Deidre was a mess when we got her home. All she could think about was the poor dead woman, not that I wasn't thinking about her too. It didn't help that the murder had taken place in a home only a few blocks from our house, which meant we'd driven past the blocked-off street full of emergency vehicles. She kept slipping in and out of time. "Andrea?" she called out in a panic when she saw the lights. "Are they there for my sister?"

"No, Aunt Deidre," Mallory said soothingly, patting her leg. "It's someone else."

I was anxious myself, memories of my mother's death flooding my thoughts, feeling nearly as fresh as the night she'd been murdered. Funny how I'd think I'd finally gotten over it, only for the horror of it all to come swooping back in.

I heated up lasagna for lunch, while Mallory sat with Aunt Deidre and got her calmed down enough to sit at the dining room table. While we were eating lunch, an officer showed up at the door, saying Officer Forrester had asked him to sit outside my house to keep watch.

"Should I be concerned?" I asked. "Is this because of the murder?"

"He didn't tell me much, ma'am. Only asked me to watch for any unusual activity."

"Tell Officer Forrester that we appreciate his concern for our well-being," Mallory said from behind me. "Thank you."

I shut the door and turned to face her. "I bet you're wishing you'd stayed in Nashville, huh?"

She made a face. "No. I'm really glad I'm here for you, but I have to tell you, I really don't want to get murdered."

"That's fair," I said. "I really don't want to get murdered either. But Officer Coolidge is outside watching over us now. We're fine."

She glanced out the living room window, and I looked over her shoulder to see the police car parked directly across the street. Satisfied, she pushed away and headed back to the dining room.

We finished lunch, and since Aunt Deidre was still worked up over the tragedy, I gave her a sedative and took her upstairs to take a nap. Mallory told me she was going to brush up her résumé, so after I got my aunt settled, I went to my room to try to read a book I'd started the week before. I'd only gotten through a few pages before my phone rang with a number I didn't recognize.

"Hello?" I answered tentatively.

"Ms. Baker, this is Ted Roberts, Steve Campbell's attorney."

"Oh." Why on earth was he calling *me*?

"I know this is highly unusual," he said, then cleared his throat, sounding uncomfortable. "But Mr. Campbell would like to speak to you in person."

"What? Why?"

"He said he would like to explain things to you."

"I don't—"

"Like I said, I realize it's unusual, but he said if you come speak to him, he'll give you the money he owes you."

Was he serious?

"Can I actually hold him to that?" I asked in disbelief.

"I have his checkbook, and Mr. Campbell plans to make the check out to you as soon as you arrive. He said he'll include interest."

This had to be a trick, but if there was any chance it was real, I didn't see what harm it could do. And as for being in danger, I suspected the county jail was safer than my own home.

He continued, "Since he hasn't been arraigned, you won't be able to see him on your own. I'll need to be present the whole time. You can come with me when I meet with him at the jail before his interview with the detective."

I *did* want answers, but I'd have to speak to him with his lawyer there. I wasn't sure if that was a good thing or not. But I was struggling to believe that a man I'd lived with for several years had actually tried to kill me. I needed to see him face to face. "Okay," I said. "But if I don't like how it's going, I'll leave."

"That's fine," he said. "I'm at the county jail now, actually. Can you be here within a half hour?"

"Yeah," I said reluctantly. "See you then."

How was I going to explain this to Mallory?

I headed downstairs and took the seat next to her on the sofa. "Don't get mad, but I'm going to the jail to speak to Steve."

"*What?*" she exclaimed. "Have you lost your damn mind?"

"His attorney called and said he wants to see me."

"I'll *bet* he does," she said with plenty of snark.

"His attorney also said he has Steve's checkbook, and he plans to write me a check for what he owes me, plus interest."

She rolled her eyes. "Oh, because you can definitely trust your ex-boyfriend's defense attorney."

She had a point.

"How do you know he actually has that much money in his account, anyway?" she went on. "How do you know it won't bounce?"

Mallory: Two points. Me: Zero.

"I guess I'll find out Monday morning when I deposit it into my account." When she didn't answer, I said, "The thing is, I really need to see him. I need to look him in the eye and ask him if he tried to kill me."

"Seriously, Maddie," she said in frustration. "Do you really think he's going to admit it if he *did*?

"I don't know," I said helplessly. "Probably not, but I still have to see him. I need closure, and I think this is the way to get it. Not necessarily from him—I'm over him—but my money. And I can't help feeling like the past few years of my life were a total waste. I think the money is just something tangible he took from me, something I can focus on getting back. Plus, as broke as I am, the whole money thing has been bugging me for months, and when I found out he sold the house..." I put my hand on hers. "I need to do this."

She glanced up at the ceiling toward Aunt Deidre's room. "I'd go with you, but..."

"That's okay. I need to do this on my own."

She reached over and gave me a hug. "I love you, Mads. Be careful."

"Thanks."

She pulled away from me and said, "That officer out front will probably follow you to the station."

Somehow, I'd forgotten about him. "Nah, I'm going to leave him here. The sheriff's station isn't that far out of town, and maybe I'll call Lance and ask him to escort my car out there." I didn't want to leave Mallory and my aunt in possible danger.

"No, you won't."

She was right. "I love you, Mal."

"Let me know when you get out there, okay?"

"I will. I promise."

Getting past the officer was actually easier than I'd expected. The officer told me Lance had told him to watch the house, so he didn't have a problem with me leaving. But I genuinely didn't want to put myself in danger, so I called Lance as I pulled out of the driveway. My call went to his voicemail, but I told him everything about my arranged meeting with Steve and said I'd text him as soon as I got there so he'd know I was safe.

I watched my rearview mirror the whole drive. At one point, I thought a car three car lengths back was following me, but it turned off onto a road several miles before I reached the county jail. I parked in the lot and walked inside, then sent a group text to Mallory and Lance, telling them I was inside the station—and included a selfie of me in front of the receptionist's desk to prove it.

I tucked away my phone and noticed a middle-aged man in a suit sitting in the corner of the waiting room. He looked very out of place.

"Ms. Baker?" he asked, getting to his feet.

"Mr. Roberts?"

A tight smile lifted his lips. "That's me."

I lifted my chin. "I want proof you have Steve's checkbook."

He reached into his jacket and pulled out a checkbook and handed it to me. "You can hold onto it if you'd like, but I'll have a better chance of getting it into the interview room."

I looked over the blank check to make sure it was really

Steve's, then handed it back. "Why do I feel like I'm being bamboozled?" I asked dryly.

"You and me both," he muttered under his breath.

We headed back, passing through the x-ray machine. I checked in my purse and phone and was then aggressively patted down. Mr. Roberts didn't get the same kind of workup I did, but then again, I suspected they didn't foresee Mr. Roberts trying to break Steve out of jail. Guess they didn't realize there was a far greater chance of Steve's attorney busting him out than me.

A deputy led us to a room with a table, two chairs, and a door on the opposite side of the table. Mr. Roberts gestured for me to sit, and he stood while we waited.

"Don't you need to sit to talk to him?" I asked, gesturing to the legal pad tucked under his arm.

"I'll let him make out the check to you and say his peace. Then I'll have you leave before I talk to him."

"Afraid I'll hear some things that I can take to the deputies?" I asked with more than a bit of attitude.

"Honestly, I've never met the man in my life, so I have no idea what he's about to tell me—or you for that matter. I guess I'll let him be the judge of what you hear."

A few minutes later, the other door opened, and Steve walked in wearing a wrinkled orange jumpsuit. The collar was askew. I couldn't help snickering as the deputy unlocked his handcuffs and then shut him in the room with us.

"Orange is really your color."

He gave me a dirty look but didn't say anything. Instead, he glanced over at Mr. Roberts. "I presume you're my attorney? R.C. Roberts?"

"You presume correctly," Mr. Roberts said dryly. "Let's get to business, shall we?" He plopped Steve's checkbook on the table as well as a ballpoint pen.

Steve sat down and slid the checkbook closer to himself before he looked up at me. "Maddie, you have to know this is all a misunderstanding."

"I have no idea what you're up to, but I just want the money I was promised and for you to tell me the truth—without putting the Steve Campbell spin on it. Then I'm out of here."

"You need to listen to me before I give you the money. That was part of the agreement," he insisted.

"That wasn't what I was told, but fine. Say your peace, but get to the point. We don't have all day."

He placed both hands flat on the table and looked me straight in the eye. "I didn't try to kill you. You have to know that."

"Honestly? I don't know what to believe anymore."

"I didn't do anything, Maddie," he pleaded. "I swear."

"Look," I said in exasperation. "I know why you want to marry me, and I know how embarrassing it would be for you to have to cancel the wedding. My death would be a very convenient excuse to cancel. *Especially* if I was murdered."

His eyes flew wide. "If I planned to kill you, do you really think that I'd come down and let everyone know I was in town— the first time I've been here in years—and murder you while I was here? That's idiotic. If I were going to kill you, I'd have made sure I had some semblance of an alibi in Nashville, then snuck down, killed you, and made it look like an accident."

"Mr. Campbell," Steve's attorney warned with an alarmed look on his face.

I stared at Steve in shock. "Put some thought into it, have you?"

The look on his face suggested maybe he had. "My gun was *stolen* from my motel room, Maddie. I swear. The police don't believe me, but it's true. I heard another guest say things were stolen out of their room too."

"*You had a gun?*"

"I know how bad it looks," he pleaded, "especially since I followed you out to the Christmas tree farm—"

"You did *what?*" I asked.

His attorney interjected, "As your attorney, I *highly* suggest you stop talking now."

Steve ran a hand through his usually manicured but now disheveled hair. "The police already know. I already told them."

"What do you want from me, Steve?" I asked, suddenly exhausted by the whole thing.

He leaned closer and gave me a soft smile. "Surely you can remember when we were good, because we were really good at one point."

I felt some of my resolve soften. He was right. There was a time I'd thought I'd been happy, but I realized now that I'd only convinced myself that I was. In reality, I'd been searching for something more, and I'd mistakenly thought marriage was it. But to be fair, that was on me, not him. "I was, or at least I thought I was," I admitted. "But I haven't been happy for years."

"All because I wouldn't put a ring on your finger?" he asked, but his tone wasn't as angry as I would have expected. "What difference did the ring make, Mads?"

"I want a *family*, Steve."

"We *were* a family. You and me. Sure, we didn't have the kids you wanted. Yet. You spent so much time wanting me to marry you, you didn't see what was already there."

I started to protest, but I couldn't help acknowledging that some part of what he said was true—although not in the way he meant it. I wouldn't have been happy if we'd gotten married. I would have been *miserable*, but if I hadn't been so focused on getting a wedding, then I might have figured that out a whole lot sooner.

I felt like a total idiot.

"You're right," I said.

He looked like I'd just announced I planned to become a nun. "What?"

"You're right," I grudgingly admitted. "I was too focused on how I thought things were supposed to be. I forgot about the here and now."

Excitement filled his eyes. "The thing is, Maddie, I *do* want to marry you! It just took missing you for me to realize it."

Same old Steve trying to manipulate the situation to his advantage. "You're forgetting I know about Serendipity. You invited your boss to the wedding you're planning, and I know you'll be humiliated when I don't show up on the big day. You hate being humiliated, not to mention all the money you're going to lose. But, despite all that, would you kill me? I don't know if you'd go that far."

"Oh my God, Maddie!" he protested. "Do you really think I'm a cold-blooded killer?"

I looked into his eyes, then I gestured to the checkbook. "I'd like my check now."

"If you marry me—"

"I'm giving you one last chance to pay me back, Steve. For once in your life, *please* just do the right thing."

"Maddie..." he pleaded.

I'd been stupid to come here. Even if he'd tried to kill me—which I honestly believed he didn't—he would never admit to it. And I could see now that he'd never intended to pay me back. I was like his dog, and all he had to do was dangle a treat to get Maddie to come running. And good for him, because it had worked. But I was done. No more. Shaking my head, I got up and faced Mr. Roberts. "I'm leaving."

"Maddie!" Steve shouted.

But Mr. Roberts knocked on the door, and it opened seconds later.

"Maddie! Come back!" Steve called after me as I stalked out.

"I'll see what I can do to make him keep his word," Steve's attorney said as I walked out the door.

I wasn't holding my breath.

Chapter Forty-Four

Noah

It didn't take long to get a search warrant for the Garfield property. While Lance stayed back at the station to go through the surveillance footage that was coming in, I headed out to walk through the house with Brent and Tripp. Brent had tried to notify the property owner—Peter Castillo—about what was going on, but so far the sheriff's department hadn't had much luck locating him. Lance hadn't gotten a chance to look since we'd been called to the robbery on Tuesday.

We parked on the road and walked up to the door. Jake didn't answer, so Tripp had the deputies bust it open.

The living room was a mess—even worse than when I'd seen it through the window a few days ago. More fast food bags and plates covered in dried food. The carpet had to be a couple of decades old, and the traffic patterns were well worn. The ratty looking Christmas tree was still on a table in the corner.

A TV sat on a stand, but an empty TV box leaned against the wall next to the stand.

"Looks like Jake got himself a new TV," Brent said. "This

wasn't here when we searched the house after Jackson Garfield's arrest."

"And it looks like he bought it," Tripp said.

I was starting to have serious doubts that Jake Garfield was our man. "Why would he buy a TV when he could have just used one he'd stolen?"

"Maybe this one is special," Brent said. "You know, like 4K or 3D, or mega pixels, or whatever's the latest and greatest."

Tripp walked over to the box and used his gloved hand to move it away from the wall. "It has a Walmart price tag that reads $399.98." He gave Brent a wry look. "Not that special."

"Or he could be working for someone," I said. "There was a matchbook left under the abandoned van. It had a rooster on it, and our narc guy said he's heard of matchbooks being passed out to some people at Cock on the Walk." I glanced over at Brent. "Find any evidence that Boomer frequented Cock on the Walk?"

"He liked to go out there for drinks with his cousin. He occasionally brought his girlfriend."

"What about Jake? Did he spend time there without his cousin?"

He pulled a face. "That I'm not sure about. We were focusing on Boomer. We know Jake used to go there with Boomer, but not whether he ever went alone."

"So if one or both of them was working on the burglaries, they might have been taking the stolen goods to someone out at Cock on the Walk," I said.

"Doubtful," Tripp said with a frown. "The Brawlers don't like to get involved in anything outside their drug business."

"But what if it wasn't the Brawlers? The matchbook had the name George on it, and our narc guy said he's never heard of a George."

Brent and Tripp considered it before Brent shrugged. "I guess it's possible."

"Did you find any close friends or family who might be harboring him?" I asked.

"We checked all the usual places, but we haven't checked Cock on the Walk. He could be hiding there, but we don't have enough evidence to get a warrant for the place."

"Let's see if we find anything else here," Tripp said.

We walked into the kitchen and started going through cabinets and drawers. Nothing jumped out at me, but I left Tripp and Brent to continue looking while I headed to the bedrooms.

It was easy to figure out which room had been Amy's because of the pile of women's clothes on the floor. It looked like it had been shoved into a corner. The drawers were mostly empty except for some men's underwear, T-shirts, and sweatshirts, which looked like they'd been shoved in. Finding Amy's clothes on the floor seemed consistent with Boomer's claim of a robbery on Monday. The new TV did too. If she'd come home Monday night and been beaten and raped, then I doubted she'd tidied up. She'd probably thrown some clothes into a bag the next morning and then gotten the hell out. Then again, the sheriff's department had searched the house after Boomer's arrest. They could have trashed it too.

Still, there seemed to be a lot of women's clothing. Why would she have left so many clothes behind?

"Hey, Brent," I called out as I moved to the closet. "Did you find a suitcase and plastic bag of belongings in Amy Davis's car?"

"Yeah," he said, standing in the doorway. "A small carry-on bag with some clothes stuffed inside, and not very neatly at that, and a bag with some toiletries."

I frowned as I took in the hanging clothes in the closet and the pile on the floor. "Why didn't she take all of these things?"

"It *was* a carry-on bag," Brent said.

I looked through the closet but didn't see any other suit-cases. Maybe he had a point. Still, I would have expected her to fill another bag with clothes and not just toiletries.

"Do you have an inventory of the items she packed?"

"I haven't seen it yet," he said.

"I'd like to take a look when the list is available."

"Yeah," he said absently. "Sure thing."

"Does the room look the same as it did the last time you went through it?"

He glanced around. "Seems like it."

I squatted and started sorting through the clothes.

"We already looked for bloody clothing."

"I'm looking for underwear."

"Excuse me?"

I glanced back at him. "With the previous two break-ins, the underwear was on the bed with the photo."

He shook his head. "Not the one this morning."

"Right, but then he didn't need it, did he? In the past, he got some sexual gratification from the underwear. Today, he got it from the rape." I tossed the last piece of clothing aside. "No underwear."

"Duane didn't see a photo when he was here Monday night," Brent said.

"Maybe he hadn't advanced to the photos yet. Maybe he was still focusing on the underwear. I don't see any here."

"She could have packed them," Brent suggested.

"Which is why I really want to see that inventory of the items she packed." I stood up.

"I took a quick glance at the contents," Tripp said, walking into the room. "I don't remember seeing any."

"You just might not remember it correctly," Brent said.

I nodded. "For argument's sake, let's say she didn't take all her underwear with her. Why would Boomer remove it from his own house?"

"To get rid of evidence," Brent suggested.

"But what kind of evidence could be on her underwear?" Tripp asked. "Sure, if he raped her, maybe that pair, but even if his semen was on her underwear, they're in a committed relationship. It wouldn't be outside the realm of possibility."

"Maybe Jake took them," Brent said. "Maybe he had a thing for Amy, but she was his cousin's girlfriend, which made her off limits. So maybe he raped her on Monday night, and that set him off. Or maybe it was something else, but it made him unbalanced enough to lose it during the break-in on Tuesday morning, and he trashed the place. Then maybe he was on his way back from the break-in and encountered Amy when she was leaving Tuesday morning. He pulled her over and things escalated from there."

"Or," I said. "It was someone else entirely."

"Either is possible," Brent admitted.

"I want to talk to Boomer," I said. "We know he didn't kill Lindy Fleming, but I want to see if he incriminates his cousin."

"Yeah," Tripp said. "Fine with me."

"Same," Brent said, sounding discouraged.

"The Cockamamie police chief is having a press conference at six. He's going to release the images we have of the suspect. Hopefully, that will bring us some leads, because even if Jake is involved in this, it's almost certainly not a one-person job."

"True," Brent said with a sigh, then straightened his shoulders. "You go talk to Jackson Garfield. We'll let you know if we find something."

"Ditto."

Chapter Forty-Five

Noah

I called Lance as I walked out of the Garfields' house toward my car.

"How'd it go at Jake's house?" he asked.

"We didn't find much." I shared my thoughts about the clothes and our discussion about Jake's potential involvement. By the time I'd finished, I was in my car, starting the engine. "I'm headed to the county jail to question Boomer. Want to meet me there?"

"Funny you should ask. I'm in my car headed out to the county jail to intercept Maddie."

"Say *what?*"

"Maddie went to the county jail to have a chat with Campbell."

I'd started to put the car in drive but stopped. "She did *what?* What about the officer parked outside her house? Didn't he try to stop her?"

"I told him to watch the house. He took it literally."

"Fuck me," I grunted. "Call her and tell her to stay put. When we're done with Boomer, you can follow her home."

"Already on it."

We hung up, and I headed toward the county jail, resisting the urge to call Maddie. What had she been thinking? He was a suspect in her attempted murder! How'd she even get inside to see a suspect who hadn't been arraigned yet?

Lance's car was already in the parking lot when I pulled in, and thankfully—or not, since she shouldn't have been there in the first place—so was Maddie's.

I walked into the building, telling myself I was going to let Lance handle the situation, but when I walked in and saw her, my resolve broke. I was terrified the person going around raping and killing women had Maddie in his sights. How could we protect her if she was gallivanting all over the county?

She and Lance were huddled together in a corner of the waiting room, speaking in low tones. Relief washed through me, quickly followed by anger.

"What the hell were you thinking?" I demanded as I walked up to them.

She turned to face me and her cheeks reddened as her eyes flashed with fury. "Excuse me?"

Lance rolled his eyes. "Noah, go get checked in," he said in exasperation.

"Do you have any idea the potential danger you're in?"

Her shoulders tensed as she clenched her fists at her sides. "Well, I've just verified that none of it's from Steve Campbell, so you're welcome."

"You're damn right he isn't a danger to you," I ground out, probably turning my molars to dust. "He's behind bars."

"He didn't do it, Noah," she spat out. "I know the man, and he didn't try to kill me. Did anyone follow up to see if there'd been break-ins at his motel?"

It wasn't our case, and I'd been focused on finding the burglary suspect. I glanced over at Lance to see if he knew.

"Yeah," he said, responding to Maddie and not me. "I

checked the reports and talked to a motel clerk. There have been a few reported break-ins, but the clerk said a lot of the break-ins aren't reported because the thefts often include illegal items."

"Like drugs?" she asked, her brow wrinkled in confusion. When he nodded, she asked, "Where the hell was he staying?"

"The Bluebird Inn."

Her jaw dropped. "What?"

"If he lost his job and is working a low-level position at the new one, he probably doesn't have much money," Lance responded.

"But he sold that house," she protested. "He made so much money..." Her voice trailed off, surprise replaced by resignation. "The wedding. He put it on the wedding." Her anger reignited. "Just how much money is he spending on it?" It was a rhetorical question, because she added, "I can't believe he'd stay at the Bluebird. I'm surprised he didn't choose to sleep in his car over that."

"Well, if Steve wasn't behind your assassination attempt, all the more reason you shouldn't have left your house," I ground out, frustrated all over again. "What the hell were you thinking?" I repeated.

"It was fine!" she insisted, but she didn't seem to be putting as much effort into the argument. "I was in my car. What's the danger in that?"

"Only Amy Davis was in her car too," I said, grinding my teeth again. "And someone probably intercepted her in her car right before they killed her."

Maddie's face paled.

Lance shot me a dark look, then turned to Maddie. "You're not safe. Not until we find out who's doing this and catch them." He glanced back at me, then turned to her. "Noah and I have to go talk to Boomer, but I want you to wait here, okay? When we're done, I'll follow you and make sure you get home okay." His voice softened. "Will you wait for me?"

Her gaze shifted to me for half a second before returning to his face. "Yeah. I'll wait."

Lance released a breath of relief. "Thank you. This might take a little while. Maybe call Mallory and tell her the plan. She's called me three times already."

Maddie's mouth lifted into a grin, and her eyes lit up. "I suspect that wasn't as much of a hardship as you're making it out to be."

He released a nervous laugh and rubbed the back of his neck. "Maybe not."

That caught me by surprise. Lance and Maddie's friend Mallory? Then again, she seemed like a spitfire, and I could see why Lance would be intrigued.

I reluctantly left Maddie in the waiting room and let the staff know we were there to interview Boomer. He hadn't yet retained an attorney and had rejected the public attorney assigned to him, so we didn't have to wait for anyone to show up.

Boomer was already in the interview room when we walked in, his orange jumpsuit stretched over the muscles of his chest, shoulders, and arms. It looked like the seams were about to give way. He looked glum as he sat in his chair and rubbed his bare wrists. He still had marks from the handcuffs he'd worn for his walk from his cell to this room.

"Boomer," I said, taking one of the chairs. Lance sat next to me. "I'm Detective Noah Langley with the Cockamamie Police Department, and this is Officer Lance Forrester. We'd like to ask you some questions about your cousin Jake."

His eyes flashed with surprise. "Jake? Why're you asking about him?"

I gave him a tight smile. "How did Amy and Jake get along?"

He seemed surprised, then he shook his head. "There you go again, barking up the wrong tree. There's no way Jake killed her."

"That's not what I asked, now is it?" I asked, keeping a calm demeanor. "I asked about their relationship."

He scratched the top of his head. "They got along."

"Really? Because that's not what I've heard," I said. That was a flat-out lie, but he didn't need to know that.

His face contorted with anger. "Who told you that? That fucking busybody neighbor, Barbara? She can't keep her fucking nose out of anything. Always trying to stir up shit."

"Stir up shit?" I asked in confusion. "How so?"

"She was a little too friendly with Amy." His face fell, and tears filled his eyes. "Why are you in here asking questions about Jake instead of finding the fucker who killed her, because I. Didn't. Do. It." He pounded his fist into the table to emphasize each of his last four words.

"Do you have any idea who might have wanted to kill her?" Lance asked sympathetically.

"No!" he wailed, starting to cry. "That girl didn't have an enemy in the world. Everyone liked her."

"What about you?" I asked. "Did *you* like her?"

"I loved her!" he shouted through tears.

"But you got a little frustrated with her at times," I suggested. "I mean, women, right? You want things done a certain way, and you tell 'em time and time again, yet they still don't get it right."

He didn't answer.

"Did you like things done a certain way, Boomer?" I asked.

His tears began to subside. "Doesn't everyone?"

"Sure," I said. "Take me. I'm a bachelor. I like things in their place. If a woman moved in with me, I'd have a hard time adjusting to having her stuff in my space."

He shook his head. "It wasn't like that with Amy. She was neater than me and Jake, but we sure did like it clean after she started doing it."

"Bet she was a good cook too," I suggested.

He shrugged and wiped under his nose with the back of his hand. "She was all right."

"It must have been great having a third income to help with things," I said.

"She didn't make all that much," he said. "And she was eating food and using electricity."

"True," I said. "But you loved her, so it was worth the hassle."

He nodded, his head lowered.

"Do you have a temper, Boomer?"

His gaze jerked up to mine.

"I mean," I said slowly, "you just yelled at me when you told me you loved Amy. You're probably under a lot of pressure. New relationship—and you're living together. This woman's now in your space, so you're trying to figure things out. And I bet there were clashes with Jake. What did he think about Amy moving in?"

Boomer looked away. "He didn't mind."

"But it had been a while since a woman had lived with you, right?"

He nodded, staring down at the table.

"I bet Jake liked it being just the two of you. I bet he resented Amy moving in with you," I said. "At least, that's what I heard."

He jerked his head up. "Who told you that?"

I shrugged. "Doesn't matter where I heard it. Only that it's true. Did you two argue over Amy?"

"Sure, he didn't like her being there in the beginning, but after a month or two, he got used to it."

"So you're saying they became friends?"

He made a face. "I'm not sure I'd say that, but he didn't resent her being there anymore. He liked that she cooked and cleaned."

I'll bet he did. "Where do you work, Boomer?"

He shifted in his seat. "Palmer Garage Doors. I install garage doors."

Garage doors? It piqued my interest, but the burglars hadn't broken in through the garage doors—they'd only left that way. Making a connection there felt like a stretch. "How long you been doing that?'

He shrugged. "A couple months."

Shortly before the break-ins started.

"Do you drive your own car to do the installations?"

"No," he said, shaking his head. "I get a company truck. Why are you asking about this? I already told those other two guys."

"I'd rather hear it straight from you. How many installs do you think you do a day?"

"It depends on a lot of things. Some days are slow, and some installs are harder than others."

"Do you make your own schedule?"

"Not really," he said. "I have a list of homes to go to, and I tell dispatch when I finish a job and I'm going to another."

"So you have some flexibility between jobs," I said. "You could take your time getting to the next one if you had an errand to run or something like that."

He took a moment before he said, "Yeah, I guess."

"And Jake, how often is he out making deliveries for the auto supply store?"

"Just about every day," he said.

"Did you two ever meet up during the day?" I watched him carefully to see his body language when he responded.

Confusion filled his eyes. "You mean, like, for lunch?"

"Yeah, or to meet up at someone else's house."

His confusion deepened. "Why would we do that?"

"It was just a question," I said, holding out my hands. "Did Amy have any other jobs other than at the grocery store?"

"Nope. She talked about getting one since she wasn't full time there, but I told her I liked her being home."

"Did she spend much money?"

"Nope, and that's one of the things I like about her." Tears welled in his eyes. "Liked." He started to cry.

"So if she was making extra money, where do you think she was getting it?"

His brow furrowed. "There was no way she was making extra money."

"What if I told you that her body was discovered with a large amount of cash?"

"What?" He shook his head. "No way. She gave all her money to me, and I gave her a hundred dollars every paycheck."

Pretty damn generous, I thought sarcastically, but kept it to myself. It wasn't time for animosity yet. I needed him to think I was on his side.

"Does Jake contribute to the household budget?" I asked.

"You're asking if he pays for groceries and such?"

I nodded.

"Yeah. And half the rent." He narrowed his eyes. "Why are you asking about Jake?"

"Did he do odd jobs to make extra money?"

"He's been working at the Christmas tree farm. His friend Travis's parents own it. And sometimes he helps in the summer, tending to the trees."

"No other part-time jobs?"

"No."

"Has he had any extra cash lately?"

He stilled. "I don't know."

He was lying. I smothered my excitement. "Did he show up with any new toys over the last few weeks? TVs? Game systems?"

He hesitated, then said, "He bought a new PlayStation last week, but it got stolen on Monday."

"What else did they take?"

"Our TVs, Jake's iPad, the PlayStation, like I told you."

"Anything of Amy's?"

"She didn't have nothing to take, but whoever broke in tore the place up pretty good. Clothes dumped out of drawers and the mattresses shoved off the beds like they thought we were hiding the family jewels under them." He snorted.

"So you think they were looking for something?"

"Maybe? Or just being thorough. I guess that's what I'd do if I was robbing a place. You hear about people hiding money under mattresses and such." He paused. "I got home before Jake and called the sheriff. The back door was busted open, stuff was missing. Jake came home while the deputy was there, and he got pissed that the sheriff's department was in our house. After they left, Amy never came home that night, so then Jake accused *her* of tearing the place up and stealing our stuff. He thought she'd fenced our stuff to run away."

"Do you think that's what happened?"

He considered it for a moment. "No. She wouldn't do that," he said softly. "That's not in her. The stealing part anyway."

"Your neighbor said she saw Amy leave your house on Tuesday morning."

"I'm telling you! Amy never came home on Monday night!" He took a breath, then sounded calmer. "But I *do* think she came by the house on Tuesday morning."

"Why do you say that?" I asked.

"Because her suitcase was lying on the bedroom floor Monday night, as though someone had searched it. But when I came home from work on Tuesday, it was gone. I figured she'd found someplace to stay on Monday night and had come over to get her things the next morning while I was at work."

"Do you think Jake could have intercepted her when she came to get her stuff?" I asked. "Maybe he was still pissed, thinking she'd stolen his new PlayStation?"

He didn't answer.

"Was he still mad on Tuesday night?" I asked.

"No," Boomer said. "He'd calmed down, but he seemed jumpy. Kind of nervous."

I didn't say anything, letting the silence fill the room for nearly ten seconds before I asked, "Why do you think he was nervous, Boomer?"

He looked down at his lap and picked at the skin next to his thumbnail. "I don't know."

"Did Jake ever hit Amy?" When he didn't answer, I said, "We know she was beaten several times after moving in with you. Multiple witnesses have come forward."

He didn't respond.

"I get it," I said with plenty of empathy. "You come home after a *really* long day. People bitching at you because they think their newly installed garage door opener's too loud. Or they don't like the look of the remote. We both know people have ridiculous demands."

He nodded slightly.

"So you're tired and frustrated, and all you want to do when you get home is kick back and have a cold one while watching a game or maybe zoning out with TikTok. But then your girlfriend starts whining that she wants to go out to see a movie, and your temper flares. You didn't mean to hurt her, but dammit," I said, starting to get worked up, "you've had it up to here with people demanding shit from you." I held my hand over my head. "So you don't mean to hit her, but you do, and it's not your fault. If she'd just read the damn room. Am I right?"

He didn't answer.

"But then your temper subsides, and you tell her you didn't mean to do it. You say you're sorry, and it won't happen again. And you mean it. You really do, but then the next time."

He looked up at me with tears in his eyes. "What's your point?"

"You hit her," I said with a harsh edge. "I want you to man up and admit it."

"I hit her!" he shouted, then his face fell, and he whispered, "I hit her."

"And did Jake hit her?"

He shook his head. "No."

"Did you strangle her?"

Tears welled in his eyes. "I didn't kill her. I swear!"

"But you did choke her, didn't you? On Monday night Amy asked a self-defense instructor to teach her how to get out of a chokehold."

Shame filled his eyes and his face turned red. "I may have gone too far a couple of times." He sounded broken. "But I didn't kill her. I swear. I loved her too much."

"And what about Jake?" I asked. "Was Jake in love with Amy?"

He released a bitter laugh. "Jake isn't capable of loving anyone other than himself."

"So did he want to sleep with her?"

He drew in a breath and pushed it out. "He never said, but yeah, I think so. I saw him looking at her, and he hated that she didn't even like him."

"Do you think Jake was capable of killing Amy?"

He looked up at me with tears streaming down his face. "Yeah. I think maybe he was."

I turned to look at Lance. We needed to find Jake Garfield ASAP.

Chapter Forty-Six

Noah

The chief's press conference, planned for six, was aimed at calming the public, but I wasn't sure their fears could be appeased. A monster was still on the loose, and people needed to be on guard.

Thankfully, he planned to speak to the cameras himself, but he texted me at about five-thirty, saying he wanted me on the sidelines in case he had any questions. Which meant I needed to book it from the county jail to make it on time. Lance wasn't required to be there, so he followed Maddie home, then planned to tell the officer on duty that no one was allowed to leave the house.

I called Brent on the way back to the police station to tell him about my visit with Boomer.

"You think Jake killed her?" he asked.

"Honestly," I said, "I don't know. Maybe have him take a polygraph. But after talking to Boomer, I'm starting to believe that Amy didn't come home the night before she was murdered."

"What about the neighbor and her friend seeing her the next day?"

"I think Amy spent the night with a friend and came back in the morning when she figured Boomer and Jake would be at work. Boomer said her suitcase was on the floor Monday night, and gone the next day. Then the neighbor saw her after she'd packed."

"But the neighbor said Amy came home on Monday night," Brent reminded me.

"Maybe she was mistaken. I think I'm going to talk to the neighbor again after the press conference. Maybe she's confusing Monday and Sunday night." Then I added, "If that's okay with you. I know it's your case."

"Hey, the more hands on deck, the better. Besides, it looks like it might be tied to your cases. I actually tried to talk to the neighbor after we finished with the Garfield house this afternoon, but she wasn't home."

"I'll tell you how it goes."

I showed up at the police station with a few minutes to spare, making sure the chief had all the pertinent information.

The press conference was held in front of the station. The chief stood behind a podium while I and a few other members of the police department stood to the side. The chief told the press that a murder had occurred during a home robbery, but no other information was being released. He also revealed that we had a vehicle description and images of the suspect. He held up stills of both and said the photographs were also on the Cockamamie Police Department's website. He asked for anyone with information to call it in. I knew we'd get an avalanche of useless tips, but we might get one or two pieces of helpful information.

The conference was short and direct, and when it was over, I headed over to Mrs. Johnson's house, but she still wasn't home. Maybe the police presence next door had prompted her to flee for the day. I called Brent to let him know, then texted Lance that I was on my way back to the police station.

Lance was at his desk when I walked in. He'd picked up food for both of us, and I grabbed my burger and took a bite, realizing I hadn't eaten since that morning. "Any good tips come in?"

"Nothing useable."

I grunted, not surprised. We worked a couple more hours, then I called it.

"We're spinning our wheels. I'll leave word for the night crew to get ahold of us if something good comes in, otherwise, we should head home and get some sleep so we can tackle this fresh tomorrow."

He readily agreed. We shut down our computers and walked out together. When we got to the parking lot, he stopped and turned to me. "Campbell promised to write Maddie a check for what he owes her if she came to see him," Lance said. "He didn't give it to her, by the way."

I didn't respond.

"That's it?" he said, starting to get angry. "You have nothing to say?"

"What do you want me to say?" I shot back. "Am I surprised the asshole promised to pay her and didn't? No. And I feel badly for her, but what do you want me to do?"

"You seriously want to pretend you don't give a shit?"

I closed my eyes and sighed in exhaustion. "What exactly do you want from me, Lance? I don't want kids. She does. I'm not putting anyone else through that."

He narrowed his eyes. "Through what?"

"My father did this job, and he sucked as a parent. My mother was basically a single mom."

Frustration filled his eyes. "So you're basing this decision on your father's behavior?"

"Not entirely, but partially, yeah."

Putting his hands on his hips, he stared at the building

before turning back to me. "Sure, we're working late tonight, but most nights, we're done by five or six. And I hate to jinx us by mentioning this, but murder and mayhem aren't the norm here in Cockamamie. It's usually much more boring." He paused. "Unless you're planning to go back to the big city."

"Some days, I'm not sure." I missed my mother, my sister, and her kids, and even though I was only a few hours away, I still didn't go back much.

"If you don't want to have kids because you don't want the responsibility, or they don't fit into your life plan, then that's your choice, and don't let anyone shame you for it," he said. "But if you don't want kids because you had a shitty dad, then I think you should reconsider your stance." He held my gaze and gave me a weary smile. "I just don't want you to throw away an amazing woman because your father messed you up."

"I've been messed up by more than my father," I said bitterly.

"Maybe instead of whining about it, you should try to fix it." Then he got in his car and shut the door.

I had to admit he had a point about all of it, but now wasn't the time to tackle it. I needed to go home and get to bed.

My phone rang around three a.m., and I jolted awake when I saw Brent's name on the screen.

"What's up?" I said, answering it, still groggy.

"We located Jake Garfield."

I sat up and turned on the light. "Have you questioned him yet?"

"Not unless I find a medium somewhere. He's dead."

"Shit," I grumbled. "How?"

"Gunshot to the temple. It was set up to look like suicide."

"Set up?"

"Come see for yourself."

I slid out of bed and headed to the bathroom. "Where was he found?"

"Same lot where you found the white van."

"I'll be there in about twenty minutes."

I dressed in record time, calling Lance during the process to let him know, then headed out the door. "I'll pick you up on the way."

He was ready for me when I swung by his house, holding two thermal mugs. He got in the car and handed me one, then we drove to the scene in silence. I was lost in thought.

Finding Jake dead was far from ideal. He'd likely taken a lot of secrets to his grave. Secrets we needed to know.

The property where we found the van was full of sheriff's deputies' cars. Some were parked in front of the outbuilding, shining spotlights on something behind it. I parked on the street, and Lance and I headed over. I flashed my badge to one of the deputies on the perimeter. "Detective Taylor called us in."

He handed me the log-in sheet. After we both signed it, the deputy motioned us forward. "He's over by the truck."

We walked around the building and saw a pickup truck parked next to it in about the same place the van had been, only the truck was farther back. Brent and Tripp were standing next to the open driver's door, talking too quietly for me to hear, but they stopped when they saw us.

"We have to quit meeting like this," I said with a grim smile.

Tripp made a face. "Feel free to take a look."

Lance and I moved closer.

"A deputy found the truck about an hour and a half ago. He couldn't see it from the road, but he remembered the van had been found here and decided to check for signs of Garfield. He found the truck, approached the vehicle, and found Garfield in the driver's seat."

I peered in and saw the man slumped in the seat. I shone my flashlight inside. Blood splattered the right side of his coat, but from what I could see, there was no blood inside the actual truck cab. A gun was cradled on his lap. I let Lance look after me.

"We already tested him for gunshot residue," Brent said, then yawned.

"Negative," Tripp filled in for him.

"Both hands?" Lance asked.

"Yep."

"Definite setup, especially when you factor in the lack of blood splatter in the truck."

"So he was shot somewhere else and brought here," Lance said.

"Looks like it."

"Any clues as to who might have done it?"

"That's the weird part," Brent said. "We were practically given a road map." He picked up a clear plastic bag from a box, then retrieved a wallet from it. "It doesn't belong to Garfield." He picked up another baggie, this one containing a Tennessee driver's license. "Gil Hoffman, last known residence in Murphy."

Murphy was an unincorporated town in Wayfare County, about fifteen miles to the east of us.

"We've filed for a search warrant for his property. We're just waiting for the judge to sign it."

"Do you really think the perp would be so careless?" I asked.

"I don't know," Brent admitted. "But take a closer look at the photo."

Lance and I leaned in.

"Shit," Lance exclaimed. "It's our suspect."

"Thought you might want to be in on the bust," Brent said with a grin.

"Hell, yeah we do," Lance said enthusiastically.

I wanted to be as excited, but something about this felt wrong. After all the misdirection and secrecy, it was wrapped up too neatly. Then again, we hadn't caught Gil Hoffman yet.

In the process of filling out the search warrant, Tripp discovered that Hoffman rented from the same landlord the Garfields did—Peter Castillo.

"That can't be a coincidence," I said. "Did you track the guy down?"

"Nope," Brent said, "but we plan on it after this bust goes down. Maybe he's the mastermind behind all of this."

The search warrant was approved, and Brent and Tripp coordinated with the deputies to create a plan for executing the warrant. Tennessee had banned no-knock warrants—a decision I'd fully supported. There were too many instances of things going wrong for the occupants and for law enforcement, but knocking on the door in the middle of the night was still potentially dangerous. We didn't know anything about the suspect either, which made it harder to plan the execution. Ideally, there would have been surveillance done on the house so we could track the occupants' comings and goings. Obviously, we didn't have time for that, so the plan was to head over to a church parking lot half a mile away from the house on a one-acre lot surrounded by trees. Two deputies would park in a car close to the house to do reconnaissance.

It was getting close to dawn, and it was much easier and safer to apprehend a subject once they came out of their residence. Less chance for law enforcement to get hurt, and safer for the suspect too. But we knew nothing about Gil's work schedule—if he had one—and we didn't want to let him get away or drag this out forever.

The deputies scoped out the ranch-style house and saw the red Nissan Quest parked under a carport. Everything looked quiet, so we decided to move. We surrounded the property, stationing deputies in the woods behind the house. Then, donning bulletproof vests, Brent, Tripp, and several deputies approached the front door, with Lance and I pulling up the rear.

I had a bad feeling about this.

They knocked and shouted, "Wayfare County Sheriff. Open up!"

When there was no answer, they called out several more times before using a battering ram to smash in the front door. We rushed in behind shields, prepared for gunshots as we made our way into the house. None came.

The house was furnished with older furniture that looked like hand-me-downs or garage-sale finds. But it was fairly neat and clean—except for the red-bearded dead man sitting in the brown fake leather recliner and the blood splatter on the wall behind him. A rifle was propped up on his lap, the barrel pointing toward his chin, which had a gaping, bloody hole. He hadn't been dead for long, so he was recognizable as the man in the surveillance footage. This was Gil Hoffman.

"Shit," I spat out. "Goddammit."

I turned around and walked out of the house, staring at the sunrise to the east.

Lance followed and stood beside me for several long seconds, not saying a word. He didn't need to. We both knew we were fucked.

We spent the next several hours watching as county processed the crime scene. The medical examiner processed Jake Garfield's body first, then came out to Gil Hoffman's place. Dr.

Mueller agreed with our assessment that Jake hadn't killed himself in the truck, but his preliminary findings suggested that Mr. Hoffman *had* killed himself. The wound was consistent with a self-inflicted wound, and the evidence left behind also fit, from the blood and tissue splatter to the gunpowder residue on his hands. When they conducted a sweep of the house, they found a chair with ropes in the basement, as well as a sheet of plastic on the floor covered with blood splatter. Jake's work name tag was found on the floor, tucked partially under a shelf by the chair. We deduced that Gil Hoffman held Jake hostage and killed him for whatever reason, then staged his body on the property.

We also found multiple pairs of women's underwear and more Polaroid photos of Gil Hoffman, his face showing in some of them, masturbating with the women's underwear. There were photos of the women's houses, including Amy Davis's bedroom, but the most incriminating photos were of Amy and Lindy dead. Amy was naked on a bed that looked remarkably like the bed in the master bedroom upstairs.

It was getting tied up with a nice big bow—Gil Hoffman was the rapist who'd killed and murdered Amy Davis and Lindy Fleming, and he'd taken photos to prove it.

The working theory was that Jake and Gil Hoffman had committed the burglaries together, then Gil had turned violent. We still didn't have a reason for his escalating behavior, but it fit with Jake becoming increasingly anxious. We theorized that Jake had tried to kill Maddie because they saw her as a threat, then Gil had gotten nervous that Jake was going to turn him in, so he'd kidnapped and killed him to forestall that from happening.

But there were things we weren't sure about. One, how had Gil gotten back to his house after dropping off Jake and his truck behind the garage on the other property? And second, where was all the stuff they'd stolen?

We hadn't found any money in either the Garfield or Hoffman residences. We theorized that Amy had somehow found the money and stolen it, and Gil had tried to get it back from her, raping and murdering her in the process.

Brent and Tripp determined that the rash of burglaries at the Bluebird Inn had been part of their burglary ring, and that was how they'd gained possession of Steve's rifle. They'd used it to shoot at Maddie at the Christmas tree farm, but it was also the gun Gil Hoffman had used to kill himself, so Brent and Tripp planned to release Campbell that evening.

I intended to be there when he got out. I wanted to question him about possibly being the third party, but in this instance, I planned for my visit to be more personal.

Chapter Forty-Seven

Maddie

After Lance followed me home from the county jail on Sunday, I told Mallory everything. She opened a bottle of wine and poured me a glass without a single "I told you so" or even insinuating it.

"I'm here now, Mads. I plan to sublet my apartment, move my things into storage next week, and officially move in with you. I'll help with the bills. I'll help with everything."

We ordered pizza and watched a movie with Aunt Deidre before bed.

Since Mallory was staying with us, I didn't need to wait for Linda to arrive before I left for work in the morning. I got to the coffee shop at 6:50, ten minutes before it opened.

Petra and Chrissy were both surprised to see me. "What are you doing here so early?" Petra asked.

I explained about Mallory living with us for the foreseeable future, and that she'd be available to watch my aunt in the mornings. "I'll be able to pull my weight now," I said. "At least until Mallory gets a job."

The morning flew by, and by noon, rumors were swirling that the sheriff's department had caught the rapist. I considered calling Lance to confirm, but I figured he'd let me know when he could.

I got off work and walked out the back door, digging through my purse for my car keys when I finally got the call from him. "It's over, Maddie."

"You caught the burglars?" I asked, pulling my coat tighter. The air had turned cold again, and from what I'd seen, there was a slight chance of snow in the forecast.

Lance paused. "Let's just say they won't be bothering anyone else anytime soon."

"They're dead?" I asked in surprise, leaning my butt against the trunk of my car, the keys forgotten.

"The sheriff's department just made a public statement that the two suspects were victims of a murder-suicide."

"Two?" I swallowed the bile rising in my throat. "Who were they?'

"This is confidential information until the next of kin can be contacted, but the man you saw driving that van was Gil Hoffman, a thirty-seven-year-old man from Murphy. He was unemployed. The other was Jake Garfield."

"Jake?"

"We believe he saw you at the Christmas tree farm and, for whatever reason, decided to kill you. Maybe Hoffman had told him about you?"

"Or he thought I knew more than I did," I said.

"Could be. I guess we'll never truly know."

"But you're sure it was him?"

"Either him or Gil Hoffman. The casings found at the

Christmas tree farm match the gun Hoffman used to kill himself."

"Oh."

"Yeah," he said quietly. "Looks like they went to high school together and had recently reconnected."

"And started burglarizing homes?"

"We don't know what instigated it, but yeah." He was quiet for a moment, then said, "There's one more thing you should know. The gun he used belongs to Steve Campbell."

My heart nearly exploded. "*Steve was part of this?*"

"We're not sure, but the sheriff's detectives don't think so. At this point, we've got nothing to link him to the suspects other than his gun, but I *will* say that Noah and I think there was a third party involved in the burglaries."

"Steve?"

"Again," he asserted in an official tone, "we've got nothing to link him to the crimes other than his gun. Detectives Taylor and Donahue are springing him later this afternoon."

"But how would he have gotten involved with two people from Cockamamie?" I asked. "He hasn't been here for years."

"We don't know, but Noah and I plan to dig a little deeper. Steve was pressed for money, and there's no evidence of the stolen goods being sold around here. Maybe he was fencing them in Nashville. Like I said, we plan to look a little deeper. But I wanted to warn you." His voice turned soft. "Campbell's being released in an hour or two. Did you file a restraining order against him?"

"What?" I asked in confusion. "No."

"So Brent was bluffing," he said under his breath. "Okay, well, I suggest you file one first thing tomorrow morning. I can walk you through how to do that, if you like."

"Yeah," I said, pulling my coat tighter. A chill ran through my body, but it wasn't from the sudden gust of wind. "Thanks."

"I'll come over to help with that, but I also plan to sleep on your sofa again. I want to make sure he doesn't bother you before he leaves town."

"I suspect he'll head back to Nashville right away." Then again, maybe not. He'd been pretty desperate to convince me to marry him, even yesterday at the jail. "You said I have another hour or two before he's released?"

"Yeah, why?"

"I want to go check on Amy's neighbor. She seemed so distraught over Amy's death when I talked to her on Friday. I just want to make sure she's doing okay with this latest information. It has to be distressing to find out you lived next door to a murderer."

"Alleged murderer," he said. "And you didn't hear this from me, but we think Hoffman was the actual rapist and murderer. We suspect Garfield had nothing to do with any of that."

"Still," I said, starting to shiver. "Miss Barbara blamed herself for not helping Amy, and I can relate."

"You did everything you could, Maddie," he insisted.

Everyone kept saying that, but it didn't make me feel any better. I was pretty sure Miss Barbara felt the same way.

"Don't take too long out there," he said. "We'd prefer you get home before Campbell is released."

I still couldn't see Steve as some criminal mastermind, let alone a physical danger to me, but I decided to trust Lance and Noah. "Okay. I'll stay a few minutes and leave."

I hung up, found my keys, then got in the car. While the engine warmed up, I sent Mallory a text.

> Steve's being released in about an hour. Lance is worried that he still might harass me, so he plans to sleep on our sofa again tonight.

But as I sent the message, a part of me couldn't help

thinking it wasn't too much of a hardship for him. Mallory's immediate text helped confirm it.

> I'm making dinner. I'll make sure there's enough for him.

I laughed.

> Don't hold dinner for him. It sounds like he's still working, so I have no idea when he'll be over. But in the meantime, I'm heading out to check on Miss Barbara.

> Well hurry. It's starting to snow.

Specks of snow were falling as I drove out of the parking lot, and they'd turned to flurries by the time I made my final approach to Miss Barbara's house. I flicked on my wipers to keep the windshield clear. The temperature was cold enough for the snow to really stick this time, and I almost turned around, but I figured I might as well stop and quickly check on her, since I was almost there. Besides, I could drive in a little bit of snow.

It didn't look like anyone was home when I pulled into the driveway. The sky had darkened, but there weren't any lights on inside, nor did I hear the usual sound of the TV. I knocked anyway and waited.

Miss Barbara didn't answer the door.

I knocked again and waited, still no response, so I headed back down the steps and toward the driveway. Before I reached my car, I heard a loud thump behind the house.

Was she out back?

I nearly left anyway, but crime scene tape flapped in the wind next door. I was sure the constant reminder of Amy's murder had to be painful for the older woman. I really did want to make sure she was okay, so I started to walk around the house to see if she was back there. The snow was sticking to the grass, making it slippery, so I took slow, deliberate steps as I walked around the side of the house and toward the back.

There was a large outbuilding set about fifty yards behind the house. I'd seen it before but hadn't thought much of it. I probably still wouldn't have if the door hadn't been open with a light shining through the crack.

"Miss Barbara?" I called out as I made my way toward it, but a gust of wind hit, carrying my voice off with it. I moved closer, pulling my coat tighter. The wind had a bite that stung my cheeks, and again I considered turning back, but what if Miss Barbara needed help? She was a frail older woman. A wind that strong might blow her over.

When I reached the building, which had doors wide enough to drive a tractor through, I stopped next to the cracked door and peered inside. A U-Haul was parked in the interior with plenty of space to spare. TVs, computers, and a mess of other electronics were spread along one side of the building. I could see the back of someone dressed in a brown work coat and a ball cap, carrying something into the truck.

"Oh my God," I whispered to myself. Someone was using Miss Barbara's outbuilding to store the stolen goods.

I took a step backward and sent a text to both Noah and Lance.

> I'm at Miss Barbara's. She's not home, but there's someone in her outbuilding, loading a U-Haul full of TVs and computers. I think I found the stolen stuff.

Noah texted back immediately.

> Have they seen you?

No

LEAVE NOW, then call me when you're safe

I had to agree with him on this one, so I spun around and started to run back to my car, but my foot slipped on the snow, and I fell face first to the ground. I reached out my hands to break my fall, and my phone went flying across the yard. Pain shot through my wrist.

Crap.

I considered taking a moment to find my phone but decided to just leave it. I started getting to my feet when I heard a voice behind me say, "Get up and turn around, nice and slow."

I did as the person asked, my heartbeat pounding in my head, but when I turned around, I gasped in shock. "Miss Barbara?"

She wasn't stooped over like she usually was, and stood a lot taller than I'd thought her to be.

And she was pointing a rifle right at me.

"What are you doing here, Maddie?" she asked, her voice deeper and more authoritative than the one she'd used with me before.

"I...I came to check on you," I said in dismay, taking a step backward. "I was worried you'd be upset that Jake had something to do with Amy's murder."

Her head tilted to the side, and she studied me like a rat about to be dissected. "Why'd you have to go and be so sweet, Maddie Baker?"

She knew my full name, but I'd never given it to her. Just my first name.

"Then again," she said with an exaggerated sigh, "I suspected you might come back. You just came back too soon for me to set my plan in motion."

"What are you talking about?" My voice had an edge this time. My shock was subsiding, and my survival mode was starting to kick in.

"I think we should have this talk in the barn," she said, motioning to it with the tip of her gun. "We're out in the open here, and this seems like a private conversation, if you know what I mean."

I knew exactly what she meant. Barbara Johnson had no intention of letting me walk away from this, and it would be a whole lot less messy for her to shoot me inside that building. The accumulating snow on the ground would make it hard to hide the blood I'd leave behind.

I lifted my chin. "I think I prefer it out here."

"I shot at you before," she said with a sneer. "I have no qualms about shooting at you again." Her mouth tipped up into a menacing smile. "Only this time there's no trees in the way, so I won't miss."

"That was *you*?"

"I'm sure they're going to pin it on Jake or Gil," she said. "That's the beauty of a murder-suicide. Dead men don't tell tales." She jerked the gun again. "Get moving."

Would she shoot me out here? We were behind her house, but I could see parts of the road on either side. Still, we were both wearing dark colors that would blend in with the trees around us—if people were even looking. It wasn't like we were having this showdown in the front yard. Or that many cars came by. My only hope was that Noah or Lance would come out here to look for me.

"Okay," I said, then took a step toward the barn and released a fake cry of pain. "I hurt my wrist when I fell, and I think I sprained my ankle." I took a hobbling step and glanced back at her. "Why'd you try to kill me at the tree farm?"

"Because you were asking too many questions, and then that

moron Gil fucked it all up by leaving Amy's car where it could be found. I *told* him to dump it in the lake with the body in the driver's seat. It would take longer for them to find her, if anyone found her at all. After the detective stopped asking questions, you were the only person looking, and you kept picking at it like it was a scab. I was worried that detective would start digging deeper, so I had to shut you up." She shoved me with the tip of her gun. "Get moving!"

"But you tried to kill me after they found her body," I said, taking another limping step. "And I had nothing to do with that."

"No, that fool Jake called it in anonymously after he found out that Gil had killed Amy and where he'd dumped her body. Said he didn't want his cousin to suffer. Damn fool didn't think they'd tie it to the robberies. He thought Boomer calling the sheriff to report their house being robbed would throw them off." She jabbed me with the gun. "More walking and less talking."

I took another step. "Did Amy work for you?"

"Are you kidding me?" she asked with a bitter laugh. "That girl was too damn straight and narrow to work for us. But she helped me rake leaves and must have found the money in the barn when she was putting the rake away. I noticed it missing a few days later. Figured one of the boys had taken it. Then Jake accused her of it at the store, and she said she'd get it to him." Barbara winked. "You supplied that little piece of the missing puzzle when you stopped by on Friday. That's when I knew Jake had become a liability. He told us Amy didn't know nothing about the money." She shoved me hard with the gun, and I fell forward on my hands and knees. "Get your ass up and start moving, or I'll shoot you in the leg and give you something to limp about."

I slowly got to my feet, my left wrist aching and my knees

stinging from their contact with the ground. I took one tentative step, then another.

"Amy didn't come home on Monday night," I said. "You and your friend lied."

"Connie didn't lie," she scoffed. "She *did* see Amy's car leaving, just like I planned it, but Gil was driving it. That helped sell my story. Jake was looking through her purse for the money, and found one of your self-defense fliers. When she didn't come home on Monday, he figured that was where she was at, so he called Gil, who nabbed her when she came out to her car."

And since she'd stayed late, no one was out there to witness it. I felt like I was going to be sick.

"I knew Boomer would claim she'd never showed up on Monday night," she continued, "and I needed to buy some time to throw off suspicion from Jake or Gil, since Gil didn't kill her until Tuesday around lunchtime."

I took another couple of steps, playing up my fake twisted ankle. How long would it take for Noah or Lance to get here? "Why'd he kill her?"

"Well, she had to go. Obviously. She took our money, and she knew too much. Gil tore up their house looking for the money, and Boomer thought they'd been robbed. Jake was planning to get a new TV and had moved the old one over here to fence. Jake decided to run with it. But I never condoned Gil raping the girl. Or that woman on Sunday. That's when I knew he had to go too."

"You killed Gil? They're saying he committed suicide."

"That's what I wanted them to believe. When the toxicology report comes out, he'll have a bunch of drugs in his system, but not enough to make them think someone else set it up. It was ridiculously easy. He fell asleep in his chair, and I put the gun in his lap and used his finger to pull the trigger. Never knew what hit him." She chuckled. "Or, in this instance, shot him."

We were almost to the barn, and there was still no sign of Lance or Noah. If she killed me, would they realize she was responsible?

"How did you plan on getting away with this?" I asked, taking more slow steps. "You said you had something set up."

"I planted some of my blood in my house to make it look like a break-in gone wrong. They would have assumed I'd been kidnapped, my body dumped. Now I'll make it look like you interrupted them." She released a barky laugh. "Which is actually true."

We'd reached the door to the barn, and I knew in my gut that she wouldn't waste any time before killing me. I considered trying a defensive kick so I could run, but the closest cover was about twenty feet away. She'd have plenty of time to shoot me in the back. But if I ran into the barn, there were a lot more places to hide.

I had to do something.

I turned and kicked her knee as hard as I could. The gun went off, and I raced into the barn.

Chapter Forty-Eight

Noah

I was waiting outside the county jail processing area, leaning my shoulder against the wall, when Steve Campbell walked out, slipping his watch onto his wrist. He seemed surprised to see me, but then a sleazy grin lit up his face.

"Don't look so disappointed, Detective."

I gave him a dry look. "You think this is disappointment? Hardly. It's utter disgust. Then again, I've heard you're not very good at reading people. Or at least you really suck at reading Maddie." I pushed away and walked up to him.

"Are you here to threaten me, *Detective?*" he asked, having to lift his head a little to meet my gaze.

"First, it's important for you to know that I'm here as Noah Langley, Maddie's friend. There's nothing official about this chat."

His brow lifted slightly, and amusement filled his eyes. "Why do I get the impression you'd like to be more than just friends with my fiancée, Langley?"

My palms itched with the need to punch this fucker in the face, but that wasn't why I was here, not to mention it would likely land me behind bars. He wasn't worth it.

But Maddie was.

It wasn't lost on me that the man was still deluding himself. If he still thought they were engaged, then nothing I said was going to change that.

"Think what you want about my intentions," I said, keeping my voice calm yet direct. "You've jerked Maddie around enough. She said she's done with you, which means you need to leave her the fuck alone. But before you get in your fancy BMW and head home, try doing the right thing for once in your life, and give the woman the money you owe her."

"Once we're married, her money will be my money. She'll come around. I just need to wear her down."

"Here's the thing, Steve," I said, holding his gaze. "Unlike Maddie, who likes to see the good in people, I've been around enough to know that some people need a little motivation to do the right thing. Here's yours." I pulled my phone from my pocket, woke up the screen, and showed it to him. "This is a drafted email from Detective Noah Langley and Officer Lance Forrester addressed to your boss at Serendipity. It's letting him know you were arrested for stalking the woman you claimed was your fiancée, who has turned you down multiple times, and to whom you owe money you've refused to pay. This email also informs him that Maddie has filed a restraining order against you." It hadn't happened yet, but Lance planned to help with one first thing tomorrow morning. "I'll also inform him that she is in the process of suing you for twenty thousand dollars." Before he could protest, I added, "She's collecting that interest you owe her."

Hatred filled his eyes. "You wouldn't send that."

I chuckled, but it was dry and menacing. "Oh, trust me, I would. But I might be persuaded not to do it if you fulfill your promise to her."

"How do you expect me to pay her?" He held his hands out at his sides, still sounding glib. "I don't have my checkbook."

"No, but from what I understand, your attorney does, and he's currently at the courthouse. Get it from him and write out a check for twenty thousand dollars. Leave it at the Cockamamie Police Station, and we'll be sure to get it to Maddie. If that check hasn't been turned in by eight o'clock tomorrow morning, I'll hit send on this email." I winked. "Oh, and when you leave the check at the station—made out to Maddie, of course—be sure to get a receipt."

I didn't give him time to answer. I just turned and walked away. I was stepping out of the building when my phone vibrated. I was so pissed that I nearly ignored it, but I wasn't in the habit of doing so. The moment I read the screen, my heart began to pound against my ribcage. It was a text from Maddie.

> I'm at Miss Barbara's. She's not home, but there's someone in her outbuilding, loading a U-Haul with TVs and computers. I think I found the stolen stuff.

Shit. We hadn't looked at her place for the stolen goods or anything related to Amy or the Garfields—not that we had a warrant. Sure, Lance and I had our suspicions there was a third party involved in that operation, but we'd never once suspected they might be using the building next door.

What the hell was Maddie doing out there? But that was a moot point right now. She was in danger.

> Have they seen you?

> No

> LEAVE NOW, then call me when you're safe

I started running for my car, terror flooding my veins. What if I didn't reach her in time? What if I lost her?

But I didn't have her, did I? I just pined for her like a stupid teenager with a crush. Only I knew what I felt for her was no crush.

I jumped in my car, barely starting the engine before I shot out of the parking spot, tires squealing as I sped toward the street. I turned on the emergency lights embedded in my detective sedan's grille. A few snowflakes were falling from the sky.

Fumbling with my phone, I called 911 and told them who I was and what was happening. They assured me they'd send deputy cars out, but there had been a bad accident a few towns over, and it would be at least fifteen minutes before a car would arrive.

I drove faster and called Lance, telling him about the texts.

"She texted me too. I'm headed out there right now," Lance said. "She's not answering her phone or texts."

"She's a smart woman. She can handle it," I said, more to appease myself than him. "County is sending deputies now, but I'll get there before them."

"What's your ETA?' he asked.

"Ten minutes or so. Yours?"

"I think I'm a few minutes behind you. Be careful, Noah."

"I plan on all three of us going home tonight."

"Me too. But Noah, there's one more thing."

I heard the hesitation in his voice. "What?"

"Maddie told me she was going out there to check on Mrs. Johnson, but it was before I found out more about Peter Castillo."

My breath stuck in my chest. "What?" I forced out.

"Peter Castillo is Barbara Johnson's son."

"That old woman's son is part of this?" I asked in shock. "He's the third person?"

"Doubtful." He paused. "Peter Castillo is in a coma in a nursing home in Lynchburg. Six months ago, he hit a tree going eighty miles an hour and suffered head trauma. He has the mind of three-year-old, and he'll never get better."

I wasn't sure how to respond to that.

"The two rental properties were his father's. He recently inherited them. Manuel Castillo was Barbara Johnson's first husband."

"So who's the master..." My voice trailed off as a horror hit me. "Barbara Johnson was behind this all along. She purposely misled us to cover her tracks."

"Yeah," he said, his voice breaking. "I think so, and I let Maddie go out there with my blessing."

I swallowed the bile rising in my throat. "This isn't your fault. We both know if Maddie wanted to go out there, she was going to do it, blessing or no blessing."

"But if I'd found out sooner," he choked out.

"She's going to be okay," I said, more to convince myself than him. "Just get your ass out there, ASAP."

I hung up and forced myself to concentrate on driving. I couldn't let myself think about what was happening to Maddie. I had to believe that she had gotten away, and if she hadn't, I'd get there in time to save her.

Thankfully, there weren't many cars on the two-lane road out to Barbara Johnson's house. Whenever I came upon another car, I laid on the horn to warn them I was approaching and then passed them. The last thing I wanted to do was turn on the siren and alert whoever was at Miss Johnson's house that I was approaching.

The snow started coming down harder, and the road had turned curvy, forcing me to slow down. I wouldn't do Maddie any good if I crashed into a tree, but my imagination ran wild.

Maddie hadn't called or texted, so I tried calling her. Twice.

Both times, it rang and went to voicemail, and I tried not to panic.

The house was up ahead, and I was the first law enforcement to arrive. I turned off my lights as I slowed down and pulled into the driveway, parking behind Maddie's car. Snow had already covered her windshield. I'd hoped she'd gotten away but had lost her phone. Now I wasn't sure what to expect. I only knew she didn't have much time.

I got out and opened my trunk, quickly shrugging on my bulletproof vest and grabbing my rifle and ammunition. I inserted a clip, shoved more into my pockets, then left my trunk open as I approached Maddie's car. No sign of her.

Where was she?

A wave of panic knocked the wind out of me. I took several deep breaths, forcing myself to calm down and think this through. She'd said the perpetrator was in the outbuilding, so if she wasn't in her car, they must have found her and taken her into the barn.

Treat this like your job. This isn't personal.

Only it *was* personal. There was a very real possibility that I could lose Maddie before I'd even let us have a chance. I'd let her get close, only to hurt her when I ran to protect myself. I'd hurt her because of my cowardice, and I vowed I wouldn't let that happen again. But I had to save her first, because if I didn't, I'd have to live with the pain and the regret of hurting her for the rest of my life.

But right now, I had a job to do, and yeah, it was personal, so all the more reason to get my shit together and do it.

A hard resolve tightened my chest. I was going to bring this bastard down.

Squaring my shoulders, I headed around the side of the house, looking for any sign of an ambush, then moved around to the back, hugging the side of the building.

I didn't see anyone, but then I heard a gunshot go off in the barn, and I took off running, barely processing that a phone was lying on the ground. I didn't stop until I reached the door, then forced myself to slow down and listen.

"Come on, Maddie. Don't make this harder than it has to be," called out a woman with a deep voice.

Barbara Johnson? I struggled to believe that frail old woman was part of this, but relief washed through me like a tidal wave. At least I knew Maddie was still alive. I could still save her.

I took a quick peek around the door and saw the U-Haul parked to the left side of the space. The right wall was lined with electronics. On the far left side were stacks of boxes and metal shelves.

I glanced down at the ground and noticed a few drops of blood in the snow, and my heart lurched. Whose blood? Maddie's or the woman's?

I took another peek around the door and saw the outline of a person at the back end of the U-Haul, coming around the corner toward me. I lifted my gun and aimed it at them.

"Police!" I called out. "Drop your weapon."

They fired several rounds, and I got off a shot of my own before ducking back around the corner outside the building. When I looked again, the person was behind the truck.

"Sheriff's deputies are on the way," I called out, very aware that Maddie was likely in there somewhere and every bullet fired put her at risk. I needed to try to end this peacefully. "Soon you're going to be surrounded. If you give yourself up now, you have a better chance of getting out of here alive."

"I'd rather be dead than rot in prison!" She sounded nothing like Barbara Johnson, the old woman I'd spoken to days ago, yet something in her voice sounded familiar.

"The DA wants answers, you know," I said, trying not to let my desperation show. If the woman was willing to die rather than be brought in, there was a good chance Maddie could get caught in the crossfire. "You could work out a deal. Get some time shaved off."

"Like I'd trust a pig," she sneered. "You're all a bunch of liars, and what part of 'I'd rather die than go to prison' do you not understand?"

"Okay," I said. "Suicide by cop. I get it. But Maddie's innocent. Don't bring her into it."

"She's the reason it all went to shit! She scared Gil with all the questions you two were asking, and he dumped Amy's car somewhere it was too easy to find. Maddie stirred up shit that should haven't been stirred."

"Someone would have looked for Amy," I called out.

"*No one* would have looked for her," she sneered in disgust. "Jake had convinced Boomer that Amy had left him. And no one at that grocery store gave a damn about her. Everyone would have believed she went back to Georgia. It would have died down. But that bitch kept stirring the pot." A gun went off, and the bullet didn't land anywhere near me. Had she found Maddie? I didn't hear any cries of pain, but a new wave of terror reverberated through me. This woman blamed Maddie for sending her empire crashing down. I doubted she planned to let Maddie leave here alive.

I noticed movement close to the house and saw Lance wearing a bulletproof vest and holding his service AR-15. An overwhelming sense of gratitude hit me center mass. I trusted Lance more than I'd trusted anyone in a long time. I knew he'd do everything in his power to help me get Maddie out of this alive. I motioned him toward me, and he took off in a sprint until he reached me.

I leaned into his ear and whispered, "Maddie's inside, but she might be injured. I think Barbara Johnson has her holed up in there."

"Fuck," he groaned.

"She must have been putting on a front when I talked to her," I said, "because she seems pretty spry and a whole lot less fragile now. She blames Maddie for her enterprise's downfall. She doesn't expect either of them to walk out of there alive. I haven't seen Maddie, but the suspect was calling out for her when I arrived, as though Maddie's hiding from her. Barbara is armed and dangerous. She's not only taken a few shots at me but also a couple inside the building, presumably trying to hit Maddie."

"You haven't seen or heard from Maddie?"

"No." I swallowed a lump of fear. "But there's blood by the door."

He stared at me, his face grim. "She's going to be okay."

I had to believe that, but it was up to us to make it happen. "The suspect has been hanging out toward the back of the building, at the rear of a U-Haul. I'm not sure if there's a door or window back there—"

"On it," Lance said, then took off around the building.

I needed to create a distraction, so I called out, "Barbara, what's your end goal here?"

"I want this bitch dead, and I want to get out of here."

"Then how about I just let you go?"

"Like you're really going to do that," she sneered. She was still at the back, behind the truck, which was good if Lance could find an opening. "Besides, I may have already accomplished my first goal. She's bleeding like a stuck pig."

I resisted the urge to rush in and try to find Maddie. The blood on the floor scared me more than I was willing to admit. I forced my panic down, and instead of rushing in, I pulled out my phone and called 911, whispering as I told them we needed medical assistance for a possible gunshot wound. If she was hurt, I needed to make sure medical help was here when I got her out.

I heard a crackle and realized I smelled something burning.

"Barbara?" I shouted, peeking around the door. I could see a glow in the far back corner. "How are you doing in there?"

"It's a little cold outside, so I thought I'd warm things up some."

Shit. Now I really had to get Maddie out of there, which meant I had to go inside. I couldn't see Barbara anymore, but she was still in the back. There was a fifty-gallon drum close to the front door, so I darted through the door and dove for it.

Several bullets whizzed past me.

"Not a good move, Detective," Barbara shouted. "I take that as a sign of aggression."

I didn't respond. Instead, I peered around the garage, trying to figure out where Maddie might be hiding. I let my eyes adjust to the light and saw a small pool of blood in front of the truck.

My stomach dropped. *Dammit.*

Focus! Freaking out won't save her. Do your fucking job!

"I swear to God," I said. "I'll let you run out that door, if you just leave now."

"Throw out your gun."

I hesitated.

"I think I've figured out where Maddie's hiding, and it would be an easy thing to unload my clip in that direction."

I wasn't sure I believed her. I suspected she would have done it by now if she was sure. Then again, I didn't know how much ammo she had left.

She fired her gun, and a box toppled on the left side of the garage.

Where was Lance? I didn't see any openings for him to come through. For all I knew, he'd needed to circle around and was at the front door. I couldn't rely on him intervening in time.

The flames in the back corner were growing larger, feeding off the boxes, and the tall ceiling was starting to fill with smoke.

Jesus, Maddie might die of smoke inhalation rather than gunshot wounds. I had to get her out of here. *Now.*

Sirens sounded in the distance.

"The deputies are almost here, Barbara," I said, my eyes starting to burn. "This could be your last chance to escape."

"Throw out your gun!" she shouted, then began to cough.

I could wait for the deputies to arrive and get into position, but the fire was spreading too fast. I doubted we'd have enough time.

I heard a cough over to my left behind the boxes, and Barbara released a couple shots in that direction.

Dammit. At least I knew where Maddie was, but I had to keep Barbara from killing her...and get her out of here before the smoke could harm her. I couldn't waste any more time.

I took the clip out of my rifle and stuffed it into my pocket. "Okay. Here it is!" I tossed my rifle onto the floor. It skidded toward the front corner of the U-Haul. As soon as I released it, I reached for the gun in the holster at my waist. "You've got my gun. Now go."

"I know you have a handgun. Throw it out too!"

I had two, so I grabbed the gun in my ankle holster, removed the clip, and tossed it out. "You have both. *Now go!*"

The smoke was thicker now, and I could hear her coughing. "I'm coming out, but don't try anything funny."

I pointed my gun in her direction, waiting for her to come out, but flames were licking up the walls, and the smoke was becoming denser. I could barely make out a figure coming from the back. They stooped close to where I'd thrown the gun. I considered taking a shot, but I couldn't make them out. Unlikely as it was, it might be Maddie. I couldn't take the risk.

The figure rose and moved closer, and when I could make

out Barbara Johnson's face, I pointed my gun around the drum. "Drop the weapon and put your hands up!"

She aimed her rifle in my direction and let loose a round of bullets that hit the drum and the wall behind me. I curled into a ball to keep from getting hit, hoping the contents of the barrel would slow down the bullets enough to protect me.

The gunfire continued but was no longer pointed in my direction. A rain of bullets hit the boxes where Maddie was hidden. I reached around the barrel again and released multiple rounds toward Barbara just as more gunfire came from the doorway. She fell to the ground, and a figure rushed into the smoke-filled room.

"Noah?" Lance called out.

"Here," I said, scrambling to my feet. "I think Maddie's over by the boxes!"

Lance leaned over Barbara's body to check her pulse, kicking the guns away from her fallen body in the process, while I ran over to the boxes. The smoke was so thick here, I had to cover my mouth and nose with an arm while I squinted to see.

"Maddie!" I started throwing boxes, trying to find her. "*Maddie!*"

She didn't answer, and I started to panic. Had one or more of Barbara's bullets hit her? The blood on the ground suggested she'd already been hurt. What if...

The double doors of the garage opened, releasing some of the smoke and letting in more light. Then Lance was next to me, throwing boxes several feet in front of the U-Haul.

"Are you sure she's here?" he asked, shouting over the roar of the flames.

"I heard her cough!"

"You keep looking here. I'll check some other places."

The fire was building, the whole back of the room was engulfed in flames. What if Maddie was back there?

"I found her!" Lance called out, kneeling in front of the U-Haul.

I clambered over to him, coughing nonstop as I pressed my chest to the concrete floor and found her sprawled on her stomach, one hand flat on the ground, her coat wadded up and in front of her face.

"Maddie!"

When she didn't respond, I crawled under the truck and reached for her hands. Snagging one, I started to pull. She moaned, and even though I hated that she was in pain, I was light-headed with relief that she was alive. Lance slid under and grabbed her other hand.

Several deputies ran up behind us as we pulled her out the rest of the way.

Lance called out to them. "The suspect's next to the truck. Dead. This is a victim."

"Maddie," I said breathlessly as I rolled her to her side, terrified of what I'd find.

Her left shoulder was drenched with blood.

"I'm here. You're safe," I said, pulling her into my arms, partially to comfort her, but also to assure myself. I looked down into her ashen face. "I've got you."

She opened her eyes and quirked an eyebrow. "Took you long enough."

Chapter Forty-Nine

Maddie

Noah refused to relinquish me to anyone else's care, carrying me straight to an ambulance parked in front of Barbara Johnson's house. I couldn't say I hated Noah fussing over me. He'd looked terrified as he pulled me out from under the van, and he hadn't let go of me since.

He stayed with me while the EMTs looked me over. They told us what I already knew—I'd been shot in my shoulder after I'd kicked Barbara in the knee. Although it looked like I'd lost a lot of blood, it didn't appear to be life-threatening.

He sagged with relief when he heard the news. Still, even though the danger was (mostly) over, he insisted on staying with me until the ambulance took me to the hospital. Before it left, he said he had to give a statement but would be there to check on me soon.

Honestly, I wasn't sure I believed him. I'd learned by now that big feelings usually sent Noah running. It was as though he was terrified to care about anyone, particularly me, and after his confession about what had happened with Caleb and his dog, I understood why. This whole situation had clearly sent him into a full-blown panic attack, and I was sure he would back away from me again.

To my surprise, he didn't.

An hour later, he showed up in my ER room, still wearing his soot-covered jacket. Streaks of soot covered his face and neck, as though he'd tried to wipe them off in a hurry and missed a few places. Smears of blood blended in with the ash on his jacket, but the smudges on his shirt were more glaring. He reeked of smoke, but so did I, despite the fact that the nursing staff had removed my clothing and given me a hospital gown.

He took hesitant steps when he walked in, as though he wasn't sure he should be there.

"I'm fine," I assured him as he took in the bandage peeking out from my gown and the IV in my arm. "It wasn't even really a bullet wound. More like a scratch."

"Actually," a nurse said as she walked into the room behind him, "the doctor said it had clean entry and exit wounds, and you're lucky you didn't need surgery."

"No surgery's a good thing," I said. "I can't afford surgery." No doubt I would be off work for at least a week or two.

The nurse started checking the IV monitors and recording something on the tablet in her hand.

"I thought Mallory or Margarete might be here," Noah said, his gaze landing on the empty visitor's chair.

"I'll tell them when I get out of here. No reason to freak them out."

The hint of a grin cracked his serious expression. "Where exactly do they think you are?"

I swallowed. "With you."

Surprise flickered in his eyes, and he took a few steps closer, stopping at the end of the bed.

"I'm giving you some pain meds," the nurse said as she withdrew a syringe from her pocket and took off the cap. "They might make you groggy for a bit." She inserted the needle into the port of my IV and injected the medication. As she withdrew the needle, she turned to Noah. "We want to watch her for another hour or two while we wait for some blood work, Mr. Baker. Then you will be able to take her home."

Noah started to protest, but she had already bustled out of the room.

"She called you Mr. Baker," I said with a strained laugh. I wasn't sure what to make of the fact he'd actually shown up, and it was making me anxious.

A smirk lit up his eyes. "I've been called worse."

"Some even by me," I said wryly.

"I've heard a few, but not the full list."

"I can alphabetize them, if you like."

A grin spread across his face. "Why do I think that might take a few days?"

"Because you're a good detective."

His face fell. "Maybe not good enough."

I'd suspected he would try to pin some of the blame for all this on himself. "Noah, there was no way you could know."

"Her story didn't line up with Boomer's, and I just took her word for it. Her friend too."

"If it makes you feel any better, I spoke to her *multiple* times, and I didn't have a clue. I believed her, and for what it's worth, her friend didn't lie. Connie *did* see Amy's car pull out of the driveway and head down the street. She didn't realize Gil Hoffman was driving it."

"Sounds like Connie needs to get her eyes checked," he said with a forced laugh.

I held his gaze. "Barbara confessed her part in all of it to me. She was the one who tried to shoot me. I think she was the mastermind of the whole thing."

His brow shot up. "She confessed?"

I nodded.

Rubbing the back of his neck, he stared at the wall for a long moment, then turned back to face me. "Detective Langley would sit down and start taking your statement, and then in an hour or so, you'd have to give it again to the sheriff's detectives." He moved closer to the side of my bed. "But I'm not here as Detective Langley right now. I'm just here as Noah."

My pulse quickened as I stared at him in disbelief.

A grin twisted his mouth. "Actually, apparently, I'm Noah Baker." He took a step closer, turning more serious. "And I don't want to take your statement right now, Maddie, as much as I want to know what happened. What you tell me right now is up to you, because I'm only here as your..." He looked down and swallowed before he stared back up at me. "I'm here as whatever you want me to be."

A lump filled my throat. Was he saying what I thought he was saying?

He reached for my right hand, his fingertips lightly interlocking with the ends of mine. "I..." he started, then stopped. He took a breath and tried again, his face looking softer than usual. More tender. "I know that having a family one day is important to you. And I told you I don't want to get married or have kids, but you made some valid points about Caleb and my father a few nights ago, and Lance also pointed out that my reasoning behind the decision to not have kids is flawed." He turned his gaze to our hands while he lightly stroked my fingertips. "I also agree that I knew deep down Monica wasn't the right woman for me, so I equated my feelings against marrying her with not wanting to marry at all." His hand stilled. "Still, marriage feels like a legal formality. If you love someone, why do you need the marriage certificate and the ring?"

"Health benefits," I joked, slightly lifting my arm and wincing. "Kidding."

He studied me for a moment as though processing what I'd said.

"I'm not serious, Noah," I insisted. "When I get married someday, I want it to be to a man who loves me so much he can't imagine spending the rest of his life without me."

His brow wrinkled with confusion. "But why do you need the ring to have that?"

He had a point. I thought I needed that with Steve, and look where it would have gotten me. I still wanted to get married and have kids, but I could also see his point about the formality of it all. If you truly loved someone, couldn't that be enough? "So you're saying you want a relationship with me, but you're still opposed to marriage."

He stared at me with raw emotion on his face. "Maddie, all I know is I can still be terrified of losing someone, even if I'm not married to them. Trying to shut down my feelings doesn't make them any less real. Ring or no ring." He ran a hand through his hair in frustration. "I thought I could stay away from you and not get hurt, but today..." His voice broke, and he blinked back tears. "Today, I realized that I could be missing out on something that could be amazing. That not giving us a chance would be the biggest regret of my life." He paused, then said quietly, "And while I realize that potential marriage is part of the future, it doesn't scare me like it did before." He squeezed my hand. "I think I had to find the right person to consider it."

Tears pooled in my eyes. "It's a little early to be proposing, Mr. Baker. We haven't even gone on a date yet."

He laughed and sat on the edge of my bed. "I know, considering I'm usually a very cautious man when it comes to relationships." He turned serious. "As for kids..." He lifted his shoulders into a half-hearted shrug. "I'm not sure I'll change my mind on that," he said softy. "You need to know that going in. But I *do* know I need to reexamine my reasons for not wanting them." His lips tightened. "The sins of the father and all that."

I slid my hand into his. "And *I've* realized that some of the most miserable people in the world are married, so marriage isn't a guarantee I'll be loved. And kids...yeah, I *do* want kids someday, and let's be honest, my biological clock is ticking, but I also realize there's no guarantee I'll even be able to *have* kids." I tightened my grip on his hand. "I can't throw away the potential for something that might turn out to be truly amazing for the chance of something else. I think I'd regret it for the rest of my life if I did."

He stared at me as though what I'd said was too good to be true.

"I want you in my life, Noah," I whispered. "I want to see if we work, but you can't keep running from me every time you get scared. You have to promise to stick around and tell me how you're feeling."

His grip on my hand tightened. "When I thought you might be dead, all I could think about was how much time I'd wasted and how much I'd hurt you while I thought I was protecting both of us." Earnestness filled his eyes. "But it didn't work, Maddie. In that barn when I thought you might be dead...I was still scared to death." He stroked the back of my hand with his thumb. "I don't want to waste any more time." He leaned over and lifted my hand, kissing my knuckles, as he stared into my eyes. "I can't promise that when I get scared, I won't run, at least for a little bit, but I *can* promise that I'll always come back."

A lump filled my throat, and I whispered, "I can live with that."

Hope filled his eyes. "Does that mean you'll turn Brent Taylor down when he asks you out on a date?"

I grinned. "He's planning on asking me?" I gave him a

playful look. "On second thought, maybe I should keep my options open."

He leaned closer, his face full of tenderness as he closed the distance between us and pressed his lips to mine.

It was a gentle kiss. It spoke of patience and hope. The promise of not only the passion I'd felt between us a couple nights ago, but of something deeper. As I kissed him back, I realized I might be trading in one dream for another, but something told me it might be worth it.

For now, I could live with that.

Find out who killed Maddie's mother in the final book of the series, *Echoes of Her*.

To read bonus content, click on the QR code below.

Acknowledgments

I started to call this book cursed. I had so many issues, y'all. First, I just couldn't figure this book out. It took me seven months to write it, the longest it's ever taken me to write a book. I revised it at least five times before I even got one-fourth into the story, and then as is typical for me, I wrote the last half in three weeks. That's about sixty thousand words, y'all, or about 225 pages. (This book is LONG.)

And that's not all. Word ate one full day's worth of work while I was revising this book. A full day of line edit acceptances and rejections, not to mention a HUGE chunk of words I'd added to the scene in Maddie's kitchen when Noah tells her about his past. Gone. It took me two days to get the gumption to go back and rewrite it all. And then, my editor, Angela, lost a chunk of the edits she did on a section I sent her, and she had to redo those.

Cursed, I tell you.

Until it wasn't.

I've only recently talked about the health issues I've dealt with over the past four years as I've struggled with high blood pressure. I'll spare you the long story, but recently, I think my healthcare providers have acknowledged the cause and hopefully have the fix. (It's looking good so far.) But I've also realized that my blood pressure or one of my medications—or possibly both—have made it difficult to focus and given me a bit of brain fog. Finding my creativity has been like finding water at the bottom of a dry well. It was during the writing of this book that we figured some things out and changed my medication. For the first time in years, I feel like I can FOCUS. My head is much clearer, and I hope my brain is back on track. I'm feeling hopeful for my future books.

I'd like to thank my editor Angela Polidoro (also known as Angela Casella), for her patience as I blew past deadline after deadline. She accommodated me even though I know it hasn't always been convenient for her. I'll forever be grateful.

I also want to thank Ray Kaelin, a former sheriff deputy of nineteen years, who advised me on several legal technicalities. He helped me make sure Noah and Lance were following proper procedures. I look forward to utilizing him more in the future.

Thank you, dear readers, for putting up with me as I've pushed out deadlines while I've worked through all of this. I never want to put out a subpar book.

About the Author

Denise Grover Swank was born in Kansas City, Missouri and lived in the area until she was nineteen. Then she became a nomad, living in five cities, four states and ten houses over the course of ten years before she moved back to her roots. She speaks English and smattering of Spanish and Chinese which she learned through an intensive Nick Jr. immersion period. Her hobbies include witty Facebook comments (in own her mind) and dancing in her kitchen with her children. (Quite badly if you believe her offspring.) Hidden talents include the gift of justification and the ability to drink massive amounts of caffeine and still fall asleep within two minutes. Her lack of the sense of smell allows her to perform many unspeakable tasks. She has six children and hasn't lost her sanity. Or so she leads you to believe.

denisegroverswank.com

Don't miss out on Denise's newest releases! Join her mailing list.